WHAT WE KEEP

JENNIFER MILLIKIN

ISBN: 979-8-9909048-1-1
www.jennifermillikinwrites.com
Cover by Okay Creations
Editing by Emerald Edits
Proofreading by Sisters Get Lit.erary

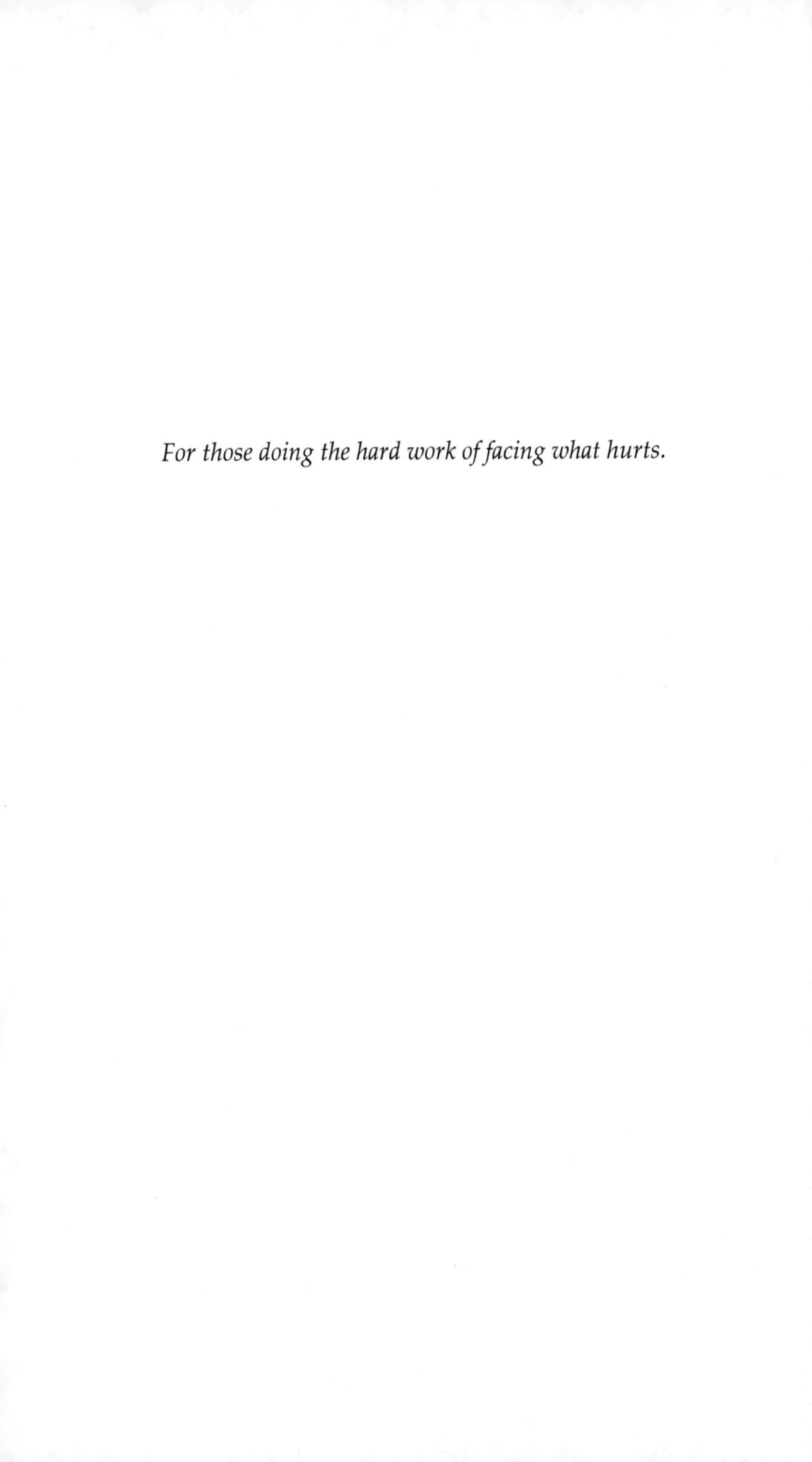

For those doing the hard work of facing what hurts.

AUTHOR'S NOTE

Dear Reader,

There may be themes in this novel that some readers find triggering. If you'd prefer to go in blind, please skip the following paragraph and begin reading.

Trigger warnings include, but are not limited to: alcoholism, divorce, death of a sibling, parental neglect.

Playlist

Burnin' Up
Jessie J, 2 Chainz

Wicked Game
Jessie Villa

Wild (Featuring Gary Clark Jr.)
John Legend, Gary Clark Jr.

Don't Worry Baby
The Beach Boys

Stand By Me
Florence + The Machine

Wreckage
Nate Smith

Burning House
Cam

Monster
Shawn Mendes & Justin Bieber

Look At Us Now (Honeycomb)
Daisy Jones & The Six

I Will Always Love You
Whitney Houston

Birds Of A Feather
Billie Eilish

Come As You Are
Moontricks, Frase, Fawna

Wish You Were Here
Pink Floyd

Ride Or Die
Infinity Song

Better Man
Leon Bridges

The Promise
Tracey Chapman

Crazy Love
Van Morrison

Make You Feel My Love
Adele

The Bones
Maren Morris

Baby I'm Yours
Cass Elliot

Visit Spotify.com to access the playlist.

PART ONE

Love is a fire. But whether it is going to warm your hearth or burn down your house, you can never tell.

JOAN CRAWFORD

SESSION ONE

DESERT FLOWER THERAPY

It is humbling to be the person sitting on the couch.

The man in the chair opposite me directs his stare my way, his eyes a glacial, almost translucent blue. *Dr. Ruben Sandoval.* A distinguished name, one that calls to mind good manners and sweater vests.

Despite having eyes the color of an iceberg, he is affable with his graying hair in need of a cut and his eyeglasses rimmed in thin gold wire. He looks like a reserved, intelligent young grandparent.

"It's nice to meet you, Avery." A brief dip of his chin accompanies his greeting.

"Likewise, Dr. Ruben." I offer him a friendly smile. "I'm a therapist, too," I add, seeking common ground.

Dr. Ruben nods slowly, just once, not letting on if he already knew my job is (*was?*) the same as his.

My hands fold on my lap, my legs cross at my ankles. I'm not sure if he's agreed to see me as a favor to Joseph, and I don't want to ask. I don't want to bring up what drove me to seek his help. Not right away, at least. It will make its way out eventually. It must.

What brought me here, to this emerald green velvet couch, isn't the low point of my story. It is one of many low points, a rock bottom that continually turns out to have another layer beneath it.

What would I give to get my life back? To have Gabriel in my arms, my home, my bed?

If a hero would sacrifice their love to save the world, but a villain would sacrifice the world to save their love, what does that make me?

What would I sacrifice to get it all back, to save my husband?

The answer is easy. *The world.*

In an effort to delay the start of our session, I direct my attention to the desert scenery beyond the window. The palo verde trees are in full yellow bloom, the cacti pushing forth magenta flowers. Soon the saguaros will offer their white, waxy blossoms. Spring in the desert is something to behold.

I'm aware of the symbolism. New beginnings, the emergence of a fresher, better self. Me, here in this office, attempting my own new beginning.

Politely, Dr. Ruben asks, "What do you practice, Avery?" The pointer finger on his right hand taps his thigh. On that finger is a gaudy gold ring in the shape of a buffalo head. It's so far past ugly, it has reached the point of being cool.

I toy with the end of my long brown hair as the weight of what I'm really doing here presses in on me. Less enthusiastic now, I answer. "Marriage and family."

Again, his response is to nod once.

This damned smile still stretches across my face, the corners tightening. "I know, I know." My hands lift in feigned protest. "Doctor, heal thyself."

He squints one eye and shakes his head in a subtle back and forth motion. "It doesn't work that way. Heart surgeons don't perform open heart surgery on themselves."

A dissenting sound sits at the top of my throat, but I hold it in. "I wouldn't call this open heart surgery."

"Wouldn't you?" He sips his hot tea. The tag hanging from the cup swings. Chamomile. "You of all people know you're here to cut yourself open, expose your organ, and fix what went wrong somewhere in the past. So—" He shifts in his chair and tucks his wavy hair behind one ear with his free hand. "Why are you here?"

My brain forms a safe answer, a cheeky response like 'I was hot and in need of air-conditioning,' but it's overrode by the sudden and pressing desire to bare my soul. *Heart surgery.*

"A fire." Something inside my chest cracks. Perhaps it's the veneer I've used to cover the thousands of fissures in my heart. Years have passed, but the unraveling begins with a single look at the wound. "My life changed the night my house caught on fire."

Without a trace of emotion, Dr. Ruben says, "Let's begin there."

CHAPTER 1

The scent of smoke wakes me.

I'm confused, sitting up and dimly grasping to reconcile the darkness of my room with that pungent and unmistakable smell. Is Sabrina cooking before the sun comes up? Fumbling around for my phone, I locate it under my pillow.

2:47 a.m. Sabrina is burning something in the middle of the night?

Tossing off my sheets, I plant my feet on the floor. Each second I'm awake brings me closer to full consciousness. The smoke does not smell like burning food. More like a campfire. And…plastic? Also, Sabrina does not cook.

Oh my God. Ohmygodohmygod.

What do I do?

Help.

I grab my phone, frantically dialing 9-1-1.

"9-1-1. What's your emergency?"

"I think my house is on fire," I choke out the words. My hands shake, my heart pounds. "I smell smoke."

The operator asks for my address, name, and number, and I blurt it out as fast as I can make my lips move.

"Are you alone in the house?"

Her calm tone does not match the way my heart batters my breast bone. I open my mouth to tell her about my roommate, but it hits me that Sabrina isn't here. She stayed the night at her boyfriend's house.

"I'm alone."

"Does your room have a window you can climb from safely?"

"I'm on the second floor. First door on the right."

"Get on the ground and stay there. Do not open any doors or windows. The fire department is on the way."

"Thank you," I whisper, dropping to my knees and sitting back on my heels. "Will you stay on the phone with me?"

"I'm not going anywhere," she says reassuringly.

"I don't have on a bra." I look down at my pajama top as I lower my face to the ground. It's flimsy, but at least it's not white. Why is that what comes to mind right now? Shouldn't there be more important thoughts, like what valuables I should save from the fire? Except I've been told to get down and stay down, and I'm not about to break rules now.

The operator doesn't laugh. Maybe it's not funny. Or maybe she's not supposed to laugh. I'm not sure. She says, "I don't sleep with my bra on either."

"My grandma always said to make sure I leave the house in matching bra and underwear in case I get in an accident and they have to cut my clothes off me, and I never do that." I'm whispering for no reason except that

I'm terrified, and bent at the waist with my nose against the carpet.

"I don't know many people who do." There's that steady voice again, rock solid, a life preserver.

Sirens pierce the smoky air. "I hear them." Hope tinges my tone.

"Stay put," she reminds me. "Let them come to you."

I nod, knowing she can't see me, but my ability to speak has disappeared. There are noises outside, sirens and horns and yelling, and my fingers shake as the heavy reality of the situation sinks in.

"Help is there, and I'm right here," the operator says. I cling to her smooth calmness.

What if she is the last voice I hear? The thought is a knife to my stomach. My eyes wrench open, my head whips around the room. Suddenly I want something. Anything. I want to hold something I love.

Leaving my phone behind on the ground, I crawl to my nightstand. Inside are two photos of me, my sister, and my mother. I choose the one where we're smiling. If I have to save something, it won't be the photo that makes me sad.

My purse. It's here too, lying on top of my nightstand where I dropped it last night when I came home. I lift an arm and find it quickly, the feel of the metal chain strap unmistakable.

Tucking the photo in my purse and ducking my head through the strap, I wind it across my body, then crawl back to my phone and place it inside. I keep my head down, like the operator said, and I don't lift it again until my door opens. Black boots and yellow pants fill my vision. Smoke billows into my room, burning my eyes.

"I've got you," a voice says, a man I think, and his arms wrap around my body. Hope and relief surge through me as he lifts, draping me over his upper back. He steps through my bedroom door, and even though the danger is still present, it all feels like it will be behind me soon.

Another firefighter meets us halfway up the stairs. "The fire is at the back of the house," he yells. "But the wind shifted, and it's coming this way."

With my thighs and arms pinned to the firefighter's body, he hurries down the stairs.

From my upside down position, I see it. Fire. It is not mesmerizing or beautiful or any of the nice things I thought about fire before now. It's a monster, eating its way through my home, swallowing the kitchen and licking at the dining room walls.

The firefighter exits the front door, sideways first and then turning to face the street. He clears the house, hurrying down the narrow path that bisects the front yard.

Applause. Cheering. Shouting.

Police officers. Blue and red lights flashing on the top of an ambulance. A crowd of pajama-clad neighbors.

He sets me on my feet, but I buckle. He catches me. My eyes burn as I try to orient myself, tearing though I don't think I'm crying. Someone takes me from his arms. I lean heavily on them, and then I'm lifted. I'm wheeled away, then lifted again, and now I'm in the back of an ambulance.

An oxygen mask goes over my nose. I am examined. A flashlight shines in my eyes. My pulse is checked. Questions lobbed at me. I do my best to answer them.

An EMT grips both doors, moving to close them. My

arm shoots out, my other hand sliding the oxygen mask from my mouth.

"I'm fine," I croak. It's the first time I've spoken since I was on the phone with the operator. My phone, tucked safely in the purse fastened around my body. But all my other belongings. Oh God.

Beside me, the EMT who examined me speaks. "You've experienced a lot of smoke inhalation. We're going to get you checked out by a doctor." She nods at the man standing outside, next to the open doors of the ambulance. A second person stands beside him.

The firefighter? My eyes are tearing so badly, I can only see an outline. I cannot tell if he is looking at me. And I have no idea if he's the man who saved me.

The doors close, and I'm whisked away from the nightmare. Funny thing is, the nightmare is still there, the blaze still burning. The only difference now is that I'm no longer a part of it.

CHAPTER 2

MY LITTLE SISTER YELLS MY NAME A SECOND BEFORE SHE flings herself into the emergency room bay.

Camryn, brown hair wild around her face and wearing a pajama top that reads *No Drama Llama*, rushes to my bedside. Her gaze slides over me, frenzied. "Your neighbor called. Not the busybody who watches everyone, the other one who knows Dad. Nancy." She assesses me head to toe. "Are you ok?"

It hurts to speak. I touch my throat, hoping she gets the message, and offer a thumbs-up.

Her eyes flare. "You can't speak? But your throat is ok, right?" She grabs my hand with one of her own, shaking it over the clean but worn sheet. "You could speak if you had to?"

I nod again, more emphatically this time as a scene from The Little Mermaid dances somewhere in the back of my mind.

"Thank God." Camryn glances at the ceiling, dropping my hand to park prayer hands in front of her chest. She looks back at me. "Nancy told me your house caught fire." Tears shine in her eyes. "She said the flames went into the sky."

Cam waits for me to confirm Nancy's assertion, but I was too busy being inside the house to know what it looked like from the outside. If I could speak, I'd say that, and then Camryn would give me a dirty look. I settle for shrugging, and the doctor who examined me when I arrived strides into the bay.

"How are you feeling, Ms. Burke?" Dr. Booker assesses me with a quick glance. He's young, handsome, and no-nonsense.

"Ok," I rasp.

Camryn steps to the end of my bed. She smiles shamelessly, forgetting what she's wearing and the state of her hair. "Can you tell me more about what happened to my big sister? It hurts her to speak, so I'm still mostly in the dark."

I'd roll my eyes if they didn't feel like someone poured hot desert sand in them.

A smile tugs at the corner of the doctor's mouth. I'm not surprised. Camryn can charm the skin off a snake, according to our father.

"Your sister was in a house fire. She experienced smoke inhalation, but I wouldn't call it an injury. The only prescription for it is time and rest." He looks at me. "I've seen much, much worse, Ms. Burke. You're very lucky."

"Thank you," I manage haltingly.

He nods at me. "Thank goodness for firefighters." Glancing at his wristwatch, he says, "Discharge might take some time, so hold tight."

Camryn comes back to my side as the doctor walks from the room, sweeping the curtain closed as he goes.

"Stop," she commands, frowning.

My hands lift in confusion and innocence.

"Don't judge me for flirting." Her eyes drift down to my chest. "You're the one who's not wearing a bra."

———

AFTER I'M DISCHARGED from the hospital, Camryn drives me to the house we grew up in. It's not far from where I live (lived?), just over the invisible line that separates Phoenix from Scottsdale.

She hasn't moved out, despite graduating from high school a year ago. She doesn't go to school either, choosing to spend her time working at the locally owned coffee shop a few miles away. Sometimes I wonder if the reason my dad hasn't either forced her to go to college or kicked her out is because he doesn't realize she still lives here. He buries himself in work, and his vision tunnels. He might know she's present, but he doesn't actually see her.

"Home sweet home," Cam announces when we walk inside the ranch style home. My legs haven't stopped feeling like sticks of Jell-O, and by now I'm upright only by sheer force of will.

"Remember," Cam says, shuffling past me. "You don't have a bedroom here anymore."

My dad didn't keep my room intact when I left for college. Within a few months of me moving out of my childhood home and into my dorm at Arizona State University, the four walls I'd grown up in transformed into a home gym. Carpet ripped up, and squishy yoga mat material laid down in its place. He installed a mirrored wall, and added everything a person could need to either get or stay in shape. He'd been dating Patricia, a personal trainer and fitness blogger. She was beloved by women who were squarely in their mid-life reawakening, fresh from the death of their first marriage and ready to rediscover the woman they'd lost when they became wives and mothers.

Patricia was nice enough, but Camryn and I knew better than to put too much stock into the relationship. Not shockingly, we were right. They lasted eight months. To my knowledge, Dad still uses the home gym, albeit with less frequency.

My father has an aversion to being single. If asked, he'd scoff and say this is untrue. I don't know how he denies it, given all the evidence to the contrary. Evidence being *women*. No opinions here, just cold hard facts. I think he doesn't want to face how lonely he is since our mom died, and denying the symptom also denies the underlying illness.

The fourth bedroom in the house is an office, not that my dad ever uses it. He's constantly traveling for work. Currently he's in Japan.

The urge to call him sweeps over me, and I voice it to my sister.

Camryn shrugs. "Why? He won't jump on the next flight and come home."

She's right.

Camryn gives me fresh pajamas that don't smell like smoke and lets me use her expensive cream face wash. I'll shower tomorrow. My hair is tied on top of my head, the lingering scent of smoke clinging to my bound tresses.

Camryn pulls back the covers of her queen size bed and crawls to the far side, making room for me. "Snuggle time," she mumbles, yawning.

I get in beside her, worry settling over me like the comforter I'm wrapped in. Does Sabrina know about the fire? Did someone call her? The police? Were the police there when I was carried out? I can't remember. What about—

"Go to sleep, Baxter."

A wisp of a laugh rushes between my lips. Baxter was the name of our neighbor's adopted rescue dog who had an affinity for humping my calves. Camryn called me Baxter as a joke, and the name stuck. She rarely uses it anymore, and I think I know why she's using it now. Comedic relief can soothe near-tragedy. And what almost happened tonight?

It would've been tragic.

In the tiniest voice, Cam whispers into the darkness, "You're the only mother I've ever had, and you could've been gone. Just like that."

Around the lump building in my throat, I say, "I didn't, Cam. I'm still here, and I'll still be passively aggressively trying to make you go to college, and finding flaws with every guy you date."

She sniffs. "And telling me you hate my shoes."

"You always choose the ugliest shoes." The words barely make it out before I'm crying.

Heaving sobs contort my face and fill my chest. Camryn rolls over, pulling me in to her. She holds me and lets me cry. At some point we fall asleep, our roles reversed. So many nights we fell asleep with me holding her this same way.

SESSION TWO
DESERT FLOWER THERAPY

"You must have been terrified," Dr. Ruben says, displaying just the right amount of empathy.

"Have you ever been in a life or death situation?" Typically, the patient does not ask many questions of the therapist, but this is different. I feel more like his equal than a patient.

Then again, *I'm* on *his* couch.

He shakes his head. "Not truly, no."

"Me neither, until the fire. Maybe it's not this way for everybody, but for me, the fear didn't come first. It was shock, more than anything else. Utter shock."

"That makes sense."

"You're supposed to validate me."

A tiny smile, perhaps even a smirk, lifts one corner of his mouth. His bushy eyebrows climb up his forehead. "How about we make a deal? I won't feed you bullshit, and you don't tell me how to do my job?"

I nod once. I like this guy, and his straightforward approach. "Deal."

Dr. Ruben says, "Your little sister sounds like she has a lot of personality."

Camryn's sly, knowing smile pops into my head. "She's a character. I used to worry she would have a hard time in life, but I think she's going to be alright." The slightest twitch of Dr. Ruben's eyes has me hearing my answer through the lens of a therapist, and hustling to hedge my statement. "I'm sure you're going to tell me it's not normal for a big sister to worry about something like that. Leave the parenting to the parent, right?"

He slides his glasses halfway down his nose and looks at me with detached curiosity. "Are you going to do my job for me?"

My palms lift. "Sorry, sorry."

He pushes his glasses into place. "I'm not going to tell you what's normal and what's not. The bell curve leaves a lot of room along the spectrum." He uses his hands to demonstrate a bell shape. They flare out at the bottom, and he says, "As long as you're not living in the tails of the curve, there's plenty that can be considered perfectly normal for the individual."

I nod. I like that.

"That said, do you want to tell me why you sound more parental than a typical big sister?"

"Well, I don't think I'm living in the tails here—" I pause for his reaction. I'm pretty sure he's biting back a smile. "But my mom died from an aggressive cancer when we were young. I took over her role."

"Where was your dad?"

I shrug. I don't like talking about my dad. It feels wrong, like an unintended betrayal. "Around."

"Was he the same dad you were used to having before your mom died?"

I poke at the rip in the thigh of my jeans. How did Dr. Ruben manage to drill down to the center of it? This guy is *good*. "A few things changed. Others stayed the same."

"Did this upset you?"

"I was more upset by what didn't change, than what did."

"How so?"

"He traveled a lot for work, and he kept traveling after she died. It seemed to me he should have found a job that allowed him to travel less. Or not at all."

"You stayed with your sister?"

"We had a neighbor who would come and stay in the guest room when he traveled overnight. She was an old woman, widowed. Very nice. I think she was there so my dad could say there was an adult in the house."

"Then she'd leave in the morning?"

I nod. "I got us off to school, then met Camryn in the afternoon and walked her home. We were on our own until the evening, when either my dad came home or the neighbor showed up to sleep over."

"You were how old?"

"Ten."

His eyebrows raise.

"I know how it sounds," I say quickly, "but I was capable of making easy dinners, sandwiches and bagged salads and things like that. I knew how to dial 9-1-1 in case of an emergency, which"—I make ta-da hands—"turns out I needed, but not until much later."

"So you took care of your sister?"

I feel it. How my chest puffs out. "Yes." I cannot mask the hint of pride in my voice.

"Who"—Dr. Ruben leans forward, pressing his hands together between his open knees—"took care of you?"

"Me." I've always felt a deep sense of pride at having taken care of myself and Camryn. But right now, the pride is gone. It's the first time in my life I've felt sad about it instead.

Dr. Ruben sits back, letting the revelation simmer. "What happened after your sister took you home from the hospital?"

CHAPTER 3

THE BACK HALF OF THE HOUSE IS ALMOST GONE. BURN MARKS decorate the rest, as if the flames became fingers and caressed the home. From my spot here on the sidewalk I see directly into my room. Weirdly, it looks intact, but I know better than to try. The stairs are not safe enough for me to climb.

On the drive over I scoured the internet, reading about house fires. Between the extreme heat and the smoke, even minor fires leave more damage than you'd think.

There is nothing here but a ruined home. I should be crying, but the receding shock has returned. There is no other explanation for the feeling of numbness where anguish should be.

I still haven't showered, and I've changed into Camryn's clothes. Sweatpants, and an oversized sweatshirt. Being unshowered and in unfamiliar clothing only adds to this out of body experience.

Sabrina's parents arrive at the same time as Sabrina. Her mother bursts from the car, running as if she herself can go back in time and put out the fire, or stop it from happening at all. When she sees me, she changes course and comes to me.

"Avery," MaryAnn cries, taking my face in her hands. She is beside herself, her eyes wide, her face a mixture of shock and disbelief. I feel a pang of guilt for not having called my father yet, and a second feeling, far more uncomfortable than the first. Sabrina's mother's reaction makes me miss my own.

"Everything is ok," I say, covering MaryAnn's hands with mine. "Well, maybe not. But I'm ok."

MaryAnn's lips press together when she releases me. "What happened?"

Sabrina and her boyfriend Cross are here now, followed by Bill, Sabrina's dad. Camryn hangs back, gaze going from me, to the house, and back again.

I do my best to explain it all to them, but I don't know much either.

"What happened to the smoke alarm?" Bill asks, eyebrows drawn.

Sabrina shrinks away from the accusation in his tone. "It was beeping, so we took it down. I meant to get batteries, but I forgot."

Bill tucks his hands in the pockets of his khakis and rocks back on his heels. He takes a deep breath, then two more before pulling out his phone. "I'm calling the insurance company," he says, and steps away.

Sabrina and I walk around the house. She cries, and I stop to hug her.

"You must have been so scared," she says, voice wavering.

I nod. "It was really awful."

"I've thought about fires before." She pulls back and wipes under her nose with the back of her hand. "Growing up, I imagined being home by myself and my house suddenly being on fire. I planned out what I was going to grab on my way out." She sniffs. "What did you grab?"

I look up at the house, where my room sits half-exposed, and picture myself with my face pressed to the carpet. "There wasn't a lot of time to save anything. The 9-1-1 operator instructed me to stay down. But I did crawl to my nightstand and take a photo of my mom."

Sabrina considers this. "I would've grabbed my grandmother's locket. Not my fancy red-bottomed shoes, or that expensive purse Cross gave me for Christmas. Isn't it funny what we hold on to? That locket isn't even real gold." She looks wistfully at the room that was hers. It is next to mine, just a little closer to the back of the house. In terms of damage, it looks an awful lot like mine.

"You might find it," I tell her. I don't actually have much hope, but it seems like the right thing to say.

"Avery," my sister calls. She's coming my way with a petite, dark-haired woman I don't recognize.

"This is Domenica Santiago. She's a reporter for the Arizona Times."

Domenica smiles wide and shakes my hand enthusiastically. "I came by to see what I'd heard about this morning in the newsroom, and saw you all here. Would it be ok to ask you a few questions?" I must be making a face, because she adds, "Not now, of course. When it's convenient for you. I thought it might make for a good story."

I'm not sure what about it all makes for a good story, and on a normal day I'd be irritated by the way she's smiling in front of the wreckage of my home, but my exhaustion is creeping in and I'm too tired to care.

Cam gives Domenica my phone number and we agree to talk tomorrow to set up an interview.

She leaves, and we rejoin Sabrina's parents. Her dad has hung up with insurance and is now talking with the fire investigator.

"Faulty wiring where?" he asks.

"Where?" MaryAnn whispers forcefully.

Bill turns away from her, frowning. "The security lamp near the back door? That's impossible. I installed it myself."

MaryAnn hurries around to face her husband, eyes lit up with fury. "I told you to hire an electrician," she hisses, pointing an accusatory finger at his chest. He walks away, and she follows him.

"Ugh," Sabrina groans, watching them. Her dad is waving her mom away, but MaryAnn is unfazed, continuing a steady stream of griping. "How can they be fighting right now, of all times?"

It seems to me right now is the perfect recipe for a fight. Frightened? Check. High stress? Check. Frazzled nerves? Check.

Sabrina shifts her attention to our charred home. "Did you get a chance to see the firefighter who saved you?"

"Everything was too chaotic." I can see him in my mind's eye, but his features are undefined. Between his large suit, his helmet and his face shield, he is only an outline of a man. "I'd like to thank him, but how can I find him? I don't know his name." It feels like an imbalance, to not know the name of the person who saved my life.

"I bet you could show up at the nearest fire station and

ask around. I think firefighters have weird schedules, like they work a day and then have two off. If he's not there, someone will know what you're talking about."

"What if he doesn't want to see me? What if he just wants to do his job and move on?"

Sabrina shakes her head. "I think anybody in public service would love to be thanked for their contribution. Especially when it's dangerous."

"When you put it that way…" I nudge Sabrina. "I'm really sorry about all this. Your house. Your things."

She stares at the misshapen mess in front of us. Homes bring feelings of safety and security. You lock your doors and you're supposed to be safe inside your home. But what about when the danger originates inside?

"We don't know the extent of it all yet." Sabrina plasters a smile on her face. It's too bright to be authentic, but I appreciate her positivity. "Besides"—she wraps an arm around my shoulders—"most of it is just stuff. It's replaceable. You are not replaceable. And you're here. Everything else is noise."

CHAPTER 4

MY STOMACH HANGS SOMEWHERE NEAR MY KNEES. THE FIRE station feels off-limits, a place I'm not supposed to go.

But where else am I supposed to find the man who saved my life? Taking a deep breath, I open the door and step inside before I change my mind.

"Can I help you?"

A man, tall with closely cropped thinning salt and pepper hair, stands near a red fire truck.

"Hello." I smile at the man and walk closer. He's built like a wall with a shirt that reads 'Captain.' The mustache on his face looks like it's lived there a long time. "I'm looking for someone, um…" I swallow against my awkwardness. "Last Saturday night there was a fire at my house. I was inside, and he rescued me." It's not a question, but my voice lifts at the end and it comes out sounding like one.

His head cocks sideways. "On Vista Buena?"

"Yes, exactly."

"That was Woodruff. He's in the kitchen. Let me grab him."

He leaves me in the bay. To keep busy, I study the equipment. A long yellow tube hangs from the ceiling, and off to the side a pole leads up to the second story. I don't know why, but I'd always thought that was fire station lore. I guess not.

A door to the left opens, and the firefighter I'd been talking with walks out. He's followed by two men, dressed the same, and about the same height.

The second man steps sideways, coming into my full view. His dark brown hair shines like glazed chocolate in the overhead light, and even from this distance I see what his gear hid. This man is attractive, a brand of handsome that knocks a person sideways and requires them to recover.

His eyes find mine. The warmth in his gaze settles into me, the pleased surprise on his face flooding my senses. His strides are long and certain. Two feet from me he stops, extending a hand. He doesn't smile, but the corners of his lips lift. Somehow, in a way that defies reasoning, I know this man has a deep soul. I feel it in my own.

I place my hand in his waiting palm, and when his calluses scrape my skin, my breath steals up my throat. I find my voice, and say, "Last Saturday night… Thank you for what you did. If it weren't for you, I…" The unsaid portion of my sentence hangs in the air. He knows just as well as I do what could've happened if it weren't for him. "You're a hero."

He releases my hand. His teeth capture the side of his lower lip and he shakes his head. "I was only doing my job."

A sliver of something slips through me. Something *delightful*. "Then I guess I'm very happy you're good at your job."

Now he smiles, a closed-mouth, almost shy grin, as if the flattery pleases and embarrasses him in equal measure. A thin white scar stretches from the top of his upper lip to his nose, lifting his lip a fraction on that side. It makes an otherwise handsome face appear rugged. I like it.

Quiet falls over us, and normally I'm good in these situations. I can chat, fill a space, but my unexpected attraction has robbed me of my talent. The silence stretches across a handful of seconds, awkwardness building, and the older firefighter nudges him. The third firefighter, who I've nearly forgotten is present, grins and urges, "Come on, hero."

He doesn't react to the nudge or the teasing. His gaze stays locked on me and he says, "I didn't catch your name?" His hands tuck into his pockets, his eyebrows lift.

My name? Do I have one? Oh, right. "Avery Burke."

"Gabriel Woodruff."

The hero has a name. It's a good name, too. Solid. Stable. "It's nice to meet you, Gabriel."

"You as well, Avery."

He says my name with care and purpose, his voice a warm caress around all five letters.

I force myself to step back into reality. "I said what I came here to say, so I won't keep you." My gaze swings over the three men. "Thank you for doing what you do."

I turn to the exit, retracing my steps. There's movement behind me, the soft swish of fabric, but when I don't hear footsteps I keep going.

My hand is on my car door handle when I hear my name.

"Avery?"

I turn, tenting a hand over my eyes to block out the sun. Gabriel walks closer. The light of day makes him more handsome, illuminating the arch of his eyebrows, allowing his high cheekbones to form shadows.

He stops a few feet from me. I have the uncharacteristic urge to close the space, to run my palms over the expanse of his chest and let my fingertips explore the back of his neck.

"Sometimes, after people have had the experience you had a few days ago, it helps them to talk about it. Would you, uh…" He nibbles the side of his lower lip again, and it makes me smile. Gabriel has a *thing*. A nervous habit. I don't know why this thrills me, but it does. "Would you want to talk about it with me?"

My smile stretches my cheeks. I don't think I've ever wanted anything more. "I would love to."

"Great," he says, breathing the word in relief. "That's great." He pulls his phone from his pocket. "Can I have your number?"

I recite my number, trying to keep my excitement from my voice and embarrassing me.

He slips his phone back into his pocket. "I'll talk to you soon."

He backs away, waving, and I climb into my car. He disappears into the fire station, and I melt into my seat. "Oh my God," I whisper, pressing a hand to my chest and taking my first deep breath since the moment Gabriel walked into my line of sight.

My phone dings. I take it from my purse.

> Hi. It's Gabriel. Am I supposed to wait a few days before reaching out? Oh well. I'm off work the day after tomorrow. Would you like to get coffee?

My grin splits my face. My stomach backflips, my arms quake as adrenaline spreads.

> Coffee sounds perfect.

Should I include an emoji? An exclamation point? I hit send before I can overthink it any longer. He sends another text, proposing a location and time. I agree to it, and just as I'm about to break into a dance in my car, it hits me he might be able to see me. Are there windows? Surely the fire station has windows. No dancing, then. I back out of the space, keeping my gaze straight ahead, and pull into midday traffic.

I'm driving, but all I see is tan skin, brown eyes fringed by the darkest of lashes. Assertive eyebrows and the gentle nip of a lower lip.

SESSION THREE

DESERT FLOWER THERAPY

"This might be where it really begins. My story, I mean." I shift on the couch. "I know I said it was the fire, and technically it was. But some days I wonder if Gabriel *was* the fire. Because it honestly felt like after I met him, my entire world was engulfed in flames."

"You had chemistry." Dr. Ruben says it simply, but that one word cannot encompass all we had. All we were.

I trail a fingertip over my forearm. Even now, I feel it. That heat, just from talking about Gabriel. "It was like I came alive when I met him. Like I was asleep, and he woke me."

Dr. Ruben frowns, disapproval in the parentheses formed on either side of his mouth.

I don't ask why.

I know why.

He gestures for me to speak.

CHAPTER 5

The day of my coffee meeting with Gabriel coincides with my last interview for my research project.

I'm in the final stretch of my degree program to become a marriage and family therapist. The end part of the program is completing a research project, and I've chosen to study longevity in marriage. Much of my research has been conducted through interviews of people who've been married far longer than I've been alive.

The Bergmans, married fifty-two years next month, appear to be two halves of the same whole. Albert spoke only once, but Ingrid chatted long after I finished taking notes. She showed me their four children and twelve grandchildren, one of whom is expecting. She talked proudly about their occupations and adventures, and her opinion on all of it.

When I finally mentioned I had a date I was going to be late for, she shooed me from the room.

A lump has parked itself in my throat for most of my

drive to this coffee shop. I pull into a parking spot, flipping down my visor and checking my makeup and teeth in the mirror.

My heart and my pulse? Different story. My heartbeat is everywhere, all at once.

I go on dates, but this one feels big in comparison. Like all dates before today were practice. This one? It's the real thing.

Gabriel sits at a table for two in the corner. He wears dark jeans, and a light-blue shirt. I can't decide if he's more breathtaking in or out of uniform. He smiles when he sees me, a grin that doesn't hold pretense. My knees wobble as I make my way over. He stands when I'm halfway there, running his hands once down his thighs. His nervousness is both disarming and endearing.

"Hi, Avery."

He steps out from his side of the table, surprising me by reaching for my hand. He takes another step at the same time he pulls me in for a hug.

It's a real, solid hug. Nothing flimsy or awkward, where only our sides meet. This is a full on, chest to chest hug.

I melt into him. Into his wide chest, round shoulders, and the feeling of safety that comes part and parcel with this man. Beneath the fabric is hard muscle, ridges and bumps I could get lost in, and a scent I never want to forget. He rubs my back, his hand moving up and down, and I allow the feelings to wash over me, both the vulnerability and the soothing. Two things I rarely allow myself, but letting Gabriel be the liberator of both feels like a foregone conclusion.

He releases me, but not for long. He takes my hand, leading me through the tables of people and to the counter to order. He gestures for me to go first, so I recite my usual. Cold brew, no room.

Gabriel orders and pays. I could have paid for mine, but I like the way he pulled out his wallet and handed her a ten, as if me paying wasn't in his realm of thinking. We take our coffees back to the table.

"So," Gabriel says, leaning forward. He props his elbows on the table's edge, his palms gripping his coffee. "How are you? I've been in plenty of fires, but never the way you were."

"Would you mind if we didn't talk about the fire? I know we made this…" I falter on the word. I don't want to say 'date.' "…*plan* to meet based on the idea of talking about what happened, but…"

"Ready to not have it be the center of all your thoughts and conversations?" He lifts his eyebrows as he guesses my feelings.

I nod, relieved he understands. "Exactly." The fire terrorizes my sleeping hours, and I'd like to keep it from my days. Last night I dreamed help never arrived, and I woke myself up before my dream-self leaped from the bedroom window.

Gabriel pushes at his shirt sleeves, sliding them up to the middle of his forearm. The fabric strains against the muscle, and a light dusting of dark hair peeks out. "Are you in school?" he asks, sipping his coffee.

He's doing what I asked of him, and I appreciate that. "I'm in my second year of graduate school at ASU."

"Studying?"

"Marriage and family therapy."

"Uh-oh." His eyes narrow playfully. "That involves psychology. Are you psychoanalyzing me right now?"

I laugh. "Yes."

His eyebrows lift. "Results?"

"Inconclusive."

He nods. "I guess you'll need more time with the patient."

One corner of my mouth lifts in a grin. "I guess so."

Gabriel sits back, one palm on his thigh, the other wrapped around his cup. "Second year? So you're almost done?"

"Almost over the finish line. I'm wrapping up a research project right now."

Gabriel sips his coffee. I like watching the bob in his throat when he swallows. "What are you researching?"

"Success in long-term relationships."

"How do you study something like that?"

"Interviews." I cross my legs and lean back. "I just came from one. A sweet old couple who've been married fifty-two years."

Gabriel's eyes widen. "What was their secret?"

"From what I can tell, different people need different things from their spouses. And the ones who make it long-term are the people whose spouses give them what they need, whatever that might be. But at the end of the day, I think it's all distilled into compassion. You have to have compassion to see and meet needs."

He nods his head slowly. "Compassion. Hmm."

The way he says it makes me think he doesn't believe it. "Why do you sound like you're not convinced?"

"I've been a firefighter for five years, and started out with a lot of compassion. But over time, when you see awful things over and over, you lose some of that. I have to compartmentalize, so I can do my job."

He looks pensive, so I ask, "Do you regret that? Having to compartmentalize?"

He shakes his head. "No. I don't think a person could survive the job otherwise."

"Do you love it? What you do?" I ask because public service jobs strike me as emotionally draining, and if you don't love it, how else can you refill your cup every day?

"Love it?" Gabriel shifts. "Nobody's asked me that before. I guess I love it."

"You were frowning. Just now, when you answered." I use one finger from each hand to draw an upside down smile on my face.

Gabriel drinks his coffee, and I see it plain on his face, him feeling like maybe I've noticed too much. Like he has been too vulnerable, and he's not comfortable with that. "Maybe it bothers me, and I didn't realize it." He taps the rim of his cup with a finger. "Do you remember the guy who walked out from the kitchen with me at the station? The young guy?"

I nod.

"That's Ryan. My best friend. He loves what we do. Lives for it." A faraway look comes over Gabriel's face. He blinks three times in rapid succession, like he's bringing himself back to the moment. "Some aspects of the job are great. My dad is the captain, so I get to spend a lot of time with him. You met him. He was the person standing in the bay when you walked in." Gabriel shakes his head. "But, to me, it's a job. For Ryan, it's more than a job. It defines him."

He falls quiet, and I get the feeling everything he said is only skimming the surface.

"I've been thinking about the 9-1-1 operator," I say, to take the spotlight off him. "How her voice could've been the last one I heard. And what that might have done to her. It made me wonder if she's been in that position before."

The air between us takes on a sad quality. I said I didn't want to talk about the fire, and now I've brought it up. Gabriel opens his mouth to speak, but his gaze moves to something behind me.

He points, and I turn. A young woman sets a stack of newspapers in a wire rack. She has already positioned one so it faces out, the front-page photo of a firefighter coming out of a burning home with a person thrown over his shoulders. The headline reads, *Firefighter Saves College Student.*

Gabriel is up from his seat, grabbing a copy and tucking it under his arm. He pays for it and returns, setting it on the table lengthwise so we can both read.

"You gave an interview?" he asks, glancing over the article.

The tip of my tongue traces my upper lip and I nod. "Yesterday. My sister set it up."

Cam had communicated with the reporter, and when it was time she placed my laptop in front of me with the video call already going. Then she sat beside me, off-screen but holding my hand.

I tap the paper. "The reporter didn't tell me it was

going to be front page news. She made it sound like it was a little piece."

"Must be a slow news day." He keeps skimming. "The crew is going to love this. They've started calling me 'hero.'"

My eyes widen in apology. "Because of me?"

"Yes," he says, but he's grinning. "It's ok. There are far worse things to be called." He gets to the end of the article and looks up at me through dark lashes. "She wrote that we're going on a date."

I palm my forehead as mortification makes me want to sink into the cold tile floor. "I'm so sorry. My sister mentioned it right before the call was over. I didn't think it was part of the interview."

His thumb runs the length of his lower lip. "Don't be sorry. I don't care if the entire world knows I asked you on a date."

My toes curl, gripping my shoes as I try to keep myself rooted to this moment when everything inside me feels like butterflies and somersaults. "You don't do that often, do you? Ask the people you save from a burning building if they'll go on a date with you?" I'm teasing because I don't know how to handle the intensity between us.

He smirks, a dimple appearing in his right cheek only. "You're the first."

"I feel honored," I say in a joking voice.

"I hope you know I didn't ask you out because I expected you to agree."

"Why did you ask?"

"Honestly?"

"No, lie to me."

This earns me a laugh. I like his laugh. It's deep, almost gruff, and masculine.

"My dad and Ryan essentially shoved me out the door after you left the station."

"You wouldn't have come after me on your own?"

"I definitely would have. My wheels were turning slower that day, thanks to a beautiful woman and her even prettier smile."

A warm flush spreads over me.

Gabriel continues. "There was no way I was going to let you drive away without figuring out some way to see you again."

I gulp against the rush of endorphins, the flowing oxytocin. "Why's that? Aside from you doing your job, we hardly know each other."

He bites his lower lip. "There's something about you, something I can't wrap my mind around." His head moves back and forth slowly as he speaks. "I just knew that if I let you drive away, I'd regret it."

Words fail me, so I close the inches separating our hands. My fingers slide over his, intertwining. The newspaper lies beneath our grasp.

"Is this the right way to start something?" I ask. Am I confusing my gratitude to him for saving my life for attraction? His thumb draws a circle on the top of my hand. My core tightens.

No. Definitely not what I'm doing.

"We can pretend last weekend never happened. I met you at the grocery store, we were reaching for the same carton of strawberries. Our hands brushed. Sparks flew. You were dazzled by my wit, I was taken by your hazel eyes."

I laugh. "Have you spent some time on this?"

He shrugs with one shoulder. "I don't shy away from romance."

Lucky me. "I am dazzled by your wit."

His free hand disappears under the table and lands on my knee. His caress is gentle, but potent enough to send a shock through my center, all the way to my heart.

His head tips sideways. "I am taken by your hazel eyes."

I will my heart rate to slow, but it's no use. It is soaring, galloping, cartwheeling down a hill. "Then I guess it's settled."

Gabriel smiles. His teeth are nearly perfect, save for a lower tooth that turns in slightly. I like this imperfection, so tiny it shouldn't be termed as such. "I like your name."

I point to my chest. "My name?"

"A-very. A Very." He looks playful. "*A Very* smart and beautiful woman sits across from me."

"I've never thought of my name that way before."

"Do you hate it? I don't have to say it like that."

I shake my head quickly. "No, no. I don't hate it." I like how he has already created an inside joke for us.

"I have to get going," he says regretfully, glancing at the watch on his left wrist. "My dad bought a new couch, and I told him he could use my truck to pick it up."

"That was nice of you." My chair glides along the tile floor as I push away from the table. "Are you close with your parents?" I ask, ducking my head into my purse strap and arranging it across my body.

Gabriel's mouth opens, then closes. He spends a few seconds thinking, then says slowly, "Yes."

I want to ask him more about that, but we're short on

time, and maybe it's too heavy of a topic for a first date. Perhaps dysfunctional families are more third date material.

We walk from the coffee shop, his hand settling lightly on my lower back. I love the warmth, the gentle guidance, the heat of his hand through the cotton of my shirt. We get to my car, and I lean my back against the driver's door. He's close enough that I can reach out and take hold of his shirt. He stays that way, towering over me, gaze locked on mine.

I want him to kiss me. I've never been this attracted to anybody. All of him calls all of me to attention.

He steps closer, sliding a hand into my hair, his thumb tracing the shell of my ear. My head tips into his touch.

"Gabriel." My whisper is an invitation, and he knows it. He closes the distance at the same time I close my eyes. I know what's coming, and every inch of me is ready for it.

It's not a short I-just-met-you kiss. He lingers. His lips are perfect, and I melt against him. When his tongue pushes against the seam of my lips, I open willingly. His sweet caramel coffee flavor mixes with my bitter cold brew. I moan quietly, unable to keep myself from making the sound. He smiles against me as our foreheads press together and we share a breath. I am astounded, floored, unequivocally knocked sideways.

"Can I see you again? Soon?" Gabriel asks. His tone is urgent.

This feeling of being wanted is good. Really, really good. "Absolutely," I murmur.

He puts a few inches of space between us. "I'm off tomorrow, too. Will you have dinner with me tomorrow night?"

I nod. "Just tell me when and where and I'll be there."

Gabriel shakes his head. "I want to pick you up. Where are you staying?"

"My dad's house. I'll send you the address."

He places a second kiss, short but sweet, at the corner of my mouth. He doesn't walk away until I climb in my car. I drive home, my fingertips traversing the trail he blazed across my lips.

A kiss that promised a million more.

SESSION FOUR
DESERT FLOWER THERAPY

"I vaguely remember that newspaper article," Dr. Ruben says. "I believe it was the picture that drew my attention."

I fidget with my bracelet, watching my fingers work the clasp. "It was an arresting photo."

"Dramatic. Spectacular." Dr. Ruben pauses, then adds, "Romantic."

The image is there in my mind, ever present. I don't have to close my eyes to see the photo as clear as if I were holding it in my hands. "It sure was."

"What a way for a relationship to begin."

I drop the bracelet and look up. "I think about that sometimes. How we met in an elevated circumstance. Usually two people meet, and they take time to ramp up. Start slow, a dinner here and a movie there. Me and Gabriel, we never had that. We hit the ground running from the very first second."

"It sounds like you two had an intense connection."

"We did."

"You mentioned your research project. Is compassion what you landed on when your research concluded?"

"Yes and no. Compassion was the best word I could find to encompass it all. But it really seemed like different people needed different things from their spouses. And the ones who made it long-term were the people whose spouses gave them what they needed, whatever that might be."

"Fascinating." Dr. Ruben's eyes squint wistfully. "I always loved that part of research. Starting out in one place, and winding up somewhere you never saw coming."

"Sounds like you're describing life."

His gaze falls back to me. "I suppose I could be."

I glance at his office walls, my name replacing his on the framed diplomas. "I'm certainly not somewhere I imagined I'd end up."

He nods, eyes watchful. "Let's keep going."

CHAPTER 6

Camryn meets me in the driveway when I get home from coffee with Gabriel. At first I think she's too excited to hear about my date to stay in the house, but her panicked expression quickly informs me otherwise.

"Dad's here." Her tone holds far more than that single announcement.

"That's ok," I assure her, climbing from my car and forcing her back a few steps. He's two days early, but it's not a problem. I'll just tell him about the fire sooner than planned.

Camryn makes a disbelieving face, but I don't care. I'm still riding high from my date with Gabriel. I'm not sure my feet are touching the ground right now.

"No, it is not ok, Avery." A vein near Camryn's temple throbs. "He's brought home a woman."

The news makes me pause, but not for long. "That isn't abnormal for Dad." I stop outside the front door. "Is there something I'm missing?"

She sets fisted hands on her hips. "He says they're getting married."

I stare at my sister, determining if she's telling the world's worst joke. I'm comfortable with my dad treating his life like it's one giant round of speed dating. But getting married? I can't picture it.

"What's she like?" I whisper, in case my dad and this unknown woman have their ears pressed to the other side of the door.

Camryn's nose scrunches. "She's–"

The door flies open. My dad stands on the other side, grinning like a loon. The reason for his goofy grin pops out from behind him, as if they're performing on a variety show.

She has blonde hair, and deep smile lines. The top of her head is level with the top of my dad's arm, and her eyes are big and brown.

"Hi, hon." My dad pulls me in for a hug. "Camryn said you had big news for me, but I have some pretty big news myself." He smiles down at the petite woman beside him. I have to admit, I haven't seen him smile this shamelessly in years. Not since my mother.

"First things first." I look at his companion and offer my hand. "I'm Avery. And you are?"

"Lara." My arm rocks with the force of her enthusiasm as she shakes my hand. "I've heard so much about you and your sister. It's lovely to meet you."

"You as well." I look from Lara to my dad. "You have something you wanted to tell me?"

At this point, I'm feeling supremely grateful Camryn already clued me in to the bomb my dad is about to drop.

"Let's sit," he says, standing back from the open door and gesturing with an open arm to the living room.

"Oh no," I say in a joking voice. "Something I need to sit down for?"

Lara's laugh is a tad shrill. Camryn gives me a knowing look, but presses her lips together to keep from smirking.

Dad and Lara settle in across from me and Camryn. "I'd wanted to tell both of you girls together, but—"

Camryn interrupts. "But I walked in on them—"

"Kissing," my dad finishes.

"Not for much longer," Camryn mutters.

He gives her a stern look. His eyes move to me, and the expression in them changes. He's preparing to not only tell me about his engagement to a woman I didn't know existed until three minutes ago, but he's going to plead his case. Asking for both permission and forgiveness.

In most relationships, the parent does not ask the child for permission, and unless they have really messed up, they rarely ask for forgiveness. But my relationship with my dad is about as atypical as it gets. Not only did I become a parent to Cam when our mom died, I also morphed into the woman of the house, closer to my dad's equal than any child should ever be. It was unfair to me, and I hate how I still carry around the resentment.

He's looking at me now, trepidation in his irises as he takes Lara's hand. As if I don't see the enormous diamond shining on her finger.

"Lara and I met on the flight out to Japan. She was headed there to teach a seminar, and we got to talking," he pauses, looking down at her. She returns his puppy dog eyes with a lovesick grin. "We hit a bit of turbulence and she grabbed my arm."

Lara looks at us and grins sheepishly. "I'm a nervous flyer."

I have no idea what my face looks like right now. I hope I'm wearing an expression that is at least somewhat acceptable for the situation, because my sister is not.

"That was, what, a month ago?" Camryn asks.

I push my leg against hers. I was thinking it, but of course Camryn's the one who would say it.

"When you know, you know." Dad squeezes Lara's hand. "Right, babe?"

Babe.

Camryn knocks her knee into mine. It's super obvious, but it doesn't matter, because the lovebirds across from us are in their own world.

"So, are congratulations in order?" They tear their gazes from one another and look back to me. I nod at the small ice skating rink on Lara's finger. "Looks like an engagement ring."

"That's exactly what it is. I asked Lara to marry me last week, and she said yes. We were so excited, we flew home early so we could start telling our families in person."

I plaster a smile on my face. "Well, let me be one of the first to say congratulations."

"Thank you," my dad says, but he looks pointedly at Camryn. I'm guessing she didn't offer the same well-wish.

He continues. "Lara has two boys from her first marriage, and we're planning to tell them tonight."

"They're about the same ages as you two," Lara adds. "Eighteen and twenty-two. They go to college in Texas, but they're here for the upcoming long weekend." Her smile dips just enough for me to see that she's nervous.

"After that, well"—Dad stares into Lara's eyes—"we don't want to wait too long to marry. Something small, intimate. Maybe even here, in the backyard, before it gets hot."

"It's mid-November," I say, trying to keep from sputtering. If they want to marry before it gets hot, that means they're targeting a March or April wedding.

Oh my God.

My pulse pounds at different points in my body, my breath turning shallow as thoughts skitter around my brain. *Dad is getting married. I don't have anywhere to live. I don't have a job. And I'm graduating in May.*

The panic must be obvious on my face, because my dad's chest puffs out, eyebrows cinching in defensiveness mixed with a dash of indignation.

"I don't need your permission, Avery." His voice turns to sandpaper, covering up the softness of his hurt feelings.

"Dad," I begin, my tone kind but firm as I step into territory that is familiar for us. "This is a big surprise, so you should expect us to feel surprised. A lot of emotions happening here," I gesture from me to Camryn. "It doesn't mean we aren't happy for you and Lara."

He nods, mollified. Lara's gaze darts from me to my dad. She's taking in the exchange, cataloging the volley and understanding the dynamics.

"Right, hon. Sorry, I should've known that. Guess I just really want you to be happy your old man has finally found someone to spend his life with."

I don't bother pointing out he already found someone to spend his life with, and her life was cut short. Or that if he'd remarried while I was still a kid, maybe I could've spent more time being one. Instead, I look at my sister and say, "We are, right Cam?"

She nods slowly. "We sure are. In fact..." Her eyes light up. I can see it now, this idea she's getting. "We should throw you an engagement party. Avery can bring her boyfriend."

I close my eyes and shake my head. Stirring the pot is Camryn's favorite pastime.

"I guess now I get to be on the receiving end of the surprise," my dad comments, eyebrows lifted. "Since when do you have a boyfriend?"

My mouth opens to answer, but Camryn is there first, delivering another one-two punch. "Since he rescued her from her house as it burned down last weekend." Cam reaches over the arm of the couch, hand disappearing from sight. When she straightens, there's a newspaper in her grasp. Tossing it on the table, she announces, "Extra extra, read all about it."

My dad takes one look at the front page, using the photo itself to tell him the story. His jaw slackens, and he swallows. Hard. "This is you? Being rescued?"

Horror. That's what I hear in his voice.

"I was waiting to tell you in person. I knew you'd be home soon, and I thought it was better to learn something like this about your child when you're face-to-face with them."

Lara's hand is at her mouth as she skims the article. Her eyes are wide. "Avery, I'm so sorry you had to go through this. It must have been terrifying for you."

"I've never been so scared in my life." In my mind I see Gabriel, opening the door to my bedroom and striding inside. The memory has shifted, changed by what I've learned since. I know the face beneath the mask. The body beneath the heavy clothing. The lip bite and the expressive eyebrows and the emotions that go into the job.

It alters the memory, casting a warmth to it where there should be nothing but terror and trauma. My hindsight has become rose-colored.

My dad has twenty questions. I answer them as best as I can, but there are some, like what Sabrina's parents are doing about the house and insurance, for which I don't have a response.

"Where are you staying?" he asks.

I point to Cam, who will be on the receiving end of some grief later. "Her bed."

Guilt flits across his face. It crosses my mind to needle him a little, remind him I can't make a bed out of a weight bench, but I leave it be.

Dad threads his arm around Lara's shoulders. "Sounds like it's going to be a full house," he tells her.

I guess that means she's moving in here.

"Fine by me," she says brightly. "It'll give me a chance to get to know the girls."

The girls. Maybe one day I won't mind being called that, but for right now the motherly way she says it irritates me.

"Speaking of kids—" My dad twists his wrist to check his watch, the action pulling Lara in closer to him. He takes the opportunity to kiss her temple. "We'd better get going. Lara's boys are expecting her."

"The question is…" Camryn points at our dad and moves her finger in a circle. "Are they expecting you?"

Lara's lips twist, worry filtering into her eyes.

"We're surprising everybody today," Dad says, standing. He offers a hand to Lara, helping her upright.

"Good luck with that," Cam responds brightly, doing nothing to hide the amusement in her tone.

"Thanks, Cam," my dad answers dryly.

He steps around the coffee table, and I stand. He places a kiss on my forehead. Against my skin, he says, "I'm still processing what happened to you." He steps back and looks down at me. "The firefighter is your boyfriend now?"

I throw a dirty look down at my seated sister. "We've been on one date."

He swipes the newspaper off the table. "Quite an interesting way to meet. Very memorable."

I reach out an arm for the paper. "Don't throw that away."

"I'm saving it," he answers, tucking it under his arm and winking at Lara as he speaks. "Few people get footage of the moment their lives changed."

"Such a romantic," Lara says, pretending to swoon.

They say goodbye, leaving through the door that leads into the garage. I wait until I hear his car start up, and then I look down at Cam, prepared to give her an earful about all the instigating.

The tears rolling down her cheeks stop me. It's uncharacteristic of her, and just as I'm opening my mouth to ask why she's crying, she tugs my hand, pulling me back down beside her. She picks up her phone, opens the camera and holds it out, trained on us.

"Let's take a picture. You heard Dad. Not everybody gets footage of the moment their lives changed." She sniffs. "And our lives just turned upside down."

She snaps the photo. Neither of us smile.

"I don't think our lives are upside down," I tell her when she slips the phone into her pocket.

She trains her wide-eyed gaze on me. "You know when you break glass, even if it doesn't shatter, it never goes back together perfectly? Alongside those big pieces are tiny shards that have a big impact? That's what this is. Even if you don't go on another date with Gabriel, which I can already tell that won't be the case, or if Dad suddenly drops Lara because her boys are adult hellions, we can't revert to who we were last week. You were in a nearly catastrophic house fire, and Dad has shown us he is capable of really moving on from Mom."

"Cam," I say as gently as possible. "I don't understand why you're upset. You don't remember Mom."

"Exactly," Cam half-shouts, her hand in the air. "And now her memory is one step further from me."

"Irrevocable shifts," I say, as a buzzing sound comes from inside my purse. I grab my phone and open the text from Gabriel.

> I was wrong. I can't wait until tomorrow to see you. Please tell me you don't have plans for dinner tonight.

I smile at his impatience and begin typing my response. Camryn chuckles softly, and I look up. "What?"

"You're smiling so hard at that phone screen it's making my cheeks hurt. Told you." She shrugs as she walks away. "Upside down."

I finish my text to Gabriel and hit send. Camryn leaves soon after, promising she'll meet Gabriel next time. She sails out the front door when her friend Danielle pulls up in her car and idles at the curb.

An hour later, Gabriel knocks on my front door.

"Hey, hero."

He grins. He's so handsome, standing there with his hands in the pockets of his jeans, filling the space without even trying.

My stomach hovers around my knees and I think maybe I could float away at any moment. Upside down is not enough to describe how I feel. Backward and inside out, also.

I am on the cusp, the edge, the precipice.

Gabriel reaches for me, and I sail into his arms, allowing him to tuck me into his warm, solid body. He kisses me like he has missed me for years.

And I throw myself over the edge, to whatever waits for me below.

SESSION FIVE
DESERT FLOWER THERAPY

"How did you feel about your dad getting remarried?"

I sip the coffee I've brought to today's session. "Like I wish he'd done it sooner."

"Why?"

"If he'd remarried while I was still a kid, maybe I could've spent more time being one. I know that sounds incredibly selfish. I'm sorry."

Dr. Ruben shakes his head at me. "You don't have to be sorry in here. And you don't have to be afraid to say how you feel. No self-censoring necessary."

I muster a smile. "I feel bad for wishing he'd gotten over my mother faster. She was a good person, and she deserved his grief."

"Did you deserve his neglect?"

The emotional punch of his words leaves me breathless. "No."

Dr. Ruben watches me, assessing, and when a full minute passes without me speaking, he says, "Let's keep talking about Gabriel."

My eyebrows pull together. "I came here to move past what happened with Gabriel. Not remember how we fell in love."

Dr. Ruben stays silent, tipping his head and watching me.

"Fine." I throw up my hands. "I know, I know. You must go back before you can go forward."

"You need to go back, Avery. Remember how you ended up in my office?"

One side of my nose begins to scrunch, but I force it down. "Right. Ok. I get it. Let's do this." My heavy sigh punctures the air. "Down the rabbit hole we go."

CHAPTER 7

"W‌HAT DO YOU THINK OF THIS ONE?" S‌ABRINA GRABS A white dress off a rack and holds it up.

"We're supposed to be replacing clothes you lost in the fire." I punch a hand through the cutouts in the bodice and ask, "Where is the rest of the dress?"

She makes a face at me. "We are replacing clothes I lost. Starting with a sexy dress for my anniversary dinner."

"Gotcha." I hold up a dress with a longer hemline but a deep v-cut chest. "What about this? And then we'll pick out something really sexy for underneath."

Sabrina replaces the white dress on the rack. "I love that idea."

I hand her the dress I chose, and she drapes it over her forearm. "Can we please talk about Gabriel?"

Even thinking his name puts a fluttery, pitter-patter feeling in my chest. "What about Gabriel?" I ask, holding a pair of jeans to my waist. Gabriel is incredible, almost too good to be true, and I'm keeping him tucked away. Like a squirrel stockpiling for winter, I am both saving and savoring.

"You've been inseparable for a month now." Sabrina's eyebrows lift. "Your dad thinks he's a real life superhero, and he's even won over Camryn, which says a lot."

"She's tough," I agree.

Sabrina scoffs. "Nearly impenetrable." She runs a hand over the fabric of the jeans I'm holding. "I like those. They're soft."

"I'm going to get them." I add them to the little pile laid over my forearm. It's half the size of Sabrina's. "As for Gabriel…" I breathe deep as I gather my thoughts. "I don't want to jinx anything. He's…well, he's everything."

Sabrina nods knowingly. "You love him."

"It's only been a month," I say, as if that's a valid argument.

She shrugs. "So? Look at your dad and Lara. They're getting married in March."

"Don't remind me," I groan. "My head is full of articles on how to make a second wedding special."

Sabrina grins. "I like her."

"You like that she agreed to be a reference on your résumé, and put in a good word for you with her school's principal."

"True," Sabrina draws out the word. "Job prospects aside, I think she's good for your dad."

"It's not all roses. Her sons aren't loving that their mom is getting remarried."

"You met them?"

I nod. "Last week. We went to brunch. They're ok, I guess. Standoffish." I shrug. "My dad and Lara's dreams of a Brady Bunch situation have been dashed. We're all a little too old for that anyhow, and besides, they live in Texas. Proximity wins this round."

"I bet her sons will come around. They need time to see how happy their mom is."

My nose wrinkles as I think about the happy sounds coming from their bedroom early this morning. I hadn't been able to sleep, so I got up to make coffee. The hushed but insistent string of vowels I heard as I passed their door had me walking away double-time.

"I heard them having sex this morning." I push aside some shirts on a rack and glance up.

Sabrina smirks. "I know it's gross, but everyone has sex."

"Including your parents," I point out.

She makes a face like she's going to be sick. "Now you've gone too far."

I laugh. "Anyway… I've been looking for someplace else to live. Camryn's always staying the night with her friend Danielle, so it's not like I'm really sharing a bed with my little sister, but it's time. I can't live in a house with the soon-to-be newlyweds any longer. Camryn has the right idea by arranging to be gone as much as possible."

"I'm sick of living with my parents, too." She jingles a necklace on a hook, making it clink against the others. "Insurance is being difficult about the house. My dad's been on the phone with them nonstop. His voice is tense but polite when he talks to them, and when he hangs up he makes a full sentence out of curse words."

I laugh at the thought of Sabrina's reserved father spewing expletives.

"Speaking of sex…" Sabrina steps closer to me. "Are

you going to talk about what that's like with Gabriel? Or are we supposed to avoid that subject, too?"

I clear my throat. I knew this was going to come up today. Sabrina and I have never been shy about talking about our experiences in the bedroom, though mine are far tamer and more limited than hers.

"We haven't had sex yet," I tell her quietly. "I live with my dad right now, remember?"

This isn't an actual reason, and Sabrina knows it. "Gabriel has a house."

Irritation rises, but it's not directed at her. "I'm aware."

"Hey," she says gently, touching my shoulder. "I'm not trying to upset you. We don't have to talk about this."

I sigh and apologize. "It's not you. I'm frustrated. With Gabriel. When he kisses me it's…it's…" I don't want to say out loud what it's like, but the truth is that when his lips are on mine it's like he's setting fire to my body.

We lie on his couch and kiss until my lips are sore. He stops there and pulls away, leaving me burning up with desire.

I haven't had a lot of sex, and I most definitely haven't had any good sex. I can tell Gabriel will be different. His patience, his slow hands, the way he tastes my mouth and my neck. The writing is on the wall. He is going to blow my mind.

"Have you asked him about it?"

I shake my head quickly. Saying *those words*, whatever they may be, is the last thing I want to do. When it comes to matters of intimacy, I clam up. Can't Gabriel be the leader? I most certainly cannot.

I step around Sabrina, pretending to consider a gold

braided belt. "I don't have the vocabulary for a question like that."

"That's ugly," Sabrina says, taking the belt from my hand and replacing it on the hook. "And you have the vocabulary. You just don't have the voice."

Pursing my lips, I nod. "Right. Also, maybe he's trying to be a gentleman?"

"Maybe he's nervous? Grab a bottle of wine, have a glass to brush off the nerves. Then—"

I shake my head. "Gabriel doesn't drink."

A 'v' furrows between Sabrina's well-tended eyebrows. "Why not?"

"He hasn't said why. He just doesn't."

She frowns. "Everybody drinks."

I make a face at her, a desire to defend Gabriel's choice rising inside me. "Not everybody." I point at myself. I rarely drink. My tolerance is low, and I don't like how I feel after.

"Fair," she concedes. "But most people have a reason for not drinking."

"Why does he have to have a reason?"

Sabrina stops thumbing through a table of perfectly folded shirts and looks at me. "Why do you sound like that?"

"Like what?"

"Like you're angry."

"I'm a little annoyed at having to talk about Gabriel's alcohol intake, or lack thereof."

"Why?"

"Because a person should be able to not drink and have it be a non-issue."

Sabrina holds up her hands. "Agreed."

We go back to shopping, but it's not as fun as it was prior to the Gabriel conversation. My annoyance with Sabrina has faded, and now I'm uncertain it was ever directed at her in the first place. It's me. It's *my* curiosity that's bothering me. I, too, want to know why Gabriel doesn't drink. And I don't want to ask him, because right now Gabriel is the best thing in my life.

What if I don't like the answer?

CHAPTER 8

"AVERY." CAMRYN SNAPS A FINGER IN MY FACE. I FROWN AND knock her hand out of the way.

"Where the hell are you lately?" She grumbles something unintelligible.

"I'm right here in front of you."

"You're with Gabriel."

I run a finger through the air, parallel to my body. "Try that again."

"You're with him mentally." Cam grabs a notebook and flips it open to a fresh page.

We're supposed to be planning a simple food menu for the wedding, but I'm distracted.

"Lara should be here any minute," Camryn says, glancing at the front door. "Before she arrives, I think we should talk about a little surprise bachelorette party. Small and tame, you know, but..."

Gabriel and I are seeing a movie tonight. Maybe he needs a clear sign, an unmistakable green light. I can use my voice, for once, and actually ask for what I want. My stomach turns at the thought. Maybe not.

"Oh my God," Cam wails, dropping her pen. "Just go. You're no help. Go to Gabriel, you hormone addled, lovesick fool." She throws her hands in the air. "It's bad enough I have to be around Dad and Lara, but at least they have sex and then function in life." She steers me toward the front door. "Go get laid, and then come back here. I want you sated and ready to work."

I shake my head, trying not to trip as I walk backward. "Cam, you don't understand, Gabriel and I—"

Cam shakes her head back at me. "Haven't done that yet? You'll be fine. It's sex, not swimming with a pod of killer whales. It's meant to be enjoyed. Go." She grabs my purse from the entryway table and pushes it to my chest.

I stop at the threshold. She drops her arms and reaches around me, opening the door. "I've never had good sex," I admit.

Camryn's head tips to the side and she shrugs. "I don't know much about good sex either. I've only done it once, and it was awful. But everyone seems obsessed with it, so there must be a reason. Go find that reason."

A throat clears behind us.

Lara hovers a few feet back, holding three brown paper grocery bags. "Hi, girls." Her smile wavers. She has definitely overheard us.

"Some advice, Lara?" Cam calls. "As far as I know, you're the only one of us having good sex."

Lara's cheeks flame.

"These walls are paper thin," Cam adds.

A boiled lobster blush hits Lara's cheeks.

She tries to recover, taking a step closer and clearing

her throat. "Well, I, uh—" She looks at me. "I think you should do whatever you want to do, and don't do whatever you don't want to do. Sex between people who love each other can be really special." She gulps, looking from me to Cam and back again.

Obviously, she's talking about our dad. While it makes me want to vomit, it's also kind of sweet.

"Gabriel hasn't even tried," I admit.

"Men are funny that way," Lara says. The red in her cheeks has faded to pink. "When sex doesn't mean anything, nothing stops them. When it means something, it terrifies them."

"See?" Cam says. "That makes perfect sense. Now, go see Gabriel and drop it like it's hot right onto his firefighter lap. He'll know what to do with you." Cam lightly shoves me out of the house. "Lara and I have work to do."

Lara winks and sidesteps me, going into the house.

Cam closes the door in my face.

I'm mildly annoyed, but I'm not sure with who anymore. Cam for being insistent, Gabriel for not being insistent enough, or me for not being able to be direct.

Gabriel answers when I call, and says he's changing the oil in his truck.

I don't tell him I'm on my way over. We make small talk, and I say I have to go.

This turns out to be a good move on my part, if the look on his face right now is any indication.

He's grinning, happy to be surprised, as he steps away from his truck's hood. He runs a red rag over his hands, watching me climb from my car.

"What are you doing here?" he asks, meeting me in the driveway. He kisses me. "Not that I'm complaining. It's a good surprise, but you said you were helping your sister today." He's wearing sweats stained with motor oil, and nothing else. He's dripping in masculinity, in that rough caveman way.

I press a fingertip to his chest, drawing a heart. "I was having some trouble focusing. She kicked me out."

He chuckles and motions for me to follow him into the house. He stops in the closest bathroom and washes his hands. The outside air temperature isn't yet hot enough to make him sweat.

I lean against the doorframe, holding on to it as his muscles flex simply from soaping up and rinsing his hands. I have never, ever wanted someone the way I want Gabriel. I didn't know it was possible for all my cells to yearn for something. For *someone*.

I can do this. Open my mouth and use my words. Tell Gabriel I will melt, right here and right now, if he doesn't take me to bed.

Gabriel finishes drying his hands and tosses the towel on the counter. He faces me, reaching up to grip the top of the doorframe with one hand. "Trouble focusing?" He leans closer, the timbre of his voice rattling my chest. "What's the problem?"

My shallow breath turns to honey, sticking in my throat. "I...um...I..."

Something passes over his face, maybe it's understanding, or maybe it's what I've been feeling since the moment I met him.

Like it's all so big, so much, so overwhelming. Like we are us, but we are also a mammoth wave, hurtling our direction, preparing to sweep us out to sea. We will be the ones to drown ourselves. That is what this feels like. A storm we've created, and willingly put ourselves in its path of destruction.

I drag in a heavy breath, and my tongue slips out to moisten my lips. This small movement tips the scale, and Gabriel hauls me flush against his chest. We pivot, my back against the wall, and Gabriel's mouth is on mine. I open for him, and his tongue sweeps inside. This action isn't new for us, but the tone is different. Somehow he is both tender and demanding, hands on my cheeks, my neck, sliding down my rib cage. My hands roam too, over his perfect chest and his even better shoulders, wrapping around him as I press myself as close as I can get with our clothes on.

"I want you," Gabriel whispers, slipping his hand under my shirt. "Is that ok?"

I answer with, "I want you, too." Look at me, using my words. Kind of.

He pulls my shirt over my head, stares at my breasts with open appreciation, and buries his face between them. "Want you so badly," he groans against my skin.

"I thought maybe you didn't, because..." I falter when he looks up at me. Desire burns in his eyes. The sight of it sets an ache at the apex of my thighs.

His tongue swipes over the top swell of my right breast, his teeth sinking lightly into the flesh. "I was trying to take it slow," he says against my skin. "Be a gentleman."

My fingernails rake through his hair. "Don't be a gentleman with me. Not right now."

Gabriel locks eyes with me, holding my gaze, and I see the moment it happens. He goes from sane to crazed. His hands slide down my body, cupping the backs of my thighs and lifting me onto him. When he gets me situated, he reaches for my bra, flipping down one of the cups. Through his house we go, my flesh in his mouth and my hands twisting in his hair.

We make it to his bedroom, and my back hits the soft sheets of an unmade bed.

Gabriel dips a knuckle into the hollow of my throat, dragging it down the centerline of my body, his gaze heavy and steady on mine. He keeps it there until he comes up against my jeans. He flicks them open and tugs them over my hips.

I sit up, reaching my fingers into the waistband of his pants. They drag back and forth, not going any lower, and he takes a sharp breath. I end the torture, and push his sweats down. He steps out of them and kicks them away.

He is beautiful. Every inch of his olive skin is muscled, taut. Hunger sweeps through me. I reach for him, and he folds over me, urging me to lie down.

Gabriel kisses me softly and pulls back to look at me. His eyes rake over my face. "Are you good?"

Considering I have the most incredible man I've ever met naked and on top of me, I'd say I'm better than good. I'm fantastic.

I lift up on my elbows, catching his lips with mine. "I'm so much better than good."

He smiles against my lips. Two of his fingertips slide over me, pushing their way into the seam of my thighs. I open for him, the same way I opened my mouth for him in the hallway.

He moans quietly when his fingers hit their mark. His eyes remain locked on mine while his first finger goes to work. "You're gorgeous, Avery." I am his focus, his attention undivided, and something about that elevates the experience.

I gulp, my breath hurtling from my throat, as his second finger joins his first while his thumb works in tandem. It's a delicious, exquisite sensation, and he watches me experience it. With one palm flat against his chest, fingers curled around his muscle, I tip my head back and rise.

Higher.

Higher.

Higher.

Then I'm there, weightless and floating. My thighs quake, my hands tremble as I fall back to earth, shattered in the very best way.

I open my eyes.

A lopsided smile tugs up one corner of Gabriel's mouth, brown eyes deep and dark. "I love watching you. You're beautiful."

Maybe I should feel shy, but I don't. Not under his gaze that's simultaneously worshipping and extracting from me a part of myself that is mostly unexplored.

I wrap a hand around the back of his neck and pull him down to me. He kisses me reverently, tasting and enjoying, and all I want in this exact moment is everything.

Gabriel leans over onto one forearm, using his other hand to push my hair back from my face. He hooks an arm under my knee and lifts, pressing himself against me. He moves, just enough to cause friction. Leaning down, he kisses the corner of my mouth. "Please tell me you're on birth control. I have condoms, but"—he shakes his head, and he's still rubbing our centers together, and I'm on the edge again—"there's no way I can allow a barrier between us. I have to have you, Avery. All of you."

"It's our lucky day." My hands grip his shoulders. "I'm on birth control."

Gabriel enters me, so slowly, sucking a breath through his teeth. His head swings side to side like he's in disbelief. "I knew you'd feel this good."

My mind is a mixture of thoughts, but they all pale in comparison to the emotion hurtling through me. Gabriel's words, his actions, his presence and his scent, it all mixes to create a heady experience.

Gabriel rolls over, taking me with him. He sits up, and I am astride him. His hands are on my hips, guiding me. We are forehead to forehead, nose to nose, lips to lips. I swallow his moans and he drinks in my gasps. I'm there again,

climbing,

floating,

falling,

and Gabriel is with me, jerking and stilling.

We come out of a daze we created, and still he holds me, fingers brushing my back and soft kisses dotting my shoulder. I'm draped over him. My bones have liquified, rendering my limbs useless. "That was so good," I murmur, my lips on his neck.

"Yes." He's still catching his breath. "Incredible. I knew it would be."

"Why did we wait so long to do something that good?"

"Sometimes, fires are too hot to enter." He kisses the top of my head. "That's what you feel like. Or, what I feel when I'm with you. My feelings for you…they're intense.

If I had to compare it to my job, I'd say it's the hottest fire I've ever come up against."

Wow. That answer definitely works.

"Avery?"

"Hmm?"

"Is it too soon for me to tell you I love you?"

Surprise makes me regain the use of my body. I pull back to look at him. He looks serious, and vulnerable. Happiness bursts inside me, and I tell him, "I don't believe love has a timeline. So, no, it's not too soon."

He tucks my hair behind my ear. "Then I love you."

My smile spreads slowly, like melting chocolate. We're naked, but I lay it all down, baring my heart and my soul. "I think I've loved you since I met you, hero."

Gabriel closes his eyes, a low moan vibrating his throat. "Baby, we're in trouble."

I kiss the space beside his ear, my heart flip-flopping at how he called me *baby*. "What kind of trouble?"

"The kind that buries you alive, and all you can do is hope rescue never arrives."

"I like that idea."

"Being buried alive?"

"Being inundated. That's what I want to be. Inundated with you. By you."

Emotion moves over his face. I'm not sure how to define it, except to say that it's good. I lift myself up and kiss the scar above his lip. "How did you get this?"

"Microform cleft lip."

When I don't say anything right away, Gabriel adds, "I was born with it. It was minor, no surgery needed."

I kiss it again. "I like it."

"I hated it when I was a kid, but I honestly don't think I've noticed it in years."

"Funny how things stop mattering after a while." I lift my forearm. "See these white spots?" I point at my polka-dotted arm. "They're called reverse freckles. I hate them."

Gabriel rolls me over. He grabs one arm and studies it. "They're barely noticeable."

"And yet I hate them."

His lips press against the inside of my wrist, mouth skimming my forearm. "I like them."

"Why?"

His lips remain on my skin, but his gaze finds mine. "Because they're on you."

The love I feel from Gabriel opens up a floodgate, and everything rushes forward. What I've been missing my whole life is suddenly right in front of me. I need only to reach for it.

So I do.

SESSION SIX
DESERT FLOWER THERAPY

"You fell in love quickly." Dr. Ruben's head tips sideways as he speaks, like he's making a query. He's not. I like how he can make a statement based solely off my retelling.

"With Gabriel, it was painless. No obstacles. He was so damn easy to love." I stare at the tiny flecks of brown in the cream carpeting, then look up. "He was pretty much perfect."

Dr. Ruben raises his eyebrows at me. I wonder if he treats all his patients with a casual familiarity, or if it is just because I once occupied the same role. "Nobody is perfect."

I blink twice, exasperated.

He shrugs. "Trite, but true. Why did you think he was perfect?"

"He was exceptionally kind. Empathetic. Not everyone is emotionally intelligent, but he was. He was patient. Funny, but not too silly. Sensitive, but still masculine." Goose bumps dot my legs at my description of him.

Dr. Ruben dips his head, making a show out of pretending to acquiesce. "Sounds perfect. When did you realize he had a flaw?"

"The night I met his mother."

CHAPTER 9

I'm meeting Gabriel's parents tonight.

For weeks we've been trying to come up with a night where everyone was free, but it was difficult with Gabriel and his dad, Doug's, schedules.

But here we are. Three months into our relationship and I'm finally meeting his parents. My dad insisted on meeting Gabriel within the first week of us dating, so he could thank the man who saved his daughter's life.

Gabriel spends the last few minutes of the drive coaching me on his mom. "She'll be friendly, but she's…" He pauses, carefully choosing his words. "Critical." He scrunches his nose when he says it, like maybe that's not the best fit descriptor.

I nod to show him I'm not fazed. Birth order was covered in my Family Communication class. I'm expecting critical, overprotective parenting, maybe even a side of 'nobody is good enough for my Gabriel' vibes.

Reaching over, I rub his arm to reassure him. "Par for the course with an only child."

Gabriel pulls into the driveway of an older model single story home. The lawn is mostly landscaping rock, with a hedge of white oleander on the far side. He cuts the engine and turns to me. "About that." His eyes hold genuine concern. He sighs and rubs the back of his neck. "I wasn't always an only child."

I flinch in surprise at his admission. "You had a sibling?"

"I had an older brother. Nash." A muscle in his jaw ticks. "He had a heart condition nobody knew about, and died of a heart attack when he was twenty."

The look on Gabriel's face sets a burning to the backs of my eyes. I lean over the console, placing my hand on his arm. "I'm so sorry."

He watches my fingers drift over his skin. "I'm sorry I didn't tell you sooner. I hate talking about it. I was there when it happened, and I relive it every time I talk about it."

"You don't have to apologize for that. I understand." He looks up, and I offer an encouraging smile. "Thank you for sharing with me."

"I've wanted to for a while, but it's difficult to talk about." His gaze travels over my face. "I'm glad I did, though." The relief in Gabriel's expression twists my heart. He glances at the large window in the front of the house. "We'd better go in. I'm sure my mom has noticed we're sitting out here."

I let go of him and gather my purse from the floorboard, forcing gusto into my tone. "Let's do it."

Gabriel says my name. I turn back, a question in my eyes.

He taps a knuckle on the steering wheel. "Promise me something."

"Anything," I say quickly, because he sounds uncertain and I want to assuage him.

His teeth capture his lower lip. "Promise me you'll still love me when we get back in this car."

I'm taken aback. I don't know why he thinks not loving him is a possibility. "If you think your parents can scare me away from you, let me be the first to tell you I'm made of tough stuff." I offer him a pinky. "I promise to still love you when we get back in this car."

Corinne Woodruff opens the door as Gabriel is reaching for the handle. She has a pretty smile, sparkling eyes, and a smear of sauce across the front of her apron.

"Oh!" She looks down at herself. "Forgot I had this on." She unties the apron and drapes it over a forearm. "Pretend you didn't see that," she says to me.

Gabriel's dad strides in from a hallway, and Gabriel makes formal introductions. Technically, I've met his dad, but I don't know if the day at the fire station could really be called 'meeting' his dad. We did little more than exchange a few words.

"You and Gabriel have been joined at the hip since you met. Good thing I sent him after you, huh?" Doug asks, elbowing Gabriel in the ribs.

"I would've gone after her," Gabriel says, a trace of annoyance in his tone.

Doug misses his son's irritation and keeps going. "Probably not. Gabriel is on the shy side."

Gabriel is not shy, but I hold back my opinion. I wind an arm around his waist, feeling protective. "Gabriel has a lot of sides. And I love them all."

Corinne beams at me. "Already loving the good and the bad." She chucks my chin affectionately. "What a keeper."

I look to Gabriel for his reaction, but his expression remains unchanged. Are these low-key criticisms a normal thing? I feel like Lara the day my dad brought her home, trying to understand family dynamics.

I offer my help in the kitchen, and Corinne declines. "We're all set," she says, walking ahead of us to the dining room.

We're in the middle of small talk when Corinne asks me about school. I explain my degree to her and how close I am to being finished.

"There are a lot of therapists out there," she says, pointing her fork at me while she speaks. "And not all of them are scrupulous. Have you seen that new show on TV?"

I twist the napkin in my lap. "It's unfortunately true, though I'd argue there are unscrupulous people in every field."

"What are the job prospects like?" she asks.

It feels like an interview, but that's ok. I get it.

This past week I landed a job with a therapist, so I'm relieved to have an answer. I open my mouth, but Gabriel responds first.

"Avery has already lined up a job." His voice is snare-drum tight. "She has to complete three thousand supervised clinical hours, and then she'll be able to get her license and begin practicing."

Corinne's eyebrows lift. "Are clinical hours unpaid?"

"Yes," I admit. It's a sore spot for me. I've been saving

money for a while, knowing this was ahead of me. I don't have enough though.

"And you live with your dad?" Corinne's voice is pleasant, but there's judgment in the obvious implication.

"Avery's house burned down, Mom. You know that." Gabriel takes my hand and brings it to his mouth, where he leaves a soft kiss. "Besides, Avery doesn't live with her dad. She lives with me."

My free hand stills, fork frozen beneath the mound of mashed potatoes on my plate.

Gabriel squeezes my hand and smiles playfully, nodding across the space separating us. "She's moving in this weekend."

My initial shock recedes, and I nod my head to support Gabriel in the farce. "I've been busy packing my things."

"Moving in together?" Corinne clears her throat and adjusts the napkin in her lap. "You've only been dating a few months."

Gabriel shrugs. "I don't see any reason to wait when I know Avery's who I want." Beneath the table, his foot rubs mine.

"Well…" Corinne pushes back her chair. She offers me a quick smile. "Let's have dessert somewhere more comfortable."

I follow Gabriel's lead into the living room. A shiny black grand piano sits in one corner, its top covered by framed photos. Corinne hands out lemon meringue pie, and after I've eaten half I make my way across the room to look through the pictures.

"Do you see that one in the center?" Doug's voice booms proudly.

There, larger than the others, is a photo of Gabriel and Doug in their uniforms. Doug's arm is slung around Gabriel's shoulders. "That was right after Gabriel became a probie."

I turn back to the three Woodruffs, all still seated. "Probie?"

"Probationary firefighter," Gabriel clarifies.

"Gotcha." I nod. We finish dessert, and I excuse myself to the restroom. Corinne points down a hallway, telling me the closer bathroom is in the middle of a repair.

The hallway is lined on either side with school photos. One in particular has a not-so-great haircut, so I stop and get a closer look, just so I can tease Gabriel later. But it's not Gabriel, so it must be the brother. Nash. I look to the next photo. Also not Gabriel. Down the hall I go, peering at each picture and not seeing Gabriel.

I don't want to judge other people's grief, but this seems odd. Imbalanced. There aren't any pictures of Gabriel except one, near the end of the hall, next to the bathroom door. He and Nash smile at the camera. Nash, presumably at high school graduation, wears a special sash and honor cords around his neck, arm laid over Gabriel's shoulders.

I move on into the bathroom, trying to shake off the discomfort I'm feeling. When I rejoin the group in the living room, Gabriel gives me a long look. I take a seat beside him while Corinne talks about whether she'll have time to mulch the flower beds this weekend.

"Did you see the shrine?" Gabriel murmurs in my ear.

"It'd be hard to miss," I whisper, pretending to adjust the strap on my sandal.

Later, when we've said our goodbyes and we're driving down the street, Gabriel reaches over the center console and winds his fingers through mine. We come to a stop at a red light, and he tugs my hand, pulling my attention to him.

He looks vulnerable in the red glow of the stoplight. After that experience, I'm not sure what to say to him. There's a lot more to Gabriel's relationship with his parents than I would have guessed.

"I'm sorry," he says.

I force my voice into a tone that conveys I don't know what he's talking about. "For what?"

He gives me a long look. "You know what for."

"Your mom?" I thumb behind myself. "She just wants to make sure I'm the right person for you. I'm not offended."

"I don't just mean her questions." Gabriel's gaze softens. "Every time something good happens to me, such as bringing a girl like you home, I can see them thinking about Nash. About how he'll never do whatever it is I'm doing." His shoulders dip. "They wish it had been me."

"No," I say immediately. "That's not true." Parents don't do that, right? Because that would be awful.

The light turns green and Gabriel lets off the brake. I wish we weren't driving. I want to crawl into his lap, to melt into him and find every one of these destructive thoughts and demolish them.

Gabriel stares at the road, his jaw set. "Honestly, I don't blame them. Nash was the best person. Outgoing, funny, confident. He had a million friends. Everyone loved him." He runs his thumb over his brow. "He was an all-around good guy. The kind of person you knew was going to do great things."

He says it like only Nash was capable of being great,

and if Nash isn't here, the greatness can't happen. "Nash may have been those things, but so are you." Reaching over, I rest a hand on his thigh. "You could've been describing yourself just now."

His gaze flicks over to mine, then back to the road. "Do you ever feel like you're watching yourself live life? Like you're standing on the outside and looking in?"

"That's how I felt after my mom died. I've always loved to read, so I pictured myself as the main character of a book, and I would narrate as I went through my days. Each day was a blank page and a pen hovered above the page, filling it in as the day passed." I've never told anybody that, not even Camryn.

"You don't talk about your mom much." His thumb taps the steering wheel. "Why is that?"

Before I answer, I spend a moment picturing her collar-bone-length dirty blonde hair, the way she would bend over me and tickle my midsection. "Sometimes I feel confused when I remember her. I was young, so I only have a handful of memories. After she died, I had to help raise Camryn. My dad disappeared, too, but in a different way. He went into himself and stayed there for a long time. I filled my mom's empty role, and it's hard to process someone's death when you're filling their shoes."

Gabriel's lips twist into a sad, wistful smile. "Sounds like our parents did a number on us."

"All parents do, in one way or another. Nobody escapes childhood unscathed. Or life, for that matter."

Gabriel takes my hand as we drive down his street. "You're wise. It's hard to believe you're only twenty-three."

"Old soul." I shrug. "And all that research on longevity

in marriage. It opened my eyes to the complexities of relationships."

Gabriel pulls into the driveway and cuts the engine. He shifts in his seat so he can face me. At first I think he's going to keep talking about Nash, but he takes me aback when he says, "About moving in together—"

I wave my hand. "You were giving your mom a hard time. I know. It would be crazy to move in together so soon."

Gabriel's quiet at first, then says, "Would it?"

"Um, yes?" I don't sound sure. Quite the opposite, actually.

"What if we didn't pay attention to arbitrary rules about when things are supposed to happen? Your house burned down and you went to stay with your dad, except he showed up out of nowhere with a fiancée. It feels a little like"—he shrugs—"fate."

"Fate," I echo. I like the idea of ignoring timelines that say when we are supposed to do things in relationships. Going with my gut, following my heart, listening to my soul. However it's termed, it sounds a lot better than hearing my dad and Lara having sex.

The more I think about it, the more I love the idea of living with Gabriel. I want to wake up to him, place my toothbrush next to his, add my favorite salad dressing to his collection in the fridge door. There is one detail though, that I have to mention.

"I'm not going to be able to contribute financially. Not much, anyway. I didn't pay rent at Sabrina's house, just my share of the utilities." I cleaned the house, too, because I felt bad about not paying rent.

Gabriel's shaking his head before I finish speaking.

"I'm not worried about that. I'm serious about you. About us. You're starting your career, and I want to support you. Financially, and in every other way."

"Are you sure?" I glance at Gabriel's house. "This is a big step."

"Yes, I'm sure. I'm not afraid of big steps. Why stop with moving in together? Let's get a dog, too."

"Hah," I laugh. "No dogs. No way."

Gabriel's eyebrows lift. "Are you telling me you don't like dogs?"

"Is that a deal breaker?" I grin.

"No, but…do you really dislike dogs? I'm genuinely curious."

"Dogs are fine, I guess. I've never had one as a pet. We had a neighbor who had an awful dog who humped my leg a lot and even bit me twice. His name was Baxter."

Gabriel's eyes light up with recognition. Before he can ask, I say, "That's why you'll hear Cam call me Baxter every once in a while."

Gabriel laughs, and the sound fills the truck. I love it so much, I want to tuck it away and save it for another time when I feel sad.

"That's enough," I say, pointing a stern finger at him. I push up onto my knees and crawl over the console. He adjusts himself in his seat to accommodate my body. My leg swings over, and I straddle him. "Do you promise you want me to move in? It's your space. Your home."

He shakes his head. "Not anymore."

"Then let's do it. Let's move in together." Excitement fills me and I squeal with my mouth closed, the sound coming from my throat. Gabriel's chuckle vibrates against me.

The mood in the truck has swung from somber to euphoric.

The air conditioning blasts against my back, making me shiver, but his grin heats me up. "So you still love me as much as you did before you met my mom?"

"If anything, I love you more. All I saw tonight only helped me to understand you better." I kiss his temple, run my hands through his hair. "Everybody's family is a unique brand of fucked up, Gabriel. That's what I'm learning."

Gabriel's thumbs graze my sides, up and over my chest. He leans in, the tip of his nose fluttering over my jawbone.

His hands drop to my hips, and his tongue slides over my jaw. "You taste sweet. And you smell like something I want to bury myself in."

Outside, the moon is nothing more than a sliver. The front porch lights are off, bathing the driveway in total darkness.

Gabriel's eyes flicker to the backseat, then up to the house. "Let's go inside," he says.

I leave my stuff in the truck, and we hurry through the front door. We're a tangle of limbs, and I slam the door closed with a hip. We make it to the living room, where we drop to the carpet.

Gabriel presses his face between my thighs, and in a few short minutes there are starbursts behind my closed eyes. He crawls up my body, smiling at me and running his tongue along his lower lip. "*A Very* sweet treat," he says, looking pleased with himself.

I feel the flush on my cheeks. I don't know why I'm shy now, considering where he was thirty seconds ago.

Gabriel leans down, peppering my jawline with short kisses. "Tell me what you like. What you want from me."

My breath sticks in my throat. "You know what I like. We have sex all the time." We have been insatiable since that first time, feral and starving for each other within hours of our last time.

"Tell me," Gabriel whispers, pushing hair from my forehead. "Be honest about what you want."

Honesty feels a lot like vulnerability, and I don't love that idea. But I love Gabriel, and I trust him. I trust there is a safe place to land. It's not honesty that's hard for people. It's what's at stake after they're honest.

I swallow against my instinct to withhold my desires. Gabriel glides into me, over and over, and in one breath, I say, "Slower."

His pace decreases. In the dark of the living room, the tip of his tongue drags up my neck.

"My hair," I gasp. I see the swell, knowing it's rising for me, and all I have to do is catch it. "Put your hand in my hair."

Gabriel slides a hand up my neck, fingers splaying as they venture into my long hair and scrape over my scalp.

"Pull," I whisper.

He listens. The understated burn of pain mixes with pleasure. My cheek presses against the forearm he uses to support himself, and I turn into him. He's doing everything right, so right, and soon I'm riding the wave and biting into Gabriel's bicep. He lets go, too, and I hold on to the coiled muscles in his upper back, offering up my mouth. He likes to kiss me when he comes.

"What, specifically, was Gabriel's flaw?" Dr. Ruben crosses one leg over the other, capturing his knee with his hands.

"It was the first time I realized Gabriel was capable of keeping something from me. Lying."

"Did he lie?"

"He waited months to tell me about Nash. It was a massive part of his life, this experience that shaped him. It felt like a lie."

"A lie of omission, then?"

"I suppose."

Dr. Ruben bounces his leg. "People lie all the time. Every day. It's human nature. It doesn't mean they're being outright deceitful. It just makes them human."

"So it should be acceptable?"

"That's not what I said. Most lies are told to protect a part of the person lying. To protect the ego, the image, the pain, the shame."

The last word confuses me. "The shame?"

"Oh, yes. The shame most of all. We tend to protect our

feelings of shame, because we abhor it and never want to show it to others. So we cover it up, we create stories around it. Lies, fibs, half-truths, call it whatever you want. At the end of the day, they are stories."

My stomach twists uncomfortably. I can take all of what Dr. Ruben said and apply it to Gabriel, but that's not what has me feeling nauseous. It can all be applied to me.

"So when Gabriel told me about his brother…?"

"He was pulling back the curtain. Erasing a lie and replacing it with truth. He was showing you that which shames him."

I nod slowly, thinking back over the conversation from that night. "It humanized him. Which was a good thing, I suppose. Until then he'd been this mythical person. The realization that he was human was, I don't know, a little unnerving."

"Tell me, Avery, do you think it was fair to hold Gabriel to this high of a standard?"

"No, it wasn't." I sigh, disappointed in myself. "He had so many wonderful qualities, and I didn't want them to be marred by anything that wasn't positive."

"Good people can do bad things, and bad people can do good things. One does not exclude the other. In fact"—Dr. Ruben holds a finger aloft—"several things can be true at the same time."

I'm still processing, but Dr. Ruben continues. "So, you go on and move in with Gabriel?"

"Yes. Pretty soon after that. Like the rest of our relationship, we didn't waste any time."

"How'd your dad handle it?"

"Better than I would've guessed."

"Why do you frown when you say that?"

CHAPTER 10

I'D THOUGHT MY DAD WOULD CARE A LITTLE ABOUT ME moving in with Gabriel three months after our first date. But, no.

He's leaning against the kitchen counter, arms crossed. He's smiling.

His wedding is in two weeks, and I think he's high on love. And on Gabriel, if I'm being honest. Gabriel is every father's dream. Respectful, chivalrous, employed, home owner. Also, that part where Gabriel saved his daughter's life? Automatic entry.

I don't want my dad to put up a fuss, but some push-back would be nice. Just enough to let me know he doesn't want to give up his little girl, but not so much that I have to dig in my heels.

"You sure you're ok with it?" I ask.

Dad chuckles. "Lara moved in here the second we got off the plane."

I stand beside him at the counter. "So it's not a 'do as I say, not as I do' situation?"

He shakes his head. "Not at all. Besides, you're an adult." He slings an arm over my shoulders. "You've been an adult since you were a kid."

I frown at the pride in his voice. Children are only adults because they were forced to become them. Newsflash, it's the last thing a kid should have to be.

Yet, here he is, tucking me into the crook of his arm, jostling me affectionately. It's as if he likes the trajectory of my life thus far, the way I took care of Camryn after our mom died.

I wish I could say all this to him. It would feel so good to release the words and their emotional toll. But then I picture his crestfallen face, the hurt springing into his eyes, and I know I never will.

"I'll probably be out by this Sunday." Stepping away, I reach into the fridge for a jug of tea. Lara makes a mixture of green tea and black tea, and it's become my favorite thing. "It's not as if I have much to pack."

I've been slow to replace anything that isn't pertinent, due to space constraints. Lucky for me, most of my childhood belongings were boxed and left behind in my dad's garage. The fire affected most of everything in my room. Even if things weren't touched by flame, everything reeks of smoke or melted from the heat. I wasn't able to salvage as much as I'd originally hoped, but in a stroke of absentmindedness I'd left my backpack holding all my work and my laptop in my car that night. Between the photo of my mom and the backpack being left in the car, my loss was minimal. It was Sabrina, or more specifically, Sabrina's parents, who experienced the most loss. Even the furniture in my room didn't belong to me, but to them.

"Gabriel is a good man," my dad says. "It's not easy for

a dad to let his daughter go, but knowing you're going to a man like Gabriel makes it a hell of a lot easier."

"I guess I know how to pick them," I respond.

When I arrive at Gabriel's with a car full of my belongings, I find he's cleared out half his closet. What this really means is that he's pushed together all his clothing and made space for me on the racks.

He pulls out the top two drawers of his dresser. "All yours." He smiles excitedly, his full grin showing his teeth.

"Two whole drawers?" I place my hands on my cheeks and widen my eyes playfully.

His arms go around my waist as he chuckles. "What can I say, I like to spoil my girl."

I press my nose to the front of his shirt. It smells clean, with a hint of his spicy cologne. "Mmm," I moan softly. "You make me so happy."

Gabriel drops a kiss on the top of my head. "Good. Because making you happy has become my number one pastime."

Gabriel and I make dinner together that evening, but it's more like he cooks and I assist. We bump into each other in the kitchen, laughing and apologizing. The fourth time it happens, Gabriel says, "I'm bumping into you on purpose."

"Is that right?" I wind my arms around his neck, a spatula in one hand and a spoon in the other. "Is that the cooking equivalent of chasing me on the elementary school playground?"

Gabriel rubs my back, warming me. "Something like that. What I really want is a kiss."

I place a quick, soft kiss against his mouth. "All you have to do is ask."

"Let's assume every time I pass you when we're cooking, I want you to pause and kiss me."

"I think we're at serious risk of burning whatever we're cooking if we do that." I hand him the utensils he asked for.

He takes them from me. "I'm willing to take that risk."

Joy bubbles up inside me, and I laugh. I've never been so happy in my life. "Then you have yourself a deal."

We end up burning dinner. It's less the fault of the momentary kisses and more the fault of the lovemaking on the kitchen table.

Gabriel chews his burned dinner and refuses to make a face. I make no such attempts.

"This is awful," I say, covering my mouth with my hand and wincing as I try to power through it.

Gabriel shakes his head, still not acknowledging how bad it is. "Delicious. I don't know what you're talking about."

We do the dishes and cuddle under a shared blanket on the couch. I rest my head on his shoulder, and the next thing I know I'm being carried to Gabriel's bed.

A thought creeps into my sleepy haze. *I've never slept in a bed purchased by me.*

I don't know why it matters, but suddenly it's filling my mind, taking over in an unwelcome way. I went from my dad's house, to college, to Sabrina's home, and then a short stop back at my dad's, and now here. Gabriel's home.

He lays me down. My thoughts must be showing on my face, because Gabriel asks what's wrong.

I frown sleepily. "Everything in here is yours."

He pushes hair out of my face. "It doesn't have to be

that way. We can go shopping. We can get on a home goods website and order stuff right now. I'll put your name on the deed tomorrow."

I like how quickly he solves the problem, how willing he is to be generous. Taking his hand, I press it to my heart. "You're so good to me."

"I'm serious," he says earnestly. "I'm calling the title company first thing in the morning."

My upset evaporates. Who cares if I've never purchased my own bed? Or much of my own anything?

My home with Sabrina burned, and I don't know how long it will take for me to think of Gabriel's home as my own, but it doesn't matter.

Because I have Gabriel.

He is my home.

SESSION EIGHT

DESERT FLOWER THERAPY

"Why do you think it is you made Gabriel your home?"

I look down at my cherry red fingernails. I don't like Dr. Ruben's question. It's making me think about things I don't want to think about. "Home is the place where you can relax and be yourself. That's what Gabriel felt like to me. He was my person."

"That's not what you called him," Dr. Ruben points out. "You called him your home."

I shrug. "He always took care of me. Comforted me. Loved me. Isn't that what your partner is supposed to do for you?"

"All relationships are different."

I frown at his noncommittal response. "What are you really asking?"

"I'm asking why you made Gabriel your home."

My head shakes. "No, you're not. You want me to realize I was codependent. Fine." I hold my arms out to the side and blow out a breath. "I was codependent. I shouldn't have made Gabriel the end-all be-all when it came to my happiness."

Dr. Ruben taps the end of his nose with his fingertip three times. "Bingo. Now let's take it a little further. Why did you make him the end-all be-all when it came to your happiness?"

I know this answer. It's buried down deep, beneath layers of hurt where I don't have to look at it too closely. "Because my happiness was not prioritized after my mom died. And I found someone who would make me a priority."

Dr. Ruben squints and beats back a grin. "There you have it."

"Let me guess. I'm in control of my happiness, no matter what anyone else says or does."

Dr. Ruben opens his arms, the silvery hair on his forearm glinting in the overhead light.

He doesn't say a word, but the motion speaks for itself. *Connection made!*

"Honestly, Dr. Ruben, why am I even here anymore? I can do this myself."

He looks at me pointedly. "You know why you're here."

Shame hits me square in the chest. I'm not proud of what happened.

Silence descends, and I know he's waiting for me to speak. I sit back, running my finger along a seam in the couch cushion. "Have you ever been married?"

I've noticed his ring finger is bare, but maybe he has a life partner. Maybe he's been married four times and given up on the idea of finding his soul mate. Or, maybe he doesn't believe in the institution.

"I was married once."

"But not anymore?"

He shakes his head, and says no more. It piques my curiosity, but I know better than to push. Especially since this session is supposed to be about me.

"The last time you were here, we talked about you and Gabriel moving in together. Let's pick up there."

My mind dips into my memories, and even though it hurts, I smile. For me, there is very little happiness that exists without pain when it comes to Gabriel. "My dad married Lara, and Gabriel came with me to the wedding. Everyone loved him. Even more, they loved how we met. My dad told the story to anybody who would listen. It was like we were extra special because of how we met, and it made him extra special in a third-party way. Cool by association."

"Did this bother you?"

"Yes, but it didn't surprise me. My dad enjoys attention."

Dr. Ruben motions for me to continue.

"I graduated. There was a month between graduation and when I started my clinical hours. Gabriel surprised me with a trip to his grandparent's place in Palm Springs." Wistfulness pokes at my chest. This is the easy part to tell. Soaring, head over heels, with no desire to ever stop. It is the best, most beautiful part of our story.

The part where we crashed will be much harder to talk about.

CHAPTER 11

I gaze at Gabriel's profile as he steers us west, away from Phoenix. His right hand alternates between gripping the wheel, and reaching for my hand to hold. Or brushing aside my hair and massaging my neck. Or running the backs of two fingers down my arm. Everything about him screams loving and capable, attentive and alert. I've been alive for twenty-three years, but it isn't until Gabriel that I feel awakened. To life, to love, to possibility. Six months with this man and I'm already a better version of myself.

Gabriel drives on, and the hours stack up. We're at four now. Palm Springs is our destination.

"Almost there," he says, winking at me. He taps his thigh in anticipation. I think he is as excited as me.

He follows the directions on his phone, but he drives like he knows where he's going.

"Are you ok with getting groceries later?" Gabriel asks, turning the wheel. "Right now, I just want to get there." He gives me a look, lust darkening his already dark eyes, and my thighs clench. I can't imagine a time when he no longer looks at me that way as often as he does now. Maybe we will be the lucky ones, the chosen two. We will always be this in love, want one another this much.

The road straightens out, and Gabriel pulls up to a house. It's retro, made of white stucco with a kelly green front door. Dew clings to thick blades of grass, and fuchsia bougainvillea leaves tumble across the sidewalk with the breeze.

We climb from the truck. Gabriel takes my hand, leading me. "There's a pool in the backyard." He removes a key from his pocket and lets us in.

The interior is as charming as the front yard. Spanish tile, and windows everywhere. The sparkling pool is visible from the foyer, and beyond that the mountains loom large.

"This is gorgeous," I say, when Gabriel returns with our bags.

"My grandparents don't use it much. They don't like to drive this far anymore, but they don't want to sell it."

I kiss his cheek. "Lucky us."

Gabriel pushes aside my hair and kisses my shoulder. He wraps his arms around my waist and takes in the view with me. My gaze zeroes in on a hot tub off to the side of the yard. "Please tell me that works."

"It better work," Gabriel growls against my ear. "If it doesn't, I'll figure out a way to make it."

Turns out, the hot tub operates just fine. Gabriel peels off my clothes, then his own, and we climb into the hot, bubbling water.

Our kisses make everything hotter, and when he lines himself up with me, I sink down. My head tips back, and I exhale. I feel like double the person I am when I'm on my own two feet. I'm invincible, more myself than I've ever been, better because of him. This must be what everyone is seeking, this true love that has driven people to insanity and eluded so many others. It is in songs, books, poems, and films. But for me, it's right here. It is on me. In me. Kissing me.

This is what it's like to be treasured. Cherished. It will always feel this way. It has to. Anything else is inconceivable.

Later, when we're physically sated but our stomachs tell us they're not in agreement, we venture out. We buy enough food for the next few days. At the end of the aisle in the grocery store, I lift a small bottle of Baileys, feeling buoyant and carefree. "What do you think? We could really be on vacation and add this to our coffee?"

Gabriel shakes his head. "I'll pass. But you can, if you want to."

I slide the bottle back onto the shelf. "Nah. It'll just make me tired for the rest of the day."

It isn't until we're curled around one another in bed that night that I ask him a question I've been reluctant to ask. Sabrina's words when we were shopping months ago have never fully left my mind, and I've been afraid of what Gabriel's answer might be. It's time, though. If there's something to know, I should know it. I'm careful to keep my tone flippant, like *no big deal*, and say, "I've noticed you don't drink alcohol. Is there a reason for that?"

His hand stills. He'd been running it over my back, and now all I feel is the tremble in his fingertips.

"Alcohol is not my friend," he says, each word measured.

I roll over and prop myself up on an elbow, my head

cradled in my palm. "I don't know if it's anybody's true friend. But why is it not yours, specifically?"

Gabriel takes a deep breath, his warm exhale streaming over my exposed skin. "Remember when I told you I was with Nash when he had a heart attack?"

I nod, preparing myself for what's to come.

"I'd been at a party with a bunch of guys I met the summer after senior year. Nash warned me they weren't people I should be hanging around with, but I thought he was being an annoying older brother." Gabriel hesitates, running a thumb over his jaw before continuing.

"I was drinking a lot by then, and I mean *a lot*. You wouldn't have recognized the person I was at the time." He pauses, and I can tell he's weighing his words.

I'm careful to keep my expression neutral. I am a safe place for him.

"Anyway, we were all wasted the night of the party, and someone suggested we fight each other. It started out one on one, but somewhere along the line that changed. I don't think they planned it, but suddenly I was being jumped. Alcohol, testosterone, groupthink, and pure stupidity." Gabriel presses two fingers to the bridge of his nose. "I was messed up, bloody and my nose was broken, and I called Nash for help. He lost his shit when he arrived. I looked awful. I told him to take me home, but he took me to the emergency room. We were in the waiting room, and he was sitting beside me, and he was touching his left arm and saying his chest felt like an elephant was sitting on it. I told him maybe he should add his name to the list, but I was joking. He'd tried to laugh, but then he started sweating and his body just…it just jerked, like he'd been shocked."

Gabriel's eyes fill with moisture. "I ran to the front desk, screaming for help, and the person looked at my face and started handing me tissues. I pointed at Nash, who was still sitting in the chair. She finally understood and picked up the phone. She said something, some kind of code, and then nurses were flying through the doors and into the waiting room." He wipes away tears. "Nash was already gone. My parents requested an autopsy and learned about his heart condition. Somehow he made it through life and sports without it being a problem, but on that day it was enough to end his life. No more school, no more dates, no more plans to be a firefighter like our dad. No future."

His head shakes like he still can't believe what happened. "Rationally, I know it's not my fault. The heart defect was always there. But rational doesn't have a place in grief, and I've never been able to shake the feeling that I made the defect express itself that day."

I'm crying with him. I don't know what to say, so I touch his face and wipe his cheeks. "I'm so sorry, Gabriel." His eyelashes flutter closed, and tears stick to them.

"It's why I became a firefighter," he says. His eyes remain closed. "It was Nash's dream. And my dad's."

"Was it not yours, too?"

His eyes open and his head shakes, micro-movements against the bedsheet. "The day I told my mom I got into the academy was the first time she smiled since Nash died."

"You're good at it." It's not an argument, but a statement of fact. Gabriel already knows he is good at fighting fires, at saving lives, at running in when others run out.

"Funny how that happens, huh?"

"Have you ever thought about stopping?"

"Yes."

"What would you do instead?"

"I'm not sure." Exhaustion has settled around his eyes. "I'm not trained for anything else. I have a degree in fire science."

"You could start over. You could do whatever you want to do."

"Not now. Not with you getting ready to work three thousand unpaid hours. We need to pay bills."

I see the wisdom in his words, even though it pains me to acknowledge them. I want him to be happy. His needs are important, too. "Promise me you'll think about it when I'm settled in my career. When I'm earning money. Promise?"

He nods. "I promise, baby."

He says nothing more after that. I hold him until he falls asleep.

———

GABRIEL DOESN'T MENTION Nash the next day.

As far as reasons for not drinking go, Gabriel's reason feels relatively mild. It could've been far worse than drinking too much as a teenager. What happened to Nash was tragic, but Gabriel did not cause it.

We go for a hike. We read books beside one another, our toes dipping in the turquoise pool. Gabriel assembles sandwiches for lunch while I'm on the phone, making dinner reservations. I toss my phone on the outdoor table when I'm done, then turn around to tell Gabriel what time we need to leave for the restaurant.

Gabriel is on one knee, beside the pool. He wears swim trunks, a bright smile, and hopeful eyes.

Air floods my throat as I gasp. My cupped hand slams over my mouth, quivering against my lips. Rocketing heartbeat, pulse pounding, weightless limbs. It's the whole nine for me, a full-scale physical response.

"Gabriel," I breathe his name as I step closer.

He takes my left hand, ring poised at my fingertip. The small diamond glints brilliantly in the sunshine. "*A Very* big question I'm asking of you. Will you marry me?"

"Yes," I say, and it's almost a sob. I can't wait. I want to do it all, this very minute. I want to be his wife, take his name, join our lives.

Gabriel slides the ring down, where I know it will stay until we're old. Then he stands, tucking me into that broad chest I love so desperately, and carries me to the lounge bed in the shade.

This time, when he enters me, I am not twice the person I was. I am infinite, my life exploding, the universe opening up for me. Everything is right there, ripe and bursting, waiting to be plucked.

Joy has never had a flavor, until now.

It tastes like Gabriel.

SESSION NINE
DESERT FLOWER THERAPY

"So he tells you the full story, and you get engaged. Sounds like a successful vacation."

I nod, quiet. My mind is stuck in a time that feels a million years ago. I think my heart is back there, too.

"Now we're up to your engagement," Dr. Ruben says, urging me to keep going.

"We didn't wait long to get married. Six months. I'd spent so much of my life taking care of Cam and playing house in a home that wasn't really mine, and I couldn't wait to make a life with Gabriel. To really be the woman of the house, not just occupy the shadow of the person I was filling in for. I'd been an adult for a while by then, but I felt grown-up wearing my engagement ring and coming home to Gabriel every day. My dad was right when he called me an adult child."

Dr. Ruben steeples his hands, resting his chin on his fingertips. "You know how inappropriate that was, don't you?"

"For my dad to call me an adult child?"

"For him to ever put you in that position in the first place."

"I'm aware." There's defeat in my voice.

"Have you considered telling him how it made you feel?"

"No," I answer immediately. "Why would I do that?"

His eyes widen, his chin moving left. His expression says *Come on.* "You're a therapist, too, Avery. You already know the answer."

"He can't handle hearing that he hurt me. I need to protect him from..." My lips purse, the last word in my sentence trapped.

"From?"

I blow out a breath. "Me."

"The truth."

"*My* truth."

Dr. Ruben stares at me.

I cross my arms. "I thought we were discussing Gabriel."

He folds his hands in his lap and uncrosses, then recrosses his legs. "We can discuss whatever you want. It's your session." He shrugs. "But remember, everything comes from somewhere."

"Right." Every person, every emotion, every trauma has an origin.

"How old were you when you married Gabriel?" Dr. Ruben asks.

"Twenty-four. A baby."

Dr. Ruben smirks. "Why do you say that?"

"I thought I knew it all." I cross my arms in front of myself. Vulnerability seeps in, leaving me cold. I've said so much to him, been brutally honest, but this road I'm traveling down feels slippery. A thought-provoking statement here, a realization there. This is not work for the faint of heart. Over time, I'd stopped considering the bravery and fortitude of my patients, returning week after week in the name of bettering themselves and their relationships.

Dr. Ruben clears his throat. "What did you think you knew?"

I make a face. "Everything."

"Most twenty-somethings think they know everything, which means they are certain they will never do things the way others have done them."

Hello, head of nail, here's the hammer. "Maybe it's more that I didn't know what I didn't know. And I thought I knew things I knew nothing about."

"Who told you I love riddles?"

I laugh once, but it's more of a bark.

"Hindsight is usually twenty-twenty," Dr. Ruben says. "Everyone has things they look back on with greater clarity than when they were in the moment. You're awfully hard on yourself."

"You'd be hard on yourself too, if you'd been through what I've been through."

"You don't know what I've been through." His voice doesn't contain irritation, or any trace of anything really. He is merely pointing out a fact.

"True. I apologize."

He nods his acceptance. "Let's talk about your wedding."

CHAPTER 12

Sometimes, I'm positive I know how much love a heart can hold. I'm aware this cannot be possible, because I haven't had kids yet, and I'm certain having children will change my perspective on a lot of things.

Watching the emotion roll through Gabriel's gaze as I walk toward him, I cannot fathom a time in my life when I will love more than I do right now.

I'm almost there. Almost to him. He wears traditional black. I am equally traditional in my white. We reach the end of the aisle, and my dad has to tug me back lightly. I don't think anyone notices. I was ready to float right into Gabriel, into the safety and calm I feel when I am beside him.

I wait, impatient, while the minister and my dad complete the ritual, confirming it is he who is giving me away. I look at Cam, standing as my maid of honor, and I can tell she wants to roll her eyes at the tradition.

My dad releases me, and this is my cue. Gabriel shakes hands with my father, and then it's he and I, face-to-face.

Nothing can compare to Gabriel in a tux, the way his shoulders fill the fabric. The shine in his eyes, the bob of his throat, these are moments I will remember forever. I already know it. And the way I'm feeling, not just the fullness of my heart but the energy in my limbs, the brightness of our future, it is right here in front of us. Palpable. Unseen, but sensed.

The ceremony is a blur. Ryan stands behind Gabriel, his best man. We make promises, and vow to love each other through it all. We exchange rings, kiss, and traipse back down the aisle amidst riotous clapping. Gabriel's colleagues clap the loudest, their hands more like bear paws. It strikes me then that Gabriel may have lost his biological brother, but he went on to find a firehouse full of them.

With my hand gripped tightly in Gabriel's, I'm also stricken by the realization that I was very wrong. I can love more. Each second that passes, I love Gabriel more.

My husband.

I whisper the word to myself. *Husband.* Through hugs and handshakes with guests, I whisper the word.

We do all the traditional wedding things. First dance, cut the cake, garter toss, and the Macarena. It's seventy-two degrees, the sunset was the kind Arizona is known for, and the cake tastes nothing like fondant. There were very few things I was picky about, and the cake was one of them.

If my recently divorced aunt hadn't come to sit beside me a minute ago, the night would be perfect.

"I'm glad I got you alone for a minute," she says, in a harried growl.

"Hi, Aunt Francesca." I hope I've hidden the dread I

feel. She's ten years older than my dad, and intimidating. Picture Bellatrix Lestrange from Harry Potter with a perma-scowl and a harsh haircut and you have Aunt Francesca.

I search over her shoulder for someone to save me. Gabriel talks animatedly to my dad across the room, hands flying to help him say whatever it is he's saying. Camryn and Sabrina are doing the Electric Slide with Ryan and his wife, Carrie.

I turn my attention back to my aunt, resolute.

"A word of advice." Aunt Francesca leans forward, resting her elbows on her spread apart knees. "Don't lose yourself. Don't let your life become about him."

I try not to make a face. "Of course not. You know I graduated from college. I'm going to use my degree."

"I'm not only talking about your career aspirations. Don't lose what's in here"—she pokes at my chest, and I feel it through the bustier I'm wearing to give my breasts a lift—"because, believe me, he'll come after it. They all do. Over half of all marriages end in divorce, and the ones that don't are just two people who've settled upon an acceptable level of unhappiness."

I stiffen. On a scale of one to ten, how bad would it look if the bride tipped over the chair her aunt is sitting in?

Should I remind her I completed a research project about long-term marriage, and I can say with a good degree of accuracy the characteristics that define it? Probably not. She'll be forming her argument the entire time I'm speaking. Instead, I opt for something short and sweet, that she can't argue. "Gabriel is not Uncle Mitchell. He will not come after..." I look down at my chest, to where she pointed. She must've meant my heart. "...my heart."

She scoffs. "I don't mean your heart. Those can be broken and repaired over and over. And don't call that man your uncle. I meant your soul."

Annoyance flares. Forget the levelheaded response. Retorts float through my head, most of them containing expletives, but I hold them at bay. Aunt Francesca's divorce became official three weeks ago. My dad warned me she was on a warpath, and that nobody, including me on my wedding day, was safe from her serpent tongue.

Gabriel approaches from behind Aunt Francesca. I must have a look on my face, because there's a question in his eyes.

Gabriel stops behind my aunt. He places his hands on her shoulders, squeezing them affectionately. "Hello, Francesca."

She bristles. I smile.

"How's my wife?" Gabriel asks over her head. His eyes twinkle. Maybe my dad told him about my aunt, and he has come to save me.

"Better now that you're here." I stand up, which isn't as easy as it sounds with all this silk and lace. I'd opted for a fitted silhouette, and as stunning as it is, it doesn't allow for much flexibility.

Gabriel rounds my aunt's chair and holds my elbow while I get my feet under me. Once I'm steady, he stays by my side and brushes two knuckles down my spine. I may be steady on my feet, but his touch unsteadies all other parts of me.

Ryan and two guys from Gabriel's fire crew appear, jubilant and probably half, if not all the way, in the bag.

"Hero, hero," Ryan shouts. The others join in. Raucous and rowdy, fists pulsing the air, they chant. It reminds me of a fraternity. The chant changes to, "Kiss her, kiss her."

I'm laughing and watching Gabriel shake his head in amusement. His eyes lock onto mine and he shrugs resolutely. He winds an arm around my lower back, and one around my neck. "We'd better give them what they want," he whispers. Then he bends me backward, and I hold on.

My eyes close as I settle into the kiss. When else in life are we going to be celebrated in public for being this affectionate and romantic? Probably never, so I'm going to enjoy it while it lasts.

The guys cheer, and holler, and one of them yells, "Get it, hero."

Gabriel smiles against me. I will remember this moment for the rest of my life. A perfect space in time, a—

What is that sound? I open my eyes as Gabriel rights us.

Fake retching.

Aunt Francesca's shoulders hunch, her tongue sticks out. She looks like a bizarre salt and pepper haired child.

To keep myself from saying the words on the tip of my tongue, I turn my back on her. I am the luckiest person in the history of ever to call Gabriel my husband.

Aunt Francesca can go fuck herself.

SESSION TEN
DESERT FLOWER THERAPY

"I brought you a plant."

Dr. Ruben gazes at me warily.

"You can accept it," I tell him, holding it out. "I'm not trying to bribe you or remove any professionalism from our relationship. In fact"—I look around pointedly—"consider it a gift to myself. Your office lacks anything earthy, anything that promises more than tears and tissues. I need this plant in here."

Dr. Ruben takes the plant and sets it on a shelf behind his desk, closer to a window. "Let's keep talking about your marriage."

My fingers stretch, the thumb of my left hand tucking into my palm and rubbing the bare flesh on my ring finger. Talking about Gabriel like this doesn't hurt. It's as if someone has given me a broom, and I've swept away the dust and detritus. I'm left with something shiny. Gleaming.

There's nothing I want more than to be that way again.

"What about it?" I ask.

"Tell me about the climate."

I point left, to the window and the scenery beyond. "It's hotter than the surface of the sun out there. I'm not looking forward to getting in my car after spending this hour in here with you."

Dr. Ruben shakes his head. "You're stalling."

"This is the good part. I want to sit in it for a while. Let the flavors mesh."

"Are you talking about stew, or your marriage?"

I smile at him. As therapists go, I've lucked out with Dr. Ruben. He talks with me, not at me. I like to think I was that way, too. My turnover rate was low.

"Gabriel and I were married. I was busy completing my three thousand clinical hours under Dr. Mallory."

"You can call him Joseph, if you'd like."

I nod, glancing quickly at my knotted hands in my lap. I hope that, in time, my embarrassment over what happened will fade.

"Gabriel and I were better than good. We were amazing. My other friends who'd already married warned me the first year of marriage was the hardest. That wasn't the case for us. Maybe it was everything I already knew about marriage from the time I spent studying it, or maybe Gabriel and I were just that damn good together. At any rate"—my head tips side to side as I think of those first months, as if even I cannot believe it—"we were the kind of couple other people want to be."

"I bet that felt good." Dr. Ruben sips his tea, then sets it on a small hot plate on the table between his chair and the couch I'm seated on.

"It did. If Aunt Francesca hadn't died a year later of lung cancer, I would have rubbed it in her face."

Dr. Ruben's lips quirk up in a corner. "She certainly made an impact on you."

My eyebrows cinch. "How's that?"

"You're holding a grudge against her for what she said at your wedding."

I make a face. "She was very rude."

"How many years ago was your wedding?"

"Five."

"Can you think of any reason why what she said five years ago still upsets you?"

I think back to that evening. The sage green pantsuit she wore, the large gold hoops tugging on earlobes that already sagged.

The answer hits me, square in the chest. Suddenly there are tears, running in paths down my cheeks, and I'm shocked by their appearance. No burning sensation, no tightening around the eyes, no warning whatsoever. Yet here they are, and there are so many I have no hope of removing them with a single swipe.

"She was right," I whisper, taking the offered box of tissues from Dr. Ruben.

I blow my nose, a loud and unladylike honk, and wipe at my eyes.

Dr. Ruben gives me a moment, then asks, "What was she right about?"

I release a noisy, aggravated breath. "That we would fail." I squeeze the balled up tissues in my hands, striped black with my mascara.

"We vowed to love each other through it all. I knew nothing of what that vow entailed. I had some vague notion it meant serious illness, like...like, cancer or dementia. It seemed intangible and far away."

"But it wasn't."

"No. It was not." My heart aches, an organ in distress. Today's appointment is the most painful of all, so far.

Dr. Ruben's expression is one of sympathy. "Do you want to keep going?"

I nod, swallowing as I steel myself. Isn't that what I do? No matter what, I keep going.

CHAPTER 13

I'VE JUST ARRIVED AT WORK, TEN MINUTES UNTIL NINE LIKE always, when Joseph asks me for a moment in his office.

I settle across from him on the couch used by his patients. He's bent at the waist, tying the stark white tennis shoes he favors. Every day he wears a variation of the same outfit: khakis, a cotton-blend mock neck sweatshirt over a long sleeve collared button up, and the shoes. I've fondly dubbed it 'the uniform,' and the joke has brought a smile to Joseph's face on more than one occasion.

Joseph sits up straight, gaze falling to me at the same time his folded hands come to rest on his small paunch. Sunlight streams through his windows, making his bald head shine.

I'm positive I know why I've been called in here. I'm one month away from completing my hours, and soon I'll be fully licensed. He needs another therapist so he can share the workload. As it is, he's booking weeks out, and for some patients, that's not helpful.

"I don't want to take too many liberties here." His measured tone fills the space. "But I think it's safe to assume you enjoy working here, in this office. Yes?" He sits back in his chair, settling clasped hands over his midsection.

I nod. "Very much, yes." My palms rub together. I knew it.

"For some time now I've been thinking about what's next for this office. And me." He glances fondly around the walls. "Would you consider taking over half the practice after you're licensed? Ideally, I could eventually transition out. The place would become yours."

Disbelief tumbles through me. "I'm…uh… Well—" My brain scrambles to form a real sentence. "I don't know. It's a lot to consider. I'm just starting out, and having my own practice, it's—"

"You'd be fine. Great, even. The clients respect and trust you. You have an easy way with them. I've spent the better part of two years supervising your sessions. I wouldn't consider you to partner with me if I didn't think you are capable."

My mind races back and forth, from the enormity of his offer to the logistics. Me, in charge of a business? The leader, the keeper of successes and failures?

"I'm honored you would ask me, Joseph. Really. Would you mind if I took the weekend to think about it?"

He gestures with an arm. "Take whatever time you need. It's not like you say yes and then it happens"—he snaps his fingers—"like that. We'd have to get a lawyer and all that jazz."

Just the thought of 'a lawyer and all that jazz' overwhelms me.

When I get home that night, Gabriel is waiting for me. He's sitting on the couch, head bent to the open book on his lap. In the past year, Gabriel has become a reader. Mystery, mostly, and a thriller here or there. He jokes that in another life, he wants to be Hercule Poirot.

I walk up behind him, and his head tips back. His gaze sinks into me, and my fingertips roam over his neck.

"How's your book?" I plant a kiss on his forehead.

He drops the book and holds my face in place, adjusting himself so our lips meet. "Good," he answers. "You taste like chocolate."

I straighten and round the couch, going to sit beside him. "I swiped a piece from work." My stomach growls audibly. "Still starving though."

"Dinner reservations are in an hour."

I bite my lip. Gabriel smirks. "You forgot, didn't you?"

"No."

"Liar."

"I forgot," I admit.

"Ryan and Carrie? Oyster bar?" His eyebrows lift as he attempts to jog my memory.

I wrinkle my nose. "Do we have to go there? I hate oysters."

Gabriel raises his palms, proclaiming his innocence. "Ryan and Carrie's pick. Not mine. Want me to smuggle in a ham sandwich for you?"

"Um, yeah?"

He laughs and wraps his arms around me. "I love you."

"I love you, too."

———

IT'S AWFUL. This whole situation is awkward and awful.

Gabriel asked Ryan how he plans to use his vacation days this year, and it was like opening Pandora's box. Every couple argues, and most have a handful of hot-button topics, but this level of fighting doesn't bode well for the future of the relationship. Ryan and Carrie have only been married three months longer than me and Gabriel.

"Mexico isn't safe right now." Ryan's tone teeters on the verge of breaking. "The cartels aren't staying away from tourist towns like they used to. Don't you watch the news?"

Carrie rolls her eyes. "Do you ever get sick of being afraid of things?"

He gives her a tired look. "I run into burning buildings. You make it sound like I hide in a safe space and suck my thumb."

She blows out a loud, disgusted breath. When I first met Carrie, I thought she was gorgeous with her curly blonde hair and hazel eyes. The more I got to know her, the less I saw her as conventionally attractive.

Gabriel's hand finds my thigh under the table, and he squeezes gently. My gaze meets his, and the corners of his mouth turn up ever so slightly. *They're not ok, but we are great.* I know that's what he's saying to me. The benign smugness we share is like a shield, a notion that reinforces a truth I already know. Gabriel and I will go on when others fail. Like natural selection, but for marriage. I turn my head in his direction, my nose brushing his upper arm.

Gabriel's hand stays on my thigh after I straighten up. The air on the opposite side of the table is taut, needing only a moderate gust to snap. I'm fearful of the scene that will ensue if that happens.

"Carrie, how is work?" I ask, to steer her attention from Ryan.

"Good." She stirs the straw in her pink drink. She hesitates, then admits, "It's actually a shit show. I'm knee-deep in a tax fraud case and I just had a paralegal quit on me." Her eyes find Ryan, then skitter back to me. "I'm exhausted," she says under her breath.

I'm not sure why she's whispering. Is she trying to hide her exhaustion from Ryan? Why would she do that? He's her husband. They may be at odds on some things, but he should be the person she goes to with all her woes. Then again, considering what I just witnessed, maybe not.

I shake my head. "It must be physically, mentally, and emotionally exhausting being a defense attorney."

She nods slowly, lifting her drink. "I'm tired of a lot of things these days." Her statement tumbles out around the rocks glass poised at her mouth.

"Uh-huh," I mimic her slow nod. I like Carrie enough, but she and I have never hit it off. She's too busy to have real friends, and I don't think our personalities mesh.

"You think we need couples therapy, don't you?"

I feel my mask slipping into place, the one I wear when I'm in the middle of a session. "I think therapy is a good choice when couples are struggling to communicate effectively. An objective third party can be helpful in bridging the gap."

Carrie maintains eye contact with me for a full three seconds, then blinks and says, "Right."

She drains the rest of her mixed drink and leans forward, the table pressing into her stomach. A tiny sparkle lights her eyes, and she asks, "If you could go anywhere, where would you go?"

I glance at Gabriel, deep in conversation with Ryan. Sometimes, late at night, we lie awake and imagine our dream vacation. We describe breakfast (exotic tropical fruit) and our activities for the day (snorkeling or lying on a beach chair). Gabriel has supported both of us while I've been completing my hours, and there hasn't been money for luxury vacations. Our only trips over the past two years have been to Palm Springs. I don't feel like I've missed out. Some of our best sex, and even better conversations, have happened there. No exotic fruit plates, though.

To Carrie, I say, "We want to go somewhere in the Virgin Islands. British or US, any island will do. I'm not picky."

The sparkle in her eyes fades. My reply has fallen short.

"How about you?" I ask quickly, trying to resurrect it.

"Brazil," she answers immediately. "And I'd go alone."

———

I step out of my heels and use the side of my foot to slide them over on the wood floor. I bend over, rubbing at my instep, and wobble.

Gabriel steadies me, and I hold on to his hip while I finish massaging my aching foot. "This is a good reminder that heels are the devil's work."

"Your calves look good in them."

I stand up straight. "Is that your way of asking me not to chuck them into the desert?"

He nods vigorously. I follow him into our bathroom, where I change out of my clothes.

"What a weird night," Gabriel remarks, toothbrush hanging from the side of his mouth.

"Can we not make that double date a regular thing?" I ask, taking the toothpaste Gabriel offers.

"He's my best friend," Gabriel reminds me, as if I need the reminder.

"I know, but"—I stick my toothbrush in my mouth—"he and Carrie have serious issues. And I spend all day listening to couples argue."

Gabriel spits and rinses. He wipes a hand towel across his mouth and turns, leaning a hip against the counter. "Ryan is going to ask Carrie for a divorce."

I'm not shocked. I'm not even the least bit surprised. The contempt coming from both individuals was enough to predict this outcome.

I finish brushing my teeth and say, "Only if he beats Carrie to it."

Gabriel's eyebrows draw together. "Did she say something?"

"No. I can tell, though. There are signs for this sort of thing."

Gabriel slips an arm around my lower back and pulls me flush with him. "Oh yeah? Do we have any of those signs?"

My arms go around his shoulders, one hand snaking up into his dark hair as I shake my head. "You and I are part of the precious few."

There's a rumble in his chest, almost like a pleased purr. Whatever has touched Ryan and Carrie, will not reach us. I spend enough time listening to couples to know how the implosion begins. There will be no such occurrences with me and Gabriel, because I will always be vigilant. I will be the watchdog of our relationship, the guard.

Speaking of my job. "Joseph asked me to join him in the practice. Make it half mine. Eventually, he'd phase out and retire."

Gabriel's mouth drops open. "I can't believe you waited all night to tell me this."

"I was processing. It's a big deal."

Now he's grinning widely. "And you said?"

"I said I need to think about it."

Gabriel tips my chin up, forcing my gaze onto his. "You should take it."

"What about us? Our plans for a family? I know we wanted to have a few years to ourselves, but it's been two years already. How can I take on an enormous responsibility like that, knowing I might have to pull back soon? And the money? Where will we get the money? That's a huge loan. Transition is a prime time to lose patients. Those who were already thinking about stopping their therapy have the perfect excuse. And then what? I went to school to help people, not be a businesswoman. How do I run a business? How do I make enough to pay business-related expenses? What if the business doesn't make enough? When are you going to get to do what you want to do? You don't want to be a firefighter anymore, and you shouldn't have to do something you don't want to do. And—"

"Take a breath, baby. It's all going to be ok."

"You don't know that for certain."

Gabriel backs away, and my arms fall to my sides. He holds up one finger, and I watch him walk into our bedroom. He picks up his phone from his nightstand and thumbs around on the screen as he walks back to me. Sliding the phone onto the counter, he taps it once and pulls me into his arms again.

A song fills the air. The Beach Boys. *Don't Worry, Baby.*

He holds me, and I fold my head into his chest. He hums, and I experience it twice, both when his voice falls down around me and his chest vibrates my cheek.

Gabriel's hands ghost my back, traveling lower. He lifts my oversized T-shirt, an old one of his that shrunk in the dryer, until it gathers at my waist.

His humming ceases, replaced by the sound of his kisses feathering my neck.

He lifts me, placing me on the counter. I tug his shorts down over his hips, using my foot to push them all the way to the ground. He hauls me to the counters' edge. I bite into his shoulder when he enters me, loving every second of him. My sweet husband. My Gabriel.

"Look at me," Gabriel says.

I open my eyes. He leans his forehead against mine, his arms keeping me steady on the counter. He is tender, but rough. I soak it up like the desiccated desert surrounding us.

The song ends.

But Gabriel and me? We keep going.

SESSION ELEVEN

DESERT FLOWER THERAPY

"You bought into the practice?"

I nod. "I did. I was terrified, but I did it. After all the fear of the unknown and failure subsided, I felt proud of myself."

"It sounds like Gabriel supported you in the decision."

I look down at my hands. "He was always very supportive of my career. If only I'd made his more of a priority."

"You didn't?"

"Not the way I should have. I let him continue in a job that did nothing for his soul. He was good at it, but it took too much from him. Emotionally." Day by day, the light in Gabriel's eyes slowly dimmed. I hate myself for not stepping in back then, for not turning myself inside out to stop it from happening. "I kept letting him sacrifice for us. For me."

Dr. Ruben crosses an ankle over the opposite knee. "I've got news for you. Unless you're threatening violence, you can't force someone to sacrifice. He did that on his own."

CHAPTER 14

Before I met Gabriel, I had no idea what a firefighter's work schedule was like. Twenty-four hours on, forty-eight hours off sounds like a dream to me, if a person can get past the 'awake for an entire day' aspect of the job. They're allowed to sleep on the job, but it's rarely long, restful slumber. They are yanked from sleep, roused by the tones, and within minutes they arrive at the truck, turnout gear and game faces on.

I fear for Gabriel. For his safety, his life, his mental health. This worry drove me to seek blog posts written by the spouses and significant others of people who have dangerous jobs. There are tips and tricks, but the general consensus is that the people who do these jobs want to come home also, and they're taking every precaution to make that happen.

That helped, but not totally. Especially not at night, when the darkness casts a greater contrast on our jobs.

Right now it's halfway between tonight and tomorrow,

though technically it's tomorrow. Four-thirty. Gabriel is two-thirds of the way through a shift, and that means not only do I miss him now, but I'll miss him again when I leave for work and he still isn't home. It isn't ideal, but the reunions are sweet.

Shoving off the covers, I stand and make my way to the kitchen. The coffee brews, and I wait beside it, empty mug in hand. Maybe I can fill an IV bag and insert the strong brown liquid directly into my veins.

When it's ready, I take my full cup to the living room. I keep a notebook on the side table because I've been toying with the idea of writing a book. Fiction, probably romance. With a husband like Gabriel and a meet-cute like ours, how could I not write a romance?

I'm working on an outline, but every time I open this notebook I hate what I wrote the time before, so I scratch it out and start over. At this rate, I'll never begin actually writing the book.

My yawning begins pretty soon after I've drained my cup. I slide down on the couch until I'm lying horizontally, and bring the notebook with me.

My eyes become heavy, my blinks grow lengthier. The words on the pages meld together, an alphabet soup. I don't fight it when the notebook drops onto my chest.

"Avery?"

My eyes open. Gabriel hovers over me, propping himself up with a hand on the arm of the couch and the other along the back. Rays of sunshine beam around the room, curling around objects and highlighting the dust. Sooty streaks darken Gabriel's cheeks and forehead. His shirt is dirty, pockets of sweat collecting near the collar and underarms.

I push up on my elbows and look around, trying to find the time. There isn't a clock in the room, and my phone is somewhere else in the house. "Shit. What time is it? I'm late for work."

Gabriel shakes his head, and suddenly he's falling into me, an anguished sob escaping on his way down.

"Ryan," he moans into my chest. His shoulders shake with such force, it ripples through his upper body. I hold tight to him, shocked and confused.

"What happened?"

"He's dead."

Gabriel sinks all his weight into me, pushing me down deep into the cushions. His grief renders him incapable of consideration, and even though it hurts to handle his full weight, in this moment the pain is an aside. I barely notice it, because the pain in my heart is too sharp.

"Gabriel," I whisper, my hands raking through his hair. "Honey, I'm so sorry. So sorry."

I don't ask how Ryan died. I don't need to. Gabriel continues to cry, emptying himself of tears and emotion. Eventually, he is spent. He kisses my forehead and rolls off me. He offers me a hand to stand up, and I take it.

I'm watching him, evaluating, taking stock of the slope in his shoulders, the way they hunch forward, as if protecting his center mass. Too late. His heart is already broken.

"Take a shower with me?" he asks, his voice gritty.

I nod, and lead the way.

I wash myself, and then him. He stands still, his muscles loose. When we get out, I call Joseph and explain what little I know, and tell him I won't be in today. Gabriel sits at the kitchen table, the breakfast I made him untouched and cold, and tells me about the call they went on last night.

"He was trapped." Gabriel stares at his scrambled eggs, now hardened on the surface. "The fucking roof fell in. He was trying to reach a kid. A seventeen-year-old kid." Tears swim in his eyes. "Ryan shouldn't have kept going. He had orders to pull back. He knew it wasn't safe. He fucking knew."

I settle onto Gabriel's lap and grip his face with my hands. "Ryan died trying to save someone." My heart twists and I want to sob, but I hold it together.

Gabriel's features rearrange, settling into a look I've never seen on his face before. Hatred. "I keep thinking about Carrie."

I pause, confused, and ask, "You mean because she's lost her husband?"

Our double date with Ryan and Carrie was four months ago, and I was hoping no news of a divorce meant they decided to work on their marriage.

"You heard her that night. She asked him in that condescending way if he ever gets sick of being afraid of things. Look at what happened last night. He should have been afraid. He should have known the risks. And he did. I know he did. But he went in further anyway."

"You don't know what he was thinking. You can't blame Carrie. You can't blame anyone."

"How about me? Can I blame myself?"

"Why would you do that?"

Gabriel's tongue runs the length of his lower lip, his breath coming in terse streams. "I let him go into the house first."

I lower my face until we're eye to eye, nose to nose.

"Stop. What happened isn't anybody's fault. He outranks you." If there's anything I've learned about firefighters, it's that they abide by rank.

He's quiet, his gaze staying on me. Then he shifts, and I stand. "I'll be right back," he says, his voice hollow, a husk.

He retreats through the front door, shoulders hunched. His truck door opens and closes. I spend the moment he's gone attempting to calm myself, so that I can be what Gabriel needs. He walks into the kitchen clutching a paper bag. From it, he pulls out a bottle.

Tequila.

He eyes me. Maybe he's gauging my reaction. Maybe he's so inundated by grief, he doesn't care about my response. In a voice so thickened by pain it's hard to believe it belongs to my husband, he says, "Get drunk with me?"

No.

But…well…

Gabriel has abstained for a decade. He has matured, his frontal lobe is fully developed now. He is not the person he was when he was a teenager.

"Are you sure?" I have to ask, though of all times for him to do this, today seems fitting. Soothe, numb, and forget, if only momentarily.

"My best friend died last night. I saw it happen." Gabriel lifts the bottle, as if it's a bicep curl. "It'll just be this one time. And you'll be with me."

I don't want to tell him no. I want to get down in the grief with him, sit beside him and wear the pain like a cloak. I want to show him how much I love him.

I pull two juice glasses from the cabinet.

Gabriel twists off the top and pours. It's a bizarre sight, Gabriel with a bottle of booze, but I don't hear alarm bells ringing in my head. Like Gabriel said, it'll just be this once.

What's the harm in it?

CHAPTER 15

Some funerals are a relatively happy affair. People slap them with a *Celebration Of Life* title and imbue the event with a joyful hue.

Not this one.

This is a funeral service in the truest sense of the name. It is somber and dark. Palpable anguish, so thick it could be sliced, settles into the space between bodies packed into pews.

Gabriel's fingers wrap around mine, his grip painfully tight. If I bruised easily, I'm sure my body would bear the markings of his iron-clad grasps since the night Ryan died. Every time we're in our bed he holds me, forming a cage, as though he believes if I'm not ensnared, I'll be lost.

I uncross and recross my legs, my black dress slipping over my black tights. Four rows in front of us, Carrie's blonde hair shimmers with the quaking of her shoulders. I know Gabriel notices. I know he feels disgusted by her. More than once since the first morning, he has mentioned what a terrible person Carrie is. He hasn't reached out to her, but I have. I called her the day Ryan died, after Gabriel passed out drunk. I wasn't expecting her to answer the phone, but she did. Where I anticipated wailing, I heard only a sunken tone. We spoke for less than a minute. She accepted my sympathy, declined my offer to help in any way she needed, and we hung up. We haven't spoken since.

Gabriel's father delivers the eulogy. He tells a story of Ryan's first time cooking at the firehouse, how he'd almost burned the place down.

"We've always kept a fire extinguisher in the kitchen, but I never expected to need it." He grins ruefully, and for the first time during the service, the low hum of collective chuckling radiates through the people. It makes me happy that Gabriel's father was able to insert a moment of levity. The stuffy air needed it.

He finishes and returns to his seat next to Gabriel's mom. The minister says a final prayer, and the service ends. There is a reception afterward, and Gabriel takes his time with Ryan's parents and his two older sisters. I stand back and watch. Grief has always fascinated me. It is an emotion so layered, so nuanced. One moment it can be as soft as a gentle rain, the next, an outraged typhoon. Some people refuse to admit its presence. Others drown in it.

And then, there's Carrie. She shakes hands and hugs, nodding and wiping at her eyes. I believe her tears are real. And she uses those real tears to firmly place herself in her new role. Widow.

Carrie gazes out across the small room we're in, and finds me. She starts for me, and is stopped twice on the way. When she arrives, she doesn't hug me the way she has other people. She stands beside me, shoulder to shoulder, and murmurs so quietly I lean closer to hear her say, "He would have hated this."

I nod. "What would he have chosen instead?"

She shrugs. "I'm not sure. But I know it wouldn't be this."

From somewhere in the room, there is wailing. An older woman is led away by an equally aged man. Maybe she is an aunt.

Carrie raises her eyebrows and ducks her chin as if to say, 'See what I mean?'.

"I'm sorry for your loss, Carrie. Truly." I mean it. Alongside my condolence sits relief it wasn't my husband. I'm not proud of that, but it's true.

"It's awful," she says, clasping her hands together in front of herself. "Going through his things. Our things. But you know what?" She side-eyes me, and I tip my head back slightly, a cue for her to continue. "Now I don't have to be a divorcee. I get to be a widow."

I get to be a widow. I've never wanted to inflict physical pain on someone until right now.

"I don't mean it the way it sounds," she adds, her words tripping over themselves in her haste to fix what can't be repaired.

"Yes, you do." I say each word slowly.

"I'm just looking at this realistically." She's whispering again, more forcefully now. "We were going to get divorced. He didn't want to be married to me anymore, either."

Revulsion leaves a bitter tang in my mouth. I don't know why she's saying any of this to me, other than she thinks because I'm a therapist I'm receptive. But she is not my patient, I am not her therapist, and I am not a keeper of her secrets and innermost thoughts.

Ryan's mother motions for Carrie. "Don't tell anybody what I said," she whisper-hisses.

"I don't plan to." Though she deserves it, Ryan does not. Gossip or negativity around his marriage need not exist.

Carrie slips away, sending me a pleading look in lieu of a farewell. By the time Gabriel makes his way back to me, I'm sitting with Corinne at one of the tables set up in the church courtyard. She has hardly said a word through all this, breaking her silence once to ask for directions to the ladies room, and a second time to ask me to get her a coffee from the box provided by the church. I would imagine a funeral service for a young man is painful for her on many levels. Both Gabriel and his father have spent a majority of the last hour talking with the firefighters in attendance.

Gabriel kisses his mother's cheek and pulls me up from my seat. I say goodbye and we start for his truck. He holds my hand.

"I saw you talking to Carrie. What did she have to say?"

I glance over at my husband in his shiny shoes and black suit, and his equally dark hair. Shadows darken the skin under his eyes. "Nothing of importance."

We stop at his truck tailgate. He leans closer and says, "I don't know what I'd do if I didn't have you. I love you," before placing a featherlight kiss on my cheek.

"I love you, too." I take the keys from his hand. "I'll drive. It's been a hard day. You should relax."

"You sure? I don't mind."

"Of course I'm sure." I squeeze his forearm.

Gabriel nods in agreement and wipes a hand down his face.

I hate pretending.

But the smell of liquor on his breath? I hate that even more.

————

GABRIEL PULLS a navy blue Phoenix Fire Department T-shirt from the dryer. He shakes it out, then threads his neck and arms through. It's his first time donning it since the night Ryan died.

It's been one week since Ryan's funeral, and Doug has ordered Gabriel back to work. Everyone else has returned, and he said Gabriel was being the kind of colleague nobody wants, moping around and feeling sorry for himself. When Gabriel told me what his dad said, I picked up my phone, ready to tell Doug exactly how wrong he was. Tough love on a man like Gabriel? Terrible approach.

Gabriel shook his head at me, and when Doug answered, I told him I called him by accident.

Gabriel walks from the laundry room into our kitchen. His movements are certain. He reaches up into a cabinet, the muscles of his upper back straining against his shirt. His calf muscles, already generous and round, flex to support his reach. On the outside, he appears strong. Inside, he is soft. The two are separated only by a soluble layer. He keeps so much of himself hidden down deep, but none of it is particularly difficult to access. It is there, ready for the taking, if only people pay close enough attention.

I'm worried about what returning to the station might

mean to him. To his soul. He is good at his job, but at what personal cost?

I never mentioned the alcohol at the funeral. I don't know how concerned I should be. I don't know how much leeway he should be given, considering the circumstances. Letting it go is easiest, and right now I'll do just about anything to keep from rocking the boat.

Gabriel finishes making breakfast. He carries two plates to the table and places one in front of me. We eat quietly. Gabriel is wrapped up in his thoughts.

"Are you looking forward to work?" I ask buoyantly, my tone lifting at the end of my sentence, as if I don't know how conflicted he feels. Yesterday he told me he didn't want to go back, but today might be different. That's how grief often works. What you didn't want yesterday might be exactly what you need today.

Gabriel finishes chewing his last bite and pushes his plate away. He props an elbow on the table and reaches for me, hand curving over my cheek and tucking my hair behind my ear. He lets it rest on my jaw.

"No." I don't like his resolute tone. I can hear how he doesn't believe he has a choice.

A surging desire to remove all his pain rises within me. "Then why are you going?"

He stares into my eyes. "I've been wondering why I continue. Why I do this to myself. Then I remember you. The look on your face when I opened your bedroom door that night. The weight of your body when I carried you. The relief in your eyes when I handed you over to the paramedics. You became my world." The pad of his thumb strokes my cheek. "Every person is someone else's world. It's my responsibility to preserve that."

I open my mouth to tell him none of that matters if he's unhappy, but then he kisses me, long and slow, the kind of kiss that asks for more. We both need to go to work, but I can't stop this. His mouth, his hands, his heart, he needs to give it all to me as much as I need to have it.

I'm wearing only my nightgown, so it's a matter of seconds before I'm on my back on the table and he's inside me.

Gabriel leans over, his body bent like an uppercase L. His kisses, so tender against my neck, juxtaposed with what his lower half is doing.

I love it. I love how he gives me his soul at the same time he gives me his body. This man. *This man.* I cling to him, wrapping my legs around his back, slipping my hands under the shirt he didn't take off. I pretend my love can seep through my palms, soak into him and carry him into his day, providing solace to his wounded heart.

He finishes a moment after me, his lips on mine and his whispered *I love you* filling my mouth.

He kisses me once more, then helps me off the table. He waits for me while I place our dishes in the dishwasher, and we go to our bedroom to get ready for the day.

We leave together, pausing at the front of our cars. When I kiss him goodbye, I tell him, "I love you. I support you, always. I am Team Gabriel, no matter what."

A smile curves his lips. He hasn't smiled much lately, and I'm grateful even for this tiny one. "Who's the opposing team?" he asks.

I shrug. "I don't know. It could be anybody. But whoever it is, I'm on your team."

His eyes fill with emotion. "It's us against the world?"

I nod once. "You and me, hero."

He smiles again, bigger this time. I think I'd do anything to see that smile. He tells me he loves me, then he leaves.

I get in my car and pause, gripping the steering wheel and filling my lungs with a deep, burning breath.

Everything will be ok. The world continues turning, and Gabriel is still Gabriel. As long as those two things remain true, everything else is extra.

SESSION TWELVE

DESERT FLOWER THERAPY

"How were things after he returned to work? Did they go back to normal?"

I nibble on the inside of my cheek. 'Normal' is a relative term. "He seemed ok. As ok as anyone can be, in that situation. He wasn't as pleasant to be around." I grind the toe of my shoe into the carpet as I think about what I'm saying. "He used to tease me a lot, in a good-natured sort of way. Flirtatious. That stopped, but it eventually started happening again. He needed a lot of time when he arrived home after a shift, like he had to transition to life outside the station. He didn't tell me that's what was happening, but it's what it looked like from the outside."

"And the alcohol?"

My lower lip trembles. "I'd thought we'd escaped with just those two instances of Gabriel drinking. I was stupid."

Dr. Ruben grimaces. "It became a common occurrence?"

"Yes." My hands form fists, and I press them into my thighs. "I participated, at first. It was kind of *if you can't beat 'em, join 'em."* Derision sharpens my tone. "I didn't know what else to do, and I thought it was better than him drinking alone." My gaze falls sideways. I can't look Dr. Ruben in the eye. "I kept telling myself it was a season. That it would pass. It was the grief. But it was every night when he wasn't working. I began finding him passed out in odd places. The backyard. In his truck in the driveway, with the door wide open." A sting of betrayal hits my heart. Am I betraying Gabriel by admitting these things?

"How did he treat you when he was drinking?"

My head shakes quickly, racing ahead of my words to dispel the real question behind Dr. Ruben's query. "Gabriel never hurt me."

Dr. Ruben makes a face, but schools it immediately.

"He didn't," I insist.

"People can hurt one another in different ways." Dr. Ruben spins his gold ring in one complete revolution. "You said you drank with him, at first?"

"It made me feel awful, so I stopped."

"And Gabriel?"

"I asked him to stop with me."

"And?"

"He didn't."

Dr. Ruben waits patiently for me to dive in.

I take a deep breath. This is it. The beginning of the end.

CHAPTER 16

Gabriel has gone out with the guys from work to 'blow off steam.' It's the third time since he went back to work a month ago.

I'm sitting up in bed reading a book when I hear him come home. Normally I'd get up and greet him, kiss him long and hard because we haven't seen each other in twenty-four hours. This time I don't want to.

If he notices, he doesn't say anything. Just like I don't say anything about last weekend, when I found him passed out in a lounge chair in the backyard. Or four days before that, when I found him asleep in his truck in the driveway with the door flung open and the engine turned off. I'd sworn that when he woke up, I was going to give him hell. My argument formed in my head, my throat clogged with the words I would say to him. I'd imagined it like an intervention, and he would weep with sadness and gratitude and painful but necessary introspection.

None of that happened. He'd come to find me after he'd woken up and come inside, fresh from a shower and smelling like the cologne I'd given him last Christmas. His eyes held fear and a measure of self-disgust. I felt relieved; as long as he was self-flagellating, I could remain quiet. I'd hoped, naïve and stupid, that maybe he could dig himself out of this hole.

Now he's standing in the doorway to our bedroom, giving me a look I've seen hundreds of times. He wants to have sex. I doubt he can perform in his current state, but that's not deterring him.

My lips tug into a smile that doesn't match how I feel. I'm a fraud, both inside and out. "I don't think so," I say playfully, wagging a finger at him. "I have the worst period cramps."

Lie.

Gabriel's lower lip juts out. He tosses his wallet on the dresser, but misses it by a good twelve inches. "I hate your period."

I place my open book on my lap. "You and me both."

Gabriel bends to retrieve his wallet, and stumbles. "Whoa," he says, throwing out an arm for balance. He makes it upright, and glances at me. Childlike shame replaces the lascivious glint in his eyes, like he's a puppy who peed on the carpet.

"Who put that step there?" I joke, and hate myself for it.

Gabriel goes into the bathroom and starts the shower.

I lay my book on my nightstand and turn out the light.

I love Gabriel.

I hate his actions.

I love our marriage.

I hate who I'm turning into.

CHAPTER 17

My dad and Lara are taking us out for dinner to celebrate our third wedding anniversary. Gabriel arrived home from his shift two hours ago. He took a shower like he always does, then went out back carrying a book. He'd had a beer in his other hand, which I pretended not to see, and he pretended not to be hiding from me.

I stay in the house, scrolling through old photos on my phone. I choose one, taken a year ago. Gabriel stands behind me, his arms wrapped around me as he presses a kiss to my cheek. I'm grinning. The photo is soft focus, giving it a dreamy quality. I navigate to my social media app and upload the photo, typing out the caption *Another amazing year with the man who makes my heart beat faster.* I hit post, then close the app and cry.

CHAPTER 18

Every summer, Joseph closes the practice for two weeks. I asked Gabriel to ask for time off for a vacation, thinking we needed a change of scenery. Something fresh, and new. He said other people were already taking vacation, and he couldn't.

So this brochure of a resort in St. Lucia that Gabriel handed me a moment ago? I'm still in shock.

I stare at the printed picture with the glossy turquoise water and the woven lounge chairs. I can already feel the warm sand between my toes, even as they're pressed against our jersey bedsheets. More than that, I feel hope surging in my heart. This could be it. Our chance to turn things around. Maybe we can get back to who we once were. Salt water cures all ills, right?

Gabriel beams with pride at having pulled off this surprise. "We leave in four days."

A tremor of excitement ripples through me. It's the first good feeling I've had about Gabriel in a while, so I grab ahold of it and let it run rampant. I roll up onto my knees and wave the picture in the air. "I need to go swimsuit shopping," I yell, bouncing.

Gabriel laughs and tackles me. My legs widen to make room for him to lie between them. He rests his chin between my breasts and gazes at me.

"Six nights, seven days." His voice drops low, washing over me. "We can do whatever you want. We can lie on a beach chair and not move the entire time. Or we can do a glass-bottom boat. Or a catamaran. Or the market in Castries."

I run my fingernails over his scalp, and his eyes flutter closed. He loves when I do this. "How about a little of it all?" I ask.

His eyes are still closed. "Sounds perfect."

"We've been saving for a trip like this for a while."

One eye opens. He knows what I'm getting at. "We have enough."

I raise my eyebrows. He laughs. "Ok, maybe not *enough* enough, but almost enough."

"Why now? Why not wait until we can pay for it in full?"

Gabriel sighs, his warm breath streaming against my chest. He's quiet for so long I think maybe he's not going to answer, but then he says, "I wanted to do something great for you. I know I haven't been great lately."

He turns his head to the side and lays it on my chest. I adjust my gaze too, and watch him pick at a piece of lint on our sheets.

It makes me feel bad to watch him feel bad. I rub his back, my knuckles kneading his muscles. "For better or worse, remember?"

"I'd like to spend more time in the better category than we have been."

How much should I say? How can I tell him it hurts my heart when I kiss him and taste vapors? That I watch him surreptitiously place a hand against a surface to steady himself, or I listen to him speak and try not to wince when he slurs.

He's not hiding it, per se, because he tells me when he's meeting his friends for a drink, but it would be hard to form an argument that he isn't keeping it away from me.

Gabriel rolls off me, but takes me with him. I push up so I'm sitting astride him.

"I love you, baby." His voice rings with conviction. "With everything I have."

"I know." I really do know, but I've been considering if there may be other times when something is more powerful than love.

Addiction.

It's a word I've yet to say out loud; I can hardly think it without cringing. "I love you the same way."

"No more meeting the guys when we're off-shift. I'm going to stop drinking." Gabriel takes my hands and holds them between us. "That's what this trip is. It's my promise to you." The setting sun sends hot pinks and fiery oranges streaming through our window, lighting up Gabriel's face.

I'm both taken aback and encouraged that he's the one who brought it up. And that confidence in his voice? It's in his eyes, the set of his cheekbones, it forms a halo around him. He means every word.

"I don't doubt you will." My voice holds all my confidence, too. Relief washes through me, and it isn't until I'm submerged that I realize how worried I've been. How lonely. Survival mode pushed those feelings aside.

His head falls into the pillow, and he speaks to the ceiling. "You know this is going to be our best trip ever, right?"

"I'm certain of it." I glance at the brochure, rumpled now from where I laid on it when Gabriel tackled me. We only need to get there, to the white sand and blue water. Everything will be better after that.

———

GABRIEL'S STANDING at the airport desk, talking to the employee at our gate. Our plane departs in one hour, and I'm waiting for Gabriel so we can go into the little store by the restrooms. I need candy and a magazine for the flight.

I'm not sure why he's talking to her. He'd been sitting beside me when he squeezed my hand, whispered he'd be right back, and walked away.

He's turning around now, looking at me and smiling. The attendant does the same, adding a small wave. My automatic response is to mirror her.

Gabriel says one more thing to her, and she laughs. She looks far happier than any of the other attendants, and I don't know if that's due to her personality, or Gabriel.

"What was that about?" I ask when Gabriel comes walking over.

He rubs his hands together in excitement. "We've been upgraded to first class."

My mouth opens. "What? How?"

"I asked her if there was room. She said there were two seats available, and when she told me how much it would be to upgrade, I said never mind. Then she said she might let the cost slide if I told her how we met. She said it had to be a good story." He chuckles. "So I told her how we met."

"That's in-sane." I singsong the second word.

"Yep. I even told her she could look us up on the internet. I told her there'd be two articles she could read about us."

Domenica did a follow up on our wedding, but her first article is my favorite.

"And did she?"

He nods. "I watched her type our names into the search bar on her phone. She got really excited after that."

"Aww." I grip the back of his neck with one hand. "You're the best."

Nine hours later and one stop in Miami, our plane is descending over the turquoise waters of St. Lucia.

By the time we get to the van sent by the resort to collect guests, I'm high on life. The air is thick, sultry, so moist I think maybe I could swipe a cupped hand through it and capture water droplets. I tuck away my passport, freshly stamped for the first time in my life, and lean over Gabriel's lap to watch the scenery as we pass. Gabriel tugs at my waist, lifting me up and over as he slides left, giving up his window seat.

The high continues. We're shown to our room, but it's not a room at all. It's detached, a single structure, and it's bigger than our home in Phoenix. I don't think we're in the right place.

"Excuse me?" Gabriel says to the man carrying in our luggage. "I booked a standard room."

The man smiles. "This room was available, so they bumped you up."

Gabriel and I turn wide eyes on each other. His cheeks quake as he holds in his response, and I feel my own cheeks trembling.

As soon as the bellman is gone, we lose our cool.

"Holy shit," I yell, as Gabriel spins me around. He throws his head back, disbelieving laughter pours from him.

I peer down at him, my gaze sliding as he lowers my feet to the floor. "Did you have something to do with this, too?"

He shakes his head. "This is not my work."

"It must be our lucky day." The universe wants the best for us. I can feel it. We went off the rails, but our cart is now righted.

Gabriel's hand slips gently over my throat. His hungry gaze digs into me, and we shed our clothes with record speed.

After, when we're in the bathroom unpacking toiletries, Gabriel lifts one item out of the pile I've dumped on the counter.

He flips the small disc of plastic between two fingers, eyes on my reflection in the mirror. "What do you think about not taking these anymore?"

I stare at him. The surprises of the day aren't slowing.

"You're serious?"

He nods.

"Are we ready?" Having a baby has never been an 'if' but a 'when,' and maybe this is what Gabriel needs. A life to care for, a child to love and raise. He needs to see the world is bigger than his grief, that it needs more from him.

He nods again. "I've been talking to some of the guys at work about it. According to them, you're never really ready, even when you think you are." He takes my hand, dropping his attention from my reflection and on to me. "Let's do it. Let's jump."

Momentous. That's what this is. One day I'll look back on this very second, this tiny blip in time when we decided our future.

"Yes." I nod so vigorously my hair tickles my cheeks. I'm laughing and crying. This is our fresh start. We made it through.

I don't think I've ever been so happy.

Gabriel has recommitted to our life. He has left behind what hurts him, and us. He has chosen me.

I watched him decline a mimosa on the plane and a fruity welcome drink when we arrived here.

Everything is good.

So good.

Smooth sailing, from here on out.

Gabriel kisses me. "Best. Trip. Ever."

CHAPTER 19

Three days of island life have me convinced I want to stay here forever.

We've sat in the mineral baths, hiked the volcano, and filled my phone's camera with photos of the Pitons. We're surrounded by towering green trees and vibrant flowers. The paths are made of stone and colorful rocks, and they shine in the daytime.

I eat exotic fruit sorbet from hollowed out coconuts, and because we're all-inclusive I don't feel bad when I order the gazpacho and dislike it.

We sit by the infinity pool and read. Gabriel bought a book at the airport and is making his way through it. I packed four books, and I'm starting on the third. I plan to leave all four behind in the small library in the common area.

We're at the beach today, snuggled up on a two-person daybed under a cabana. Gabriel lazily traces a finger over my stomach, parallel to the top of my bikini bottom. My eyes are closed, letting the sun's warmth and Gabriel's touch wash over me.

"I wonder if there's already a baby in here," Gabriel murmurs, retracing the line his finger drew. "Maybe the cells are already dividing."

"I'm not sure it works that quickly." I open my eyes and take in the hopeful sparkle in his eyes, the upturned corners of his mouth. Laying my hand over his on my stomach, I say, "But if there is, and she's a girl, we can name her Lucy, after where we made her."

"I love that." Gabriel kisses my temple. "I guess it's a good thing we didn't make her in Istanbul. Or Antarctica."

I laugh. "Listen to us talking about Lucy as if she's real."

Gabriel palms my belly and playfully narrows his eyes. "Don't talk about my daughter like that."

"You're already protective of her. I love that."

"I'd burn down the world for her."

I laugh louder this time. "You're supposed to be the one who puts out the fires."

Gabriel grins. "Figure of speech."

"I love you so much. If we don't make Lucy on this trip, it's going to be fun trying."

Gabriel nips at my earlobe, and I shiver despite the sun shining on me. "I'm nothing if not determined."

Ringing comes from inside my straw tote bag. I groan. "I thought our phones were turned to silent." I turn away from Gabriel to reach into my bag.

"I thought so, too," Gabriel says when I hand him his phone.

He presses the button on his screen. "Hey, Mom."

I look out at the water, trying to push away my irritation that our island paradise bubble has been infiltrated.

Gabriel's conversation floats in and out, but it doesn't sound as if they're talking about anything of importance, so I tune them out. I pick up my book and let the world between the pages envelop me.

"Sorry about that," Gabriel says apologetically, leaning over me to toss his phone into my bag. "It's on silent now."

"Is your mom ok?" I bat away my irritation.

"Today is a hard day for her. It's the anniversary of Nash's passing. She didn't say anything, but I know that's why she called."

Shit. How did I forget that?

I sit up cross-legged and face Gabriel. "I'm sorry. Somehow I forgot."

Gabriel hooks his pinky around my pointer finger and rocks my hand gently back and forth. "It's my fault. I brought you to paradise. Bad things don't exist here."

I answer with a lopsided smile. "Do you want to talk about him?" I already know what his answer will be, but it feels important that I offer.

Gabriel flips my hand over and traces the lines in my palm. "Not really."

"Sometimes it's good to talk about the people we miss." I'm treading lightly now, knowing how easy it is to slip into the role of therapist without meaning or wanting to.

Gabriel lies back, capturing his lower lip between two fingers as he considers my offer. I'm shocked he's thinking about it. Usually he declines, or tells me another time.

Suddenly, he sits upright. "Let's go in the water."

He doesn't wait for my response. He's already standing up and brushing sand from his shorts.

I do the same. I suppose that's it for our conversation about those we've lost.

The water is warm around my ankles. We walk deeper, and my legs lose shape under the surface. We stop when I'm chest height. The water is smooth, no waves because we're tucked back in a cove, and small fish dart around my feet.

Gabriel keeps going, and I swim to him, wrapping my arms and legs around him like a koala.

He presses his cheek to the side of my head. I push my nose against his neck and breathe him in. Briny sea mixed with sunscreen, and the inimitable scent of my husband, those pheromones of his that reach deep down inside me.

"Do you remember when you said I should look for a different career once you're settled in your job?"

My arms around his neck loosen, and I pull back to look at him because this feels like a conversation that needs eye contact. "Yes."

"What do you think? You seem settled. The practice is successful. You've learned the ropes of how to operate a business and still be a therapist."

I nod slowly, trying not to show my surprise. I'm not surprised at his words or his desire. We've talked about this before, and I've always wanted him to do something that doesn't affect him as much as it does. I can't help but wonder where this is coming from. What did his mom say on the phone? Or not say?

"You should go for it. What would you like to do?"

"I'm actually pretty good at—" he cuts off abruptly, water droplets flying as he shakes his head. "Never mind."

"What? Tell me."

Gabriel tips his head up at the nearly cloudless blue sky. "Listen to me, talking crazy. Of course I'm not going to change careers. I have a family to think of."

"You could though," I tell him, because I want him to know I'm behind him. Whatever he needs to do, we'll do. I'll support us. We'll make it work. "You could quit as soon as we're back." Never mind the mountain of grief he will get from his parents, and what it will mean to his dad to have a son who is no longer a firefighter. We'll weather that storm, too.

Gabriel grunts a single laugh. "Now who's talking crazy?" His eyebrows lift, then drop back into place. "It's all good, Avery. All good. Promise."

Sadness casts a shadow on the moment. I want Gabriel to have what he wants from life. I want him to stop denying himself. I want him to stop living for Nash, and live for himself.

Gabriel turns us so he faces out of the cove, his view the ocean beyond. I snuggle into his chest. Water laps around us from my movement. His skin is warm, his muscles solid.

Gabriel is quiet, and I wish I could peer inside his head. I can tell he's holding back.

All good. Promise.

I want to believe him.

It's just that I don't.

———

I WAKE UP ALONE.

It's three a.m., and my bladder is telling me not to

drink a glass of water before bed again. I knew better, but the heat of the beach left me thirsty.

Gabriel is a sound sleeper when he's beside me. He closes his eyes, sleeps for eight hours, and wakes up happy.

That's why the thrown back comforter on his side bothers me.

I leave the bathroom and walk through our bungalow. It has three rooms, and we've used one to sleep in, and all three to have sex.

His snoring leads me to him.

Only, Gabriel rarely snores.

Is someone else in our room? Of course not. Gabriel wasn't in bed. It must be him. I'm the one who needs to go back to bed, if these jumbled thoughts are any indication.

I cross the living room, where the snoring is still as deep and rhythmic as it was when I first heard it. All the way to the couch I go, peering over.

Gabriel lies on his back, face serene, mouth open. I take a moment to study him. I've only slept beside him for two-thirds of our relationship, and it makes me remember an old couple I interviewed in college who said they hadn't slept apart from one another their entire marriage.

Gabriel's eyebrows twitch, like maybe he's dreaming. His head moves back and forth, the movements tiny but rapid.

Time to wake him up and get him to our bed.

I round the couch and crouch beside him. My plan is to kiss his cheek, gently rousing him, but a snore followed by a long exhalation stops me. I'm frozen, my lips hovering an inch above his warm skin.

I smell it on his breath.

Vapors. Ethanol.

How? The room doesn't have a mini-bar.

I sink down to the cold tile floor, my shattered heart clattering around me. His commitment to me, to us, to the life we wanted to bring into the world, *poof*, there it goes. Alcohol soluble. And with it goes every remaining shred of hope.

How can I keep loving a person who refuses to love himself?

He has a problem.

My Gabriel, my husband with the kindest soul, has a problem.

Confusion and anger fill me. Gabriel lies passed out, oblivious to my pain. He has become oblivious to it while he is awake, too.

I push the tears from my face, certain of one thing. I cannot, *will not*, bring a child into this marriage.

I get to my feet and walk away from my snoring husband.

I find my suitcase, then the smaller toiletries bag nestled inside it, and locate the plastic disc I didn't plan on using.

Tears stream down my face as I swallow two birth control pills. Tomorrow I'll take the next two.

I lie down in our bed, but I'm not alone, because I have my loneliness beside me. It has a heartbeat. It's a living, breathing thing.

True loneliness isn't being alone. It's being with someone else and still finding yourself alone.

A truth I wish I never learned.

———

WHEN I WAKE up in the morning, Gabriel is beside me. I lie there, quietly reading the news on my phone even though we were supposed to be cutting ourselves off from the real world. I figure it's fine, considering the real world has detonated a grenade in the middle of my bliss.

Gabriel reaches for me when he wakes up. I push his hand away. He doesn't try again, or ask why I'm mad.

Silently, we dress for breakfast. I don't have an appetite, but I know I need to eat. Our server delivers a Bloody Mary alongside our coffees. "A little hair of the dog," he says, winking. Gabriel doesn't touch it.

"You have a problem," I murmur, spearing a pineapple slice.

He stares out at the bright blue water in the distance. "It was the anniversary of Nash's death."

"You'll always find a reason if you're looking for one."

"You're overreacting." He tosses his napkin on the table.

I stare at him, waiting for him to remember his declaration on the day he told me about this trip. Waiting for him to remember what this trip is supposed to symbolize.

The muscles in his jaw flex. "I'm on vacation."

I say nothing.

"Give me a break," he says, teeth clenched. He pushes back his seat and leaves.

Tears pool in my eyes, blurring the happy yellow color of the fruit on my plate. He's the one who messed up, so why is it I'm sitting here feeling like I've done something wrong?

I finish my coffee, watching the melting ice turn the Bloody Mary into a soupy mess.

SESSION THIRTEEN
DESERT FLOWER THERAPY

Dr. Ruben hands me the tissues.

"I'm sorry."

"Me too."

"We can cut it short today. You don't have to keep going."

I wipe at my eyes. "We're almost to the worst of it. I might as well continue."

CHAPTER 20

"How was St. Lucia?" My dad stabs his fork into his teriyaki bowl. He chews a cauliflower floret and looks at me, expectant.

My dad, Camryn, and I are seated at a trendy restaurant, the kind with an exposed ceiling and patterned floor tile. He and Lara are remodeling their house, and he has been tasked with going to new places trying to get an idea of his design preferences.

"Beautiful," I answer, covering my mouth as I chew. "Paradise."

He sips his iced tea. "Gabriel back at work?"

I nod. "Yep."

He digs for another bite. "I bet it's not easy to start a twenty-four-hour shift right after getting home from vacation."

"Very true."

Camryn gives me a weird look, and I stuff in another bite so I have an excuse not to say any more. I haven't told her anything about Gabriel. I'm ashamed, and embarrassed.

My dad is like a dog with a bone. "Any details you want to share?"

What happened in one night there has overshadowed the entire trip, so I tell them about the first few days. I detail the excursions, the color of the water, and the glass-bottom boat tour and how I threw up over the side of the boat.

I have no desire to tell them about Gabriel. I don't want to worry them, and more than anything, I don't want their view of him to change. I also don't want their view of *me* to change.

Turns out, Avery and Gabriel's storied romance isn't so magical after all.

"What about you?" I turn the tables on Camryn. "What's up?" Using my fork, I gesture from me to my dad. "You asked us to lunch."

Camryn pushes away her half-eaten plate. "Well," she starts, folding her hands on the tabletop. "You know Danielle?"

I stare at Camryn. "Your roommate Danielle who has been your best friend for years and is about to graduate from dental school? Yes, we know her."

Cam clears her throat. "Danielle prefers to be called Dani."

"Noted." I nod.

Cam takes a deep breath. "And she's my girlfriend, not my best friend."

Dad's fork pauses in mid-air. "You're gay?"

"Lesbian," Cam clarifies.

"Since when?"

Camryn's gaze flicks to me, then back to our dad. "I don't think you want me to answer that."

He blinks twice, long and slow, then looks away. "Jesus."

"He's not here right now," Cam says.

I bite back a laugh. "Actually, He's everywhere all the time. Omniscient."

Camryn sends me a grateful look, and I wink at her.

Dad gazes across the booth at me. "Did you already know?"

I shake my head. "No, but the writing was on the wall. They're always together, and neither of them has had a boyfriend in years."

Dad holds up a finger. "Cam had a boyfriend last year. Damon?"

Guilt shadows Cam's eyes.

"Did you ever meet Damon?" I ask my dad gently.

"No." Understanding lights his eyes. "Damon wasn't real?"

"I'm sure he's real to somebody," Camryn says around her straw.

I deliver a kick to her ankle. She laughs.

"Are you mad, Dad?" Camryn acts nonchalant and makes a lot of jokes, but deep down she cares about what our dad thinks of her. About what I think of her.

Dad puts an arm around her shoulders. "Nah. Kind of relieved, actually. I was starting to think you were going to be single forever."

"Happily attached," Camryn announces.

"Does this mean you're going to have kids? Or not?"

Cam rolls her eyes. "One thing at a time, Dad."

Dad looks at me. "What about you? I'm not getting any younger, and I want to be the kind of grandpa who wrestles with his grandkids."

"I'll talk to Gabriel about it," I answer, crunching through an ice cube. I'm trying damn hard to be flippant, as if the idea doesn't feel like a hot knife in my heart.

"You'll have to do more than talk if you want to give me grandkids."

I pretend to vomit. "Please don't say that ever again."

He whispers something in Camryn's ear, then excuses himself to the restroom.

"What did he say to you?"

"He called you a prude."

I look up at the ceiling and shake my head.

"Did something happen in St. Lucia?" Cam's tone is uncharacteristically gentle.

If I was going to tell anybody, it'd be her. Even so, I can't bring myself to do that. I am consumed with managing Gabriel's image, of the face we present to the world. And so, even to the person who knows me best, I say, "Everything was great."

I'm lying to her, but the person I'm lying to most is myself.

I've placed Gabriel on a pedestal he didn't ask to be on, and now I'm experiencing his fall. I won't tell him what he's doing is hurting me, because I'm protecting him from my anger.

My dad rejoins us, settling into his seat and pressing a flattened palm on his thigh as he leans forward. Something about this familiar mannerism pushes at me, and I'm struck by a realization I don't like.

Gabriel is not the first man I've protected from my feelings, even when he deserved them.

I have done all this before.

SESSION FOURTEEN
DESERT FLOWER THERAPY

"You lied to your family about Gabriel." Dr. Ruben taps his chin as he assesses me.

"By then, I was lying all the damn time." I shrug, not because I don't care, but because *what does it matter*?

"You stayed with him."

"I loved him. And he was still Gabriel, you know? He maintained a job and our home, he mowed the lawn, paid bills. A bystander would've had a difficult time peering in and seeing his problem." I clear my throat. I feel foolish now, thinking back to what I ignored, and explained away. "I read a story about a woman whose husband was abusive, but only when he drank. She stayed for a long time, because they had kids and the abuse was infrequent. After I read it, I remember thinking everything was ok in my marriage, because my husband wasn't hitting me."

"Comparative suffering."

"Exactly. I did that a lot. I sought out stories that were worse than mine, then told myself I didn't have anything to complain about."

"Did he drink at home?"

"Not that I knew of, in excess at least, but I don't think that means much. Our schedules made it so we weren't home at the same time as often as some couples."

"What did you do during all the time you were alone?"

"I read a lot of books."

Dr. Ruben's gaze sweeps over my face. The mask of detachment he usually wears has slipped. He looks like I feel.

We have arrived at the final part of my story.

This. Is. It.

CHAPTER 21

VERY LITTLE ABOUT MINE AND GABRIEL'S RELATIONSHIP IS THE way it used to be. A rock, a boulder, a mountain sits between us now. I get home from work, and on the nights Gabriel is home, he has dinner ready. We sit at the table and make small talk. We wash the dishes and clean the kitchen. We go for walks, we watch new shows. We have perfunctory sex twice a week, checking the box. We're putting on a show, even when there isn't an audience. We've never tried harder to be normal.

A touch is no longer simply a touch. The thoughtlessness of it has disappeared. Everything has weight. Consideration. A marriage that used to be second nature has become real work.

Now, he hides it.

I want to hold him. I want to tell him I will do whatever it takes to help him get better. I can't do that, because I don't know how receptive he'll be. People with addictions don't like being told they have addictions. I see it in my practice, over and over. But Gabriel isn't a person seeking my services. And I am absolutely partial.

I don't know what to say to him, and so we dance around it. A marriage that used to feel ironclad, now is made of dust. Something about what happened in St. Lucia changed him, and us.

Every day is a tightrope walk, and I'm in a constant state of nausea. I suck on ginger candies and eat tablets of antacid as if it doesn't taste like chalk.

Every time he comes home and leans in for a routine kiss, I hold my breath so I won't taste the sting.

I hate the way we're living right now.

Maybe I wouldn't be so disappointed if I'd believed people when they told me marriage is hard. Turns out, Gabriel and I are not special. We are not lucky, or chosen.

I don't know what we are.

I only know what we aren't.

Happy.

Until now, I didn't know a person could be in a marriage, and still get their heart broken.

———

THIS IS the only place I can think to go. Still, I can't believe I'm doing this.

Desperate times, desperate measures.

"Avery?" Corinne opens the front door. "Everything all right?" Her voice is high-pitched, anxious, everything it should be when your daughter-in-law who you are not close with shows up at your front door.

"Everything is fine," I assure her, though it isn't.

She backs up from the door, inviting me in. I step

inside, into a home I don't visit often. Gabriel doesn't see his parents here, mostly because he sees his dad at work, but also because being here reminds him too much of what hurts him most.

Corinne takes me into the living room. She walks out, returning a few minutes later with coffee. I take the offered cup and thank her.

She sits down across from me. Her living room is set up for conversation, and I've always liked that.

"It's a Friday. Why aren't you at your practice?"

"My first patient isn't until eleven, so I thought I'd stop by." I sip my coffee, the liquid hot and black. The way I used to take it. Over time, Gabriel turned me into a sweet, flavored coffee drinker.

Corinne slides a coaster to me, and I set my coffee on the table in front of me. I had planned to tell Gabriel's mother everything, to ask her for help in getting through to Gabriel. Now that I'm here, I'm worried this is a betrayal of his privacy.

This experience is a mind fuck. I'm starting to not know up from down anymore.

"Gabriel has told me a little about…" The words are in my mouth, but I don't know if I should say them. The Woodruffs don't talk about Nash. Ever. "Gabriel told me he used to have a problem with alcohol."

She nods, watching me over the rim of her cup. "Yes. That's why he doesn't drink anymore." Her eyes narrow. "Why?" There's fear in her voice. Fear and hesitation and something else.

"It's just…" I run my palms down the front of my black pants. I already regret coming here. For her, and for me. Corinne holds Nash's death so close to her, and I can't blame her for that. I don't know how I'd be in the same situation, but I can't imagine the heartache of losing a child would do anything other than consume a person. Can Corinne withstand her only remaining son being less than everything she wants him to be? Everything Nash didn't get to be?

"Gabriel had a drink in St. Lucia, and I'm curious about his history with alcohol. He doesn't like to talk about it, and I don't want to ask him questions that upset him." I shrug, as if it's not a big deal. "That's all."

Corinne's eyes fill with relief. Emotions trickle through me. Guilt, disappointment, and even resentment. I have just lied on Gabriel's behalf. Again.

Her stiff posture relaxes and she settles back into the cushions. "Just the one drink?"

I nod.

"Nothing to worry about," Corinne says with a wave of her hand. She gets up from her seat and comes to sit beside me. "I can see you're concerned." She pats my leg. "Don't be. Everything is fine. It was just one drink. He doesn't have a problem."

I hear in her voice how much she needs to believe this. Now I understand, far more than ever before, why she was hard on me the first time we met.

I smile at her. "Thank you, Corinne."

She asks me about our trip, about my practice, about giving her grandkids. It's the longest we've ever spoken, and the most interest she's ever shown in me. I can't wait to leave.

Lying once is hard. Maintaining the lie? Much more difficult.

CHAPTER 22

The ringing phone wakes me.

I grab it off my nightstand, hardly registering the ten digits flashing on my screen. "Hello?"

"Avery? God, I'm sorry." Gabriel's voice cracks.

I sit up straight, catapulted to an awake state. "Gabriel?" I look at his side of the bed, confirming he's missing from it. "What's going on?"

"I'm sorry," he whispers again.

"Gabriel, what is happening?" I'm sharp with him now. Terrified.

"I need you to come get me." His voice breaks at the end.

Weight presses against my chest, my heart, my stomach. Though I dread my next question, I ask it anyway. "Where are you?"

A beat. Then two more, before he says in a garbled voice, "The police station."

A sharp inhale stabs my throat. I think I knew he was

going to say it, but hearing the words is different. They are confirmation of a fear I refused to acknowledge.

"What did you do?" I'm crying now, my voice climbing up my throat, only to tumble down.

"I'd like to tell you when you get here." He recites the address, his voice hardly louder than a whisper. "I...love you."

All I can say is, "Do you?"

I tap the end button just as I hear his hoarse whisper. "Yes."

My fingers shake as I pull my jeans up over my hips. I fumble with the zipper so many times that I yank off the jeans and stuff my legs back in my pajama shorts.

I am so beside myself that I end up in a sweatshirt, forgetting it's the middle of summer. I don't even crank the air conditioning on the drive. Thoughts of what might have happened consume me, but it's more of a distraction than anything else. I know what happened. I knew this was coming.

I pull into the parking lot and immediately spot a lone, dark figure leaning on the wall of the police station. Slowing, I put the car in Park and watch him approach.

My husband.

Gabriel opens the door. He stands in the space, hesitating. He shuffles from one foot to the other.

Why is he just standing there?

The pieces fall into place. *He's not sure he's allowed in the car.* His shame breaks my heart.

"Get in," I say.

He folds himself in the passenger seat, and we do not speak for a full minute. Then he closes the door, and I drive.

"I'm sorry," he whispers.

I look at him in the glow of a streetlight as we pass under it. He stares at the floorboard, shadows darkening the skin beneath his eyes. "What are you sorry for?"

My fingers shake against the steering wheel. I no longer want confirmation of what happened. I want to curl into a ball and cry.

"For putting you through this." Slowly his head moves back and forth, like even he can't believe it.

I ask the question, with the answer I already know. "Did you drive drunk?"

He nods, eyes still cast down.

"How much trouble are you in?" I've heard of the leniency police officers will show firefighters. Those could have been rumors though, and until now I'd never thought to ask.

Gabriel lifts his head, swinging his face to meet mine. The brokenness in his gaze doesn't appear to have a bottom, and I'm lost in those dark eyes of his, falling down into nothing and everything and whatever is waiting once we hit bottom.

His lower lip trembles. I turn right, faster than I intend, and park the car on a dark and quiet street.

My back presses against the door as I turn and face him. I wait.

"I'm in a lot of trouble."

I've never heard his voice like this. Shallow, and full of despair.

"Start from the beginning." I don't know how my voice is calm.

"I went out with Plotnik and Casella after we were

done with our reports. I know I told you I'd be home, but —" He hesitates, and I finish the sentence for him.

"You didn't want to come home."

His answering nod is tiny and regretful. "Things have been hard. Between us, I mean."

My skin prickles. Anger bubbles, but it doesn't break the surface. I'm feeling too many other emotions for anger to take hold yet.

"It's my fault." He shakes his head. It seems to be his favorite movement right now. "Everything is my fault."

"Keep going," I instruct. Fear grips my heart. For the first time since he called me, I'm beginning to understand this might be worse than I thought.

"I had too much to drink, but I didn't want to ask you for a ride. I didn't want you to know I'd been drinking. I see your disappointment every time you look at me, and I didn't want to add to it again, and…" He coughs on a sob. "And I didn't call for a ride, because then my truck wouldn't be there, and you would know." He digs into my center console and finds a travel pack of tissues. "How did you know, in St. Lucia?"

"I woke up and found you on the couch. And you reeked." I wait for him to be done blowing his nose. "I restarted my birth control that night."

He sobs once more, louder this time, filled with more anguish. I cry too, but quietly.

When he can speak, he says, "I'm sorry. So sorry." He's shaking his head again, like even he is astonished by all that has happened. "I ruined it for us. I—" His voice cracks. "I have no idea what's going to happen to me."

I take a deep breath. Reality and whatever this is that I'm doing right now do not feel like they are one and the same. This is a different me, an alternate version, and I've been asked to play her role momentarily. "Is this not a standard-issue DUI?"

More sobs from Gabriel. "Someone walked in front of my car."

Horror races through me. "Are they ok?"

"I don't know. Nobody would tell me anything. One moment I was driving, and then there was a loud sound. I never even saw them. I got out of the truck." He makes a sound, an anguished huff of emotion. "I'm the one who called 9-1-1."

I'm too shocked to think. My limbs are frozen, and simultaneously tingling. I'm no longer tethered to this earth, and I could float away.

I'm on autopilot now, turning on the car and driving us home. I want to climb in bed, wake up in the morning, and call this all a dream.

But I'm really awake. And this isn't a dream. It's a nightmare.

"Will you get special treatment because you're a fire-fighter?" How can something I used to think was unfair suddenly feel like a lifeline?

"My special treatment was them letting me go home with you and not having to post bail. I don't think there will be any more special treatment from here on out."

My wheels are already turning, making lists and plans. There is no control to be had in this situation, so I grab onto whatever I can. "We'll start making calls on Monday morning, find a good lawyer. That's the most important thing."

"I need to know if the person is ok. They were awake

when the ambulance arrived. I'm almost positive their leg was broken. Maybe I can go to the hospital—"

"Do not go to the hospital." I don't know what I'm talking about, but it sounds like a bad idea. Something a lawyer might warn against. "We don't know what the future holds, and what a case against you will look like."

Are these my words? Is it me speaking?

Our walk into our home is surreal. The placement of my purse on the entryway table is surreal. It doesn't feel real when I take off my sweatshirt, or change into a tank top. Gabriel stands in the middle of our room, lost.

"Take a shower," I say, pointing through the open door into our bathroom. He listens. When he comes back into our room, I'm already lying in our bed. I'm on my side, my back to him. The mattress dips with his movement, the comforter shifts. His gaze burns into my back. I don't know what he's feeling or thinking, and I don't want to ask.

I'm running out of compassion.

It's a slippery slope, I know, because compassion is more important than anything else.

Maybe tomorrow I'll try to find more of it. Tonight, the well has run dry.

Gabriel doesn't touch me, though I can feel he wants to. The sheets shift again, and I know it's Gabriel rolling over. Giving up.

Marriage is hard, but this can't possibly be what everybody meant. This isn't petty annoyances or differences in spending habits.

This is so much worse.

CHAPTER 23

"Gabriel, I…" Corinne's voice trails off.

The connection falls quiet, and I know Doug and Corinne are on the other end, too shocked to form words.

I stare at Gabriel's cell phone, lying on the kitchen table with the speaker turned on, and wait. I'd suggested Gabriel tell his parents in person, but Gabriel's only response was, "Nash would've never done this." Then he brought up his mom's contact in his phone and pressed send. I don't think Gabriel can look his parents in the eyes and say these words. Honestly, I don't even care. I am too broken.

"What are you going to do?" Doug asks, disbelief in his tone.

"Get a lawyer," Gabriel answers, voice soft.

"You'd better get someone good," Corinne adds, stress thinning her words. "How do you plan on finding one?"

"Avery found someone this morning. She's already left him a message."

"Maybe I should look, too," Corinne says. "I could ask—"

"No, Mom." Gabriel stretches a hand across his face, fingers rubbing at his temples.

"Do you trust her to choose a good lawyer? After she let this happen to you?"

I throw out my hands, ready to defend myself, when she adds, "She knew you were in trouble. She told me you had a drink in St. Lucia, but she said it was only one. She should've told me what was going on, and I could've prevented all this from happening."

Gabriel looks at me, head inching back as if dazed, like he's surprised I was capable of going to his mother. Maybe he didn't understand until now just how scared I was for him. For us.

"You couldn't have prevented a thing, Corinne." Stress and exhaustion make my eyes ache. "This is partially your fault in the first place." The words are whispered, so she cannot hear them, but Gabriel's gaze meets mine, and he hangs his head like he did last night.

"You knew he was drinking," Corinne says, her voice rising and falling in a panic. "For how long? How much? Why didn't you tell me?" Her breath turns shallow and shaky.

"Corinne, take a deep breath," Doug instructs.

I'm already walking away from the phone. My head is barely above water. If I stay in the conversation, there's no telling what I'll do or say.

"It wasn't her place to tell you, Mom," is the last thing I hear before I walk out the front door. I spend a quick second wondering where Gabriel's truck is before I remember it is in police custody. *Evidence.*

I sit down behind a brick pillar at the end of the porch, where I'm hidden from the view of the street. My head drops into my hands, and my eyes close.

The tenor of Gabriel's voice floats through the front door. He's still talking to his parents, and soon it will be my turn to tell my dad and Lara. The rug will be ripped from under them, just as it has been for Doug and Corinne. At least Gabriel's parents knew of his prior problem. For my dad and Lara, every facet of this will come as a shock. The same goes for Cam. I'll have to pull back the curtain, and reveal it all.

The therapist in me understands the trajectory. *Ignored grief and guilt from Nash, triggered by Ryan.* The wife in me is devastated that our life, that *I,* wasn't enough to keep him steady. I cannot comprehend all the tiny but impactful moments I saw but somehow still missed.

Me, of all people. The therapist.

I could draw a detailed map of our time together, and yet, here I am, wondering how we got here.

CHAPTER 24

"Theyʼre going to make an example out of you." Our lawyer sits back, folding his hands on the table. He is a stout man, with dark, freshly cut hair and a red necktie. Gregory Decker, though the partners call him Deck. This makes me think of a fraternity, which in turn makes me think of someone not taking their job seriously. But he comes highly recommended, and has an impressive pedigree. We're paying out the nose for him, using money we don't have.

I grip the edge of the gleaming walnut desk with both hands and lean forward. "Is that what they said?"

Beside me, Gabriel is stoic. If it weren't for the heavy set of his shoulders, the dip of his chin, someone wouldn't be able to look at him and know what we're doing.

"Not in those words, but based on the plea agreement, I'd say so." His fancy pen taps the table. "I did everything I could to get the endangerment charge dropped down to a misdemeanor, but the pedestrian was hurt. Prosecutor is adamant it be charged as a felony."

"The pedestrian was also drunk, and walked in front of his truck." My hands rake through my hair. I cannot recall the last time I've washed it. "What if we don't take what they're offering? What if we let it go to trial?"

"As your lawyer, I advise you to take the deal. Maximum sentence was seven years. This is three, with the possibility of early out at two with good behavior."

"Did you tell them about his heroic service to the public? The lives he's saved?" Desperation sinks into my voice.

"Yes, Mrs. Woodruff. That's how I got it reduced to three. This is a sensitive time. There are more eyes on the police than ever before. Oversight isn't a bad thing," he says diplomatically. "But it's not helping your husband right now."

"I'm not suggesting there shouldn't be consequences for bad choices, especially ones that endanger others, but there should be better-fitting punishment. How is sitting in a prison cell going to help his mental health? He can go to a treatment facility. AA. Weekly check-ins, an accountability partner." Hysteria dances on the edge of my words. I can't let this happen. Gabriel can't go to prison. "He has PTSD. And possibly major depressive disorder." Neither of these diagnoses are official, but it wouldn't be a stretch to make them. Especially not right now. "This man works a dangerous job so others don't have to. Because of him, most of society does not worry themselves with learning how to fight a fire, or basic emergency medical care, or, for God's sake, how to remove a rattlesnake."

The lawyers' eyebrows lift. "A rattlesnake?"

"You wouldn't believe the number of rattlesnakes this

man has removed from a frightened person's yard." I look at Gabriel. He nods once, a silent corroboration.

Gabriel has been mute since the moment we sat down across from the lawyer. He nods, swallows, his facial muscles move as he represses his emotions. He has nothing to say, and I have everything to say. Doesn't he want to fight for himself?

If he won't, I will.

"The fact is," I continue, "he, and every other fire-fighter, are on the other end of that phone call." I point at Gabriel. "He answers that call for help. Five years ago, he answered my call for help. Now he's the one asking. Who's going to do it for him? Who will answer his call?"

Appreciation glimmers in the lawyer's eyes. "Impassioned speeches aside, we have to work with what we have. The prosecutor's job is to focus on the event. My job is to paint a picture broader than the one day the event occurred." He pushes a file folder across the table to me. "That's what I did with those letters. That photo."

I take the folder, slipping it into my purse. It contains two letters, one from Gabriel's father in his professional capacity as fire captain, and one from a longtime colleague of Gabriel's. The photo is from the newspaper article, Gabriel carrying me out of a burning home.

I gathered those items. *I* requested those letters. Gabriel has done very little to defend himself. It's as though he has given up.

The lawyer taps the printed out plea deal in front of him. "Now we must work with what we have. And this is it."

"Take it," Gabriel says.

"What?" I stare at his stiff profile. "Gabriel, no."

"I've been doing this for twenty years," the lawyer says. "I've seen it all. I promise, this is the best you're going to get. Taking your chances on a trial would be foolish."

My head drops into my hands. My shoulders shake, but the tears don't come. I cried myself out before we came here, and was left with a dull headache and sharp fear.

Gabriel and the lawyer discuss logistics. For me this is still out of body, a book I could be reading about a wife listening to her husband discuss his impending prison sentence.

"I'll let you know when the hearing will be. You will show up, and answer the judge's questions. It's not like what you see on television."

The lawyer stops me as we're walking out. "You can't change the system in a day, Mrs. Woodruff. But you have good ideas. Perhaps you should consider activism."

His words slide in one ear and out the other. I can't think of anything but what is happening to my life, the implosion.

Later that night, once we're home and in our bed, Gabriel reaches for me. For hours we've been robots, going through the motions. Picking up a prescription. Making dinner. Doing the dishes. Every motion by rote, every thought sickeningly heavy.

I let him hold me. I'm not angry. There isn't time to be mad at him. Each tick of the clock is precious now.

"I don't deserve you," he whispers against my forehead. My automatic response is *yes you do,* but I'm feeling so many things, good, bad, and downright ugly. I say nothing at all.

Three years. Gabriel will go away for three years, maybe only two.

Only two.

Look at how I qualified that statement with an 'only.' It hasn't begun, and already I'm applying hope to a decrease in duration.

"Avery," Gabriel whispers my name.

I wait for what he's going to say next.

"Avery," he says again, sobbing. He rolls me onto my back, caging me in with his arms. Tears drip off his face and splash my chest. "You should move on."

At first I'm confused, but then I understand. "What? No."

His lips tremble. "You're young. Smart. Passionate. Beautiful. You have so much to offer someone."

"I'm already giving all that to you."

"I won't be there to receive it."

The tears I couldn't find in the lawyer's office are pouring now. "Gabriel, no. We're married. I'll wait for you. Three years is nothing."

Compared to thirty years, three is a blip. But three years is something. It's holidays and family dinners, waking up alone and going to bed alone. It's tiny moments in my days, the guy who will cut me off in traffic and the barista who will misspell my name and the funny bone I'll smack on a corner and the box I can't reach on the highest shelf and,

and,

and,

the list goes on.

I grip his face, the regrowth of facial hair poking my palms. "I will not move on. Ever. This is a hard situation, but I'm not afraid of hard things. It's easy to uphold your vows when things are going well. When the money flows and the sex is good and nobody is making life-altering mistakes." My thumbs stroke his cheeks. "Bonds are forged in fire, and right now, Gabriel, we're in the middle of a fire. And even you can't put it out."

"I started it." His eyes close. More tears splash onto my chest, sliding down between my breasts. "I'm responsible for the fire."

He is. But I also wonder how much of a role I played in it all. I didn't take his history seriously enough. I knew he was drinking, and I didn't stand in the way. I didn't beat the drum, sound the alarm, threaten to leave. I maintained his image at the expense of him. Is what happened my fault? No. Did I contribute? Yes.

I kiss him, and taste our tears. "Don't talk anymore about me being with someone else. I won't hear it. Got it?"

He nods. He kisses me again, more fiercely. His lips press against mine, giving to me and asking nothing in return. His hands roam my body, and in them I feel his hunger. His sorrow. His apology.

The next day, we learn his court date will be held in two weeks. There's something about being faced with the stuff of nightmares that makes everything in the present more palpable.

Joseph gives me a leave of absence, and Gabriel and I are never without one another. Each second takes on water, until it's bursting. And here we are, squeezing from it every last drop.

———

I'VE ALWAYS LOVED Gabriel's voice. Deep, clear, confident, a voice that is strong enough to know you're safe with him, with corners rounded enough to know he is also kind.

Today is the first day I do not like my husband's voice.

"How do you plead?"

"Guilty."

The word reverberates in my bones.

Guilty.

Guilty.

Guilty.

CHAPTER 25

GABRIEL HAS BEEN GONE FOR A MONTH. *GONE.* THAT'S WHAT I'm calling it.

I, too, am *gone.* Not an ounce of energy for my old life lives in my body now. Every call from Sabrina goes to voicemail. She's pregnant with her first, and I want no part of it.

Is this selfish? Absolutely. Sabrina has been my closest friend for years. She was in my wedding party. But the last time we spoke, the day after Gabriel went to prison, was like taking the knife in my heart and twisting. Not that she meant to. I'd been silent on my end of the line, with nothing to say that wasn't sad. Sabrina filled the quiet with chatter about her pregnancy. I think she asked me to be in the delivery room, but I'm not certain. I'd been living outside my body that day.

I still am. Soon, Sabrina will stop calling. She's in the happiest time of her life, and I'm in the worst. For her sake, I'm letting her be. I refuse to be an Aunt Francesca to Sabrina.

And so, I sit in my dark living room on a Friday evening, my curtains drawn to keep out the sunset. I don't want a shred of beauty around me.

"Avery?"

The closed front door muffles my sister's voice. A normal person would take a closed front door and unanswered knock to mean nobody is home. Not Camryn. She knows I'm here, sad and pathetic and sitting in the dark.

I know what's coming next.

Yep, there it is. The sound of a key in a lock. The metallic click, the bolt sliding. Door opening.

Camryn's eyes zero in on mine. The glow from the phone gives away my location. I stay perfectly still, my finger poised above my screen.

Cam sits beside me. "Dad said he's called you three times this week." She tugs the blanket from my lap, draping it across her own until we're sharing it.

I don't respond. What's there to say? Just like with Sabrina, I haven't answered his calls because I don't want to talk.

"Who's that?" Cam asks, pointing at the smiling blonde woman on the screen, standing beside an equally blonde and grinning man.

"Someone from high school." My upper lip curls at the seemingly happy photo posted three days ago.

"You're into torture now? Is that it?" Cam snuggles deeper.

"My existence is torture."

"Melodramatic." She sighs the word.

"I know. I just… I can't seem to stop." I'm sad all the time. Even when I don't appear sad, it's because I'm pretending. "Look at this caption. It's their anniversary.

She writes 'So lucky to be doing life with you.'" I make a face. "What is that? What is 'doing life'?"

"Pretty sure you've used that exact caption," my sister says, but I ignore her because I'm in no mood to be reminded that I used to be as enamored with my life.

I scroll further. "And this one. What about them?" A girl I knew in college is beaming, radiant on her wedding day. "She goes on and on about how perfect her new husband is." I flick the screen with my middle finger. "No shit he's perfect, it's your wedding day. Just wait." I glower at the glowing bride. "Just. You. Wait."

God, I'm sad. For so many reasons, on so many levels.

"It's normal."

I turn to look at Cam. She takes the phone away and tosses it aside. It lands face down. "What you're doing is normal. This grief."

Grief. I pick up the word, try it on. It fits.

I poke at a button on my pajama top. "When I learned about grief in school, it was taught in stages. Denial, anger, bargaining, depression, and acceptance. But everything I've seen in my practice, and everything experienced in life, says otherwise. Grief isn't linear. Grief doesn't have a shape. For some, it's a continuum." I sniff. "Do I have a right to grieve? My husband didn't die. He became an alcoholic who made a bad choice and now he's living with the consequences of it."

"So are you."

"Am I even allowed to be upset? These feelings, shouldn't they be reserved for people who've really lost something? A son to war, or a spouse to a tragic accident. I don't deserve to be this upset."

"Everybody's personal tragedy is their own, and they

have the right to be upset by it. Nobody gets to tell you what you grieve."

I stare at my sister's silhouette in the semi-dark. "What about you? What do you grieve?"

"Honestly?" She blows out a breath. "I grieve the most inconsequential stuff. The grocery store doesn't have my cereal? Grief. I can't find the hair on my shirt that's terrorizing my underarm? Grief. Waiting in a long line at the bakery only to find they are out of my cinnamon bagel? Serious grief."

She makes me laugh, because I know she's only somewhat kidding.

"Listen, Baxter." She takes my hand. "You need to go easier on yourself. Allow space to wade through all the feelings. And stop judging yourself."

"When did you become a therapist?"

Camryn scoffs jokingly. "I'd never be a quack."

I look at my fingernails. They are in need of care. "I don't know where to go from here."

"You take a step. And then another one. Eventually, you look back and see the distance you've traveled. And then you be damn proud of yourself, because you made it."

I bend and flex my fingers, thinking about the concept of moving forward while Gabriel is suspended in time. Camryn gets up and disappears into my room. She returns carrying my box of nail polishes. She selects a color, doesn't ask me if I like it, then grabs my hand.

I watch her paint a clear base coat. When she's finished, I say, "I'm going to see him tomorrow."

"I assumed so, considering tomorrow is Saturday and

that's when you go." She swipes bright coral over my thumbnail. "Are the visits getting any better?"

I look into her eyes. "It's once a week for two hours. There isn't much opportunity for improvement."

She paints my nails in silence after that.

I think back to my first visit. Gabriel walked into the visiting area, wearing a shade of orange that did not look good on him. It does not look good on anyone.

That visit took my mangled heart and broke it further, but a bystander would never guess. I worked double-time to remain upbeat. I plastered a hopeful smile on my face, and it never budged. It was as if I could, by virtue of sheer will, make the whole situation more palatable. Gabriel tried, but he never managed to get there. He could not force himself over that wall of pain.

I decided he didn't need to, because I would do it. I would build the muscle we'd need to be strong. And I did. I have. I have fortified and stretched, and I can do it all. I can hold his suffering, and mine, too.

It hasn't been easy. My other visits have grown progressively worse and worse. My husband looks sadder than ever before. Desolate. I want to hold him, shield him, soothe him. Sometimes I want to shake him, to scream at him for drinking again, for driving. When those feelings come up, I tuck them away.

He refuses to tell me any detail about what his life is like now, and I try not to put too much thought into why. In my head, I've placed him on an extended vacation. *Gone.* It breaks my heart to think otherwise.

"All done," Cam announces, blowing on my fingers. "Hopefully they don't chip between now and when you see Gabriel in the morning."

I pick at a fleck of nail polish on my cuticle. "They'll have to last longer than that. I'm going later in the day tomorrow. I told Dad I'd help him with taxes first."

"Good. Dad's been worried about you."

"Little late in life for that."

"I know," Cam says in a low voice. She twists the cap on the nail polish, securing it. "Look at it this way. Gabriel has already been in one month. Thirty-five more to go, but he'll probably get early release."

I press lightly on one nail, to see if it's dry. "Don't hope, Cam. Hope has no business existing."

Cam tosses the bottle back in the box. She doesn't look at me when she says, "I think I'll stay the night tonight."

CHAPTER 26

The prison is in the middle of nowhere. There is nothing but dirt and dust, and sprawling, ugly cacti. Mountains jut up in the distance, incongruous to the flat landscape.

I've made this drive for almost three months now, and each week it's harder than the time before it.

I thought I'd lost Gabriel all at once, but no. Each Saturday, I find a little less of my husband in his dark eyes. At last week's visit the vacancy in his gaze took my breath away. It is as if I'm holding an ice cube in the middle of July, watching it slowly melt and slide between the cracks in my fingers.

My husband is slipping away.

I'm here now. I park, and take the kind of breath that fills my chest and burns my lungs. I swipe on two extra coats of lip balm, after learning the hard way that false smiles crack the corners of my mouth. I pass through the metal detector while they check the contents of my purse. I step into the visitor's room, and sit down at a table to wait for Gabriel.

A man a few tables over from me smiles in this sad way and nods. I nod, but do not smile. I cannot force the muscles to move that way right now. False or not, I have to save all my smiles for Gabriel.

The man gets up, pushes in his chair, and approaches me. He stands behind the seat across from me, the seat meant for Gabriel. He's balding, his belly a paunch beneath his starched white shirt and navy blue jacket. His long fingers grip the chair, all bare save for a simple gold band on his pinky.

"Mrs. Woodruff?"

I stiffen. "Yes?" Has something happened to Gabriel? Has he been beat up? Hurt? Worse?

"I'm Peter Whalen. A family law attorney." He holds out his hand. I let it hover in the open space before shaking it woodenly.

"What's going on?" I ask.

He gestures to the chair. "May I sit?" He drops into the seat without waiting for my response. "I'm sure you're wondering why I'm here." He digs into his briefcase, coming away with a small sheaf of papers.

Instantly, I get it.

I'm shocked, but maybe not really. Not deep down.

It makes sense.

It's so Gabriel.

The lawyer straightens the papers. I clutch my purse to my chest, as though it can provide any measure of safety against the pain bending my heart in two.

"You don't look surprised." He tips his head to one side, surveying me.

"Peter…Mr. Whalen…"

"Peter is fine."

"Have you ever watched a movie where you had no idea what was going to happen, but somehow you guessed the ending anyway?"

He pulls a pen from his jacket pocket. "I don't watch movies. But I understand the point you're making." Peter taps the pen on the papers, nodding slowly as he thinks. "Gabriel's world has become tiny. He controls nothing. He hates what he's done to you."

"He told you that?" My eyebrows pull together. How long has this man known Gabriel?

"Not in those words. I've done this long enough now that I know what's going through his head."

I don't care how many other clients there were before, and why it means Peter thinks he knows my husband. "How long have you known Gabriel?"

"He contacted me a few weeks ago."

"You work quickly."

"These kinds of things can go quite fast when uncontested." He coughs. "I'm assuming this is uncontested?"

I fold my hands in my lap. "I want to talk to Gabriel."

"He has said that he would prefer not to see or speak to you."

There's a fist in my gut. I'm being punched. There's no other way to explain the pain rocking my core right now. I sit back and cross my arms. "I'm supposed to sign divorce papers without ever having a last conversation with my husband? Is that what's really being asked of me?"

Sympathy softens the corners of his eyes. "I know this is unexpected, and quite painful, and I—"

"Did he come to this conclusion alone?" I understand it

all, and yet it still doesn't make sense. It is perfectly Gabriel to think he is doing right by me. It is not Gabriel to choose not to face me.

"He contacted me. I met with him, and his mind was already made up. I didn't lead him to it, if that's what you're implying."

"This is uncharacteristic of him." For a second, I marvel at how calm I am, but I'm not really all that calm. Not on the inside. I'm scraping and scrounging, trying like hell to survive this.

Peter sighs, like he too is overwhelmed by what he's doing. "Maybe you can try to look at things from Gabriel's point of view. He's distressed by his current situation. And ashamed, from what I can tell. He was a firefighter, which means he's used to occupying the role of hero. What he's doing now…it's coming from the same place. He's trying to save you."

"From what?"

"The life you're being forced to lead, I presume."

What will happen, if I refuse? Should I do it? Force his hand? What will that look like?

I picture months of pain, of showing up here to visit and him refusing to see me. Would he do that? How far will it go? How bad will it get? Would I end up hating him?

In the end, my own hopelessness wins out.

I say nothing. I take the pen. Did Gabriel use this pen? Has he already signed? I flip to the end, to the paper with the purple tab sticking out the side.

Gabriel Douglas Woodruff

. . .

I CAN'T BREATHE.

The pen shakes. My signature is a jagged mess. Almost illegible.

I push the papers away and stand. I take a step away, but the lawyer's voice saying my name draws me back.

He reaches into his briefcase again, this time producing a long, rectangular envelope. "Gabriel asked me to give you this."

He holds it out. I stare down at the envelope, at his knuckles covered in tiny reddish hairs.

A swell of indignation rises inside me. "If Gabriel can't face me and say what he has to say, I don't want to read his words either."

He keeps the envelope extended, as though I might change my mind. "One day down the road, you might want to read this."

I lean down, the chain strap of my purse smacking the table and making a loud sound. I take the envelope, and grab the pen I just used to sign my divorce papers. On the front, I write *A Very Heartfelt Refusal To Read*. To Peter, I say, "Please return this to Gabriel."

I want no part of what he has to say in a letter. I'm afraid if I see his boxy handwriting, his r's that sometimes look like v's, I will be taken down right here in the visitor room. It is only by sheer stubbornness that I am upright.

Peter motions to the envelope, and my handwriting. "I know you feel blindsided, but I've been in family law for a long time. You'll be ok. Everyone, no matter how hard the experience, eventually ends up at the same point. For some, the path is a lot more painful than it needs to be."

"Thank you for the advice." My tone is clipped. I push the editorialized envelope to him and tap it with one finger. "But the sentiment stands."

I make it to my car before the tears take over. They become a curtain, a waterfall, and I can no longer see. I fold my arms on my steering wheel and sob. I scream and I cry and I pound a fist on my dash.

I learned early on that life isn't fair.

But I didn't think it would be this cruel.

———

It TAKES me a week to tell Camryn what happened. I couldn't bear to let those words cross my lips, as if speaking them into the universe makes them truer than they already are. I tell her in a text message, because it's easier than watching her face process the news. I cannot hold her anguish, too.

Before the day is out, my dad is calling. I answer, taking us both by surprise. I rarely answer his calls these days.

"Hey, hon," he greets, cautious.

"Hi, Dad."

"How are you?"

Half-alive. "Fine."

He'd readily swallowed my *fine* when I was growing up, because it was a relief to him to think I didn't need anything. I saw that relief in his eyes, and understood. He needed me to be fine. So I was.

This time, he presses. Maybe it's Lara's presence in his life. Perhaps she has, at long last, awoken him from his selfish stupor. "Cam told me what happened. You're not fine, hon. You couldn't possibly be."

"This is new information to you, but I've already had a week to process."

He sighs. "About that…you've got to start leaning on the people who love you. Let us help you. Why didn't you call me right away?"

Is he *hurt*? The thought angers me, awakening me from the state of nothingness I've been in for seven days.

And then, for the first time in my life, I say what I'm thinking. My dad-filter is missing, *gone* like Gabriel.

"Why would I have called *you*?"

He makes a sound, I can't discern if it's a gasp or a sharp exhale. What's obvious is that he's hurt. *Again*. And I can't take it.

I hang up and turn off my phone, staring at the black screen.

Well, damn. There it is.

I remember being at the ocean for the first time, standing at the shoreline and feeling awestruck by its power. I pressed my foot into the wet sand, the surf broke around my ankle, and it struck me that I'd affected the will of the water simply by exerting a tiny bit of force.

My small truth, spoken aloud to my dad for the first time ever, feels like my tentative step into the breaking wave.

And yet, there's no relief to be found. If anything, I feel shittier than I did before he called.

I keep picturing the divorce papers and Gabriel's signature. I added my own to the document, and our last names matched. We've legally parted ways, but we share a last name.

Grabbing my laptop, I type *how to change a last name after divorce* in the search bar.

My body aches at the query, but I press on. There is no reason for me to keep Gabriel's last name.

Avery Burke, here I come.

CHAPTER 27

The next morning, I go to work.

The moment I walk through the door, it's clear I shouldn't be there. Looking around the small reception area, I feel a curl of hatred for the serene blues, comforting light greens, calming ivory. They all make me see red. Don't get me started on the water sculpture.

Still, I smile at our receptionist, Dawn, and split an apple fritter with Joseph. He's been careful with me since everything happened. Considerate and kind, but watchful. I insist that I'm fine. I promise him I am exercising, journaling, praying, meditating, that I am doing all the things to help me process my personal life.

I'm not lying to him. Those are all things I'm doing. They're just not helping the way I wish they would.

My third appointment of the day is when everything goes wrong.

Alicia and Kent Doyle sit across from me. He is clean cut, his slacks free of wrinkles. Cuff links peek from the starched cuffs of his obviously expensive shirt. Alicia is well kept too, but exhaustion pulls at her eyes. They are both mid-thirties, and Alicia had their third child a year ago. They are here because life isn't fun anymore, because they are noticing fine lines around their eyes, because they are exhausted and trying to understand if this is it for them, if they should dig in and do the work or raise the white flag.

If I had a quarter for every couple on this couch who fit this same mold, I'd…well, I'd have a ton of quarters.

This is their third appointment. In the time before everything in my personal life imploded, I'd have their intake papers memorized. I'd have strategies, coping mechanisms, ideas, advice. My ear and my heart would be open.

Not now. Not since Gabriel.

Each second listening to them bicker on my couch instead of their own feels like an hour. Alicia is crying. I'd like to tell her about my marriage and give her something to cry about.

"He said the ugliest thing to me yesterday," she sniffles, and I push the tissue box closer to her. She takes one, but doesn't use it. "He told me he doesn't feel attracted to me anymore, because my breasts don't look the way they used to. Can you believe that? He said I should get my boobs done."

"I don't know why you're so hurt by that." Kent throws up his arms, and I can tell they've been having this fight on repeat since he said it. "If you wanted me to"—he gestures at his lap—"make that bigger, and it was surgically possible, I would do it."

It takes everything I have not to roll my eyes.

He continues. "You used to talk about having surgery. Now you act like my suggestion is coming from left field."

I should be stepping in, calling for them to take a breath and think about where these desires are stemming from. But I don't. Because the anger I've been pushing away? It's awakening, and I'm afraid to open my mouth.

"That was after baby number two. I was having a hard time." Alicia finally uses the tissue. "I'm feeling better now, and I like myself. I accept where I am and how I look."

Kent lets out a frustrated growl. "Well, I don't. I want your body back."

Alicia dissolves into more tears. "What happens now? I have surgery or you'll cheat on me?"

He shrugs. "This isn't the life I expected. This is—"

"Enough," I shout, my arms extended, my palms open. Kent's mouth snaps closed. Alicia's red, swollen eyes widen.

"You," I point at Alicia. "Get breast implants, don't get breast implants. It doesn't *matter*. Life will find a way to fuck you no matter what you do. So do whatever you want, and do it for you only." I turn on Kent. I hate his face. "You are a dickhead. You have placed value in your wife's body, and no other part of her. She brought your three children into this world, and this is how you thank her? Your behavior says far more about you than it does about her."

The door opens behind me. I know Joseph is standing there, watching my spectacular plummet into the grave I'm digging for myself, but I cannot stop. The damage is done, I may as well go out with a bang.

I look back to the wife. "Alicia, the alarm bells are sounding. Heed them."

I get up and turn away from the couple on the couch. Joseph doesn't look surprised. All I see in those eyes is pity.

I take my purse from my desk. I don't feel bad. I don't feel good. I am numb.

"Go home," Joseph murmurs when I pass through the open door.

I spend the rest of the day alternating between sleeping and staring at the street, watching my neighbors live their normal lives. At five, my phone rings.

"Hi, Joseph," I answer. "Before you say anything, please know I'm sorry for my outburst, and the shadow I've cast on our practice. Are the Doyle's ok?"

"Hi. The Doyle's are fine. Upset, and shocked, and the wife said she felt unsafe."

I can hear the eye roll in his pause. He thinks people use the word too loosely these days.

"I explained to them you'd recently experienced trauma and you are on a path similar to the one they're following." He sighs. "More importantly, how are you?"

"You heard how I'm doing." My voice is just above a whisper. "I really am sorry, Joseph."

"I'm disappointed in myself. I was paying attention to you, but not close enough. I should've seen this coming."

"It's not your fault. I guess I'm better at surface-level appearances than I realized."

"You're good at many things, Avery. Appearing ok is one of them."

"Where do we go from here?"

"Here's what I'm thinking. You take an extended leave of absence. I'll hold down the practice."

Guilt settles like a boulder in my stomach. "But you were supposed to retire this year." He'd been waiting for me to feel comfortable on my own, transitioning his clients to me one by one.

Joseph's life has been affected by Gabriel, too.

"Shit happens." He says it offhandedly, but it must be a crushing disappointment. "You return when you feel better. But on one condition."

"What?"

"Go to therapy."

How ironic. "Do you have any recommendations?" I wish it could be with him, but there's a conflict of interest.

"I know the perfect person for you. I'll send you his info."

"Thank you, Joseph. For understanding. And for treating me kindly instead of being angry at my behavior."

"The world could use a lot more kindness, Avery. Take that with you as you go."

We hang up. A text message from Joseph comes through. He has shared a contact with me. *Dr. Ruben Sandoval.*

I go into the kitchen to make dinner. There's very little in the pantry, and even less in the fridge. Gabriel was always the cook, and when he was on shift at the station, I ordered in or bought prepared food.

I end up eating cheese and stale crackers for dinner. Instead of mindlessly scrolling my phone and hating everything I see, I get out the Cooking For Beginners cookbook my sister gifted me last year for Christmas. At the time, I'd given her a dirty look and she'd laughed. Never did I think I'd be putting it to use.

Then I do something so basic, so banal. I make a grocery list.

SESSION FIFTEEN
DESERT FLOWER THERAPY

"That's how I ended up here, on your couch." I pat the velvet cushion. Am I relieved to have concluded the tale? I don't think so. 'Listless' might be the right word to describe how I feel.

Dr. Ruben nods. "That is quite the story."

"I wish it weren't mine." I try to push away the lifelessness in my limbs, but they are leaden.

"Well, sure." He leans forward. "Having already trained as a therapist and practiced as one for a few years, you know most of what I'm going to say to you. The trick now will be putting it all into practice."

I have an idea what Dr. Ruben's advice will be, but he's surprised me a number of times since our sessions began. "What are you going to say to me?"

"You should have a conversation with your dad"—he lifts a hand because I'm opening my mouth to argue—"even though you don't want to. Either confront him, or let it go. He caused you hurt after your mom died, and you're hurting yourself now by holding on to that."

"And Gabriel? I guess I need to let go of all that hurt, too?"

"Eventually. It's still relatively fresh. You won't move forward, if you hold it close."

"Do I want to move forward?"

"Don't you?"

"Honestly, I still can't imagine a life that doesn't include Gabriel."

"I hate to break it to you, but you're living one now."

I smile wryly. "All his clothes hanging in our closet would beg to differ."

"The untangling of intertwined lives isn't pleasant, or pretty. But it's necessary. One day, you'll find yourself ready to begin that task."

I fidget with a bracelet. "Is this goodbye, Dr. Ruben? Are you going to tell Joseph it's safe to allow me back into the practice?"

Dr. Ruben cracks a smile. "I can if you want me to, but I don't think that's what is best for you."

"What do you think is best for me?" I'd like a roadmap, a guide, something.

He opens his arms wide. "That's up to you."

CHAPTER 28

One year since Gabriel divorced me, and it feels as fresh as if it happened yesterday. The only thing I've gotten better at is stubbornly pushing my way through the pain.

Today is one of those white-knuckle days.

"Why didn't you hire a moving company?" Cam grunts as she lifts a box. "I saw a moving truck the other day and on the side it said it was a company run by military veterans. The driver was hot. You should have hired him." She sets the box in the bed of the pickup truck I've rented for the day. "I'd really rather be sipping from a cold beverage while watching the hot veteran do all the heavy lifting."

A sweat-matted baby hair tickles my cheek, and I shoulder it away. "You're attracted to women."

She rolls her eyes and turns for the house. "My eyes still work, and they appreciate pretty things."

I smile and follow her up the driveway. "How much longer do I have your help?"

Cam's supposed to meet Dani to look at commercial spaces for rent. After years of saving, and pre-approval for a small business loan, Cam and Dani are ready to move forward with their dream of opening a coffee shop.

Cam props the front door open with a foot. I walk past her and into my bedroom, where more boxes await.

"That depends on how much help you need. Is it just the boxes, or do you want me to go with you to Gabriel's parents' house?"

"I can handle his parents," I tell her, grabbing another box and hauling it across the bed toward me. "I have enough experience with them."

"Yeah, but his mom is"—Cam curls her fingers and holds them on either side of her cheeks while making a bare-teeth face—"you know. Like that."

I laugh at Cam's antics, but the sound is hollow. "She's not as ferocious as she appears at first. I feel bad for her. In a way, she's lost two sons."

"Yeah. When you put it like that…" Cam grabs another box and steadies it on her hip. "I guess I can forgive her for putting Gabriel's alcoholism on you."

"She apologized for that," I remind Cam. Corinne called me the day after Gabriel went to prison to check on me, and told me she was sorry for the things she'd said.

Cam frowns. "Hmph."

"I appreciate the way you defend me."

Cam rolls her eyes. "Well, duh. What did she say when you told her you'd be bringing all of Gabriel's things over?"

"I haven't told her yet." We weren't close to begin with, but after Gabriel went to prison, the Woodruffs acted differently toward me. They started showing interest, caring, trying to provide me with support and comfort. I pushed them away, because staying close would only prolong the inevitable. One day, Gabriel will return, and then what? It's safer for my heart to keep them at arm's length. Caring for them is a losing game, and I've lost enough.

Cam gives me a long look. "Do you think surprising her is a good idea?"

"I was hoping she wouldn't be there." I know how it sounds, but facing her, handing her Gabriel's belongings, is a way of checking another box. Cutting another tie. I need to be swift, without fanfare. I don't know that I can survive it any other way.

"Very adult of you," Camryn comments, adjusting her stance as the box begins to slip. "What are you going to do? Text her a picture of boxes stacked six-high on her porch?" With her free hand she mimes someone texting on a phone. "Thanks for the memories, Corinne. P.S. Here's your son's stuff."

I groan. "Stop." What I mean is, stop telling me what I should be doing. Stop telling me what I'm doing is wrong. I'm doing my best.

"I think you should give her a heads-up, that's all. What if she hasn't thought about where Gabriel will go when he gets out? And now she's being given all his things?"

"Am I supposed to wait for him to get out before I box up his things and return them to him? I don't want to live with his stuff for two more years." For Gabriel, time is suspended. For me, the seconds tick by and turn into minutes, and the longer I stare at his clothes hanging in our closet, the harder it is to take that next step.

"I can't keep his stuff around anymore. I could be a real bitch about it and donate it all, but I don't have it in me."

I step out the door ahead of her, only so I can hide my eyes. I talk a flippant game, but that's all it is. A ruse, and the only person I'm deceiving is myself.

We finish loading up the bed of the truck. After I shove in the final box, I turn to her. "I'm selling the house, too. I'll find somewhere smaller." I can't afford to live here. Not when I'm the only person paying the mortgage.

"Makes sense, considering you don't have a job anymore."

"I'm not destitute. You know I made money when Joseph and I sold the practice." I struggled with the decision to return, but Joseph made the choice for me when he called and told me he was ready to spend his days at a beach, not listening to people bitch. I laughed, because I'd just left my last session with Dr. Ruben. I don't feel great about getting a degree and not using it, or spending all that time going in one direction only to backtrack. Losing my career didn't have the impact it would've had if I weren't already hovering near rock-bottom. There wasn't much further to fall.

"Yes, yes, I know," Cam says with exasperation. "But I can't figure out what you do with your days."

"I volunteer at the animal shelter—"

"Which is bizarre," Cam interjects.

I chuckle. Oddly, I've found a sense of purpose in helping care for these animals. "I'm helping Dad with the books for his new business."

"Consulting," scoffs Cam. "Sounds like code for 'unemployed.'"

Our dad started his own business because he wanted

to have more time, but has ironically ended up having less free time than before.

"I'm thinking about writing a book." I feel embarrassed saying it out loud. Who do I think I am? Who would want to read anything written by me? "I found my notebook, the one I used to write in when Gabriel was on shift at the station and I had trouble sleeping."

Cam's eyes light up. "That's the best idea! You know Dani's aunt is a literary agent, right? In New York. I bet Dani could get her to talk to you and—"

"Whoa, whoa," I say, but I'm laughing at my sister's exuberance. "I don't have a solid premise yet."

Cam exhales hard, like I'm exhausting. "Tell me when you have a *solid premise*"—she exaggerates the words—"and I'll get Dani to call her aunt."

"Sounds like a plan." Excitement ripples inside me, but I try to keep it at bay. I know someone who knows a New York literary agent. That is HUGE. I've read personal accounts from people who say they queried one hundred agents and never heard a peep back. It took away my desire to even try, but now? That desire is suddenly burning inside me.

"I better take off." Cam pulls me in for a hug. "I love you, Baxter. You got this."

"I love you, too."

She leaves, and I go back into my house to grab my purse and my keys. Very little has changed, at least on the surface. All the furniture is still here, the knickknacks, the rug Gabriel and I chose. He'd insisted we christen it that first time we laid it down in the living room, and I ended up with a rash on my back.

I climb in the rental truck. It's twice as big as my car,

and it takes some time for me to adjust to how much space I'm taking up on the road.

I keep thinking about what Camryn said about Dani's aunt. Storylines and ideas bounce around my mind. I'm so deep in my thoughts I nearly manage to forget what it is I'm going to do.

———

THE WOODRUFF HOME. I haven't been here since before Gabriel went to prison. They learned about the divorce through a phone call from Gabriel, and then Corinne called me. She told me she was devastated for me, for how everything turned out. There we were, two women connected by a common thread, both knowing we contributed to its downfall. And yet, we are ultimately not at fault.

I feel differently about Corinne now. I see her as a person trying to make it through the worst kind of heartbreak, clinging to memories and expectations because it was all she had.

Both Corinne and Doug answer the door. I can't tell what Doug is thinking, but Corinne has her emotions written all over her face.

"Avery." She smiles at me, tentative. This is such tricky territory. Corinne was once mine, in the way Gabriel was my dad's. Legally tethered, but connected by the heart. Does a snip through the binding mean a cut into the heart connection as well? Am I allowed to still care for his family if I'm not married to him?

Corinne looks over my shoulder at the vehicle in the

driveway. "You rented a U-Haul truck? Are you moving somewhere?"

I rise on my toes, then slide back down on the balls of my feet. This is more difficult now that we're face-to-face. "I boxed up Gabriel's things. I just thought"—my intertwined fingers form a single ball and bounce on my thigh —"that eventually he will need his stuff. And if I give them to you, and you tell him you have it all, he'll know where to go when he's released."

Corinne's lips purse. "Right." She nods. "Of course."

It hits me that Corinne and Doug will now have a second son whose belongings are in boxes. Gabriel once told me his mother got halfway through boxing up Nash's belongings, then stopped. She never restarted, and since then Nash's room is half packed, half the way it looked the last day he left it.

Doug steps out from behind his wife, and on his way by me he squeezes my upper arm. His touch is the next best thing to being near Gabriel, and the sting of tears touches the backs of my eyes.

Tucking back the emotion, I make a confession to Corinne. "I almost didn't knock. I wanted to leave everything on your driveway and make a run for it."

She huffs a shallow laugh. "I'm happy you didn't do that."

Doug returns holding two boxes. Corinne and I join in, and soon we've unloaded the back of the truck. Boxes fill one-half of the Woodruffs living room.

Corinne stands beside a box labeled *Shorts & Socks*. She taps it and says, "I guess he'll be needing these."

"He'll need everything, at some point. That's why I brought it all here. I assume this is where he'll come when he…gets out." My voice dips. "I'm going to sell our house, too, and put half the money in his bank account. That way when he gets out, he'll, uh, he'll have money."

Suddenly I feel sick. It was one thing to work through all this in my mind, but now, standing in front of people who look similar to Gabriel, it's tearing me apart.

I look away to get composure, but I'm faced with all those framed photos on the top of the grand piano. I put away all the pictures of us that were up in my house, and intentionally avoided all photographic reminders of him. Taking in his face now feels like a drink for my soul and a knife to my heart.

"Where do we go from here?" Corinne's voice is small.

I tear my gaze from Gabriel's image. "I'm not sure. We move on, I guess. I don't know what else to do."

"We move on from you?" Her voice catches at the end. "And you move on from us?"

I sniff. God, I really do not want to cry again, but I don't know how much of a choice I have. "Are there rules for this kind of thing? A standard operating procedure?"

Perhaps the disjointed timeline has been the most bizarre part of the divorce. We crossed the finish line, then I had to go back and hit the checkpoints.

Doug speaks. "We don't want to lose you, kid."

"I know. But the reminders…" I bite my lip. "They're painful. And they're everywhere. I'm just doing what I can to decrease the pain of all this. I have to do what's best for me. For my mental state."

Corinne walks to me. She takes my hand and clasps it in her own. "Oh, honey, do what's best for you. Take care of yourself first."

I hug them both, one at a time. Doug releases me

quickly. He clears his throat and walks away. Corinne holds me tightly. We're nearly the same height, but she strokes my hair and holds me like I'm a child. Her child. The one she lost indefinitely, and the one she lost momentarily.

Perhaps she, too, has been altered by this experience. Maybe for the better.

"I hope you know you're welcome here any time," she says. "In our home, and in our lives."

It's a sweet sentiment, but it has a timer. One day in the not-too-distant future, Gabriel will be released. He will come here, and restart his life. What he won't need is his ex-wife in the picture. How could he possibly move on if his parents are tied to his past?

Sometimes, the simplest acts are the most difficult to execute. Walking through the Woodruffs front door feels like a first step into unknown territory.

Yes, Gabriel was gone, but I had his things. Now I don't even have that.

As much as it hurts, I keep going. I leave his possessions behind. With every step, a little bit of my old life breaks off and tumbles to the ground.

I buckle my seat belt and reverse into the street. I am raw and exposed, and everything hurts. But there's something deep down, a newly developed but insistent feeling.

Not hope, because that would be too much to ask, but its benign cousin.

Trust.

Trust that I will be ok. I will make it. I am almost on the other side of this storm.

CHAPTER 29

"It's a seller's market." The realtor, Tracey Booth, gestures around the kitchen. "Everything is going. Old, new, fixer-uppers, you name it. In fact…" She walks from the kitchen to the small dining room, gazing out at the backyard. She wears a black knee-length skirt and ivory silk blouse, and simple gold hoops. "The bones of this place are good. Unique. I can already tell this will be purchased and renovated. Maybe even flipped. I'm telling you, Phoenix is hot right now."

"It's only January." The bad joke covers up the sadness I feel at the prospect of letting go of my home with Gabriel.

Tracey laughs. "People from cold states visit in the winter, and they suddenly want to move here. I would too, if I had to shovel several feet of snow. Been there, done that. I'm from Buffalo, but I've been here going on twenty-three years."

I look around at my home. I scrubbed every inch yesterday, including the corners and behind the toilet, the fan blades and the air conditioning vent covers, which required a ladder to reach. "It's my first time selling a house," I tell her. "I'm not sure how the entire process works, but..." I hesitate. I have to tell her, but I hate watching the absorption of the information. *Prison.* People hear the word, and they conjure an image. A hardened criminal, a dangerous man. I know, because that's what I used to do. In the time before.

Everything feels like *before.* Before Gabriel went to prison. Before Gabriel divorced me. A pivot, a point on a graph signifying an event.

Tracey waits for me to continue, eyebrows slightly lifted. Here goes nothing.

"My ex-husband's signature will be more difficult for you to get."

She doesn't bat an eye at the word ex-husband, like I've seen other people do. I know it's because, in their eyes, I'm too young to have a failed marriage. To be twenty-eight, and divorced.

"No problem. These days it's easy to get signatures from exes who've moved states, or countries. Twenty years ago, that was not the case, but now"—she shrugs—"it's all electronic, anyway."

I shift my weight to my other foot. "How about exes who are incarcerated?" My breath stays in my throat, frozen in place, as I wait for the typical reaction. A widening of the eyes, a slight jerk of the head, gazes that go everywhere but my face.

Tracey is a pro. Or a master of her facial expressions. Either way, she displays no opinion of any kind, no pity or fear.

"I can handle that, too. Has he agreed to the sale of the home?"

I nod. "His lawyer has been in contact with him."

I hate talking about Gabriel in this removed way, it hurts so damn much. He exists, but he is no longer mine. He is like any other person on this planet, an individual in their own orbit, no longer inhabiting my own.

"Like I said, everything is electronic. As long as he's in agreement, there shouldn't be a problem."

"It wasn't a violent crime." I want her to know that. I want her to understand that my Gabriel wasn't a person who hurts people. Not on purpose. He was a person with a problem, and he made a colossal mistake. "He had a problem with alcohol, and one night he drove drunk."

"Oh no," Tracey says, frowning. Pity floods her eyes. "I guess it was worse than your average DUI?"

"Someone was injured. A pedestrian. It ended up being a felony charge. I'm telling you because I don't want you to think he was a real criminal. Like, someone who was malicious."

Tracey's lips twist. She sighs quietly, reaching into the pocket of her black knee-length skirt. She holds a fist between us, palm up, and opens her hand.

A coin. White and gold, with a triangle in the center. It reads 'To thine own self be true.'

"Ten years sober, as of last week." Tracey tucks the coin back into her pocket. "My husband died before I got sober. I'll never forgive myself for not being fully present with him during those final years. I tell myself if I'd known they were the last ones, I would've done things differently."

"You don't think you would have?"

"Addiction is a beast you use to attempt to fight the

beast within, and all you're left with is a bloody disaster. You hurt yourself, you hurt others, and you justify your behavior. I'd like to think I could've quit for him, but I just don't know."

"Why did you end up quitting?"

Her eyes squint, like she's considering something. "We're veering far off the road of a professional relationship."

"I'm ok with that if you are."

With her fingers Tracey makes a twisting motion against her empty ring finger, the way she probably did countless times before when she wore a ring. "Not too long after my husband passed, I woke up in a hotel room next to a man I did not know. It was my personal equivalent to your ex-husband's accident and DUI. We all have our own threshold for rock bottom. Waking up to a man who was not my husband was mine."

My heart sinks. "I'm so sorry, Tracey."

"I'm sorry, too. For you. It's the collateral damage that pains an alcoholic the most. Knowing you inflicted pain on the people you love." She pauses to shake her head. "There's so much shame in that. Not a day passes that I don't think of how much I hurt my husband while he was alive. He asked me repeatedly to stop drinking, and I told him he was no fun. I said he was already acting like an old man, and that you only get one shot at life and I wouldn't spend it acting like a boring old person. I hurt our marriage, and he withdrew. Every time I opened a bottle of wine at home or ordered a drink at dinner, I felt the tiny accusation from him, and I resented it. And he resented me. Soon, all those resentments piled up until they blocked our vision. We hadn't spoken in three days, and he went to work one morning, fell from a ladder, and that was it. He died disappointed in the woman I'd become, and I hated myself immensely."

Salty tears sting my lips. She offers me a sad, knowing smile. "Did you divorce your ex because of the accident?"

I shake my head. "He divorced me. After he went to prison. I still can't believe it."

A knowing look creeps into her eyes. "He gave you a chance to move on. You were his collateral damage."

"I didn't ask for the chance. I didn't want it. He took away my choice."

"Fair." She lifts one pointed finger in the air. "But, consider this. Shame is a powerful emotion. It sits at the root of so much of what we do, how we act, how we respond. And everyone feels it, at one point or another. Nobody escapes it."

"I try to think about what this all might be like from his perspective, but it's hard when I don't know what that is." I look around our home, at the oven where he baked my birthday cakes, and the small basket in the corner where he'd dump his keys and wallet when he came home. His favorite coffee mug with the State Forty-Eight symbol still sits on the shelf next to the sink. I knew it was there when I was packing up his belongings, and I chose to keep it.

Tracey eyes me. She seems to understand this isn't easy. "Are you sure you're ready to part ways with this house?"

I nod immediately. "I've been running in place for a while now. It's time to move forward."

A slow smile spreads onto Tracey's face. "Atta girl."

Pride warms my cheeks. Tracey is probably only slightly younger than my mother would have been if she'd lived.

We go over specifics, like timing and asking price, and Tracey tells me she'll be in touch.

———

IT'S PERFECT. A one bedroom, one bathroom condo on the ground floor. There's crown molding and wood floors, and a charming claw-foot tub. The only thing it was missing was a second soul to occupy it. I remedied that quickly, though, during my last shift at the shelter.

Reaching over the side of the couch, I run a hand along the length of Ruby, my newly adopted yellow Labrador Retriever rescue. I knew she was meant to be mine the second she was dropped off at the shelter by a man who claimed he'd lost his job and could not afford her care. She looked in my eyes and instantly stole my heart. I officially understand those *Who Rescued Who?* bumper stickers. Ruby's adoration is pure, and sweet. It's just what I need.

She sighs, a thick and contented sound, and rolls closer.

Tomorrow I'll spend the day assembling new furniture and unpacking. Tracey was right. Our house sold in fewer than four days.

In some ways, it feels wrong to be doing all this without Gabriel. Then I remember I'm doing all this *because* of Gabriel.

But it's ok.

I'm ok.

Sometimes, ok is enough.

CHAPTER 30

Gem, my sister and Dani's coffee shop, had its grand opening two weeks ago. Since then, there has been a steady stream of customers all day, every day.

I arrived at Gem early this morning, in the hopes of actually getting a table. I've been writing at home, and I'm ready for a change of scenery.

The girl in front of me in line cranes her neck to look around. She catches my eye and says, "Isn't this place gorgeous? I love how it's earthy and moody at the same time."

I grin proudly. "This is my sister's place. Well, her and her partner."

As I say it, my name is called across the room. Cam bends over, wiping a table and pointing at it. *Come here,* she mouths. She sets a coffee down on the clean surface.

"Perks," the girl in front of me comments as she moves up to order.

I leave the line and walk to Cam. "I hope that's for

me," I say, practically begging. I was up late last night outlining an idea for a story.

"It is," Cam says, but pulls it away as I'm reaching for it. "I need your help. Dani has this idea for a hanging chalkboard." She explains, "The concept is simple: a jar where people can enter in short poems, quotes, limericks, random musings, really anything, and each week one entry will earn a spot on the chalkboard. They can email them in, too, and we will print it and add it to the jar."

"Sounds fun," I say, reaching for my drink, and this time Cam lets me have it. "Encourages patron involvement."

Cam makes a hopeful face. "I need your pretty handwriting."

"Pay me in free coffee and pastries."

"Opportunist," she mutters. "Also, Dani spoke to her aunt. She wants to talk to you."

I swallow the hot coffee. "Dani?"

Cam rolls her eyes. "No. Dani's aunt. Her name is Jill."

Excitement shimmers through me for a few seconds before reality strikes it down. "I have twenty pages of crap." I'm not kidding. I hate what I've written recently. It's like every creative bone in my body has liquified.

Cam flicks her finger against the top of my closed laptop. "You'd better get to it then." She leaves me alone after that, and I attempt to produce something passable.

Write, delete.

Write, fling silent expletives.

Write, tell myself I'm living in a fantasy if I think I'm capable of attempting this. I should go back to being a therapist and this time I'll promise not to yell at my patients.

After two hours, I give up my table to a grateful looking mom toting a toddler. I try not to think about how that could've been me, if the St. Lucia trip had gone differently.

I'm sifting through mail in my tiny entryway when I see it.

A mailer, forwarded from my old address, with the name Peter Whalen and an address stamped in the return corner. I open it, and an envelope slips out. I catch it before it falls, and turn it over. My heart thumps as I read my own words.

A Very Heartfelt Refusal To Read

I peer inside the mailer, hoping for an explanation. Why send this to me now? There's a sheet of paper, something handwritten. I pull it out. The top is stamped with the law firm's name. Below, the lawyer writes:

AVERY,

I came across this recently. I understand you didn't want it on that day, but perhaps now you've changed your mind. At any rate, it's in your possession and you can choose what to do with it.

Best,

Peter

I WALK to the living room and drop everything but the envelope onto the table. My hand quakes as I slip my finger under the paper flap, and a tiny hot pain flashes across the pad of my finger. I ignore the paper cut, and keep going, tearing my way across.

Sitting back, I extract the trifold blank sheet of white paper and unfold it. The entirety of my body feels numb, except for my rapidly beating heart.

AVERY,

I COULD SAY I'M SORRY INTO ETERNITY, AND IT WOULDN'T BE ENOUGH. YOU DIDN'T ASK FOR ANY OF THIS, AND I CANNOT CONTINUE ALLOWING YOU TO BE PUNISHED ALONGSIDE ME. I DON'T WANT YOU TO DRIVE OUT HERE EVERY WEEKEND. I DON'T WANT YOU TO HAVE TO TELL PEOPLE YOUR HUSBAND IS IN PRISON. I WANT YOU TO LIVE A LIFE FREE FROM MY CHAOS. TRAVEL. ENJOY LIFE. WRITE. TAKE OUR STORY, AND USE IT. I'M GIVING YOU PERMISSION. I LOVE YOU, WITH EVERYTHING I AM. ALL OF ME LOVES ALL OF YOU. NOW I SEE THAT SOMETIMES LOVING AND LETTING GO ARE THE SAME THING. PLEASE GO BE HAPPY.

GABRIEL

I LIE DOWN on the couch, stunned. Ruby licks my face. I should be crying, but the tears don't come. I've been turned inside out, my heart lying in a ditch somewhere. I picture Gabriel writing this letter to me. He's more than halfway through his three-year sentence now. Does he regret it? Letting me go?

My phone rings, and I have to hunt it down. I don't recognize the area code.

"Hello?"

"Avery? This is Jill Church. Dani's aunt."

I look at my own surprised reflection in the entryway mirror. "Hello, yes. Hi, Hill. I mean, Jill." I shake my head at myself. "Sorry," I laugh.

"Don't worry about it. I know you weren't expecting my call, but Dani gave me your number and I thought I'd reach out while I have a few minutes before my next meeting."

"That's so kind of you," I say, my brain tripping over itself trying to figure out what to say next.

Jill solves that problem for me. "Look, this isn't the way things usually work. Dani said she's known you for years, and asked me to give you a shot."

"Yes, she—"

"Shoot."

"Excuse me?"

"Shoot your shot. What's your book idea?"

Gabriel's letter is still in my grasp. Should I do it?

"Contemporary romance," I hear myself say. "It starts out with him rescuing her from a fire. When she goes to the fire station to thank him, he asks her on a date. Then…"

I continue on for a solid two minutes before Jill interrupts me. "My next meeting starts in one minute. I like it, though. Text your email address to this number. My assistant will be in touch. Chat soon." The line goes dead.

I stare at myself in the mirror as I slowly lower my phone to my waist.

I huff a disbelieving laugh. I shake my head. "What just happened?" I whisper. Ruby noses my thigh. I bend down so I'm eye level with her, scratching behind her ears.

"Ruby." I nuzzle her. "We have a book to write."

CHAPTER 31

"Try this," Cam says, pushing a matte black, oversized cup my way.

I peek into it. I've never seen a cup like this. Inside the cup is a little well, open on one side, and full of a light-colored creamy sauce. "What is that?"

"White chocolate sauce. The heat of the coffee is constantly warming the sauce, which in turn mixes into the coffee."

"Why don't you just put the sauce in the coffee and mix it all up at once?"

Cam blows out an irritated breath. "Because that would be one hundred times less aesthetically pleasing." She nods toward a glass canister on the counter with a little sign that says 'Treat your dog, too.' "Grab one for Ruby."

I do as she says, tucking the small treat into an inside pocket of my purse.

Cam grabs the cup and leads me to a table against the far wall. She pulls out a chair and sits down, and I take the booth side opposite her. "Ready to put that pretty hand-writing to good use?"

"I don't think it's as good as you think it is," I warn her, taking a drink. The sweetness hits my tongue, and explodes. Coupled with the caffeine, it's a formidable duo.

She waves away my protest. "Here you go." She tosses me a bag of chalk pens, then points to a huge chalkboard leaning against a wall.

"These are the entries?" I ask, nodding at the glass bowl filled with folded pieces of paper sitting on the table beside us. She reaches for it and sets it in front of me. "Choose one."

I choose one at random, and look up at her. "He who sits in jelly has his ass in a jam?"

Cam shrugs. "Dani said almost anything goes. Use common sense limitations."

I select a hot pink chalk pen from the bag and go over to the chalkboard, copying the words and adding some flair to the letters.

Together, Cam and I hang it on the wall. She pulls her phone from her pocket and backs up a couple feet. "Smile big. I'm going to spread the word on social."

I do as I'm told. Cam snaps the photo, spends a moment adjusting the filter and cropping it, then types out a caption. "Posted," she says proudly, smiling at me. "I tagged you."

"I haven't posted anything in a long time," I remind her. "Tagging me is mostly useless."

She shrugs. "Certainly can't hurt."

Cam's newest employee, Laramie, waves at her from the register. "Duty calls," Cam says, dropping a kiss on my cheek and gathering the pens and glass jar. "Stay here as long as you like. I saw you brought your laptop with you." She throws a glance at the navy blue leather case on the seat beside me.

Cam disappears, and I pull out my computer.

Jill's assistant emailed a couple days after we spoke, telling me Jill was interested in taking me on as a client. When I finished jumping up and down, I signed my name on the electronic document her assistant sent. Now the real hard work begins.

Gabriel said to use our story. Even after my on-the-spot pitch to Jill, I second-guessed using it. Is it possible to write our story objectively? No. Even so, it's a story I want to tell. So I sat down, closed my eyes, and pulled myself from inside the scene. I stood outside, viewing it as a bystander, doing my best to watch us fall in love and make mistake after mistake. That's when I decided to move forward with it.

Writing at Gem is a nice change of scenery, though I do miss Ruby's warm body lying across my feet beneath my desk. Eyes on my computer, I pick up where I left off yesterday, immediately immersed in a world I once considered pure magic.

Ninety minutes later, I blink hard as I'm siphoned from that world. Three tables away, a woman wearing earbuds speaks loudly while staring intently at her screen. A person on the screen gestures and talks. The woman says, "When did the symptoms begin?"

Hmm. Odd.

I try to tune her out, but when she asks, "Is it a burning itch?" my focus flies off the rails and crashes to the ground.

I look around me to see if anyone else is hearing what

I'm hearing. Power in numbers, or at least a shared 'Can you believe this lady?' look.

Two tables to my left, a man sits alone in front of a laptop. On his table is a scone and, judging by the full, steaming cup of coffee beside it, I'd guess he sat down recently.

Our gazes connect. He does a smiley smirk thing, side-eyeing the loud woman who is still having a one-sided conversation nobody wants to listen to. He looks back at me, and shrugs.

"I think she's a tele-doc," he says. "Her last conversation wasn't this cringey. Something about an ear infection."

"I must've missed it," I answer, glancing at my open computer.

He pushes up his sleeves, revealing a shiny silver watch. "You looked deep in thought."

His comment steals the beats from my heart. He could've made that assessment with a two-second glance, but I have a feeling that's not what happened.

I nod. "Hard at work over here." I'm not uncomfortable knowing he was watching me. It's the fact I like it that's making me uncomfortable.

He's attractive. His dark blond hair is mostly straight, with a slight wave at the bottom. It's long-ish, or at least long in my book. I'm not sure if hair that falls to the chin is really all that long. He wears a heathered dark gray hoodie and jeans. His jaw is square, his cheekbones chiseled.

He looks nothing like Gabriel.

He glances at my screen. "Do you mind me asking what you're working so hard on?"

His eyes bulge. He hears it at the same time as me, and all I can do is purse my lips to keep from laughing.

He looks mortified. "I guess I shouldn't end my sentence in a preposition."

One loud sound of "Hah!" bursts from me. The tele-doc woman sends a 'do you mind?' look over her shoulder, and I laugh again. The man shifts, folding his leg so his knee rests on the bench and he faces me. His arm lies along the back of the booth.

I mirror his posture. We're now two feet closer, simply because of a shift in our positioning.

"I'm working on a book," I tell him.

His head tips to the side. "A book about…?"

"A romance novel. Sort of."

"Sort of?"

"It toes the line of women's fiction. Possibly."

"Should I pretend to know what that is?" His tone is light, and slightly apologetic. "I mostly read science fiction."

"Women's fiction is when the journey is about the woman. Romance is when the journey is about, well, the romance."

"Ahh." He nods. "I'm intrigued. Tell me more?"

The tele-doc starts up again, as if she's not in a quiet coffee shop. He scoots closer on the bench, and now we're only a couple feet apart. Flecks of ocean blue are interspersed in his emerald green eyes, topped off with unfairly long eyelashes. He waits for my response.

I shake my head. "I'm not telling. I don't even know your name."

He smiles. A full, real, all-tooth, giving the sun a run

for its money type of beatific grin. "Hudson. Like the river. But my mom calls me Huddy."

"What do you prefer to be called? Hudson or Huddy?"

"Huddy, by everyone else." He gazes at me through those long lashes. "By you? Hudson."

I feel his answer down deep, between my navel and a part of me that disappeared a while ago.

"What's your name?" he asks.

"Avery."

"Avery," he repeats, his voice deepening.

Please do not say A Very.

He doesn't.

Something happens to the air between us. Suddenly it's heavy, thick, as if we're in the south in the dead of summer. Hudson looks at my lips. I touch them automatically, gently pinching the lower between two fingers. His gaze lifts, and he focuses on my eyes.

The tele-doc says the word 'rash' and I want to throw Hudson's scone at her.

Annoyance flickers across his face. "Do you want to get out of here?" He stumbles on those last two words, and I find it endearing.

I point at his full coffee, his open laptop. He looks to where I'm indicating. "I don't care about any of that."

I swallow, hardly able to believe what I'm about to say. What I'm about to do. "Then, yes." I haven't thought about another man since Gabriel, but it had to happen sometime, right? I wasn't prepared for that sometime to be today, but I don't think I'd ever be prepared, so…here we go.

I close my computer, tucking it back into my bag.

Hudson does the same. I head for the small counter where the used dishes go, sliding my cup across the wood grain.

Hudson appears at my side. He's taller than I would've guessed. I watch as he deposits his uneaten scone and full coffee beside my empty cup.

I turn to him and touch the sleeve of his soft sweatshirt. "My sister and her girlfriend own this place. The next time you're here, tell them you know me, and I said your order is on me."

He nods and opens his mouth to say something. Whatever it is, he changes his mind.

He leads the way out of Gem. Camryn must be somewhere nearby, because I feel holes burning into my back.

We walk out front, and Hudson motions to a restaurant nearby. "Are you hungry?"

"I'm always hungry."

Hudson smiles. "Greek ok with you?"

I nod, and send a quick text to Camryn telling her where I'm going, then I silence my phone.

The food is good, and the company is better. Hudson tells me he works in commercial real estate. He's training for a rim-to-rim Grand Canyon hike. He has a secret affinity for old western movies, and he's named after the Hudson River because his parents lived in Manhattan when he was conceived. Now they live across the river, in New Jersey. Hudson came out here for the sunshine and never went back.

There are sparks, and plenty of them. It's not like it was with Gabriel, where the attraction was more like rapturous magnetism. Hudson's fingertips graze the top of my hand while I talk about my dad and Cam. Something inside me awakens. It's been so long since I've been touched.

We leave the restaurant, and Hudson points up at a newly constructed condominium building. It's modern, with large glass windows and vines growing down the sides. "I live there."

"Nice place." I have to look up to talk to him. He has to look down to talk to me.

He says, "I'd like to see you again."

We see each other three more times after that. A movie, another dinner, and a long drive to Green Haven in search of an antique dresser for his mother. He FaceTimes her while we're in the crowded, musty store, and when Hudson trains the phone on me, I say, "Nice to meet you, Mrs. Donahue." Then he shows her the dresser he has found. I give him a wide-eyed look, and he winks back.

On our fourth date, we go back to Gem and I buy Hudson the coffee and scone he abandoned two weeks prior.

Cam comes over to meet Hudson. I've told her all about him, including how he's kissed me at the end of each date, chastely on the lips. The frustration and desire I feel at his reticence reminds me of another time, and I do everything I can to forget that.

Hudson passes Cam's test, laughing in the right way at the right time when she makes her irreverent remarks. When he tells her he lives in the new high-rise across the street and his living room window faces Gem, she asks him if he can take a few bird's-eye pictures of the shop.

"Just curious to see what it looks like from above," she says.

"You bet." He nods. "We can go do that now, if you'd like."

"What a good idea," she says, grinning and raising her eyebrows lasciviously when Hudson isn't looking.

We say goodbye to Cam and walk across the street. Hudson's place is as clean and sleek as I imagined it would be, but there are touches of warmth. Framed photos of vacations with his family. A knitted blanket thrown over the back of his brown leather couch. "My nana," he explains when I mention it.

Hudson and I stand at the floor-to-ceiling living room window, and he does as Camryn's asked.

When he's finished he sends me the photos, then slides the phone into his back pocket.

"Thanks for doing that for her," I say, hyperaware of the way the late afternoon sun burnishes his face, making him even more handsome. "I should get going."

But I don't move. Neither does he.

"Avery." The low volume paired with the husky way he says my name makes me take another step into him.

He palms one side of my head and grips my hip, gently tugging me flush against him. He leans down just a little more, until his lips brush mine. "Do you want to stay?"

I nod against him, needing not a moment to consider. I want to be held, kissed, to feel like a woman again. Is that so wrong?

I've imagined this a hundred times, *after Gabriel*, what this might be like with another man. In those instances, I felt nothing but guilt for daring to imagine myself with someone else.

And so, I wait for the guilt. It does not arrive.

Not when Hudson leads me by the hand into his bedroom.

Not even a few hours later, when he orders pizza for

us, and we eat in his bed, and he asks me if I want to stay the night.

The guilt finally comes the next morning, and it has nothing to do with Gabriel. I feel guilty over the absence of guilt. Over what that might mean.

Am I over Gabriel?

No.

Never. A person doesn't get over something, *someone,* like that.

But I understand this is normal. Natural. Stagnation is suffocating after a while. I need to press on.

Hudson leaves for work wearing crisp navy slacks and a silk-blend shirt. He kisses me where I lie in his bed, and asks if I'm free for dinner. We agree on a place, then he tells me to turn the bottom lock on my way out.

I dress slowly, sore in places I forgot existed. I stop at Gem for coffee, knowing my sister will be there. Knowing she will see me in yesterday's clothes.

"You're welcome," Cam says when she spots me.

I laugh, shaking my head as I wait for her to make my usual. "It's like you dabble in witchcraft."

She scoffs. "Hardly. I could smell the attraction coming off both of you. You just needed a push." She hands me the paper cup. "Was it good?"

I wrap my hands around the warm cup and sip for an extra moment, pausing to think about my answer. It wasn't just the sex. Hudson and I laughed. We talked long into the night. We brushed pizza crumbs from his sheets and had sex a second time. "Yes," I finally answer. "It was really, really good."

Cam stands on the other side of the slim counter, palms pressed on the quartz. "Was it weird?"

"No. And that's the weirdest part of all."

She smiles proudly. "You needed this. You needed to see that moving on doesn't have to be monumental. It doesn't have to be moving boxes and buying houses. It can be small steps, too."

I touch her hand. "Does Dani know how dangerous of a woman you can be?"

Cam grins. "She has played strategy games with me. I always win."

"I'm a strategy game?"

Cam leans over the counter and fixes my ponytail over my shoulder. "You were yesterday."

Well played, dear sister.

CHAPTER 32

Cam becomes the bride I'd never guessed she'd be. She cares deeply about color schemes, flora, and a wooden arch she has commissioned.

I'd nearly laughed when she told me about the arch, then I realized she wasn't kidding. Historically, my sister is the least romantic person on the planet. Famous movie love quotes make her skin crawl.

You complete me. What a dope, she'd said, adding an eye roll. Nobody else can complete you.

If you're a bird, I'm a bird. Dumb, she'd declared. Why be a bird? Be a tubeworm. Those fuckers live forever.

Ah, my sister. She can ruin the best movies.

When she asked me to go with her to check in on the arch, I'd agreed without asking questions. Namely, where do we have to go to accomplish the check-in?

Sugar Creek, Arizona. A tiny town two hours up the Beeline Highway.

"Well," Cam says, ducking into my car's passenger seat

and slamming the door behind her. A raindrop slithers off the shoulder of her lightweight jacket. "That was a boring drive."

I'm inclined to agree. Caravaning is not on my list of what qualifies as a good time. Not by a long shot. Neither is what we're about to do. "It was fine," I respond, because today is special for her and I don't want her to know that the further I drove from our home, the less I wanted to keep going. Inclining my head to Ruby in the backseat, I add, "Ruby and I listened to a couple podcasts."

Cam glances at her car, parked in the space beside mine. "Of course you did."

Ignoring the comment, I peer out at the nondescript building. The rain distorts the name, but I think it says Intricate Wood Works. "Where did you hear about this place?" Sugar Creek was always a name on a map, *a little town up north*, until now.

"Social media," my sister says, while her tone says 'duh.' "You ready to go in? Because I'm ready. I want to see my arch." She unsnaps the fabric strap wound around an umbrella. I slap at her hand when she starts to open it.

"Not in the car." I frown at her. "Have you never operated an umbrella?"

She sticks her tongue out at me. "Only on rare occasions."

To be fair, Phoenix doesn't offer its inhabitants many opportunities to use umbrellas. My little sister isn't a 'just in case' kind of a person, so it's not like she'd be prepared even if the opportunity arose. She doesn't keep a few dollars in the center console of her car, extra water on hand, or, in today's case, an umbrella. I'd bet all the dollar bills and extra water in my car that the umbrella she's awkwardly holding right now came from Dani.

"Give me that." I take it from her and climb out of the car, opening the umbrella as I go. Rain pelts the asphalt parking lot, bouncing back at my feet. I walk around to Cam's side of the car and hold the umbrella over her while she gets out. Then she holds it over me while I clip a leash to Ruby's collar and lead her out of the car. Huddled together, the three of us make our way through tiny streams of water flowing over the parking lot.

We pause at the front door, protected by an awning, and I hold out the umbrella and shake the water droplets from the fabric. I close it up and hand it to Camryn.

"Thanks for the lesson," she says, playfully sarcastic.

"You are welcome," I respond loftily.

She laughs and looks around. "Aside from the current weather, I'm kind of jealous you're spending the next two weeks here. Look at all these trees." Her tone conveys the wistfulness of a person who grew up in a desert. "It's just so…green."

My eyebrows lift. "Do you really want to switch positions with me?"

"No," Cam says without taking a second to think about it. "For many reasons."

After learning how far away we'd have to go to see the arch, I booked two weeks at a cabin nearby, figuring it was the perfect change of scenery I'd need to finally finish my book.

I shoulder Cam. "You can stay up here with me."

"Pfft," Cam waves away my words. "And rob you of the chance to write the second half of your book in a remote destination, like a legitimate moody author? I would never." She taps the top of my head. "I expect you to have greasy hair as your fingers fly over the keyboard. You'll be wearing flannel. And a beanie. A fire roaring in the fireplace. Can you build a fire?" She makes a bare-teeth face. "Or would you rather not? You've had enough fire to last a lifetime, probably."

My head tips sideways. "Are you done?"

She sighs heavily and reaches for the door handle. "I suppose."

Inside, rubber mats have been laid out in the entrance to accommodate for the rain. Cam and I stamp our shoes on the mats. Ruby shakes, and I wince as a spray of droplets coats everything around her.

A young receptionist watches it all from behind a desk, his mouth quirked up in mild amusement.

"Hello," I say to him, feeling mildly perturbed at being watched while I navigate this unfamiliar territory.

He grins, revealing a row of crooked bottom teeth. "You must be from the valley."

Humor replaces my irritation. "What gave it away? Our ineptitude with an umbrella?"

His gaze hops between my and Camryn's feet. "More like the fact it's raining hard and you both wore sandals."

Camryn leans into me, laughing. "Busted."

"Is it ok that she's here?" I point down at Ruby. "I didn't want to leave her in my car." As I say it, I realize I've forgotten my purse in the car. Between the downpour and the small town, it's probably not at risk for being stolen.

The receptionist flicks his wrist. "It's fine. We love dogs. She has to stay up front, though. No animals in the wood shop."

I nod. "Got it." I lead Ruby to a dry rubber mat a few feet away and instruct her to lie down and stay.

Cam approaches his desk, hand extended. "I'm Camryn Burke. This is my sister, Avery."

"Mason," he says, pointing at himself. "And I believe you"—he points at Camryn—"have an appointment to see how the arch is coming along."

Mason takes us back, past his desk and down a short hallway, to a door with a window in the top half. I follow behind my sister, repeating the pep talk I gave myself the whole two-hour drive here, which was very short and went like this: *Be happy for her, you're ok.*

"Through here," Mason says, stepping aside to usher us through the open door. We step into a cavernous room, and every direction I look holds some kind of treasure. Elaborate chairs, doors, benches, wall décor. Power tools hang from pegboards, along with screwdrivers of all shapes and sizes. In one corner sits a sawhorse with a sander on top, and a chain saw on the ground beneath it. An office is on the opposite wall, and a man walks from it. He looks like a much older version of Mason.

"I'm Joel Humphrey," he says, introducing himself. Camryn introduces us, and we each shake his offered hand.

Mason heads back the way we came, and Joel takes over. He welcomes us to his shop and tells us a little about his work and his process.

"Now, let's see what you came here to see," Joel says, rubbing his hands together. His excitement, though endearing, is nowhere near Camryn's. Her arms are crossed and she's rubbing her forearms, a sure sign she's trying not to come out of her skin.

We approach a tall object covered in a white sheet. Joel grips the fabric and yanks, dramatically revealing the half-finished project beneath.

The scent of cedar swirls around us. The arch, fastened at the joints by rough-looking metal pins, towers above my head. Joel tells us it is eight feet by eight feet, and points out the carvings in the wood.

"When it's done, both posts will match." He nods at the bare wood on the other side.

Camryn claps and rises on her toes, bouncing. Her grin takes over her face. She's looking at me, expectant. "Do you love it?"

I gather up everything I have in me, including all my memories of my own special day, and fit it into a tidy box. "It's incredible," I answer. I don't know why it hurts. I mean, I know why, but I don't know *why*. I'm past all that. I've moved on. I've lived on my own and adopted a dog and even had a whole new relationship.

Though, that 'whole new relationship' wasn't exactly successful. Hudson ended things a month ago, blaming my preoccupation with a ghost as his reason. I can't say I fault him. Or that he's wrong.

Still, my reaction irritates me. I want to claw into my chest and capture these infuriating emotions and toss them in a blender. I want to be nothing but happy for Camryn and Dani. I don't want my happiness for them to be punctuated by any holdovers from yesteryear.

It's because of Hudson. I'm certain of it. I'm…raw. If we were still together, I probably wouldn't feel this way. Being single again is like taking a step backward, and I've already taken enough of those.

"Would you like to meet the man who's been working

on it?" Joel asks. "Usually I do these custom pieces, but I hired help a few months ago and he's every bit as good as me."

"Yes, definitely," Camryn responds. She smiles at me, and I smile back. I am dying on the inside, but I'll never show it.

Joel walks away, leaving me and Camryn to inspect the post that has the carvings. My fingers bump over the wood, slipping through the valleys. It's obvious the person who worked on this put care into it. Camryn jostles me with her elbow.

"What do you think about a little surprise for Dani? Like an old-school heart with C loves D inside it, carved into the other post?"

"Adorable. You should request it."

Cam pecks around the post at me, stern eyebrows pulled to a point. "Don't get so caught up in writing that you forget you're supposed to be planning the bridal shower while you're up here."

"I have an entire notebook dedicated to the task."

Cam makes a face. "A physical notebook? How old are you? Use the notes app on your phone."

"Don't judge my process."

The clomp of footsteps sounds through the huge room. Camryn and I turn at the same time Joel says, "Here he is."

My breath, my stomach, my heart, they all disappear, leaving me hollow but somehow still heavy. Blood pounds in my ears, throbbing and pulsing.

It's impossible, *impossible*, except it's not because there Gabriel is, staring at me, shocked gaze piercing my soul in the way only he can.

He says my name. Each letter slams into me, five separate wrecking balls decimating me where I stand.

"What the hell?" my sister's disbelieving whisper catapults me into action. I'm moving, searching, trying to find a way from this place. I have to get away. There's a door on the right, it's not the way we came, but it will do.

I burst through. It's the same parking lot, but on the other side of the building. The rain hasn't let up, and I'm drenched in mere seconds. It doesn't matter. Nothing matters.

Not anymore.

Not when Gabriel is here, in the flesh.

I tip my face to the rain because I need to feel something to remind me this moment is real.

Gabriel comes through the door, charging into the parking lot, and I am his goal. He reaches me, stopping only a foot away. Wet hair hangs over his forehead, tiny rivers of rain running over the planes of his face. Heavy breath pushes his chest, his eyes are wide and brimming with emotion.

We stare at each other, neither of us able to get a handle on this moment. Then he reaches for me, and I let him touch me. His fingers wrap around my upper arms, and the memory of his touch resurfaces as though it never left. A ragged breath drags through my lungs.

Gabriel is touching me. *Gabriel.*

How many nights did I yearn for him? An ocean of tears did not return him to me, and now, here he is, his presence more impossible than I could've ever imagined. How long did I beg God for mercy on his behalf?

Months.

Weeks.

Days.

Hours.

Until I was nothing but alone, in our bed, accepting our ending.

Now here he is. He pulls me closer, and his lips are near my ear, his hands gripping my arms. The rise and fall of his chest pushes against mine. His smell. My God, how I've missed it. Even diluted by rain it is there, curling into me. Beneath his touch my skin is seared, but then the desperation for his touch subsides as the memories trickle in.

He once saved me from a fire. But when it was all said and done, he's the one who burned me down.

Camryn pulls my car alongside us. She motions for me to get in.

I take a step back. His hands fall away, but they don't go far. His grip is there between us, suspended in mid-air, and all I have to do to be held by him again is simply step forward.

I don't.

Because I can't.

I can't go back there, to that place where we existed. Not when I've come so far.

Despite it all, my heart screams for him, his touch, those eyes that did me in. And the way he looks now, his gaze simultaneously shocked and pleading...

No.

I take another step away, then two, until I'm in the car. Ruby pushes her face between the front seats, her nose pressed to my arm. My sister has the heat on blast, as if there is even a chance of drying me. I am soaked to the bone, but that hardly registers.

I feel everything at once, and nothing at all. An incongruous duality.

Cam says, "You look like you've seen a ghost." She's aiming for ironic, but there's too much shock in her tone for her to hit the mark. The comment is literal.

Gabriel's figure shrinks in the side mirror. He is rooted in place as we leave the parking lot behind.

"I have."

PART TWO

There are all kinds of love in this world, but never
the same love twice.
   - F. Scott Fitzgerald, The Great Gatsby

CHAPTER 1
GABRIEL

AVERY.

Here, in Sugar Creek. In my arms. Her warm breath heavy on my cheek as she exhaled her shock.

My heart began beating for the first time in nearly three years.

I've spent lonely days imagining what it would be like if I was ever lucky enough to see Avery again, but my imagination fell short. The relief, the love, the utter desperation was all on the mark, but I'd left out the gut punch. The reality of what I'd done poured over me when I saw her face.

When you're in a sterile environment, gray paint and block walls and barely surviving, reality drifts away. Like looking into a well, your vision narrows and you see only the dark.

One day, you're reintroduced to the light. *Here are your things,* they say, pressing your old clothes to your chest. You walk out of the gates, feeling like an intruder in the free world. Day by day, the fog burns off and realization dawns. You have made the two greatest mistakes of your life.

And then, on a rainy day that blends into all other days no matter the weather, the love of your life shows up.

Raindrops gather on her skin, catch in her eyelashes. You'll be soaked to the bone but it won't matter because…

Avery.

Is.

Here.

CHAPTER 2

AVERY

Camryn drives my car to the rented cabin, her phone spouting directions. "We'll get my car later," she explains, and I nod absently. The rain stopped a few minutes ago, and now the sun peeks from neutral clouds. She helps me carry in my bags, and Ruby's things.

"Avery?" Camryn's eyes are on Ruby as she sniffs every inch of the place. "You need to say something."

I've yet to speak a full sentence. Mostly because I can't locate enough words to form one.

"You're scaring me." Camryn's using her authoritative voice, so I know she's not actually scared. "Don't hold it in. Whatever you're feeling, you need to let it out."

How can I explain my feelings? I cannot decide if I'm happy to see Gabriel, or devastated. I think I may be a little of both, along with everything in between. When did he get out of prison? Why didn't anybody tell me? Shouldn't I have received a call from…*somebody?* Doug, Corinne, Gabriel himself? *Hi, it's me. Just wanted to let you know I'm out, in case we run into each other in a small town up north.*

"Whatever you're experiencing over there"—Cam glances my way across the living room, eyeing me momentarily before looking out of the window to the trees that surround this place—"is acceptable. All of it. It's not good or bad."

"You sound like my therapist." I'm trying to get a handle on my emotions, but they're too damn hard to put my arms around.

"Whom you don't see anymore," Cam reminds me, as if to say, *you're cured, remember?* Like I'm a solved problem instead of a work-in-progress.

"Who I might have to start seeing again, after that." I thumb behind me, unsure if I'm pointing in the right direction. "Whatever that was."

"That was your ex-husband building my wedding arch. Never knew he possessed woodworking talent." Cam sounds breezy, but her throat undulates with a hard swallow. She loved Gabriel, too. Her fisted hands float in the air on either side of her face, and she unfurls her fingers at once. "Surprise," she deadpans.

I slide a palm over my face, rubbing away one eyelid of shimmery brown eye shadow. "I hope that's the last surprise I receive for a year."

"Five years," Cam amends.

"Ten," I add. I sigh and bite my lip to keep from crying. When I'm certain the threat has passed, I say, "I keep seeing his face. The shock. And the way he followed me."

Cam nods. "He went after you like he was shot from a cannon."

"He touched me," I murmur. The sting, the bite, the unbridled electricity of his touch, even in its absence it remains.

"I noticed." Cam doesn't sound happy.

"What did the owner—Joel?— say? About the way I ran out? And Gabriel coming after me?"

"He asked what the hell that was about. I told him you used to be married."

Used to be married. I hate that sentence. I used to be young, and naïve. By most accounts, I'm still young, but my naïveté has dissolved. I didn't know what could break a couple, the weight two people could be tasked with carrying. But Lord, I sure know now.

"Why was he there?" Cam asks.

I shrug. I have no idea. "He didn't say."

"He said something to you. He didn't stand there, silent."

I look out the window to the glistening pine trees. Like Gabriel's touch, I feel his gaze and his words and his warm breath on that square of space beside my ear. Something stabs at my chest, and it hurts enough that I palm my skin. "He told me I'm still as beautiful as the day we met."

Camryn frowns, disbelieving. She pats my shoulder and grimaces. "I love you, Avery, but you're not at your best right now. You're a little *crying homecoming queen* meets *cat who fell in a swimming pool.*" Camryn is a master at making jokes to avoid emotion.

"To be fair, I wasn't at my best the day we met, either, so he's not comparing it to much." I walk to the mirror above the small table next to the front door.

Ugh. She's right. I run my hands under my eyes, but the smeared mascara doesn't budge.

Cam joins me at the mirror, looking at my reflection and saying, "Only Gabriel would find you physically attractive in your current state."

"Don't be a bitch." I push away from the mirror.

She blows out a heavy breath. "Honestly, I don't know what to say. All conversation is a landmine right now."

I hear her padding down the hall behind me, following me to the main bedroom. She begins unpacking my largest suitcase, the one with all my clothes. I open a second, smaller bag.

It holds my toiletries, my notebooks, my favorite pens. And my laptop, which contains the first half of my manuscript.

Cam eyes the laptop. "Did you send your book to Jill?" She's steering the conversation away from me and Gabriel, but it's not going very far, considering the book is about everything that happened to us.

I heft the bag onto the bed. "I sent her what I had this morning before we left to come here." Nerves twist around my stomach. Jill may very well hate what I wrote.

"Did you choose a title?"

"Not yet." I poke at a freckle on the top of my left hand. "It's a heavy decision. Makes me wonder how parents choose a name for a child."

"For real." Cam leans forward, her torso bumping the bed. "Read it to me."

"You want me to read my book out loud to you?" Knots form in my stomach. It's not your average *I feel shy about what I wrote* knots. It's more *This is my version of real events and you might not like it* knots. There are some parts she won't appreciate. Some parts she still doesn't know.

Cam presses. "It'll be like when we were kids and you wrote short stories and read them to me."

"Except this one is based on real events." There's a bit of warning in my tone. I wrestled with writing this book at all, even when I had Gabriel's permission.

"Look at it this way," she reasons, placing the clothes in a drawer, "I'm going to read the book once it's published anyhow. You might as well do me the honor of letting me hear it first."

I can't believe, after all the confusion and pain from seeing Gabriel, I'm almost smiling at my sister's convoluted rationale. "It may never be published. It could be so bad, Jill will drop me as a client." I close my eyes and press the pads of my fingers to them. "What if it's awful?" Little bits of light spring across my vision, and I open my eyes.

Cam flops across the bed, one hand propped under her head. "What if it's awesome?"

I stare at her for a moment, deciding if I'm ready to read my words out loud. If she hates it, at least she'll be on the road soon and I won't have to see her for two weeks. I tuck a pillow behind my back, cross my legs underneath me, and open my computer.

I glance at Cam, and she nods her encouragement for me to begin. "I have nowhere to be and nothing but time. Read to me."

"We need to get your car from—" I almost said *Gabriel's.*

Is that in my lexicon now? Gabriel has a physical place again?

"The woodworking shop," I finish.

Cam eyes me. She knows what I nearly said. "It's not going anywhere."

I take a deep breath and open my mouth.

Here we go.

CHAPTER 3

AVERY

My sister stares at me, slack-jawed.

Slowly, I close the laptop. I read to her for nearly three hours, pausing once to get water, and a second time for the bathroom.

"That's it." My shoulders reach up to my ears, then drop heavily. "That's all I have so far."

Cam gnaws on her lower lip. "I...I don't know what to say."

"You've been stunned into silence? I should be recording this."

Cam smirks. "Just kidding. My words are back." She reaches for my hand. "Avery, I didn't realize everything you went through. You never told me about St. Lucia."

"I couldn't bring myself to."

"I get it. If Dani was the one struggling, I don't know if I'd be able to tell people either."

"Apparently I'm ready to tell people." I gesture at the computer on my lap as trepidation washes over me. "I don't know. We'll see. Sometimes when I think about telling our story, it feels like I'm betraying Gabriel."

"He told you to use your story."

"He was in an emotional place when he wrote that letter. What if he doesn't mean it anymore?"

"I guess you could ask him."

I shake my head. "I think it would be better if I stayed away from him." Better for me. My mental, and emotional, health.

"Whatever you say, Baxter." Cam drops my hand and climbs off the bed. "I need to get going back to Phoenix. Come on."

I drive Camryn to Intricate Wood Works, where she abandoned her car to whisk me away from the sudden appearance of my past. She gives me one long look before she leaves, and hugs me hard.

"Are you going to be ok?" Her forehead creases in concern. "I can stay overnight. Cuddle in bed with you. Tell spooky stories and scare the crap out of each other."

I laugh softly. "No, I'm ok. I promise." I look over at Intricate Wood Works. Is Gabriel in there? Probably not. It's late in the day, and there aren't other cars in the parking lot, and even if there were, I wouldn't know if it belonged to him. Does he still have his truck?

Camryn follows my gaze. "You can always come home," she says, looking back at me. "You don't have to stay here."

I shake my head. "I want to stay. When else will I get an opportunity like this? To sit in the woods and focus on my book? Besides, you saw where I'm staying. There are only a few other places nearby. I'm not going to run into Gabriel again, and I'm not going to go looking for him."

Cam believes me, or at least she accepts my words. I tell her she's welcome up here at any point in the next couple weeks, and remind her to check my mail. She gives me a mock salute and takes off.

I don't have plans to go looking for Gabriel, but it'd be a lie to say I haven't thought about it. How good would it feel to look him in his eyes and demand answers? Or an explanation.

I find a grocery store and stock up on food. I'm treating this like a writers' retreat, not a trip, which means I need non-perishables. I don't want to run out for fresh produce every other day.

The cashier doesn't say much. I don't think Sugar Creek is so small everyone knows everyone else. If she recognizes me as new, she's not giving it away. I pay her and she tells me to have a good night.

On my way back to the cabin, I drive through the middle of town. It's adorable. Quaint. And crowded. People walking down the sidewalk, coming in and out of shops, eating dinner on restaurant patios.

I tell myself I'm not scanning the faces for Gabriel, but of course I am. How could I not?

A man on the sidewalk pretends to bite into an over-sized muffin painted on a glass window, and a woman stands back to take his picture. I study the map app on my phone at a red light, and marvel at how much new construction surrounds the town.

It's dark by the time I arrive at my cabin, and when I step outside my car and pause in the open door, I hear nothing. The birds have gone home for the night, it's too early in the year for the steady thrum of cicadas, and there isn't anything more than sweet silence.

Ruby's keening whine pierces the peace. She must be going crazy inside a place that feels unfamiliar.

I unload the groceries, feed her, and search for a light to illuminate the back of the house so I can take her outside. When I find it, I flip it on and step outside with her.

Ruby sniffs around for the right spot. She goes from tree to tree, bush to bush, inspecting her surroundings. I'm turning around to go inside for a sweatshirt when I hear a sound.

At first, it's a twang reaching me through the trees. Moments pass and the notes build and it becomes a song. I peer into the darkness, looking for its source, but find nothing. That's a good thing, I suppose, because if someone were close enough for me to see, it would mean they were pretty damn close. The best, and most likely, guess is that it's coming from the nearest cabin.

The music gets louder, and I listen closely. I know this song.

Wish You Were Here by Pink Floyd.

Music makes me think of Gabriel. I rarely listen anymore, but now I'm letting myself. I sink down on the bottom stair and close my eyes. I see Gabriel, sitting across from me on our first date. His eyes glimmer with excitement, and he doesn't attempt to hide it. I loved that about him, how he didn't play games when it came to how he felt about me.

The song ends and the musical notes back off, returning through the trees to their source. Gabriel's image recedes with them. Ruby joins me at the bottom of the stairs, and she gets up when I do, scampering up the steps ahead of me.

I rearrange what Camryn unpacked, and set up the

dining room table as my office. I lay out my laptop, my notebook containing my outline, and a blank poster board with sticky notes. Perhaps I need to see the story visually in order to breathe life into the second half.

The last item I lay out is the printed manuscript. Maybe having the words in physical form will be good for creativity.

I gaze down at the table, and a sense of readiness settles over me. Jill and I are scheduled to have a call tomorrow midday. Seeing everything laid out this way makes me feel a little more ready for her.

I place Ruby's bed next to my own. She falls asleep first, blowing out heavy breaths and making noises while she dreams. I stare at the dark ceiling and relive every second of seeing Gabriel earlier today. Putting myself in the moment, I allow the emotions to wash over me. I even feel the rain.

But, of course, that is not rain.

Those are my tears.

———

She hates it.

I think.

Jill sits, silent, chewing on the side of her pinky fingernail. Somewhere beyond her office, a car horn blasts.

One side of her mouth turns down. Would she have the heart to tell me my manuscript reeks? I'm certain she would. She's my agent. It's part of her job. I get the feeling she enjoys that particular aspect.

Jill flips through the pages. She must've printed them out like I did, instead of reading the electronic version I sent her. Maybe she plans to use my words, my story, to line her cat's litter box.

She frowns at a page, running her chewed up pinky nail down its length.

She hates it. I knew it.

The structure of the story is unconventional. Maybe that's the problem. Maybe she hates the way I've separated it into parts.

Or the therapist. She hates the therapist.

I wipe my palms on my tattered sweatpants and flick a fallen piece of tortilla chip off my thigh. I'm wearing a crisp white button-down blouse and three varying length gold necklaces. My computer screen only shows my top half, so I still have on my pajama bottoms. As Camryn would say, I'm fancy lady on the top, couch potato on the bottom.

The longer I stare at Jill's blunt-cut asymmetrical bob, the more my self-doubt grows from a liquid into a block of concrete.

Jill continues to page through the spiral bound stack, stopping somewhere near the end. She folds her hands on top of the open pages and finally looks at me.

"I love it," she says simply.

All the breath I'd been holding whooshes out of me. My shoulders lower from where they've been stuck at my earlobes and return to the place where they should be.

"You really know how to terrify a girl," I joke, adjusting the gold 'A' charm on one of my necklaces. "I thought you were about to tell me you hated it."

"Not at all. I loved the way you involved the therapist. I'm a big fan of normalizing therapy." Jill's hair shifts around her face as she speaks, and she brushes it back with her hands. "It's a solid book, so far. Engaging. I read it all the way through in one sitting. I needed to know what was going to happen next." She holds up a hand. "Don't get me wrong, there are some spots where I see room for improvement. I'm not sure about the ending."

My brows furrow. "The ending?"

Jill clears her throat. "Yeah. I see the ending coming a mile away."

An uncertain smile bends my lips. "Can you tell me what it is? Because even I don't know the ending yet."

Jill grins. I think she likes me, but it's hard to know. She's not an easy read. Her happiness with me could just as easily be amusement. Her long pauses are probably just her giving herself space to contemplate what she was thinking the day she took a chance on a debut author. I'm positive if she weren't Dani's aunt, she wouldn't have given me the time of day.

"Right now," Jill says, looking directly at me. I swear I feel it in my soul. "It looks like she's going to skip off into the sunset with the new guy. Do you really think it should be that easy for her? Where's the conflict? You don't want it venturing into All Dogs Go To Heaven territory."

I haven't seen that movie since I was a kid, but I understand the reference and what she's really saying. "It's a romance," I remind her cautiously. "If I don't supply a happily ever after, I'll get burned at the stake." There's also the small part that I haven't figured out the ending yet. But no matter, because Jill seems game to argue the hypothetical.

Jill's head metronomes. "It's also women's fiction. So you don't necessarily have to have an HEA."

In normal life, not everybody gets a happily ever after.

I know that all too well. But in fictional life? I'd love to send my characters off into cotton candy clouds and bliss personified.

"What would a different ending look like?" I'm curious.

Jill ticks off ideas on her hands. "Nobody gets the girl. She saves herself. She rides off into the sunset on her own white horse."

I like that idea. Love it, actually. But I'm not sure if I love it in theory because it sounds *boss bitch* and *girl power* and all that, or if it's really the path I want my character to take. There's also the matter that I haven't been completely truthful with Jill. She doesn't know how closely this book follows my journey.

I push that thought away and focus on the here and now. If I dig my heels in about the ending, I might take away my chance to tell it at all. I lift my hands in surrender. "Let's leave it open-ended for now while I work through the second half of the story."

"Sounds like a plan," Jill says. She looks down at her watch. "I have to jump. Another meeting starts in ten and my bladder is about to explode."

We hang up after I promise to keep chugging along on the second half of my book.

The problem is, I'm not sure what to write.

Because I'm currently living it. How do you write an ending to a story based on your life experience when you haven't reached it yet?

Maybe Jill is right. Maybe the ending is me riding off on a white horse by myself. It wouldn't be a bad ending. There's just this part of me, tiny but mighty, a holdover from all my years pining for the life I envisioned for myself, that's having a hard time jumping on that white horse. Maybe it's because I had that life, the one I dreamed about. Maybe it's because it *was* all it was cracked up to be. Before it was marred by pain, resentment, and the just plain ugly, it was glorious. Or, maybe it's because I saw Gabriel again.

The happily ever after has claws. Imagine that.

CHAPTER 4
GABRIEL

For the past eighteen hours I've been absent-minded in the truest sense of the word. I've made dinner and watched it burn as I relived the widening of Avery's eyes when she saw me. I forgot I was supposed to watch Joel's dog this weekend while he and his wife are away. He dropped her off with me this morning, and I pretended not to be surprised at their arrival.

Joel hasn't asked me about Avery yet, but I know it's coming. Given the way I acted when I saw her, how could he not be curious? When I walked back into work after Avery drove off, all Joel did was hand me two towels, and leave me alone. I went to the bathroom and dried off. I had packed clothes to go to the gym after work, so I changed into them. I didn't make it to the gym, though. I was too shocked to do much of anything.

In an effort to work off a little of this extra energy, I'm attempting to take Dixie for a run. It's not going well.

"Come on, Dixie." I look down at the dog beside me. She's a mix, I don't know of what breeds.

Dixie stops for the seventh time to investigate a new smell. I jog in place, waiting for her to be done. I lose patience and start running, and she catches up when she realizes she's fallen behind.

My feet kick up gravel as I round a bend in the road. It's a quiet stretch of land, for the most part. Most of the noise comes from the rental cabin next door. New faces coming and going. I don't see them much, not with all those trees and space separating the properties, but I pass the place on my way to work and notice the ever-changing vehicles.

Today, there's a white four-door sedan parked out front. Normally, the cars are SUVs or minivans. Vehicles that accommodate families. The front door to the cabin is propped open. A dog appears in the doorway, and that's all it takes. Dixie is off.

"Shit," I mutter, running after her. My calls for her fall on deaf ears. Dixie has a singular goal, and it's that dog in the doorway barking its head off.

Dixie approaches the home at full speed, and the other dog backs up. The barking has stopped and now its eyes are anxious. If it could talk, it would be saying something like *I'm sorry, I didn't mean anything by it.*

I'm running as fast as I can, but I'm no match for Dixie. She wants a friend, and there will be no stopping her. She races up the stairs and straight into this stranger's home.

I take the stairs two at a time, slowing at the front door. I peek inside. "Hello?" When I don't see anybody I step inside cautiously. Dixie and the other dog circle one another, sniffing each other's backsides and establishing a hierarchy.

I look around, but don't see anybody. Great. I can haul

Dixie away and nobody will know. I stride forward into the open area between the living room and the kitchen, where the dogs are wrestling. With any luck, the renters are down at the lake, and I can have us out of here in fewer than ten seconds.

I grab Dixie by the collar. "Come on," I command, making my voice deep and strict. She ignores me, pulling against my hold.

I stand, frustrated, and run a hand over my face. When the hand is gone, I see movement in the corner of my eye. I turn quickly, hands up in innocence, ready to tell the person I'm just trying to get the dog back.

My words die on my lips.

Avery stands in the kitchen, holding a frying pan out to the side of her body. Her eyes are wide, frozen. AirPods nestle in her ears.

It's difficult to describe what my heart is doing in this moment. The best word I can think of is *sobbing*. This woman was my world, until I went and ruined it.

Now she's here, not just here to see her sister's arch but here, in a cabin, inserted into the tiny slice of solitude and seclusion I've carved out for myself. She's supposed to be in Phoenix, thriving and living her best life.

Her arm lowers, and the frying pan bumps her calf. She removes each AirPod methodically, setting them on the counter with the pan.

She comes closer, stopping a few feet from me. Her chest rises and falls with a slow and quiet exhalation. Her shirt falls open at the top, just enough that I can see the top swell of her breasts. A place I once buried my face, kissed, and slept on. I drowned myself in this woman, and came up for air when I never wanted to.

Now here she is, standing before me. Her eyes are question marks, but she seeks answers I don't know how to give. How do you explain to someone you demolished their heart not because you didn't love them, but because you loved them too much?

The dogs, wrestling and growling and playing, bump into my feet. We both look down.

"You have a dog?" I ask, astonished. Unless… My gaze darts around the room. Is she here with Camryn? Or someone else? The thought sits in my stomach like curdled milk.

"Ruby," she answers. "She's mine."

It's the first time in years I've heard Avery speak. She didn't say a word to me yesterday. She stood in the rain, a statue, except for the pulse throbbing in her throat. Her voice curls into me now, settling back in its familiar spot in my chest the way it once did.

"You didn't want a dog. Not after…" My voice trails off. She's giving me a look that says *you don't know me anymore.*

She's not wrong.

I point out front. "That's your car?"

She nods. "My old one died." Her gaze goes to my head. "You're wearing your hair longer."

At her mention of it, I brush it off my forehead. Her hair is shorter than before, up near her collarbone. It used to hang down her back. "You got a haircut."

Her face muscles twitch like she's beating back a smirk. "I've had several."

I nod. "Right. Of course."

Quiet falls over us. What do you say when there is so

much to say? Where do you begin, when the hill that looms is really a mountain?

"Why are you here?"

I blink at her direct question. Avery isn't normally a direct person. The thought pushes at me, reminding me, just as she did a moment ago, that I don't know her anymore. Not the way I once did.

"I came after the dog. I didn't know"—I gesture at the front door—"this was your place. The door was open and —" Avery shakes her head, and I stop talking.

"No. I mean, why are you *here*?" She motions around us with both arms, and I understand what she means.

"Early release."

"How long ago?"

"Five months."

She huffs a hard breath of disbelief and makes a quarter turn, her profile in view.

I've worked hard to rebuild some semblance of a life, and now I'm watching my world shake and shift, the loose stones beginning to tumble. I reach out a hand. "Avery, listen—"

"No," she whispers coarsely, facing me. I can't help but notice the beauty in her fierce gaze. "You listen. Don't you do this to me. After everything you put me through, don't come back now."

My heart twists as my palms lift in a gesture of inno-cence, which, let's face it, is ironic. "I wasn't going to, Avery. I wasn't planning on inserting myself in your life. But then you showed up in mine." I search her face, the angry pinch of her eyebrows.

"You have a lot of nerve, Gabriel."

"This isn't about nerves." My hands rake through my

hair. I've had no time to prepare, no advance notice of seeing her again. I cannot offer my thoughts or feelings in any way that isn't messy and raw. "I don't have a choice. Not when it comes to you."

"Ohhh oh oh." She shakes her head. "You had a choice. And you made it."

"I did what was best for you."

Avery's eyes widen with her upset. "You chose what you thought was best for me. You didn't let me make that choice for myself."

I swallow against the lump in my throat. We're jumping into churning waters, and I want to swim in the shallows. I want to ask her how she has been, what she's been doing, who she is now. Instead, we're picking up where we left off, as if two years haven't passed and we're still balancing on the same string pulled taut.

"You…you…" I growl with my frustration and stare into her eyes. A mistake, for certain, because all I can do is remember how much I love her. "Everything I did was out of love for you."

"Let me get this straight." She steps closer, the tip of her finger nearly touching my chest. She pauses, and I think she realizes the proximity is a bad idea. Her familiar scent wraps around me, and it takes everything I have not to lose myself in it. How does a starving man not eat when offered food? Not drink when offered water? Avery's murderous expression is what stops me from reaching for her.

"You broke my heart out of love for me?"

Here it is. We've stripped the layers without preamble, to seep through the gauze placed on the gaping wound, and bring it all down to the crux. The truth is so damn painful, so mutilating, and that famous saying the truth will set you free? Maybe to some, but not to me. I could tell the truth, or I could lie through my teeth, and it would have the same result.

Suffocating shame.

Quietly, I say, "I broke your heart long before I divorced you."

No response. No noise. Not even a movement. She is utterly silent. We both know I'm right.

A heavy breath moves her chest, and if it weren't for that I'd believe time were standing still. She shakes her head. "You never loved me. You couldn't have."

I look into her eyes. We both know her words are utter nonsense, a falsehood not even worthy of entertainment.

I concentrate on making my voice clear, solid, and strong, because I need her to both hear and feel the sincerity of my words. "I never loved you more than the day I let you go."

"It was cowardice," she whispers. Her eyes swim with tears.

My hand twitches, dying to soothe her, but I bat away the ingrained response. My own tears sting the backs of my eyes.

"It was mercy." My voice is thick. "And I'm sorry for what I put you through."

She laughs once, an empty sound. "You don't know what I went through."

Looking at her now, at the devastation seeping from her, I recognize this might be the last time we see each other. The last time we talk, the last opportunity I get to explain myself. If I don't take this chance, I may never get another one.

Gently, I take her upper arm in my grasp. She winces, as if my touch causes her pain. Maybe it does, but I sure as hell know it's not physical.

"You're right. I don't know. Would you tell me, if I asked?"

Her lower lip trembles. I try not to stare at it, but it's nearly impossible. Like the top swell of her breasts, her lower lip is a part of her I've loved on.

"I…" She looks conflicted. "I don't know."

"What did you go through? After"—I pause, searching for a word, but there isn't one—"everything."

I see in her eyes that she is afraid to tell me. After all this time, she's still protecting me from her feelings. "Avery, please. I don't have a right to know. I understand that. Still…" I force my hand to stay where it is, to not cup her cheek and stroke her soft skin like I'm dying to do. "I want to know."

"You don't deserve it." Her whisper is sharp, slicing into my heart.

My chin drops. "No, I don't."

She's quiet, then says, "Gabriel?"

My eyes draw up to hers. She swallows and looks at the dining room table beside us. "Do you see those papers?"

I look to my left. A stack of bound paper lies open on the table.

"That's a half-finished manuscript. The book of me and you." Her head shakes quickly. "That's not the title. There isn't one yet."

I look back to her. "That's our story?"

"Half of it."

"The other half?"

"I'm still writing it."

I'm not sure what to say. In a time that feels like another life, I told her to use our story. I'd wanted to give her something, anything, to make the situation better.

Avery continues. "If you want to know what it was like for me, it's all right there."

"I can read it?"

She stares at me for a long moment, and I know she's thinking through something. "Yes," she says finally. She extracts herself from my hold, stepping over to the table. She closes the manuscript and offers it to me. I take it, tucking it to my chest like a football.

"Avery, I—"

"You should leave." Her gaze skitters to the back door. Both dogs stand beside it, asking to be let out.

I have a lot more to say, and no right to push her. "You're alone out here?" I look around the place.

Her chin lifts defiantly. "Yes."

"For how long?"

"Two weeks."

I point next door. "I'm in the next cabin over, if you need anything." I'm sure she's planning to never need anything, and I don't blame her.

She nods and folds her arms in front of herself, as if she's erecting a barrier. "Thank you."

I call for Dixie, and she ignores me. Sighing, I walk over to the dog and grab her collar. She puts on the brakes, refusing to be moved. Avery laughs, then cuts herself off as if she doesn't want to be caught finding anything funny in my presence. I end up picking up the dog and carrying her out of the house, the manuscript wedged between my chest and Dixie's.

Avery stands beside the front door. I pass her and turn around when I step outside. I open my mouth to speak, but Avery beats me to it.

"I don't think we should see each other again, Gabriel."

Panic crawls up my throat. I can't lose her again.

She must read my expression, because she says, "It has the potential to be messy. And I"—she shakes her head slowly—"I can't do messy." She presses three fingers to her lower lip, and says, "Getting over you nearly killed me. I won't survive a second time."

The admission takes my breath away. Not just the words, but the way she says them. Confident, certain, and vulnerable. She's different than she was before, in a way that's hard to put my finger on.

"I understand," I tell her, and it's a half-truth, which also makes it a half-lie. I understand her words, but I don't agree with them. She'd never need to get over me a second time, because I would never, ever do what I did the first time.

Avery's gaze drops to the ground as she closes the door, as if she can't bear to look at me one last time. I set Dixie down and we walk home.

The manuscript is heavy in my grasp, weighing so much more than just a handful of ounces. I went for a run, but I feel like I've completed a triathlon instead.

I make a pitcher of iced tea. I take it onto the back porch with me, ice cubes clinking in my glass. Dixie lies down nearby. Settling into the chair, I take a deep breath, mentally preparing myself.

I open the manuscript to the first page, and begin to read.

CHAPTER 5
GABRIEL

MORE.

It's the first thought I have when I finish reading.

I want more story.

More Avery. These words are her heart, her soul, wrung out like a soaking wet towel. As I read, I heard her speaking.

The 8 1/2 x 11 bundle of paper lies on my lap. It is still open to the last page, the final words of the half-finished manuscript shining like a beacon.

Well played, dear sister.

I blow a hard breath and shake my head. It's not surprising Camryn would stick her nose in Avery's business. She's done it before.

My second thought is more like fifty thoughts all arriving at the same time. Awe, surprise, hurt, embarrassment, jealousy. To name a few.

Somehow, though the story isn't all that joyful, I smiled in a handful of parts. Despite the agony in it all, there is happiness.

I read all afternoon and into the evening. The remaining shreds of sunlight disappeared a few minutes ago. Deep purple and pink bruise the last of the day's sky, the shadows of the pine trees lengthening. Through those trees, is Avery.

My ex-wife.

The author of this book. Our story.

She's captured our relationship here on these pages, but not perfectly. Not completely. She doesn't know what it was like for me to step into a burning home, to hurry up the stairs and find her on the floor. She doesn't know I fell in love with her right away, long before I said the words. She doesn't know the excruciating pain of being the executioner of your own marriage.

A faraway light shines through the trees. It's her backyard light. Knowing she'll be there for the next two weeks sends a sharp pain through my chest. I want to put eyes on her, even if her gaze holds nothing but anger. At least it isn't pity. For the last few months of our marriage, all her eyes held was pity, and I didn't deserve it.

I think I would've preferred her fury.

It's how I knew I needed to let her go. Avery would have gritted out the time, and I couldn't allow that. She was meant to soar, and I'd clipped her wings.

I don't think we should see each other again, Gabriel.

I wish she hadn't asked that of me. I'd be charging through the trees right now, if she hadn't said that. Even if I ignored her wishes and knocked on her door anyway, I don't know what I'd do when I arrived. What is there to say? The damage between us is irrevocable.

We can't come back from what happened. It's all there

on these pages. We started out a fairy tale, and turned into a nightmare. Because of me.

What right do I have stomping over to her cabin and knocking on her door?

None.

Dixie stands at my left, staring at me meaningfully. I have forgotten her dinner.

I push off the chair and go inside. I move through the motions, measuring out Dixie's food, and then making my own. Everything is thick and robotic, as if I'm underwater.

Avery described us as a storm we created, and willingly put ourselves in the path of its destruction.

I wonder how often people do that. Create storms and die inside them.

When Avery and I met, I was already a stealth tornado. I didn't know it, and neither did she. When you're living your life for someone else, how can you be anything but a disaster in the making?

CHAPTER 6
GABRIEL

I'VE BEEN WORKING ON CAMRYN'S ARCH FOR THE PAST THREE hours. She's requested a special message.

C loves D, with a heart drawn around it. She wants it small, hidden from a first glance. When the order for this arch came in, I had no idea who it belonged to. The details aren't my job. My job is to put hands on the wood, to carve and sand and mold. And burn.

Joel has agreed to introduce some of my pyrography pieces on his social media. I've brought my wood burning machine with me today, and a few new pens and tips. I have a handful of decorative wood slices finished, but I think custom coasters and wooden spoons will sell better. They are less expensive and easier to give as gifts.

The irony of my past life and my current life intersecting isn't lost on me. No matter what I do, I end up around fire.

Like most mornings, Avery was my first thought when I woke up. Usually my thoughts are wistful, but today I felt frustrated. Even though she's so damn close, she's still so damn far.

My fault. All of it.

Joel walks into the space where I'm set up, finishing a section of the arch. He is a kind man, quick to smile and slow to judge. Thank God.

"Looking good," he says, surveying my work. "I hate to admit it, but you're better than me."

"Nah." I wave away his compliment, but he's not having it.

"I'm serious. I thought I had a good ten years left with this business, but looking at what you're capable of…" He trails a fingertip over a curve in the wood. "You might just edge me out. And I might just let you."

I look at my feet and smile. Joel is too good to me. His wife, Kimberley, has been just as kind. She sends him to work with lunch for me, and baked goods, and random items she swears are either deeply discounted or two-for-one specials.

"Don't go retiring on me yet," I tell Joel. "There's plenty I still need you to teach me."

He points at my wood burning tools on the desk across the room. "I think it's you who should be teaching me. Where did you learn to burn wood?"

He's probably expecting me to say the big P word, except they wouldn't have allowed us to have weapons, and wood burning tools could absolutely be weapons.

"I took woodshop in high school as an elective. I wasn't expecting to love it, but it all clicked for me. The way a person can take something made from the earth and imbibe it with their own creativity. I couldn't believe I could put my hands on something so precious, and leave a mark. It felt like even if I was just this tiny human, I mattered."

"I understand what you mean. I never learned pyrography, but building and carving makes me feel the same way."

He walks around the arch, eyes roaming the details. "Thanks again for watching Dixie for us."

I returned the dog to him this morning when I arrived here at work, and Kimberley came to pick her up and take her home. I wasn't expecting how much I enjoyed having Dixie around, and I feel sad thinking about going home to an empty house. "Anytime. It was nice having her there."

Joel lingers. I can tell he wants to say something to me, so I draw out the work. I go back over what I've carved, pretending to smooth and perfect.

After a minute, he says, "That woman from a few days ago… She's your ex-wife?"

I knew we'd arrive at the topic eventually. "Yes, that's my ex-wife." My stomach lurches at the word.

He nods slowly. "I've known a lot of guys with ex-wives. I can't say I've ever seen any of them act like that when they see them."

"There's some unfinished business." There really isn't. The papers were signed. Our assets split or dissolved. On paper, we are done.

"Sure looked to be that way."

"How long have you been married to Kimberley?"

"Forty-one years."

I tap the sawhorse behind me with two knuckles. "Did you think it would be easy?"

"Never."

"I don't know why, but I went into marriage thinking it

would be easy. People talk about 'hard times,' but that concept sounded like, well, a concept. Something that couldn't be applied to me and her." So arrogant. Like Avery, I'd believed hard times belonged to other people. It didn't occur to me the hard time could be a living, breathing organism. A person. Me.

"I take it you hit those hard times?"

I laugh once, a hollow sound. "Head-on."

Joel eyes me. He knows where my story leads, but we don't talk about it much. The mention of prison makes people uneasy, and for good reason. They immediately think violence, repeat offenders, hardened criminals. Danger. Not someone making the worst mistake of their life, and paying dearly for it.

I learned all about what people think of ex-cons when I was trying to get a job after I got out. One glance at my application and out the door I went. Time after time, I watched the curtain close over their expressions, the polite head nod as they came up with a reason for why they weren't hiring. Then I remembered Drew, who I'd met on the inside, telling me about his uncle Joel after he learned I liked working with wood. Drew made it sound like his uncle was a salt of the earth guy who believed in second chances. I found a parole officer in the area, packed my bags, and drove up here to Sugar Creek. I introduced myself to Joel and Kimberley, and Joel agreed to take a chance on me.

"Do you think there's any hope for you two?" Joel asks.

My lips purse and I look down at my dirty jeans. "She said she's over me. And she doesn't want to see me again."

"Hmm."

It's a dubious sound, and draws my attention back to him.

"What does that mean?" I ask.

"If she's over you, why doesn't she want to see you again?"

"Because I remind her of a time she'd prefer to forget."

"I'm not buying it."

I smile at his insistence.

"I'm just sayin'"—he lifts his hands—"I've been alive for a long time, and I know more about women than you do. I saw that young lady's face. She's about as over you as Kimberley is over me."

"You sound like a romantic."

He pats his chest, just above his heart. "A man can't be married as long as I have and not be a romantic."

Joel's phone rings and he fishes it from his pocket. "Speak of the angel," he says, winking and walking away to answer Kimberley's call.

I turn my attention away from the arch and to my burn machine. Settling in, I create three sets of coasters, each one distinctly different designs. One geometric, one floral, and the other a monogram. I use Avery's initials.

AWR

According to her manuscript and the title page, we no longer share a last name, but I'm being hardheaded.

I'm just about to call it a day when Joel passes through. He peers over at the work, nodding his head in approval. "We'll get Mason to take the photos tomorrow."

I'm glad he has his grandson to run the social media,

because that's way out of my wheelhouse. Even before I went to prison, I never bothered with it.

"Sounds good," I answer, packing away my pens and tips.

Joel pushes off the table, and starts to walk away. He turns back. "You may be down"—he slides his hands into his pockets and shrugs—"but you aren't out."

I like that. A lot. It sparks hope into a place I'm not sure hope is allowed to be.

I finish out the day, and go home to an empty house. I make dinner for one, which is depressing because most recipes are meant for at least two. I wrap up the leftovers and store them for tomorrow. Instead of reading one of the books I've borrowed from the Sugar Creek library, I page back through Avery's manuscript, picking and choosing what I read a second time. I like how she describes our first date, and all the intimate moments. I love reading about how I made her feel. In this form, I get to relive it as much as I want.

The brightness of these parts still manages to cast a shadow. Tiny stabs assail my heart, and still I marvel at the woman behind the words.

Avery wrote this. I let her go, and look at her.

She soared.

I hate to know I was right.

It would be worse had I been wrong.

———

JOEL VOLUNTEERED me to help unload and set up tables for the county fair being held this weekend. He made a comment about needing brawn, and he would serve as the brains. Not that much of either is needed in this situation.

Which is fortunate, because only half of me is here, unloading tables and carrying them to where I've been directed to go. The other half is stuck on Avery's book, living our relationship through her eyes.

I vividly remember the day we met, too. Not in the fire, but for real, in the fire station. In my version, she was the one who stopped my breath. She wore a skirt that swished around her ankles, and a white T-shirt tied in a knot at her waistline. When she lifted her hand to shake mine, her shirt rode up and revealed a line of her skin. She stunned me that day. She stuns me now.

On my way here I drove past the cabin where she's staying, hoping to catch a glimpse of her. I didn't, but I saw her car. She was there, and somehow that was enough. Well, not enough, but it was something. More than I've had in a long time.

"Gabriel?"

I turn toward my name. Jane from Lady J Bakery walks my way.

"Where is your head right now?" The bracelets on her arm clack together as she gestures in the air. "I've said your name three times."

"Sorry about that." I duck my head at her. "In my own world, I guess."

"Mm-hmm." Her eyebrows raise. "Does this world of yours have a young lady in it?"

I palm my chest with exaggeration. "Jane, come on. You know you stole my heart the first time I stepped foot in your bakery."

Jane laughs, her lined face wrinkling further. "My blueberry muffins have a reputation for doing that."

Jane is fifty-eight, and splits her time between her bakery and church. She's beautiful, in a regal sort of way. Kimberley once told me Jane showed up in town one day, all by herself. No ring, no moving truck, no nothing. She rented a little place outside town that doesn't even have a proper address, but every Sunday she went to church. Before long Jane had melted into the town of Sugar Creek as if she'd always been there. She was gorgeous, according to Kimberley, and fielded advances from single men of varying ages, but always said no. Eventually they all quit trying. Kimberley swears Jane's true love is baking, and there isn't room for anything else.

I disagree. After Kimberley told me all this, I watched Jane every time I went into Lady J. There is something inside her that keeps her from being truly happy. She ran away from wherever she was before, and she came all the way here to Sugar Creek. How can I tell?

It takes one to know one.

I ran here, too. It wasn't just the difficulty finding a job, but everything else. Going to a restaurant and listening to someone complain about the food not being to their liking. My mother, hovering over me. My dad, slapping me on the back and telling me I needed to get back on the horse. If only it were that simple. Maybe for some people it is, but not me. I couldn't slip back into my old life. For one, there was no Avery. For two, nothing fit quite right anymore. As if all the old shapes were circles, and now I'm a square.

Jane pulls the lid of a plastic container and holds it out to me. "Hungry?"

I reach in eagerly. Jane's blueberry muffins are legendary.

"So," Jane says, putting the top back on the container. "What has you so distracted you don't hear your own name?"

I brush crumbs from my lips as I chew, shaking my head. "Memories."

"Memories," she repeats, the word heavy, as if she knows exactly what I mean. "Isn't it amazing what we'll do to ourselves with memories? How willing we are to experience pain over and over again?"

"Or joy," I add, thinking about that day I saw Avery in the fire station.

"Right," she says, and I get the impression joy isn't a part of Jane's memories. "Your memories are good ones, then?" Her eyebrows lift as she asks the question.

"Some more than others." I swallow another mouthful. "I'm sure that's typical of most people."

She nods slowly. "Anyway..." She pushes off the wall she'd been leaning on. "Would you mind setting up the awning over my table? I've been feeling stiff lately. Starting to feel my age," she jokes, rubbing at her lower back and pretending to hobble.

"You aren't a day past forty," I say, walking beside her to her table. She laughs.

It only takes me a few minutes to set up the awning for her. There are pockets at the bottom, and I fill them with rocks to keep the awning in place. Jane pays me with another muffin. Cinnamon sugar this time.

Jane looks out at the work being done to convert the space into a fair. "Do you ever wonder what it's all for?"

My eyebrows scrunch and I gesture out with one finger. "All this, you mean?"

She crosses her arms in front of herself. "Life. Everything we do. What is it all for?"

In the short time I've been in Sugar Creek, I've grown close to Jane. She's almost like a mother figure, one who doesn't judge me or wish I were someone else.

I squint at Jane, trying to figure out where this is coming from. I've never heard her sound this melancholy. "Love, I suppose."

She purses her lips as she considers my answer. "Awful lot of mess for that one thing."

In my mind, I see Avery. Our situation is more of a disaster than a run-of-the-mill mess.

"Though," Jane adds, "I guess there cannot be light without darkness."

CHAPTER 7

AVERY

I gave Gabriel the manuscript because I'd been unable to say everything I wanted to say. Isn't me giving him the contents of my head and my heart even better than speaking aloud? It's been a few days since I said he and I shouldn't see one another again, and even though I meant it, a part of me is dying to know what he thinks of the story.

Of *my* version of *our* story.

In lieu of Gabriel's opinion, I'll have to settle for Jill's. She emailed earlier today with a subject line that read "Let's have a check in!" The body of the email was empty. I wrote her back and told her I'd call her in an hour. She sent me a link for a video call.

Knowing I'm going to see her forced me to take a shower and do my hair and makeup. I've been a mess the past few days, existing on crackers and cheese and coffee. It's only partially what Camryn envisioned for me. When she romanticized me writing in a cabin, I don't think she saw me as sad and slightly depressed. Pining for a life and a person I thought I'd moved on from. I'm sure these feelings are normal, but that doesn't mean I have to like them.

While I wait for my call with Jill to start, I tidy up my little cabin. Sweep away dirt tracked in by Ruby, dry my breakfast dishes. Today I'm planning to tell Jill what this book is based on. Especially now that Gabriel's in the picture again.

Kind of in the picture, anyway. Kind of, but not really. Not really, but also, *he's right there.*

But wasn't he always? If I zoom out, he's there. He's the ghost Hudson couldn't handle. If the situation were reversed, I wouldn't let myself love someone who loved a ghost. I can't fault Hudson for asking for better.

When it's time, I log into the video call. Jill is there, waiting, her severe bob ready to cut glass. It matches her serious expression.

I wave. "Hello."

"Avery," Jill says. At least her tone is warm. "Where are you?" Her gaze leaves my face, looking at the room behind me. "Were you there a few days ago when we spoke?"

"Yes." I peer over my shoulder and back to her. "A little writer's retreat. A cabin," I amend, when her eyebrows draw together.

"Love it," she says. "Very woodsy and cute. Are you inspired?"

"Yeah." My attention flickers outside in the direction of Gabriel's cabin.

"Tell me more," Jill demands, catching on to my tone. "Is there a hot lumberjack nearby? Now that would add to your book." She laughs at her joke.

"Well…" I bite my bottom lip. "Not a lumberjack."

"But there's someone?"

"Yes?" I'm not sure why it comes out like a question.

"Who?"

"My ex-husband."

Jill is silent. I don't know if this is good or bad. I get the feeling if a person shocks Jill into silence, it might not be a good thing.

"Jill, listen, I need to tell you about—"

She holds up a hand. "Is your book based on real life?"

No sense in beating around the bush. "Gabriel—my ex —gave me permission to write our story."

Jill exhales loudly. "So the DUI? And the alcoholism?"

I nod once to confirm what she's asking.

She grimaces. "The divorce?"

"True."

"Avery." Compassion softens her voice. "You poor thing."

I push down my immediate distaste at the words. *Poor little thing.* It's all I heard after my mom died. All I heard after people started seeing how much I was taking care of Camryn. After people learned about Gabriel. *Poor thing. How sad.*

"It's over now." My voice betrays a confidence I don't feel.

"Are you sure about that?"

"We're divorced," I say, as if that's an explanation.

"And?"

"That's usually a pretty solid ending."

A smile curves Jill's mouth upward. "Avery, I've read your book. If what you wrote is even half as much of what you two felt for each other, it is most definitely not over. Where's the closure?"

"I don't think everybody gets closure. Sometimes things end, and that's all there is to it."

She crosses her arms and leans back in her chair. "You talk a brave game, Avery Burke, but you're lying through your teeth."

I blink at her blunt words. "He's given me a million reasons not to trust him with my heart. Maybe my character can take him back. But I'm afraid fact and fiction will have to diverge in this case."

Never mind that the moment I saw him again, my heart felt like it could fly. Or that when he chased that dog in here, every cell in my body stood at attention.

She nods solemnly. "My father was a raging alcoholic. I grew up watching my mom manage his alcoholism. Lying to people to cover up for him. Lying to herself, too. I guess what I'm saying is that I understand."

"And yet you think he's worthy of a second chance?" I'm surprised. Jill is no nonsense. I can't imagine her giving a man a second chance, if she were in my position.

"Is your book reflective of the real Gabriel?"

My heart skips a beat. "Yes."

"Then, yes. People make mistakes, even the good ones. Are you using any of this in the book?"

"I've written four new chapters."

"Do they include your character running into Gabriel?"

I shake my head. "No."

"It wouldn't be a bad direction to take the story."

"I thought you wanted me to ride off into the sunset on my own white horse?"

She shrugs. "Still not a bad way to go. Just not the only way."

"Gotcha."

She peers into the screen, shrewd eyes taking me in. "Are you doing ok?"

I recently saw a ghost, so, no, I'm not doing well. No matter how much I force Gabriel from my thoughts, he doesn't go far. It doesn't help that I want to see him, despite the way my brain warns my heart. I don't tell Jill that each night since I arrived, I sit outside and listen, hoping to hear Gabriel's music. "I'm struggling," I admit.

"I thought so." Jill sits back. "You should go have a little fun. Where are you?"

"Sugar Creek."

She turns to her second computer and begins typing, muttering the words Sugar Creek as she taps the keys. Less than a minute later she announces, "There's a county fair there right now. Looks like a pretty big deal. Very small town and whimsical. You should go. Step away from the story for an afternoon."

"That does sound like a good idea." I've been writing, rereading, and agonizing over my word choices since Gabriel and that crazy dog came barging in here a few days ago.

Gabriel has a lot to do with how long it's taking me to write. Lengthy sessions of staring at the laptop screen aren't helping either. The words meld together, and soon it's Gabriel's face I see.

He's still handsome, but weathered now. His eyes were always deep and wise, but now I see he knows things. Things he'd rather not know, I'm sure.

To Jill, I say, "I think I'll check out that fair. I did my hair and makeup today, might as well put it to good use."

"Go on," she urges. "My New Yorker heart is very

jealous of the small-town whimsical fun you're about to have."

We sign off, and I look up the fair. Jill is right. It's whimsical, and I'll regret not going.

I change out of my yoga pants and loose-fitting top and into a casual dress.

I heat my curling iron and put some casual curls into my freshly washed and dried hair.

I slip my feet into some casual shoes.

So casual.

If I happen to run into Gabriel while I'm there, then, you know, what's a girl to do? I'd been caught off-guard the last two times I saw him. If it happens today, I'll be ready.

"Wish I could bring you," I tell Ruby, scratching behind her ears on my way out.

A flicker of excitement sparks to life in my belly.

Gabriel might not even be there.

But also…he might.

I said we should stay away from each other, but what if we find ourselves in the same place at the same time? Loophole, right?

I probably shouldn't be going. I mean really, what am I even doing? Why am I doing it? I know better. Our marriage is over, and it has been for a while. There's really no good reason to see him again. I realize what a bad idea this might be.

The realization doesn't stop me. All I want is to exist in a world where Gabriel never hurt me, where our slates have been wiped clean, and we are together again without all the pain of the past.

I know that's impossible, and yet, here I go, out the door.

CHAPTER 8

GABRIEL

THE BIGGEST PARK IN SUGAR CREEK HAS BEEN TRANSFORMED for the fair.

Weeks of setup all for this three-day weekend.

It doesn't disappoint.

Everywhere I look is an explosion of color. Families. *Children.*

There's something about small kids that delivers an invisible gut punch. Especially ones who are around three or four. Avery and I didn't make Lulu on that trip to St. Lucia, but we would have eventually. If I hadn't blown it, Avery and I would be the happy family at the fair, eating deep fried food on a stick.

It's one of many colossal regrets.

I walk around, offering to relieve people I know who are running tables, and watch everyone else have a great time.

I've just settled onto a bench after manning Jane's booth for fifteen minutes while she took a break when I spot Avery meandering through a crowd. I stare, transfixed, like I was the first time I met her. I still cannot believe she's here. Normally I'd think maybe I'd been given a gift, a shot, but I must be out of second chances by now.

She's alone. The fabric of her dress moves around her thighs, and she holds a cone of cotton candy. I watch her pluck off a piece, pushing the sugary pink cloud into her mouth. She pivots, and her eyes find mine as if she'd been looking for me.

I see it. I feel it. The sparks, the electricity, the sheer magnetism that has always existed between us.

She stares at me, then draws back her shoulders and comes my way. I'd been certain she'd turn around and go in the opposite direction, and now I'm in shock watching her come closer. Her hips switch, and her cheeks are pink. She is different, but familiar. I'm not sure how that's possible, but it is. I've read her book, so I know she has grown in our time apart, likely in more ways than is detailed on the pages.

"Hey," she says when she reaches me. She shifts from one foot to the other, looking back over her shoulder like maybe she made the wrong choice by coming over here.

I scoot over on the bench, silently inviting her to sit.

She accepts my unspoken offer and sinks down. She pulls off more cotton candy and eats it.

"This is really cute." She motions out to the fair. "Better than the state fair. That place is always so crowded."

I watch her speak. I'm in awe of her, especially after reading her book. "I've never been."

She gapes at me. "You never went to the state fair? But you grew up in Phoenix."

"My parents didn't take us."

Avery's eyes widen at my casual reference to Nash. Prison was its own brand of hell, but it gave me an unexpected opportunity: time. Time to think, to sit deep in my feelings, to sift through all that happened that landed me in that place. When you're stripped bare, you don't need a mirror to see yourself clearly. Between my own reflecting, all the books I read, and the group therapy I chose to attend while I was in, I learned about myself and my choices.

Avery recovers. "Come on, Doug and Corinne," she says, playfully scolding my parents.

I smile. It feels intimate, the way she uses their names.

"How are your parents?" she asks, pulling off a whorl of fluffed sugar.

"Good, I suppose. My dad retired a little over a year ago."

Avery's eyebrows lift in surprise. "He loved his job."

"He loved it less when he didn't have a son to share it with. Those were his words." He'd told me during one of his visits to the prison. He probably hadn't intended to pour salt on a wound, but for me it was like adding more collateral damage to my tally.

Avery nods and offers me cotton candy, and I take some. She watches me, smiling mischievously. Cotton candy is on a short list of foods I'd rather not eat.

"How's that?" she asks.

"Sugary," I deadpan. She laughs.

"Come on, let's find you something savory." She stands, and tries to pull me up with her.

I stay rooted in place as she takes a step forward, and it stops her forward momentum. She looks back at me and drops my hand, a question in her eyes.

I squint up at her. "I thought you wanted us to stay away from each other?" For the record, I do not want to stay away from her. But I don't want to be the reason she feels any kind of pain, and she made it clear the last time we saw each other she believes that will be the result.

Avery's lips twist. "It's been hard for me these past few days, to know you're not that far away. For so long..." Her sentence dies, but I know what she was going to say. *For so long, I couldn't reach you even if I wanted to. Even when you sat beside me, I could not reach you.*

I nod once. "Same."

"Have you been reading my book?"

"Twice."

She blinks. "You read it twice? The entire thing?"

"The entire first half," I clarify. "And some scenes a few additional times." I don't specify which scenes.

A flush grows on her cheeks. "It feels weird to know you've read it."

"Reading your side of the experience is fascinating. It's like peeking inside your head."

She sits back down beside me, her posture stiff. I don't want her to feel uncomfortable, so I say, "I loved the scene in the lawyer's office."

Surprise lifts her eyebrows. "I wouldn't have guessed you'd like that one in particular."

I stuff my hands in my pockets and shrug. "I like it because I remember it clearly. I guess you thought I'd lost the will to fight for myself, and I admit I kind of had, but it was more than that. I was in awe of you that day, the way you took charge and stood up for me, even when I didn't deserve to have you in my corner. You were passionate, and you spoke from your heart. In a way, it reminds me of your writing. Gregory Decker said you'd make a good activist, but I think writer is more your style. You can slay dragons with your words."

My compliment draws a semi-smile from her. "The pen is mightier than the sword. I'm going to change the characters' names. Just so you know." She tucks her hair behind her ear. "And if there's anything you don't want me to include, you can tell me. I can change stuff around. This is the first draft, which is more me telling the story to myself. The final product will be different."

"How about the guy? Hudson. Can you press the delete button on him?" There's no hiding the jealousy in my tone. I know I should be grateful someone else came along and treated Avery the way she deserved, the way I didn't, but I can't help how envious I feel of him.

She gives me a sympathetic look. "I wondered how you'd feel about that."

Like someone else has been on the receiving end of your touch, and your smiles, and your laughter, and that smirk you get when you know you've made a really good point during an argument but you're trying not to rub it in.

I don't say that, because I gave up the rights to all that, along with so many others. "It wasn't my favorite part," I concede, and this draws a chuckle from her.

Her eyes light up. "I have an idea. How about today we act like we've just met?"

"Really?" With a history like ours, I'm not sure it's possible to put on the blinders, even for a few hours.

"Really," she confirms. "Maybe we can set aside this tension"—she gestures from me to her—"for a little while."

Am I going to argue with her idea? Hell no. I'm going to ride her suggestion until we run out of road.

She offers her hand between us. "I'm Avery. I'm twenty-nine, divorced, and I may or may not become a published author. Only time will tell."

I slide my hand in hers. "I'm Gabriel. I carve and burn wood, and I promise it's not as weird as it sounds. I'm thirty-two, and I got out of prison five months ago." My voice catches at the end. I can't help it.

Avery doesn't falter. She shakes my hand, smiles like the last part of my sentence is neither a shock nor a bother, and is the first to take a step. I fall in beside her.

We ride the Tilt-A-Whirl, the Ferris wheel, and I spend twenty-five dollars winning her a stuffed monkey. We make no mention of the past. Avery drags me to the Zipper, laughing when I eye it cautiously.

"Don't be afraid," she tells me, handing our tickets to the teenager. We climb on and go up, up, up, spinning in the air. Before I close my eyes, I see Avery, laughing with her eyes wide in exhilaration.

Unbelievably, it does feel like we've just met. This person who is laughing and trying fried Oreos and holding on to a fuchsia stuffed monkey? She is new to me.

"You're staring at me," Avery says.

I look away from her as our cage reaches the top position on the ride, and pauses to allow on new riders. "It's hard to believe I'm here, with you. After...everything."

"What do you mean?" Avery pretends not to understand. "We met today." She says it like *come on, get your head in the game.*

"Right," I nod.

The ride is still stopped. I look down, which is really

never a good idea when you're this high up in the air. Below us, the teenager grimaces at the switchboard and scratches his head. He grabs a phone attached to the switchboard, says something, then looks up.

I look at Avery. "I think we might be stuck."

"Very funny," she replies.

I point down. "I'm serious."

She peers over. I watch her take in the scene below. She straightens up, her body tense. "You weren't kidding."

I shake my head. "I wish I were."

"What do we do now?" Panic edges her tone. "Gabriel?"

I like how she says my name and asks me this question, even though I have about as much control and influence over this situation as she does. The fact she's looking to me to solve a problem ignites some biological instinct in me to protect her, to make everything better.

"Folks," a voice blasts through the air. Avery and I look down at a man standing below, holding a bullhorn to his mouth. The teenager stands beside him. "Nothing to worry about, but we're going to stay put for a few minutes while we work out a technical difficulty."

"Nothing to worry about?" Avery scowls. "Easy for him to say. He's not the one dangling in the air in a metal container." She pats her hands on her thighs in rapid succession, her feet bouncing.

I withdraw my phone from my pocket, choose my music app, and pull up a list of my favorites. I hit play, and the first notes drift out into the air. Avery looks over, her hands and feet ceasing their movement. A tiny smile tugs at the corner of her mouth.

"Gabriel and his music," she murmurs. The affection in her tone is clear.

I didn't choose this song on purpose. *Better Man* by Leon Bridges. It's the first in a long list of favorites.

Avery listens, watching me. Her chest moves faster with her breath, and she suddenly says, "Why didn't you come for me five months ago? Why wasn't I your first stop?"

How can I explain it to her? There are a million words I can choose from, but they all fall flat. Instead, I choose a story. "You have a yellow dress with blue flowers printed on it. It has sleeves like a T-shirt, but it's low-cut." Using the pointer fingers on both hands, I demonstrate a deep 'v' going down the front of my chest. "It reaches half-way down your thighs, and you look like an angel when you wear it."

Her eyes widen. "I bought that dress last summer."

My heart beats double time. "You were my first stop."

Her breath comes in short, panicked gasps. She covers her face with her hands, her head shaking back and forth. "You're not supposed to be here, saying all the right things. I'm not supposed to want you to say all the right things. I've moved on."

Gently, I pull her hands from her face.

Tears drip down her cheeks, tumble off her jaw, soak into the fabric of her dress.

I cannot watch her agony and not attempt to soothe it. I was made to love this woman. Closing down the space, I fold her into my body and cradle the back of her head in my palm. My cheek presses to the side of her head, my fingers curling and stretching, slipping through her hair.

Her shoulders hunch forward, as if she could curl in on

herself, and I continue to hold her. Her sobs subside, her quaking chest evens out, but still something rocks us.

It's my body, jerking with silent sobs.

My wife. My Avery. My everything.

"Gabriel." My name on her lips is a mangled whisper.

I pull back to look at her. She wipes away the tears that stick to my eyelashes.

"I came back for you." I need her to know, even if all knowing does is bring her peace. "I went to that place, the one with your favorite flowers. I thought *'she's probably going to use these to slap you.'*" Avery smiles after I say it, but smiles when a person has been crying don't look anything but sad. "I was standing in line, and I looked out the window. There you were, across the street. A hostess was leading you and some guy to an outdoor table. He had his hand on your lower back. He pulled out your chair. Held your hand across the table. Ordered your drink. I remember thinking 'They're comfortable with each other.'" The knife in my heart twists. "You were smiling at him. You looked happy. And I'd already done enough to you. I didn't want to cause more damage."

Avery presses her fingers to her lips as she listens.

I'm replaying the scene in my mind, but it's morphing into an alternate reality, where I cross the street and interrupt the date. Where would we be now, if I'd done that? I don't have a good answer. Maybe we'd be nowhere. Maybe we'd be somewhere.

"Fuck," I murmur regretfully. I tip my head closer, and we're forehead to forehead, nose to nose. Her warm breath streams against me, and she smells of sugar. I wish the sweet smell of her were my only thought, but it's not. I hate myself for what I've done to her, and it's keeping me from being fully in the moment. "Why are you here with me? Why are you letting me be in your presence? Why don't you hate me, Avery?"

"I could never hate you."

"I hate me."

"That's why I can't."

I shake my head. The tip of my nose moves across hers. "You should."

"Don't tell me what to do," she whispers.

She doesn't move. Her lips are an inch from mine, and it would take almost nothing to close that gap. She's waiting for me, and I don't need to be asked twice.

Without warning, the ride moves. Avery tumbles back in her seat. She grimaces and rubs at the back of her head as she looks down. "Guess they fixed it."

I bite my lip and nod.

We're quiet all the way to the bottom. The operator opens the cage door and makes a sideways comment about us behaving ourselves up there. He looks away quickly when neither of us respond.

We walk a few feet from the ride, and Avery stops. She looks up at me. "I need to get back to writing."

I tuck my hands in the pockets of my jeans. "Understood. I guess the game of pretend is over? You don't want to see me again?"

Avery stares at me, and I can't tell what she's thinking. The seconds stretch on, then she nods curtly. She takes a step away, but stops, turning back to me. "You think I should hate you, but let me tell you something I've learned. Once you separate the action from the person, clinging to hate becomes a more arduous task."

She turns, and I watch her walk away. I watch until she

disappears, swallowed up by the crowd of children with dancing balloons, tired adults, teenagers high on life.

I give her a lengthy head start, then I leave too. Being a party of one doesn't sound so great anymore.

———

MOST WEEKS, the faces are the same. Especially in a town that doesn't have a lot to choose from in the way of meetings.

We're seated in a semblance of a circle in a church library. The air smells stale, but also of bitter black coffee and books. Twelve pairs of kind eyes and expectant expressions are on me.

I nod at the room. "I'm Gabriel, and I'm an alcoholic."

"Hello, Gabriel," the group recites.

Alcoholics Anonymous is a condition of my early release. Even if it weren't, I'd attend anyway. For myself. And everyone else in the world.

Two days a week, I can be found in this musty library. Some of the people here I only see when I step foot in this room. Others, I see throughout the week as we carry on with normal life. None of them look like a reformed drunk, whatever that means. Add that lesson to the list of what I've learned over the past few years. Alcoholics can present as functioning adults. Contributing members of society. Some alcoholics may teeter around public sidewalks in the middle of the day gripping a paper bag, but so far I haven't met one.

I've learned the kinder term for alcoholic is 'alcohol use disorder.' Like Avery said yesterday, it's separating the action from the person. 'He's an alcoholic' versus 'He has alcohol use disorder.' I've also learned the symptoms of the disorder vary from person to person, and have varying levels of rapidity and severity. This was all courtesy of group therapy and recently published books I read.

AA is old-school.

Here, in this meeting of people with alcohol use disorder, there is an accountant. A grandfather. A young mother. A veteran of the Vietnam War. A landscaper, librarian, two dentists, a teacher, and a newspaper editor. And me, the former firefighter.

The twelfth person here tonight is a baker.

"Good to see you again, Gabriel," Jane says, approaching me after the meeting has wrapped up.

"You too, Jane. How did the fair treat you?"

"Well. I sold out of everything. I was up most of the night baking enough to be able to open the shop"—she yawns—"this morning."

"By yourself?"

She nods.

"Ask me for help next time that happens. I'm not half bad in a kitchen."

Jane's head tips sideways, her eyes curious. "Speaking of the fair. I saw you with someone."

I nod slowly. "She's my ex-wife."

Jane's eyes widen, but she quickly gets control of her reaction. "Huh. I wouldn't have guessed that."

Jane knows about Avery. Jane knows about everything. "Why is that?" I ask.

Jane stacks the AA booklets on a nearby table. They are there in case someone new comes to the meeting, but that rarely happens. The last time someone here was new, it was me almost five months ago. Jane straightens. "It looked like you were on a date. Judging by your body language, because that's all I could see from under my tent."

Was it obvious I had to glue my hand to my thigh to keep it from straying to Avery's lower back? I try to imagine me and Avery, walking side by side, but I fail. I can only see her from my viewpoint. Brown hair loosely curling over her collarbone, eyelashes dark and thick. "She's in town for another week, working on her book."

"She's a writer?" Jane sounds impressed.

"She is." I nod, pride flowing through me. "She's halfway finished with her first book, and she already has an agent. I've read it," I say, excitement hastening my words. "I've read what she's written so far, and it's good."

Jane gives me a knowing smile. "What's it about?"

"Uh…" I stall, suddenly not sure if I'm supposed to be saying what it's about. "It's a love story."

Kind of. Maybe.

Jane's knowing grin ratchets up to full on know-it-all. "Is that right?"

I see where she's going with this, and I nod.

Another person stops by to say hello to Jane, and I excuse myself. On my way out the door, Jane calls my name.

"People tend to write what they know," she says, with a wink.

CHAPTER 9
AVERY

I'M STUCK.

My manuscript is going nose-down, on its way to a fiery explosion. The right words elude me. Just like real life, I hadn't planned on Gabriel's character returning. Not including it feels untrue, even if this story isn't supposed to be entirely factual. I'd planned on taking the skeleton of our real story and filling it in with fiction. Right now, what I've written is pretty damn close to fact.

Even Jill admitted how good it would be to use this development in the story.

I've recounted seeing Gabriel again, the dog running into my cabin, and the fair yesterday. It's almost as if, by writing about it in this semi-removed way, I get a different view of it all. I control the circumstances, the happenings, and the outcome. Considering I know nothing about what might happen in real life, that control feels good right now.

I get it all down on the page, then sit back, stretching

my arms above my head. I need a break. After a few hours of writing these tense, emotional scenes, I'm left with a pulsing buzz zipping through my veins. I need to move.

I think it's time to explore Sugar Creek.

———

LUCK MUST BE on my side today, because I've found a parking spot at the end of the busiest street in town. I slip my phone and wallet into my back pockets and tuck my purse and laptop under the passenger seat out of big-city habit, likely an unnecessary precaution here.

I browse boutique after boutique, buying a pair of turquoise earrings and a braided leather belt. I thread the earrings through my ears and cinch the belt around my waist, then continue on down the street.

Something sweet hits my nose, growing stronger with every step I take, as if there is sugar floating in the air. I follow the scent to a bakery, the one I saw from my car my first night here. It doesn't look fancy from the outside, but it appears sturdy. Made of brick, like the other storefronts on this street, and glass windows showcasing the treats inside. Passersby know exactly what they're going to get if they go in. It just so happens coffee and a muffin are what I need to refuel and get back to my manuscript.

The door chimes when I step through, and the scent of warm sugar wraps me in a comforting hug.

"I'll be out in a second," a voice from somewhere in the back of the store yells. I'm perusing the cases of muffins and other baked goods when there's a crashing sound from the back, the unmistakable clink of metal hitting the floor.

Cautiously, I round the counter, slowly pushing through the swinging partition to the back. A woman sits on her backside, her hands at her face. A large sheet pan lies sideways on the ground, propped up by her leg. Muffins are strewn around her.

"Can I help you up?" I ask, offering a hand.

She drops her hands from her face and looks at me. Recognition glimmers as she allows me to help her to her feet. "You're Gabriel's wife. Ex-wife," she amends. "Sorry."

I nod to let her know her faux pas is forgiven, but my curiosity rages. Who is this woman who seems to know about Gabriel? And me?

She wipes her palms on her backside and surveys the mess on the floor. "I didn't sleep much last night. Guess I'm just a little clumsy today."

She kneels, and I follow, retrieving the scattered muffins. We load them onto the sheet pan, and she slides the entirety into a nearby trash, a forlorn look on her face. "I got up an hour early to make those." She tucks the pan under her arm and looks back at me. "If you'd like to take a seat out there"—she gestures to the front of the store—"I'll be by in a moment with a coffee and a muffin. Does that sound ok?"

"Lovely," I respond, making my way out to a small round table. The woman approaches a few minutes later, tray laden with two saucers and cups, a white porcelain creamer and coffee carafe, and two warm muffins.

I help her set down the cups and saucers, and she arranges the rest. "One is cinnamon spice, the other blueberry." She points at each muffin. "Take your pick, and I'll have the other."

I reach for the blueberry and nibble at the side, sighing at the incredible flavor. "You made this?"

"Yes." She takes the empty seat across from me. "Everyone chooses the blueberry. Except for Gabriel. He asks for whatever needs to be sold." Her grin holds the affection of a mother.

I reach for the cup. "I don't mean to sound rude or anything, but…who are you?"

She smiles in this slow and patient way, and says, "My name is Jane. This is my bakery."

"And you know Gabriel?"

Her cup pauses at her lower lip. She nods. "He's only been here a short time, but he's slipped into the workings of this place like he was a part we've been missing all along and didn't know it."

"How do you know him? Because he comes in here?" I have this sudden desire, this insistent nudging, to know more about Gabriel. Who he is today, the person he has become.

She nods again. "That, and he helps me when he can. He chopped firewood for me this past winter. He'd said he'd never done it before, but he caught on quickly. After that he came by every other week and did it. Sometimes I arrived home and it was there, neatly stacked, waiting for me. And Joel"—she waves a hand—"he's really helping out Joel."

"How so?"

"He works for Joel's business, but I don't think he knows what that's doing for the man. And his wife. Their son died thirty years ago in the Gulf War. I think they've been slowly dying ever since then, too. Gabriel…" Her head shakes slowly, teeth running over her lower lip. "He fills a void."

I have a strong sense she's not only talking about Joel and his wife anymore.

My thumb traces the rim of my coffee cup. "Gabriel is a very good man."

That's never not been true. Even at his worst, he was good. Bad decisions are not the property of bad people.

"He's finding his footing. I'm happy to see that."

A stab of jealousy cuts through my chest. Gabriel is out in the world, muddling through and figuring out who he is now. He's learning to chop firewood, working with his passion, and choosing near-expiration muffins. And he's doing it without me.

I blink against my own thoughts, confused by them. I've known I still love Gabriel, but I told myself it was in that way where, once you've recovered from the heartbreak, you think of them with a nostalgic fondness. This doesn't feel fond. Or nostalgic. It is sharper, more combative.

I do not know what to do with it.

I sip my coffee. "Do you know much about me and Gabriel?"

"He's been open with me. Or as open as he wants to be, I suppose."

This surprises me. The Gabriel I knew kept his hurt close to his chest. "How open?"

Jane smooths back her hair, runs her fingers across the top of her opposite palm, shifts in her seat. Her obvious discomfort throws fuel on my curiosity.

"That question is better asked of Gabriel. I don't want to betray a confidence."

I try not to frown as I bite into my muffin. I'm glad she's being respectful of Gabriel, but it's getting in the way of me understanding more about him. About why he would confide in Jane, and what he's told her.

"Are you married, Jane?" Her ring finger is bare, but she works with food. She likely doesn't wear it when she bakes.

She sweeps an arm around the shop. "Sure I am. To this bakery."

I huff a soft laugh. "That's not what I meant."

"Once upon a time, I was married." Something in her eyes recedes, like a waterline pulling away from the shore. There's a vacancy there, a haunting, something she tries hard to suppress. I haven't known her long enough to draw such a conclusion, but it's obvious to me, this pain she wears on the inside.

"Do you want to talk about it?" My register drops, getting deeper and softer, measured. I may not practice therapy anymore, but that way of thinking is never too far. I see now that it wasn't just the job, but me. Listening and problem solving is a core part of who I am.

Jane shakes her head. "Some problems simply exist, and that's all there is to it. Talking about them won't help."

"Talking about them almost always helps."

"Who?" Jane's eyebrows lift. "Who does it help? It can't help the victim if it's the victimizer doing the talking."

Interesting. It sounds as if Jane has slotted herself in the offensive role. I don't love the term 'victimizer' because it's more commonly used to describe someone who's committed a crime, but since Jane's used it I'll roll with it. "The victimizer doesn't deserve to be heard?"

Jane eyes me. As I watch, the curtains she uses to keep herself from being seen too deeply fall into place. The pain she keeps inside goes back the way it came, and a light filters into her gaze. She is the muffin lady again.

Jane sweeps crumbs off the table into her waiting cupped palm. "You're an author? From Phoenix?"

I say nothing about the abrupt subject change. "I'm not an author yet," I answer. "I'm not published. And yes, I'm from Phoenix."

"Sure hot down there." Jane tosses her muffin liner in the trash.

I don't think Jane wants to talk about the searing heat of summer. I dip my chin a fraction, the way Dr. Ruben used to, a way of silently acknowledging what I'd said without giving it too much attention. I stay quiet, and I wait, and after a few seconds of silence, I'm rewarded with, "I used to live there. Smack dab in the center of the city. Not that it's much of a city"—she raises a hand in a vertical line, indicating tall buildings—"but you know what I mean."

"I do." I finish my last bite of muffin. "Did you own a bakery there?"

"No." She chuckles, as if the idea is absurd.

"What did you do?"

She stares at my chest, but I don't think she's seeing me. Her eyes gloss over, and she takes an odd-sounding breath, like she's suppressing a sob. Her eyes meet mine. "You're good," she says, pointing a shaking finger at me. "Gabriel said you were."

"I'm not practicing anymore." I swallow the last of my coffee.

"It doesn't seem like you need an office to practice."

A smile tugs up one side of my mouth. "Once a therapist…"

Jane takes my empty cup. I throw away my liner and my napkin. "Thank you for the coffee and muffin, Jane."

"My pleasure. It was nice to put a face to the name. I've heard a lot about you."

"I hope that's a good thing," I joke.

She places a hand on my upper arm. It's warm, comforting. My mother's young face flashes through my mind. "It is, honey. It really is."

I say goodbye and go back to my car. I'm walking quickly, because I've been struck by something precious and fleeting.

Inspiration.

———

I HADN'T PLANNED to work from my car for two hours, but that's what I did.

I wrote two thousand words, and good ones, too. Not words that'll be deleted later in favor of something snappier, wittier, more succinct.

I stretch out my fingers, my hands, my wrists. They are sore in the best way.

Children play at the park across the street. I'm parked in a church parking lot, under the shade of a tree. My windows are down, and a breeze streams through my car.

Now that I'm not focused on writing, Jane rolls through my mind. I can see why Gabriel thinks well of her. She's interesting. While it's not uncommon for most people to carry a burden, Jane's seems different. Heavier, more far-reaching. She has cast herself in the role of villain.

Why? Why is she here, spending her life alone? Why did she leave Phoenix?

And then there's Gabriel. All this time I thought I was writing about him in past tense, and one day, that ceased to be true.

I'm drawn to him. It's that simple. Despite everything that has happened between us. Why is it I want to go toward the source of pain? Shouldn't I be running the other way?

Right now, sitting here in this car after talking to Jane and writing, I want Gabriel. I want his touch, the way he'd curl a knuckle and run it down my arm, or cup the back of my neck and draw me to his mouth. I want his smile, his introspective gaze, his eyes that see into my soul. I want my life back. I want my husband back.

But my husband doesn't exist anymore.

Gabriel experienced a significant, life-altering event. Firefighting Gabriel who put everybody else's happiness before his own is now Woodworking Gabriel who lives in a small town and I have no idea what he does with his happiness.

Maybe that's why I'm drawn to him, even when it seems like I shouldn't be. He's someone new, an iteration of the man I didn't think I could breathe properly without.

Maybe, if Gabriel were still the man he once was, it would be easier to stay away from him. I could use the past to inform the future, learn the way most humans learn. By experience.

But he's not. This version of Gabriel is better than the previous. Likely subtle to others, but glaringly obvious to me, this new Gabriel seems content. Less internal chaos, more peace with who he is as a person. Still one to do good for others, but not at the expense of himself.

The corners of my mouth creep up, and instead of resisting, I let it happen. Let that warm, cozy feeling reverberate through my chest. Let myself contemplate the question forming in my mind.

Can I fall in love with the same person a second time?

CHAPTER 10
GABRIEL

Joel walks into the room as I'm carefully packing a custom bookshelf.

"How goes it?" He watches me wind packing paper around the piece and secure it with heavy duty tape.

"Everything is good. I should be able to get the truck packed up and sent off before the snow makes an appearance."

Ernie, the truck driver who transports our large pieces across the state, paces twenty yards out from the building. He lifts a hand in greeting, a cigarette dangling from his lips.

Joel waves back. "Can't believe it was nice enough to wear shorts last weekend, and now it's going to snow."

"I guess the weather changed her mind." As I say it, I think of Avery. We're not supposed to get so much snow that it should be a problem, but Avery is a desert girl. The most she's dealt with snow is seeing it on the tops of the mountains north of the city.

"Might as well take tomorrow off," Joel says. He disappears into his office and comes back with a small box. "Kimberley said to give this to you."

I smile and take the box. "What did she make this time?"

"Cookies, I believe."

"Tell her I said thank you."

"She knows you're thankful."

I scratch at my eyebrow with my thumbnail. "I'm still going to say it."

Joel claps a hand on my shoulder. "I heard you and a beautiful woman were stuck at the top of a ride last weekend at the fair."

Small-town life. I switch the box to my other hand. "Avery and I were on a ride when it stopped working."

"That right there"—he points at my chest—"is why I don't ride roller coasters."

"It wasn't a roller coaster, but I agree. I like to keep my feet planted somewhere."

"You and Avery, huh?"

I nod. I'm not sure what to say next.

"I don't know a lot of people who go on rides with their exes."

"She doesn't know anybody else in this town."

He eyes me. "Something tells me she'd still choose you even if she knew every single person in this place."

My neck grows warm, and I hope the thrill I feel at his comment doesn't show on my face. "Maybe you should spend the snow day writing poetry to Kimberley."

Joel laughs, a hearty guffaw that shakes his broad chest. "Maybe I will." He steps away, signaling to Ernie that we're ready to load the piece. "Maybe I will," he echoes.

We get the truck packed and sent off, then Joel says we should call it a night. I stop at the grocery store and pick up a few items. I'm not sure if Avery knows snow is coming, so I grab a few things for her, too. She might not even like this stuff anymore, but I buy it anyway.

On my way home, I talk myself out of it. I haven't seen her since last weekend at the fair. She knows exactly where to find me, and she stays away. Am I supposed to do that, too?

It takes all my strength, but I force myself to drive past her cabin, where her car is parked out front.

I force myself to unpack the groceries.

I force myself to make dinner, watch a movie, take a long shower, and go to bed.

I don't attempt to keep her from my mind. The strength of the world could not suspend the memory of her.

———

THE FORECASTERS WERE WRONG.

The snow came earlier than expected, and it's falling quickly. I've been watching the sky since I woke up a few hours ago, waiting to see if it's going to run its course early. Judging by the blue-gray clouds blanketing the sky, I don't think that will be the case.

I pull on my heavy waterproof coat, my boots, and my beanie. On my way out the door I grab my gloves, and Avery's groceries.

CHAPTER 11
AVERY

I DIDN'T KNOW ABOUT THE SNOW UNTIL LATE LAST NIGHT, when I checked the weather app just before I fell asleep.

"What do you think?" I ask Ruby. She's looking up at me, eyes excited as her tail slaps at the table legs, making loud, thumping sounds. "Do you know how to manage snow?"

Ruby spins in a circle, as if to say *Yes.*

I grab the one jacket I brought with me and shove my arms through. I don't have boots, but I have tennis shoes, and those will have to do.

As soon as Ruby is done going potty, I'll run into town and grab groceries. I'm out of nearly everything except coffee, and while coffee is vital, I also need food.

"Come on." I motion for Ruby to come with me. She races to the back door, making it there first.

A blast of arctic air smacks me in the face when I open it. "Sweet Jesus," I hiss, my breath taking shape in front of me. "That is sharp."

Ruby bounds outside. I stand in the doorway and watch her. There's no way I'm going out there with her.

The fallen snow covers Ruby's favorite spots, so she has to make a big production and reacquaint herself with the landscape. I wait, teeth chattering.

Ruby lifts her head, ears pointed, her body at attention. She pauses, listening, then takes off running at full speed.

I call her name, but it's useless. "Dammit," I mutter, hurrying down the stairs. The snow is soft, my tennis shoes falling through as if it's made of marshmallow. I follow Ruby around the house, then freeze in place.

Gabriel lifts a grocery bag in the air, keeping it away from a bounding Ruby. He hasn't seen me yet, so I take the time to drink him in. He's laughing, and wearing a beanie and boots, and dammit if he doesn't look so at home in this setting. Mountain man looks good on him. Sexy, in fact.

He looks up, and his gaze finds mine. I wave. So does he.

"What are you doing outside?" he calls, frowning slightly as he closes his car door with his foot and walks closer. "You're not wearing a coat."

Seeing Gabriel made me forget I'm cold, but now I've remembered and my toes are curling in my shoes, my shaking arms crossed over my chest.

Gabriel meets me in front of the house. Snowflakes land on his shoulders and hat. And in his eyelashes. One on his lower lip. My stomach twirls, butterflying. My heart trips, flips, explodes.

"Come inside," I manage, leading the way to the front door.

Gabriel follows, and Ruby, the traitor, traipses along

beside him. I watch as Gabriel toes off his boots and makes his way to the kitchen. "I was at the grocery store last night and picked up some stuff for you."

I pause, taken aback. "What? Really?"

He shrugs, like it's not a really sweet thing to do. "You might not like these things anymore. It's ok if you don't, I just thought…" he trails off.

I walk to the bag he's set on the counter and unload the items.

Pre-sliced apples.

String cheese.

Smoked almonds.

Chips and salsa.

Gabriel watches me. "Do you still eat any of that?"

"All of it." It's hard to explain what I feel in this moment.

Known.

That's the best word I can think of, and even that falls short.

Seen.

Loved.

That last one takes my breath away. To cover it up, I busy myself putting the cheese and apples in the fridge, and everything else in the pantry.

I turn back to look at Gabriel. "Thank y—" The gratitude dies on my lips. Gabriel stands in the middle of the small kitchen, arms crossed in front of his chest, legs slightly wider than his hips. His presence fills the space, his signature smell invading my nose. There's no way to describe Gabriel's scent. He doesn't smell of body wash, or cologne, or masculine deodorant. My attraction to his scent is biological, and on another level. Apparently, time has not affected it. If anything, it has increased. Perhaps that, too, is biological.

I duck my head, forcing my eyes to find another subject. The corner of the kitchen floor will do. Even better, a piece of dried pasta that never made it into the pot of boiling water last night.

Gabriel backs up until he meets the edge of the kitchen counter. The smell dips fractionally, and I become brave enough to test the air.

Much safer. My head clears with my next breath, and I try again. "I appreciate you bringing all that by. I'm low on food, and I was going to make a run to the store."

Gabriel thumbs outside. "You were going to drive in that?"

I look out the window, to where the snow falls steadily. "Umm…yes?" It's clear what a bad idea that would have been.

Gabriel doesn't speak, but he nods his head slowly. "Well, now you don't have to." He pushes off the counter, thumbs hooking in his pockets. "I'll see you around, Avery."

"Wait." My arm shoots out to stop him. "Are you going to drive in that?"

He stares at me for a full two seconds, a smile playing on his lips, then says, "I drove in that to get here. And I've lived here for a winter now, so I have some practice."

"Right," I nod. My clasped hands bounce on my thighs. "It's just that, there's a lot of chips and salsa, and almonds, and I can't eat them by myself." What am I doing? Why am I doing it? I know better.

Gabriel's hopeful expression makes the wrong feel right. "No?"

I shake my head. "No."

He reaches up, sliding the beanie off his head and running a hand through his hair. It tumbles into messy waves. "Do they have any games?"

My eyebrows pinch. "They?"

"The owners of this place? It's a rental, right?"

"Yes, yes." My head bobs, clearing out the cobwebs. "I found a game cabinet my second night here." I leave the kitchen, which means I have to pass Gabriel. I sail six inches from him, and he doesn't move. No wide berths found here.

There's a small cupboard in the dining room. It's stacked, from bottom to top, with games. I open it and step aside so he can see.

Gabriel comes closer. He sinks down, balancing on the balls of his feet, and peers into the cabinet. "I know better than to suggest Monopoly."

He's right. I despise the game.

Gabriel stands, a pack of cards in his hands. "War?"

I clear off the dining room table, pushing aside my notes, and my laptop.

"Are you making progress on the book?" Gabriel asks, shuffling the cards.

I sit down and draw my knees into my chest. "I've written a few more chapters."

"I'm curious to know what happens next."

I watch his hands deftly arrange the cards into a neat pile. "It appears the story is going in an unexpected direction."

Gabriel swallows hard. "Why is that?"

"Plot twist." I bite the side of my lip. "The main character's ex-husband showed up out of nowhere."

Gabriel splits the deck in two. "That changes the story?"

"It's starting to look like it might." It may be a stupid thing to say. Should I be giving hope to Gabriel? It's hard not to, when I feel the tiniest flicker of hope igniting in me, too. The more I write the story, the more I see what's possible. The difficulty is in all the ground the characters will have to cover. How much hurt there is to unpack. And, ultimately, forgive.

Gabriel holds out my cards, and our fingers touch when I take them. It's not an electricity I feel, but a pull. I'm drawn to him in a way that doesn't make sense. It surpasses everything I know about attraction, and brain chemicals, and trained responses. It wipes out my fancy degree, my hundreds of hours of studying and researching, thousands of hours in my previous career, and leaves it at its most basic level. This connection between me and Gabriel just *is*. It exists. As essential as food, air, and water. Nothing we know about why it's there can fully encompass that it is there at all.

"So your story," Gabriel says, setting his cards on the table in front of him. I do the same. "Do you know the ending?"

"No." I flip over my first card. A nine.

Gabriel does the same. A two. We keep going.

"Do you have a sense of what it will be?"

I shake my head. "There are a few possibilities. I have to think about what I want for the main character. Is she supposed to move forward on her own, or find love? With who? A man? Which one?"

"Which one?" A muscle in Gabriel's jaw tics. "I'd hoped he was temporary."

I'm not sure what to say. Hudson may not have been permanent, but he was important. To my heart, and my growth as a human. I can't deny that.

It's my turn, so I flip over my next card.

"So, Hudson, huh? The guy from your book." Gabriel's tone has lost all warmth. "Is that his real name?"

"Yes." I'm trying not to like his jealous tone, but it's useless. I do. I like it very much.

"Is he the man I saw you with that day? At the restaurant?" Gabriel lays down a seven.

"Yes." I flip over my next card. A seven. Time to battle. I lay out three cards. Gabriel does the same. Neither of us lays a fourth card, the way we're supposed to. Gabriel stares at me.

"You cared for another man." He sounds heartbroken and indignant, but it's an empty indignation. Like he knows it's true, but still can't believe it.

I stare back at him. "You let me go, remember? You weren't my husband when I met Hudson. You aren't my husband now."

Gabriel's lower lip tugs with an emotion I can't name. "You're always going to be mine, Avery. I'm always going to be yours. I don't need a piece of paper or a ring to tell me that." He taps two fingers over his heart. "It's in here."

I can't wrap my brain around his words. His facial expression. It sets loose a roller coaster of emotions in me. Buried amongst it all is a twinge of pleasure.

"Then why? Why give me up? If I'm always going to be yours, why let me go at all?"

Gabriel flips over his next card and lays it down. A queen. "Where is Hudson now?"

I flinch at his subject change. "I'm not sure."

"You're not together?"

"He broke up with me. He said he needed space." Hudson was right to protect himself. If he was sick of competing with a ghost, how would he feel knowing the ghost took human form?

"What did he need space from?" Gabriel's upper lip curls, his tone communicating how little he already thinks of Hudson.

"My…" I search for the right word. It's not easy. "Preoccupation."

"With what? Writing?"

I swallow the boulder in my throat, shaking my head back and forth and lifting my gaze to meet his.

Gabriel nods slowly, understanding. I proceed with the game, flipping over a fourth card.

An ace.

Gabriel pushes all the cards my way. "You win."

It's an interesting word, considering we've both been losers for years. "There isn't a winner." I sound bitter. I feel bitter.

The muscles in Gabriel's jaw clench. "When are you going to let yourself be mad at me?"

I frown. "Of course I'm mad at you. I've never not been mad at you."

Gabriel shakes his head. "I don't just mean angry with me and my choices. I mean irate. Red-hot, fucking fury."

I know what he means. I felt it. When I found him passed out drunk in St. Lucia. When I got the call about his accident. When he divorced me without laying eyes on me. The fury filled my organs, spread throughout my body and singed my veins. I'd pushed it away, because I didn't want to feel it. Didn't want to feel something so powerful and ugly toward someone I loved more than myself.

Shouldn't he be grateful I haven't acted on this feeling? "Why do you want me to hate you? To be irate?"

Gabriel pushes up his sleeves, eyebrows drawn like he's trying to work out what he wants to say. "You used to look at me like I was a hero. Like you knew I could keep you safe. Your human shield. From bad guys, from pain. Then the look in your eyes changed. I was the one causing you pain. And you pitied me. I wanted your anger, your hatred, even disgust with the way I was acting. Anything but your pity. I couldn't take it. Your compassion was suffocating, because I didn't deserve it."

"My compassion suffocated you?" How can a person's mercy and kindness suffocate someone?

I push my cards aside and stand up. "You want some fury? Here it is. It's bullshit that you can call out my compassion as your reason for letting me go." I smack a palm on the table. "Do you think you're the only person in this world who has been looked at with pity? Because you're not." Even now, chest heaving with heavy breath, I see the people at my mother's funeral. My teachers making special exceptions knowing my mother had passed away. The neighbors inviting me and Camryn to eat dinner at their house because they knew my dad would work late and we were alone.

And then, of course, the pity on everybody's face after Gabriel went to prison. Cam, Dani, Joseph, my dad. Everyone I knew wore the same expression. The only person who didn't look at me that way was Gabriel, because he caused it all, but I can only imagine that—

Oh, my God.

Even remembering it, I feel small. Tiny. Isolated. Like a person without power or agency.

I'm Gabriel, and…

…I'm afraid to go home and face my wife.

…I have hit someone with my vehicle, and injured them.

…I have hurt my beloved spouse beyond measure.

…they refuse to be angry with me, even when it's impossible for them not to be.

…they choose to pity me.

…I feel ashamed and pathetic.

…and I hate it.

"I am mad at you." My voice wobbles. Dr. Ruben told me I'd have to deal with this, but I didn't think it would be in this form, in a moment that looks like this. "How dare you? How fucking dare you take my marriage from me? It was mine, and your addiction ruined it."

My hands tremble. I must look like a crazed woman, overtaken by her emotion. I gesture up and down the length of my body. "Is this what you want from me?"

Gabriel stands, rounding the table and placing his hands on my shoulders.

"I want whatever you feel." His gaze is intense, imploring me. "That's all I wanted back then, I just didn't know how to ask for it. I was buried in my own self-hatred. I still am in some ways, but I'm trying. I really am."

I look into those dark eyes, trying to understand Gabriel. What he experienced back then. What he's experiencing now.

"I'm sorry, Avery." His voice reverberates with meaning. "I can't take it back, and I'll never stop being sorry. It kills me to know I hurt you."

"You did so much more than hurt me. I wanted a life and a family with you. You tore apart my dreams."

Gabriel only nods, accepting everything I'm sending his way. This is what he wanted from me. My acknowledgment that he split my life into pieces. What good is it doing for him, though? He knew all this already, even when I refused to say it. He knew what he did, how he shattered everything.

This is for me.

Gabriel is asking me to walk through my pain and offering himself up as a target for fury I did not want to feel toward him.

Something else rises through these unpleasant emotions. A tiny memory, poking its way out from the recesses of my brain, something I learned when I was researching longevity in marriages.

My throat is too damn dry to speak, so I go to the kitchen for a drink of water. It gives me time to think. Gabriel's eyes are on me as I go. Snow falls fast outside the kitchen window.

I return with water for both of us, and hand one to him. "Have you ever heard of a near enemy?"

He drinks all his water and sets the empty glass on the table, then shakes his head.

I lean against the edge of the table and cross my legs at the ankles. "It's a concept in Buddhist psychology. It refers to a mental state that mimics a positive emotion but actually undermines it." I feel sadness creep onto my face. "Pity is a near enemy of compassion." I drink half my glass of water, then set it down beside his. "I'm sorry I pitied you."

"You have nothing to be sorry for, Avery. The fault is all mine."

I shake my head at his words. "There's more. I didn't take you seriously when you told me you didn't drink. I drank with you when Ryan died. I got drunk with you. I shouldn't have agreed to that. I should've known better."

Gabriel steps in front of me. His hands go to my shoulders, his gaze insistent. "That was not your fault. That was all me."

"I contributed to that. I was complicit. Maybe you would have done it anyway, if I'd said no. We'll never know. But I have to own my part."

Gabriel leans his forehead to mine. His breath is a warm stream against my lips, the tip of his nose nuzzles mine. "I'll never stop being sorry for what I did to us."

"I know."

We stay that way, absorbing one another's emotions.

Apologies.

Sorrows.

And, eventually, desires.

It's me. I move first. My palms find their way to his chest, then spread out to his arms, sliding up until my hands are running through his hair.

My heart settles in, returned to its rightful place at long last.

Gabriel takes a deep breath. His hands leave my shoulders, slipping down over my back, hauling me in until I'm flush against him. His lips hover over mine.

"Say the word, Avery." The low growl of his voice washes over me. "Tell me this is what you want."

"I want you. This. Us. I want it."

He kisses me, and something inside me awakens. I thought I'd moved on, but I see how wrong that was. There is no moving on from Gabriel. There is only a reshaping, making room for today, this moment.

I press against him, desperate for every inch of me to touch every inch of him. All my waiting, all my wanting, at long last relieved. My fingers dig into his coiled back muscles as I settle into our kiss. He tastes like old times, and I cannot get enough of him.

He groans into my mouth, as equally famished for me as I am for him, and the reverberation travels down my throat.

All the way into my heart.

Deep down to my soul.

CHAPTER 12
GABRIEL

The only kind of addiction I'll ever have again.

Avery. Her skin, her taste, her touch, her scent. I want to drown in it.

I know her by heart, but somehow she is new.

Her gasp when I tip her head back is committed to memory, but the first time I've heard it.

Her soft moan when I press my lips to her neck is imprinted on my soul, but the vibration has never been felt before.

Her heavy-lidded gaze when I bring my mouth down on her is tattooed on my heart, but the sight of it feels like another beginning.

I lift Avery, setting her down on the table without breaking our kiss. Her arms wrap around my neck, fingers dragging through my hair.

I work my way down to her jaw, kissing a path over the ridge that leads to her throat. She tilts her chin up, giving me access. Dragging my lips along the delicate length of her neck, I pause when I feel her pulse, racing beneath the tip of my tongue.

I groan at the feeling of this vital part of Avery, so exposed to me. Fuck. I fucking love this woman.

Avery responds to my groan by pushing into me, pressing her breasts against my chest, eliciting from me a groan that sounds half-crazed.

"I'm trying to take it slow," I murmur, running my tongue over her collarbone. Honestly, I don't know if I can. It doesn't feel possible right now. I've waited so long for this moment I thought I'd never have again.

Avery's fingers curl in my hair as my lips skim lower. "I don't want you to take it slow," she says raggedly. "I want you to fuck me like you used to."

Her words have me pausing, my lips hovering at the top of her breasts. I lift my gaze to find hers already on me. I know she's thinking what I'm thinking, about all the times I encouraged her to speak up and say what she wanted from me when we were intimate.

Here she is now, doing what I asked of her.

The least I can do is exactly what she's asking of me.

Avery reaches down, dipping her hand into my waistband, gripping me. I work her shirt over her head, kissing her neck while unclasping her bra. I mutter an expletive at the sight of her, and she smiles.

"I won't last long if you keep that up," I murmur, looking down between us. "The last time with you was the last time."

Understanding dawns, and she slows but doesn't let me go. "Take them off," she instructs. "My leggings. Take them off."

I peel them away, along with her underwear. She

releases me and lies back on the table, wincing at the hard wood against her back. I shake my head. "Bedroom. We deserve a bed." I bend over and scoop her up, and she wraps her legs around me. She is wet and warm against my stomach. Palming her backside, I lift her up an inch, down an inch, over and over. She whimpers the softest, sweetest little moans into my ear and hangs on to me.

The sound of her, my Avery, making noises I know by heart is nearly enough to finish me right then.

It takes everything I have to hold off. I manage to get her down the hall and into her bedroom, inching her up and down my midsection the entire way.

Her hair fans out around her when I lay her on the bed, and my breath sticks in my throat at the sight of her, naked and rosy-cheeked and *here*.

Avery is here, with me.

"What?" she asks.

I shake my head in disbelief. "You… You're stunning. You take my breath away. That's what you do. You always have."

Her eyes shine. Her lips curl into a smile.

I crawl up onto the bed, kissing her, kissing my way down her body, kissing my way to the apex of her thighs.

"Gabriel," she whispers, her hands in my hair. Every inch of this woman's body has a place in my memory, but especially right here. This is my woman, *my wife*, and I know exactly how to make pleasured cries sing from her lips.

That's what I do, until she's squirming and twisting, and I'm smiling against her.

"Need you," she manages to say. "Right now. Please."

I crawl up her body. She runs her hands over my chest,

my abdomen, around to my back. Her gaze locks on mine as I come over her, holding my weight with my forearm as I reach between us. She reaches with me, her hand wrapping over mine as I guide myself to her.

She gasps at that first inch, then wraps her legs around my lower back and urges me along, until there's no part of me that isn't inside her.

My forehead drops to hers. "Fuck," I groan.

"I know," she whispers. "I feel you…*everywhere.*"

This woman. She is a part of me, an extension, to a point where I cannot tell where I end and she begins.

Each movement, every stroke, is better than the last, and I wish I could press a pause button and linger in this moment with her.

"Come," Avery whispers. "I know you need to."

Supporting myself on my forearms, I wind my fingers into her hair and run my thumbs over her cheeks.

She waits until she knows I'm coming, then she captures my lips and kisses me through the crescendo.

When my orgasm ebbs, I stay where I am, dotting her face with soft kisses.

I don't know what she's ready to hear, so with my body I tell her I love her.

I issue her a promise.

I will never, ever again be the person responsible for hurting you.

CHAPTER 13

AVERY

My feet, cocooned in my fluffiest socks, pad over the scratched wood floor and into the kitchen. Ruby gets up from where she was sleeping in the living room and leans against my thigh, asking for an early dinner.

"Might as well," I say to her, giving her a belly rub and filling her bowl.

While she eats, I prepare a pot of coffee. It's mid-afternoon, but the snow outside leaves me wanting something warm to drink.

The coffee brews, Ruby eats, and I lean against the kitchen sink, staring mindlessly at the world beyond the window. Like a television with just one channel, the only thing playing in my brain right now is Gabriel.

A part of me is shocked at what happened between us. A larger part of me is more shocked that I'm shocked at all.

What does it mean?

Should it mean something?

Should it mean nothing?

I'd been the one to knock down the metaphorical dam. *I want you. This. Us.*

What about—

"Overthinking."

I turn. Gabriel stands in the entrance to the kitchen, leaning against the wall. His hair is mussed from our post-coital nap, his eyes not yet fully open. "You're over-thinking."

"I don't know how not to." The coffee gives a final whir, and I busy myself pouring two cups. "I hope you feel like afternoon coffee. I want something to warm my core. Kind of chilly in here." I shudder to prove my point.

"I'd love a cup," he says, his tone warm and sated. His gaze is on me, and I feel it deep down, bypassing my skin and diving straight into my heart. "What were you thinking about? Your shoulder blades were pinched together."

"What do you think I was thinking about?" We both know what had my shoulders drawn, but are we ready to name it?

He reaches past me, grabbing the coffees and carrying them to the couch. He sets them on the coffee table, then starts toward the fireplace. The logs are in place, but I'm clueless as to how to build or start a fire, so I haven't touched it.

Gabriel palms the mantel. "Do you want me to get this started?"

"Yes, please." I settle on the couch, tucking my legs under me. "You're good at that," I comment, as Gabriel rearranges the logs and drops a lit match from a box on the mantel.

He turns around and gives me this look, part pleasure at my compliment and part flirtation. "I can put out fires, and start them."

I say nothing of his euphemism, but I can't control the smirk appearing on my lips. The fire pops, the flames beginning their ascent up the split wood. He backs away, retrieving his coffee cup and handing me mine before settling beside me.

"Do you want to talk about…" He points toward the bedroom. "Or should we pretend it didn't happen?" His voice is strained, and I wonder if he knows he's frowning. "Call it a mistake? A moment of passion?"

I study the droop of his shoulders as he prepares himself to hear me backpedal. "Why are you giving me an out?"

"In case you need it. In case you want it," he adds.

"I don't need or want it." I sip from my coffee, then admit, "I don't know how to label us sleeping together. I only know how not to label it."

He nods slowly. "I can accept that."

Ruby comes to sit between our legs. She props her head on the couch and gives me her 'I need to go outside' look.

"Ruby has needs," I say, setting my cup on the table and standing.

Gabriel gets up with me. "I'll get out of your hair."

"No," I say quickly. It's the second time today I've discouraged him from leaving. "I mean, if you don't have anything more to do, you should stay. Keep me and Ruby company."

Gabriel smiles. "I would love that." He glances out the

window. "There's enough snow to sled. The owners have sleds somewhere around here. I've seen people using them."

I don't know what constitutes enough snow to sled, but it sounds like fun. "You lead the way," I say, gesturing outside.

Gabriel looks for the sleds, while I get dressed in more appropriate attire. I grin at the bed when I walk in the room. It's rumpled, and the sheets are tossed aside. Gabriel never did like making the bed.

I pull on jeans over my leggings, and a sweatshirt over a long-sleeve shirt. I find Gabriel in the one-car garage. There isn't space for a vehicle, because it's packed with other things. Bicycles, an old dresser, and a disassembled bed.

"Found them," Gabriel announces, holding up a bright red sled. A burnt orange sled leans against his leg.

He carries both out the back door, Ruby at his heels. She doesn't know what's going on, but she's here for it.

I grab my jacket from the back of a chair and pull it on as I follow Gabriel out. I make a sound when I step out, something unintelligible. It's cold.

Gabriel looks back at me. He pulls his beanie from his pocket and slides it over his head. "Do you have a hat?"

I shake my head and tuck my hands into my under-arms. "It's April. I thought I was safe from snow."

Gabriel pulls off his beanie in one swift movement and hands it to me. "Wear this."

"What about you?"

He dismisses my question with a small head shake, as if there is no way he'll wear a hat when I don't have one.

I slip the fabric over my head while I follow Gabriel around the house, to a spot between our cabins.

He tosses the sleds on the ground and looks back at me. "You ready for this?"

"Will you show me how to do it?"

"All you need to know is to lean one way or the other to direct where you go. I'll go first."

Gabriel sits down on the orange sled and pushes off. Toward the lake he goes, sliding to a stop twenty feet from the waters' edge. He rolls over on the sled and looks up at me. "Come on," he yells.

I copy what Gabriel did, pressing my palms into the soft snow and pushing.

Air whooshes past my head. I'm probably not going as fast as I think I'm going, but it's exhilarating. The cold bites at my cheeks, and my bare fingers.

"Lean left," Gabriel yells, hands cupped around his mouth.

I do as he says, but it's too late. I'm heading straight for him, and he scoots out of the way with only a second to spare before I hit his sled and am dumped on my back in the snow.

Cold seeps through my clothes as if they're not there at all. I cover my face with my arm, laughing and blushing. Gabriel's feet crunch through the snow, and he drops down beside me. I lower my forearm enough to peek out. Gabriel's on bent knee, smiling down at me.

"I crashed."

He chuckles. "You sure did."

My lower lip juts out, and he taps it with one finger. I capture his finger between my teeth, biting down gently. His eyes darken, his face heats.

The frigid air changes. I stop feeling the cold, and instead feel the intense desire to have Gabriel again. Right this second.

Apparently, Gabriel can read my mind. He pulls off his coat, laying it down on the snow. He guides me to lie down on it, and I don't feel the cold at my back anymore. His coat is far more suited to the weather than mine.

On my back, with my leggings and jeans pulled down just enough for him to gain access, he slips inside me. The heat generated by our bodies is enough to warm me, but Gabriel worries about me anyway.

"Are you cold? Should we stop?" His lips press to my neck as he questions me.

"No, no, don't stop," I whisper. "I'm perfect."

Gabriel looks into my eyes. The tip of his nose nuzzles mine. His weight is balanced on one forearm, and with the other he strokes my cheek.

Somewhere above us, birds emerge from their shelters, and begin to call to one another. Between parted clouds the sun peeks out, sending its rays across the snow and creating a smattering of sparkle across everything.

Without warning, tears form in my eyes.

Gabriel stills inside me. "What's wrong?"

"It's just…I didn't spend much time reflecting over our relationship before because it was over, and it hurt too much." My fingers move across his cheekbones as I speak. "Everything I pushed away back then is coming up now. And I was looking up, and seeing you and all this beauty surrounding us, and feeling you inside me, and it hit me."

Gabriel places a soft peck at the corner of my mouth. "What hit you?"

"When we were together before, I wanted to be pretty

for you. All the time. Not just physically, but every other way too. I wanted a life that was shiny, that looked good. And in doing so, I created a world where you could not be ugly with me."

Gabriel's lips twist and purse. He hasn't moved, but still he fills me. I wait for him to deny my words, because that would be typical for Gabriel. He never has allowed me any wrongdoing.

The more I think about it all, the more I need to be in the wrong. I need to be in the space where mistakes are made, where humanness is allowed. I need to shoulder this burden with Gabriel. I need him to allow me to sit in the dark with him.

I breathe the same air as Gabriel, watching him absorb what I've said. His expression changes, micro movements in his cheeks and the pull of his eyebrows. Finally, he says a single word. "Yes."

I kiss him. "I'm sorry. So sorry for not leaving space in our relationship for ugliness."

Gabriel kisses me back. "I've had a lot of time to think about this. And it's not ugliness. All the mistakes that make us human, they're not ugly. They're as beautiful as all the pretty things we do."

He resumes movement. Filling me, leaving me empty, filling me again. The entirety of my brain and my body and my heart focuses on what's building in my center. Gabriel must know this, and he does what he did before, when I was his and he was mine. A tuck of his hips, as if he could lift me off the ground, and I shatter, arcing up to the snow-stacked treetops and plummeting spectacularly back to earth. I'm recovering from my high when Gabriel jerks, groaning my name against my neck.

I smile up at the sky. "Snow sex is definitely going in my book."

———

We eat chips and salsa for dinner. Apple slices for dessert. Gabriel locates packets of hot chocolate in the pantry, left behind by a previous guest. He heats milk on the stove and pours in the mixture. He kisses me after my first sip, swiping his tongue in my mouth and telling me I taste like chocolate.

Gabriel builds a new fire. He sits on the couch, motioning me over. I pick up a blanket as I round the couch, then crawl on his lap and drape it over us.

Gabriel cradles me, and says, "Should we address the elephant in the room?"

I look up at the side of his neck. "Which one?"

My head bumps against his chest with the movement of his laughter. "My sobriety."

I'd wanted to ask, but how does a person ask a stark question like that? I guess you just say the words. So I do. "Are you sober now?"

"I'm sober forever."

I focus on his five o'clock shadow and push back against memories I wish I could erase. I don't want to have them now. I want to live here, in the present moment. "I'm proud of you."

He grunts. "You shouldn't be."

I shift, sitting up and looking down at him. How I wish I could snap my fingers and remove the shame from his eyes. "I've never been addicted to anything." *Except you.* "I don't know what it's like. But I've watched someone I loved suffer from the disease, and it looked very, very painful."

Gabriel reaches for a lock of my hair, slowly letting it slip through his fingers. The second time he picks it up, he says, "Loved?"

His eyes search mine. His one-word question is a reservoir, containing so many more.

I can't answer him, because I don't know how. Capturing his face in my hands, I tell him, "You are not the sum of your mistakes. You need to give yourself a little credit."

"That's a difficult task. Sometimes, it all feels like a weighted blanket, holding me down." The short growth of facial hair scrapes over my palms as he speaks, but I keep them in place. I like the painful tickle. I nod, urging him to continue.

"I want to leave it all behind, but it's always there. Clinging to me. It's a thorn. Many thorns."

My hands move to his shoulders and I lean back slightly. "Every day we are alive, we are experiencing. The joy, the struggle, the strife. We take little bits of those experiences, and we walk on into the next day. We can't control what happens around us, or what other people do, but we make choices. We choose the hurts we cling to, the truths and lies we allow to mold us and shape us. You can allow the shame you feel about your mistakes to weigh you down and keep you from growing, or you can pick out what lessons you want to learn from them, and keep those instead. It's your choice."

Appreciation shines in his eyes. "There you go, being far too kind."

I shake my head. "I've made mistakes, too. I lost my career, remember?"

He brushes my lower lip with the pad of his thumb. "I've been meaning to ask you about that. Did you really yell at a couple during a session?"

"I really yelled at a couple. I'll change it to liposuction or a nose job or whatever else in the final draft, though, so it doesn't violate their privacy. And change names and descriptions, obviously."

Gabriel chuckles. "I would've paid good money to see that."

"I can reenact it for you," I joke.

"What about your dad? Did you have a heart-to-heart with him, like the therapist suggested? Or was that fiction?"

"I did, actually. It was a difficult conversation. He acted hurt, and surprised. It helped having Lara there. She guided him through it. It was oddly cool to watch." I already liked Lara, but that was the day I began to love her. "He apologized eventually, once the hurt wore off."

Gabriel's hands go to my hips, his thumbs stroking my waist. "You took a leave of absence from work? Sold our house? Started your book? Like the manuscript says?"

I nod. "In that order."

Gabriel watches his thumbs as they move over me. "I felt sad when the lawyer brought me the papers for the sale of the house."

Our eyes lock.

Gabriel blinks and nods, breaking the heaviness of the moment. "Thank you for setting aside money from the sale. It was helpful when I got out. It gave me options, and time."

"It was the right thing to do. Even though Sabrina told me to take the money as restitution."

Gabriel breathes a laugh. "How is Sabrina?"

"Good, I guess. I don't talk to her much anymore. She's busy. Two kids." I shrug away the pinch of sadness that flits across my heart. I'd done too good a job pushing Sabrina away, and damaged our friendship irrevocably. What I know of her life now is gleaned from social media. "We're at very different stages of our lives. It wasn't easy to maintain a friendship after…everything." It's my fault. She was married and having babies, chasing a toddler and nursing a newborn, and it was a reminder of everything I didn't have. I stopped returning her calls and texts. She stopped sending them.

Gabriel exhales a heavy sigh. He opens his mouth, most likely to lament about why Sabrina and I are at different stages, but I place a finger against his lips.

"That's enough elephants for one evening."

Gabriel's thumbs stray from my waist, traveling up my rib cage. "What do you want to do instead?"

"I have some ideas." I trail kisses along his jaw. I'm ready to stop communicating with words. It's time to let our bodies do the talking.

What is it they're saying, though? I don't yet know. All I know, and all I really want to know right now, is that I'm tucked up in the snowy mountains with a man I never thought I'd see again. It's like magic, or an alternate reality. Fantasy land. For the rest of tonight, that's where I want to live.

Gabriel turns into me, and we kiss slowly, as if we have all the time in the world. As if we never had to stop. That familiar feeling tugs at my chest, and I press against the growing hardness I'm seated on. Gabriel winds a hand in my hair and pulls gently.

I rock against him, and let myself pretend nothing ever came between us.

As if my last name is still Woodruff.

As if Gabriel's mouth and heart and hands is all there is, or will be.

As if I'm not going home in a matter of days.

CHAPTER 14

GABRIEL

Avery's in my arms. According to the clock on the dresser, it's nine-thirty in the morning. I never sleep in. Never. I also rarely sleep through the night, and guess what? Last night, I did.

Her head is heavy on my chest, her hair cascading off the side. I remember what this was like, to wake up next to her on days when I wasn't waking up on an uncomfortable excuse for a bed at the fire station.

It's not hard to remember, because I never forgot. Avery was always only as far away as my open eyes. Close them, and there she was.

But this? A million times better.

She makes a soft noise, a tired moan, and shifts. Her cheek drags over half my chest, and she turns, eyes on my face.

The corners of my lips turn up at the sight of sleepy Avery, but the look in her eyes stops me. It's fleeting, this look, and she's already replaced it with happiness, but still. I saw it.

She slides up a few inches and places a delicate peck on the corner of my mouth. "This is a dream, right? Waking up with you?"

I can tell she means it. She's thrilled it's my face she saw when she opened her eyes. But first, she was surprised. She woke up next to Hudson for months. I'm assuming, anyway.

This is the first time I've fleshed out this idea of Avery in a different relationship, and what that entails. In my imagination, they did what we did.

She woke up next to him. She knows his favorite food, has likely had dinner with his parents. They've probably been on vacation together.

Avery's two fingers brush over the skin between my eyebrows, smoothing apart the furrowed skin. "You look upset." She props herself up and looks down, the ends of her hair tickling my chest.

"It's nothing." I don't know what we're doing, or how long this will last, and I don't want it marred by unpleasant feelings.

A stern look comes over her face. "Don't do that."

"Don't do what?"

"Don't hold back because you think I won't like what you have to say. Because you think what you say might cause me to feel a certain way."

She's good. She's even better than she was when she was practicing. Maybe it was all that therapy she went through for herself.

I toy with the end of a strand of her hair, and say, "You were surprised to see me when you woke up. I could tell."

Her lips purse. "Yeah," she admits, her voice soft. "Sorry about that."

"Nothing to be sorry for."

She shrugs. "True or not, I still feel bad." Her fingertips trace over my chest. "It's ok for me to feel bad. You didn't cause that."

I open my mouth, but she shakes her head. "Please don't say anything more. That feeling is mine. I own it. And you can't take it away, or make it better." She taps her finger on a large freckle on my chest. "For the record, I was surprised for a nanosecond. I feel very happy to wake up and see you."

I reach for her face, molding my palm to her cheek. I have the strongest urge to ask her what the hell we're doing, what this all means. Do I dare read into the past twenty-four hours? I'm not willing to risk an answer I won't like, and the question tumbles back down into my throat. "Do you want to come to the shop for a few hours today? I need to finish up a barn door."

"I would love to." She smiles when she says it. "Mind if I bring my laptop? I need to work for a little while, too."

"I don't mind." I look at the clock again. "I should run home. Shower, do a few things around my place. Can I pick you up at noon?" My lower lip draws in between my teeth, and I chew. Avery eyes the motion knowingly, and lightly tugs at my lip until I release it.

"Nervous?" she asks.

"A little," I admit. This is reminding me of our first date, the way I asked her out in the parking lot at the fire station. I'm as nervous now as I was that day.

"Noon is perfect." She presses a light kiss to my mouth, then starts to pull away. I catch her hand, pulling her back, and she doesn't protest. I think she was waiting, hoping I wasn't done with her.

I'm not. Not by a long shot.

Gently I guide her onto her back and make love to her.

There isn't a chance I'll be wasting any opportunities with this woman.

———

I'VE CLEARED off a work table for Avery.

She sits, click-clacking away on her keyboard, while I work on the custom barn door order we got last week. I catch her looking at me. She's adorable in the safety goggles and ear protection I made her wear. We share a smile, then go back to what we were doing. We repeat this process in ten-minute increments, as if we are teenagers.

Eventually Avery tires of this and gets off her stool. She points to her head, asking if she can take off the safety gear. I nod my yes, and she sets them beside her computer, then walks closer. I set down the jointer I'd been using, and she looks over the pieces of the door I cut earlier.

"Did Joel teach you how to do this?" She sounds impressed.

"Yeah. He's taught me a lot. Some stuff I learned on my own. The internet can teach a person just about everything."

"I have a love/hate relationship with the internet."

I chuckle. "Why is that?"

"It can be intrusive. Grant access to people who you'd otherwise not have access to. And them, to you."

This opinion had to be formed from experience. It's too specific.

"What happened?" I ask.

She looks down, gently knocking the tip of her tennis

shoe against my steel-toed boot. "I received letters after you went to prison. They were well-meaning, but they were from random people. Mostly women, telling me they were sorry for how everything worked out. Some men"—she pauses, shudders—"offering their services, should I require them."

"What the fuck," I mutter, my face scrunching in a mixture of anger and disbelief. The audacity of people.

"It was those stupid articles from—"

"Domenica."

We're quiet for a minute.

"I'm sorry I rained on our parade. I didn't mean to bring all that up." Avery grabs the box with my burn tools and machine from the next table, holding it out. "What is all this?" There's a desperate edge to her voice, a need to change the subject.

"Woodburner." I point to the machine. "And these are the tips. Each one produces a different effect."

"Did Joel teach you this, too?"

"I learned wood burning in high school."

"Were you good back then?" Her inquiry is soft, almost hesitant. "Did you love it?"

"Yes. And yes."

She reaches into the box. Her hand stills and she sends me a questioning glance.

"It's ok," I say, gesturing to the contents of the box.

She pulls out a tip, turning it over and examining.

"Spear shader," I say.

Her eyes meet mine, then go back to the implement. "Did you start with woodworking and…" She searches for the right word for wood burning.

"Pyrography," I supply.

"Pyrography," she repeats. "Did you move on to pyrography when you knew you liked working with wood?"

"The teacher saw I was talented. He suggested something that required more artistic skills. I think he was grateful there was a student who didn't see his class as a waste of time."

"And you were naturally good at it, weren't you?" One side of her mouth turns up in a smile. "It wouldn't surprise me. You've always been that way. Naturally capable."

My limbs heat under her praise. "I'd like to say yes, but no. My first attempts were garbage."

She laughs once. "I bet that's not true."

I give her a knowing look. "It's one hundred percent true. But I got better. I kept practicing. My teacher let me come into the classroom after school and work. I didn't think about it until now, but I'm sure that meant he stayed late." My heart pinches at the realization.

"Did your parents know you were good at it?"

I nod once. "They thought it was a little hobby. They called it whittling."

Avery snorts derisively. "Sounds about right. When did you stop?"

"After Nash died. I put all my focus into becoming a firefighter."

"And then you put all your focus into allowing me to step into my career." She stares down at the box.

I coax her gaze up with a finger under her chin. "Don't feel bad. Choices, remember? I made mine."

She nods, but she still feels guilty, and I don't know how to change that.

I let go of her chin, removing my chisel and writing tips from the box. "The next order is a sign for a wall. I think it's a wedding gift. Want to watch?"

Avery grabs the stool she'd been sitting on and places it beside me at my bench. She sits down and grips the edge of the stool with both hands, leaning forward. Her hair falls over her shoulders, hanging in the air.

I point at the hair tie on her wrist. "May I?"

She looks at me, not understanding what I mean.

"It's not safe to have your hair hanging near tools." I work the hair tie over her hand. Stepping behind her, I gather her hair. My fingers brush the nape of her neck.

A pleased sigh filters out from her. Her head tips left, and my fingers slide around her neck, moving gently back and forth. Avery's closed-mouth groan curls into me, making me think about things we can't do here.

"You'd better stop," she murmurs.

"Or?" My hand dips lower, skimming the tops of her breasts.

The back of her head meets my chest. "I don't know. I don't have anything good to say next."

I smile at the top of her head and take back my hand. "We can't do anything in here anyway." I finish the job of tying back her hair and take my seat.

"Out of respect for Joel, you mean?"

I lay out the rectangular slice of walnut. "Mostly, yes. Joel has been good to me."

"What about your parents?"

"What about them?"

"How have they been to you?"

I flip on my woodburner, adjusting the dials to my preference. "Supportive, I suppose. As much as they can be." I start in the right-hand corner, pressing the chisel into the wood. "They try. They just…"

"Fall short?"

"I've disappointed them. And I'll never measure up." I continue the length of the wood, turning it forty-five degrees when I get to the lower corner. "I don't see that changing."

It used to hurt like hell to think about my parents, and all the ways I've let them down. Now I feel bad for them, more than anything else. They're choosing to miss out on their only child, because they can't get over what happened to Nash. Maybe they have the kind of broken heart that will never heal. Maybe they fear healing, because they think it means leaving Nash behind. I don't know what it's like to be them, to be parents who've lost a son. I do know what it feels like to lose a brother, to have half of your heart ripped out and wonder how the world keeps turning when he's not in it.

I pause my work. Avery's frowning. She always felt defensive of me, always hated the way my parents had an obvious preference for Nash. I liked the way she disapproved of their attitude, the way she'd go to bat for me. If this feeling in my chest is any indication, I still do.

"Do you ever think about telling them how you feel?" Avery shrugs one shoulder. "If I can tell my dad, maybe…"

"I think about it. I can't imagine actually doing it, though. My mom… I don't know if she can handle it. It would hurt her to hear how I feel." It would require me to say Nash's name, something we all go to great lengths not to do around her.

Avery smiles in this tiny, sad way. "I said the same

thing to my therapist. I didn't want to hurt my dad by telling him how he hurt me."

"But you did. Tell him, I mean."

"I thought I was supposed to protect him. Like I was being selfless." She shakes her head. "It's the other way around. He was supposed to be selfless and protect me, but his grief crippled him in the parenting department. Our relationship is better now that I was honest about how I felt."

"My mom…" My sentence trails off. I don't know how to say what I want to say.

"You fear what will happen if you say something. I get that. But look at what happened when you didn't speak up." Avery rubs a hand over my shoulder. "People are more resilient than we think. Especially when it's asked of them."

I survived two years in prison, a place where resilience is key. Perhaps I've been selling my parents short. They too, can hear they messed up, and remain standing.

And if my parents can be resilient, and Avery's dad, and Avery, and me… What about our relationship? Can we resurrect it?

"Avery," I say, my tool poised above the wood. She lifts her gaze from where she'd been watching, waiting for me to resume. "Can I take you to dinner tonight?"

Her steady, clear-eyed gaze is on me. "Yes."

CHAPTER 15
GABRIEL

Sugar Creek doesn't have a lot in the way of fine dining. We have charm, though, and Avery happens to love charm.

She smiles up at me and points at a hedge of colorful roses on our way to our table. "Pretty," she whispers excitedly, as we follow the hostess to our table in the back corner of the outdoor seating area.

Avery orders sparkling water from the server. Tapping the underside of her menu, where the wine is listed, I tell her, "You can order wine, if you want." I don't need her to adjust her behavior for me.

Avery's attention remains on the menu as she says, "I rarely drink."

The server returns and takes our order. Avery leans back in her seat when he leaves, looking around at the people at nearby tables. "I met Jane a few days ago, from Lady J bakery. She thinks highly of you." There's curiosity in Avery's tone.

I nod. "Jane's a nice lady."

Avery pinches her bottom lip. "She seems…regretful?"

My eyebrows draw together. I don't want to say too much. Jane's story is hers to tell. Avery is perceptive, so I'm not surprised she has taken notice of Jane's hidden pain. "How so?"

"Hard to say, exactly. There's something to her, though. She carries something down deep." Avery pats her chest.

Avery couldn't be more correct. Jane carries regret, and guilt, in the marrow of her bones. She dreams of going back and righting her wrongs, though she believes that's not possible.

Jane's alcoholism differed from mine. She hid it from everybody she knew, and she hid it well. Her husband, her daughter, her friends. Jane drank to soothe horrific childhood memories. She thought she was handling everything fine, until she realized there were parts of her days she was unable to recall. Then came the day she turned on the gas stove improperly and forgot she was supposed to be cooking dinner. She passed out on the couch, and her eight-year-old daughter woke her up with complaints of a headache and her tummy feeling funny.

Jane convinced herself the best way she could love her daughter and husband was to rid them of herself. She ran here, to this sleepy town, and she hasn't gone back. I am the only person who knows this story, who has seen a photo of her daughter. Perhaps it was my colossal mistakes that made Jane trust me with her own.

I can't betray Jane's confidence, even to Avery. I say, "Jane lives a quiet life, bringing smiles to people's faces with those blueberry muffins of hers."

"She said you eat whatever is nearing expiration." Avery smiles at me. "I like that." Her gaze wanders over the walls of the restaurant. "And I love that this used to be a house. Nobody had to build a new structure to make this place."

"Joel told me the woman who owned this property lived in the home her entire life. She passed away ten years ago, and the place was left to her granddaughter. When her granddaughter didn't want it, her great-granddaughter moved in and turned it into a restaurant."

"That's amazing." Avery squeezes the lemon in her sparkling water and sips. "Something old gets a new life."

I nod. "A second chance."

A flush sweeps over Avery's cheeks. "A second chance," she echoes in a low voice.

This is it. Here goes nothing. "Avery, I—"

Her eyes widen, pointing over my shoulder. "Oh my God, Gabriel. She's choking."

I turn around. A woman is standing, bent over her table, grabbing at her throat. Her face is panicked, and she doesn't make a sound. The woman seated across from her yells for help.

I reach her in a few seconds' time, and notice the telltale swell of her stomach. She's pregnant. "I'm going to help you," I say, then use the heel of my hand to deliver a solid smack between her shoulder blades. When five attempts does not dislodge the food, I wrap my arms around her from behind, and position one fist at the base of her breastbone. My other hand covers my fist, and I begin quick pushes, in and up, and after a few interminable seconds, a ball of partially chewed food hits the table. I take a step back.

There's a loud sound of breath being sucked in, followed by a sob, then more sharp breathing. The other woman who'd been eating with the pregnant lady has her arms wrapped around her, and she finds me over her shoulder. "Thank you," she says loudly. "Thank you thank you thank you."

I look around and realize I have an audience. People are clapping. The back of my neck heats. They're looking at me like I'm a hero. As is Avery. I wave quickly and duck my head, trying to communicate that it's not a big deal. I take a step toward my table, but I'm stopped by a man who shakes my hand. Another person who pats my back. This goes on the entire way back to my table.

Avery stands beside my seat, waiting for me. She places a kiss on my cheek. "You're awfully good at that."

I pull out her chair and she takes her seat. "The Heimlich?"

She gives me a look meant to communicate that she knows I'm deflecting. "At saving lives. At knowing what to do when something goes wrong."

I replace my fallen napkin on my lap, shaking my head at her praise. "I'm sure several people here know how to perform the Heimlich."

Avery's eyebrows arch. "On a pregnant woman?"

I shrug and look away. Avery touches my arm and pulls my attention back to her. "She's coming this way."

I look up, and the woman who was choking just a few minutes ago is making her way over, her friend in tow. I stand.

Her eyes are shiny. "You saved my life." She palms her swollen stomach. "And my baby's. I don't think I can say thank you enough times." Her head shakes with astonishment. "What can I do? How can I repay you?"

"No repayment necessary. I'm glad I was around when you needed help."

"Can I have your name?" she asks, palm sliding over her swollen midsection. "I want to at least be able to tell my husband the name of the man who saved us."

I open my mouth to respond, but Avery's already answering. "His name is Gabriel."

The woman's friend smiles. "Like the archangel."

The pregnant woman nods. "We'll let you get back to your dinner. But thank you. Thank you." She presses a hand to her chest and smiles at Avery.

"I feel like everybody is staring," I whisper to Avery after they walk away. My back is to the restaurant.

"They are," Avery whispers. "As someone who has been the recipient of your heroics, I understand the fascination."

"That's why you married me, isn't it?" I'm making a joke to take away from the headiness of the last ten minutes. I realize belatedly that my joke might fall right to the ground.

Avery grins. "That, and your cute butt, hero."

Hero. My old nickname. The guys at the station called me that to tease me after the first time Avery visited to thank me, but Avery used it as a term of endearment.

I loved when she called me that, and if this happiness spreading over my chest is any indication, I still do.

Throughout dinner, a few people visit our table and offer words of appreciation. The server brings us all four desserts without us ordering them, and when I request the check, he tells me there isn't one.

"That woman you saved was the cousin of the head chef. She's visiting, and called him to tell him what happened. He's not working tonight, but he called the restaurant right after and said to comp your check." The server stacks our empty plates and backs away.

I leave a big tip on the table under my empty water glass, and Avery and I walk out. We reach the front of my truck and she turns to me, tugging lightly on the front of my shirt. "I know dinner is over, and it's late and getting chilly, but I wouldn't mind taking a walk. Maybe getting coffee or hot tea?"

I look down at her. "You're not finished with me?" I mean it lightly, a joke, more like *you aren't sick of me yet?* but that's not how it comes across. Now that I've said it, I realize I mean it both ways.

She blinks, long lashes fluttering, and shakes her head back and forth. Words teeter on the tip of her tongue. I can almost see them, threatening to tumble out. Her eyes widen and her pupils dilate as wisps of alarm settle on her face.

To ease her discomfort, I wind an arm around her waist and kiss the top of her head. "Hot tea sounds great."

CHAPTER 16
AVERY

He sees it.

These things I want to say.

How easy it would be to loosen my hold on my thoughts. On everything. Can I grant clemency to the barrel of misdeeds that sits between us, and move on?

You're not finished with me?

The double-meaning rang like a bell, echoing through my chest. I panicked, and he let me off the hook.

A long sigh sticks in my throat as I stretch out in bed. My hand glides over the sheets in search of Gabriel. When I don't find the warm, hard body I'm looking for, I pull myself to sitting and look around the room. His shirt dangles from the footboard, his shoes lined up neatly next to the open door.

Last night, after hot tea and a long walk around town, he drove me back here and I invited him in. We ended up in bed, like I knew we would. Sometimes, communication between bodies is as effective as the spoken word. And boy, do we communicate well.

It was different, though. The question of 'What are we doing?' has permeated both of us, creating an urgency and tenderness that wasn't there before. The exultation of our reunion is fading, revealing what's been lurking all along. The hard stuff.

I find Gabriel in the kitchen cooking eggs. His posture is stiff, his back muscles coiled. He's frowning at the yellow mixture in the pan.

My heart constricts at the sight of him. How good it feels, to wake up and see Gabriel's belongings, and find him in the middle of a mundane task. As if our lives are as cozy and lived-in as they used to be.

"Hey, you." I walk up behind him, wrapping my arms around his waist and pressing my face against his tense muscles. "What's wrong?"

He moves the pan off the burner, and I step back so he can turn and face me. The side of his mouth tugs, and he looks so sad. "You're leaving in four days."

I nod, a tiny up and down bobbing of my chin.

"There's nothing for me in Phoenix." His head shakes slowly as he speaks. "Not right now."

I nod again. I've already drawn the same conclusion. Sugar Creek suits Gabriel. He has come here to rebuild, and he's not finished building.

My heartbeats ricochet through my chest. This is the part I didn't plan for when I asked Gabriel to stay when it was snowing. Or when we finally had our overdue reckoning. Or when we let our bodies speak volumes, over and over. "What do we do?"

His expression is unfathomable. He settles both hands on my waist, fingers flexing. "I don't want to lose you again." His voice is rough. "And if you asked me to go back to Phoenix with you, I might."

My breath hangs in my throat, waiting for the rest of what he has to say.

"It wouldn't be the right choice for me. I'm getting my feet underneath me here." His voice is rough, resigned. "I would throw all that away for you, Avery, but please don't ask that of me."

"I would never." The words are out of my mouth quickly, and they're almost completely truthful. A sliver of me sees the possibility of coaxing him into leaving his oasis in the mountains, returning him to the city where he's from and the life we created.

A lump forms in my throat. I cannot ask anything of him. He might say yes, and saying yes for the wrong reasons is a recipe for disaster.

I push back the stinging feeling behind my eyes, shifting my focus from my loss to his gain. "I'm proud of you, Gabriel." When his head begins to shake in argument, I palm his jaw and say, "No, really, I am. And you should be, too. It's not wrong to put yourself first sometimes."

"Maybe it's not wrong, but it doesn't feel right, either." Gabriel kisses my forehead. "Let's eat, before it's cold."

We don't bother to sit, choosing to stand at the counter and stare outside as we devour fluffy eggs. When I'm finished, I feed Ruby. She must sense the climate in the room, because she is abnormally calm.

Gabriel takes my plate to the sink with his. He begins the cleanup process, his back muscles flexing with his motion. I want to bury my face there again, against his warm skin that smells like my old life. He's facing the sink when he says, "You could stay here." His voice is tentative, his sentence lifting at the end with a hopeful note.

I've already thought of that. Could I slip seamlessly into small-town life? I think so. But what about my dad and Lara? Cam and Dani? What if my book is met with a round of emphatic declinations from every publisher Jill presents it to? I'll need to get a job, and how big can the pool of openings be in Sugar Creek? All those questions pale in comparison to the biggest question of all.

What are we doing?

Gabriel pushes off the sink, spinning around and propping his hands behind him. Tiny soap bubbles slide off his fingers onto the lip of the counter. "I know…" His chin tips up and lowers slowly, just once. "Cam. You won't leave her."

I shake my head. "She's grown. Cam doesn't need me."

Gabriel's eyes lock on mine. "It's me, isn't it?"

My heart fractures at the resolute disappointment in his tone. How can I explain something I hardly understand myself? "It's…everything. I don't know what to make of this"—I gesture between us—"and I'm confused. But I'm only confused if I pause to think about what's happening up here, tucked away in this charming mountain town."

"And if you don't pause? How do you feel?"

My gaze drags up his body, from his legs crossed at the ankles to the stubble on his neck. It puts a warm, ambient glow in my belly. "Happy."

Gabriel nods like he knows. "Anything else?"

"Content. Like I've been treading water for a long time, and I've finally reached land."

Relief floods Gabriel's eyes. "I feel the same."

I lean my elbows on the counter, rubbing my hands over my face. I wish this were easier. I wish I could move up here and forgive and forget. I wish he'd never done what he did. I wish he didn't have an addiction. I wish I hadn't enabled and encouraged and ignored.

I wish.

I wish.

I wish.

Gabriel holds out a hand for me. I take it, stepping over his crossed legs and capturing them between my own. "We can make it work," he begins earnestly. "I'll drive down to Phoenix on the weekends. You can come here. We'll talk on the phone. You'll send me ridiculous things Cam says, and I'll reply with a string of emojis you'll have to make sense of. We'll miss each other like crazy. And then—" Gabriel stops, as if all the air has disappeared from his lungs. He shakes his head slowly. "I can't survive on that, not after we've had it so much better."

"Me either." Tears sting my eyes, but I don't want to waste time crying.

"Where do we go from here?" A pained look crosses his face, as if he can hardly bring himself to say what I know is inevitable. "What are we doing?"

Four words, ripe with emotion. It's not just a question. It's a challenge, a call to examine, and decide. We can no longer avoid it.

"I…" My fingertips trail over the planes of his bare chest. "I don't know. I don't know what I'm doing here, or with you. I don't know where to go from this point. I wasn't expecting you…" I palm his heart. "This. All I know is that I can't do anything halfway with you. No long distance." My voice catches, and I'm motioning between us, attempting to put words to emotions I can barely identify.

Gabriel gently touches my chin, guiding my gaze to meet his. My lower lip wobbles. Here it is. The beginning of yet another ending to me and Gabriel.

"Four days," he says, an echo of the first words that began this conversation. His cheekbones lift, his eyes squint. "We're going to make the most of these next four days."

His head dips and he finds my mouth. He kisses me urgently, like there is nothing more important in this world than his lips on mine.

Right now, there isn't. Not really.

CHAPTER 17
GABRIEL

I did all I could to squeeze every drop from our time together.

I touched her with hungry hands. I loved her with a ravenous mouth.

My foolish heart thought *Maybe*. Just maybe…

But, no.

At the end of the lane, her brake lights flash. My heart leaps to my throat, my knees bend as I prepare to break into a run.

Her car pushes forward, turns, disappears.

She is gone, my heart her hostage.

CHAPTER 18

AVERY

Camryn called twice during my two weeks in Sugar Creek, but I didn't answer. She texted me after the second call, saying everything was fine and she only wanted to see how things were going. Three days later, after I didn't respond to her message, she sent a follow up requesting proof of life. I sent her a picture of my foot.

My guess is the foot picture is the reason she's frowning right now.

Camryn makes certain to hold the frown for another beat, then steps back from her front door. "Come in. I'll go grab your mail."

I follow her into her house, Ruby at my feet. I'm shocked Cam didn't immediately point out my puffy eyes. I'd done my best to keep from crying when I said goodbye to Gabriel. The moment I pulled onto the interstate the floodgates opened and I cried the first hour of my drive. It might not have been goodbye forever, but it was goodbye for now. An open-ended farewell, a sentence ending in ellipses.

Camryn talks as she walks. "We tried to change the chalkboard, but the handwriting was not half as good as yours."

"Who did it?"

"Dani." Camryn shoots a warning look over her shoulder. "Don't tell her I said that. I love that woman, but a calligrapher she is not."

My sister's teasing tone is the familiarity I need. Her voice feels like the hug I could really use right now.

"It's good to hear your voice." I blink through the moisture forming in my eyes yet again.

"I have been told I sound like a symphony," Camryn jokes. She opens the back door and Ruby bounds outside.

Cam grabs a tall stack of what is largely junk mail and spins around. Her eyes bulge. "Why are you crying? Please don't tell me you loved Sugar Creek and didn't want to come home. I get that it's a cute town and all, but it's a hike to get there and I don't like driving."

Her rambling forces a smile into my upset. "That's not why I'm crying."

She hands off the mail to me and crosses her arms over her chest. "You saw Gabriel, didn't you?"

I nod.

"You banged him, didn't you?"

I give her a withering look.

She returns it. "Make love," she says, adding air quotes.

I snort a laugh. "I missed you."

"So? Is that what happened?"

I nod again. I open my mouth but she holds up a warning hand. "I don't want details."

"I wasn't going to give them to you."

"Good. What were you going to say?"

"That it was amazing. Just like before. Maybe better."

"The sex? Or everything?"

I sigh, glancing down at the small mountain of mail in my arms. "Everything."

"Are you screwed? Figuratively, I mean. I already know about literally."

I shake my head. "I left. I mean, I chose to leave." I couldn't sound more conflicted if I tried. "I left."

"You said that already."

I frown at her. "Don't challenge me."

She holds up her hands. "I'm not challenging you."

"Yes, you are. You're pointing out I'm repeating myself."

"Not a challenge."

"Coming from you it is."

She wraps an arm around my shoulders and directs me to the kitchen table. "I can't decide if I like how well you know me, or if it's a colossal inconvenience."

"The former." I lay the mail on the table and it tips over, scattering. "You could've thrown away the junk."

She shrugs. "How am I supposed to know what constitutes junk for you?" She holds up a bill. "I happen to think this is junk."

I stare at her, and she laughs. "Ok, you're right. I was being lazy." She takes the seat beside me. "I knew you'd get together with Gabriel up there."

I groan loudly. "You should've dragged me home with you the day you left."

Her head cocks sideways. "Why?"

My legs cross under the table and bump into Cam. She allows me space to bring my legs up onto the chair, tucking them into my body and resting my chin on my knees. "Because now I'm wondering if it would've been easier to never see him again." My poor, mangled heart. We were doing ok before Sugar Creek. Not great, and maybe we were still muddling our way through, but we were ok.

"Why?"

"Because he broke me, and I don't think I should go backwards. I should go forward."

"Why?"

"Because that's what I'm supposed to do."

"Why?"

Her repetitive question is grating on my nerves. "Because it is."

"Why?"

"Say something else!"

"Why do you believe you should go forward? Why do you believe by being with Gabriel you are going backward?"

I sit back, considering Camryn's questions. "When I think of Gabriel, it's hard to see a future, because he consumes all of my past."

"Not all of it."

I squint at her. "More, please."

"You were twenty-three when you met Gabriel?"

I nod.

"You lived twenty-two years without him. Not just without him, you didn't even know he existed. You had other boyfriends, you weathered Mom's passing, you practically raised me, took care of the house and Dad. You got yourself to college, you graduated and went on to earn your Master's. Gabriel doesn't own those things. He does not consume all of your past. Just a piece of it. An admittedly huge part," she allows, "but not all of it."

Even if I understand everything Cam is saying, I have a hard time believing it. "Gabriel's portion weighs more."

"Fair." She nods. "But he's not all of it. Just remember that. You were Avery Burke long before you were Avery Woodruff."

"I'm still Avery Burke."

She completes a half eye-roll. "You know what I mean."

"Jill wants me to use what happened in Sugar Creek in my story."

Cam frowns. "You told Jill before you told me?"

"Timing," I explain. "I happened to talk to her before you."

"Because you didn't answer my calls. Because you didn't want to talk to me and tell me what you were really getting up to."

I shrug.

Cam smiles smugly. She knows she's right. "Is Gabriel ok with you using it?"

"He's fine. I've already written it. My time in Sugar Creek was productive—"

"In between the banging."

I lightly punch her in the boob. She laughs. "Speaking of Jill, did you see she RSVP'd for the shower?"

"I haven't looked recently." Planning Camryn and Dani's bridal shower was supposed to be the other task I completed in Sugar Creek, but then Gabriel showed up, and, well…

Cam looks unhappy. "Start looking. The shower is in

one month and you're hosting it. I did my part. I sent the invites."

"Are you sure you don't want to host it somewhere other than Gem?"

Her eyes narrow. "Why?"

"You're getting married there, too."

"It's free," Cam reminds me. "So please shut that mouth of yours and start planning."

I sit up straight. "I'm on it. I promise. Notebook is brimming with…notes. You're going to love everything I have planned."

Her frown deepens. She knows I'm bullshitting. "Tell me if I should ask Dani's friends from dental school. They've offered to help already."

I wave her off. "I'm good. Lara volunteered to help if I need it."

Cam doesn't look convinced. If anything, she looks concerned.

"Don't worry about your shower. I promise, everything will be fine."

"That's not what I'm worried about."

My eyebrows lift and I hold my hands out to the side, silently asking her to explain.

"What is going on with you and Gabriel?"

I groan. "I'm not sure, Cam. It's messy, and confusing."

"How did you leave things?"

"We both agreed we can't do long distance, and—"

"You'd consider taking him back?" Astonishment widens her eyes. "After everything?"

I bristle. "Don't judge me."

Cam holds her hands in front of her chest, palms out. "Not judging. Just surprised. Riding the bang train to closure town is one thing, forgiving him and taking him back is another."

"It's not that simple, Cam. It's not a snap of the fingers, or, like, an epiphany." I mime the brain-exploding emoji.

"I know, Avery. It's just…he hurt you. Badly."

"We both made mistakes."

"He made more."

I nod. "Is this your way of telling me you don't think I should ever give Gabriel another chance?"

"Nope."

"Then what are you saying?"

"I'm neutral. I only want you to be happy and healthy. Whatever that means for you."

"Chickenshit."

She barks a laugh. "Not usually, but maybe a little in this case."

I gather the mail and stand. Cam brings Ruby inside and walks us to the front door. "Be happy Hudson removed himself from the equation. Otherwise, this would be messier than it already is." Cam lightly presses a hand to my arm, her forehead creased with concern. "What do you plan to do about it all?"

My shoulders curl inward, and my head is heavy as it swings back and forth. "The only thing I know to do. I'm going to bury my head in my computer, write my little heart out, and throw you the best bridal shower you've ever seen." I lift my drooping head to deliver a kiss to her cheek. "And copy the next Spill The Beans on the board."

"Tomorrow," she says, mouthing the word please.

"I'll swing by Gem in the morning."

"And be ready to see Dad and Lara this weekend. They want to have dinner."

I frown as my head fills with a fleeting vision of me providing my dad and Lara with a sanitized summary of my trip to Sugar Creek.

Cam sees my expression and asks, "Are you going to tell Dad about Gabriel? I think his heart was as broken as yours when everything happened."

"No. I don't know." I sigh. "Not yet, at least." What, exactly, is there to tell? I don't want to rope him into my angst.

Cam pretends to zip her lips.

I go home. I unpack. I float through my routine, my movements on autopilot. When I take a shower, I wash my hair with body wash instead of shampoo. To Ruby's delight, I feed her three cups of food instead of two. I spend an hour on the internet looking at cute matching shirts to force Camryn and Dani to wear at their shower, then forget to order them.

My mind is approximately one hundred and seventy-eight miles away.

CHAPTER 19

GABRIEL

The arch is finished.

I stand back, arms crossed, rocking forward into the steel toe of my boots. Seemingly simple, yet intricate upon further inspection.

Joel lightly smacks one side of the arch. It's sturdy and solid, a masterpiece. "Think you can deliver this next week? Ernie's on vacation."

"Sure." I don't mean for my tone to sound gruff. "No problem," I add, softening my voice. Delivering the arch to Camryn might mean seeing Avery.

It's not that I don't want to see her. The opposite, actually. I'm dying to hold her again. Feel the melody of her pulse as I press a kiss to her neck.

It's just that… Well, I don't know. I'm struggling to put into words how I feel. It's a heady mixture, this self-doubt and shame, and its shadow reaches far. Without Avery here to look at me like I'm her hero, her man, her soulmate, it's more difficult to trust I am those things.

Joel tucks his hands in his khakis. "I can't help noticing how different you've been recently. Are you all right?"

I tug the heavy canvas over the wood. "I've had a lot on my mind."

Joel nods. "Yep."

I haven't told anybody about what happened with Avery, and it's starting to get to me. "Avery left a couple weeks ago, and I haven't talked to her since. It's almost like it didn't happen. Like I dreamed it." I've picked up my phone a hundred times, hoping to see a message from her. I haven't reached out to her because I'm trying to give her space. I'm not quite sure what exactly I'm giving her space to do, but it feels like the right choice. I'm terrified if I push, I'll lose her. I'm scared if I don't push enough, I'll lose her.

"I'm sorry to hear that," Joel says.

I shrug. "I don't know what I expected. We're divorced. I'm the reason for everything. It's all on me." Avery believes she contributed to what happened, and it's not that I think she's completely wrong, but I don't know that she's right either. Can a person be culpable and innocent at the same time?

"Why don't you go back to Phoenix?"

I rub the nape of my neck. "My work is here."

"No, it isn't."

I look around at all the pieces I'm working on. My hands have been on at least half of the pieces in this room. "Unless I dreamed this place too, I think this is where I work."

Joel guffaws. "Gabriel, this is a rung on a ladder. A stop along your path. Do you really believe Sugar Creek is where you'll make your home?"

"It seems as good as any other place. Better, really. I have a place to stay, and a job. That's more than I have anywhere else. More than I can ask for."

"What about all your friends?"

Friends... My crew tried. They called, they texted, a few of them stopped by when they heard I got out. I didn't answer calls, I ignored texts, and I was already on my way to Sugar Creek when they showed up at my house. I felt bad, but what was there to say? They'd tell me what's new in their lives, and then what? How was I supposed to respond? Tell them what it's like to be alone with your thoughts until they drive you crazy, until you're consumed with everything you did wrong in your life, and you pray for the chance to make it up to the people you love the most?

Sometimes I wonder if any of it would've happened if it weren't for Ryan dying. There's no way to know, but my best guess is *yes*. I was a tinderbox. Ryan was the accelerant. The fire came in the form of tiny sparks accumulated over years.

I shake my head at Joel. "I don't have friends anymore."

Joel presses on. "What about your parents?"

I shrug and look away. They love me, but I don't think they like me. Nash never would've disappointed them the way I have.

"What"—Joel pauses, placing a hand on my shoulder and compelling me to look at him—"about Avery?"

I shake my head. "Maybe I should look at the two weeks Avery was here as an unexpected gift. As closure." My throat tightens on the word. *Closure*. It's the last thing I want from her.

One side of Joel's mouth turns down, and he looks like he feels bad for me. "Can I make one suggestion?"

"Please."

"There's a lot more life out there for you. Don't hold yourself back because you think you don't deserve more. If you're not careful, you'll become your own jailor."

Joel releases me, stepping back to give me space. He eyes me for a few more seconds, then slips his hands in his pockets and returns to his office.

For the rest of the day, Joel's words play on in my head. *You think you don't deserve more...you'll become your own jailor...*

In prison, I spent a lot of time going over it all in my head. I started at the end, and went backward, step by step. The further I went, the more patterns and truths emerged. Those steps all converged, until they ended at the same destination.

It all goes back to Nash.

———

"Surprise!"

I blink against the sun, the shock, and my parents on my front porch. My mother's arms are open, my father stands behind her.

"Mom, Dad. Hi." I step back, grabbing my shirt off a chair and pulling it over my head. I'd been ready to go for a run when they knocked.

"Sorry about dropping in on you," my dad says, looking around the small living room.

"I don't mind. You're always welcome." I watch my

mom take in her surroundings. Her lips pinch disapprovingly, obviously unimpressed with where I'm living.

I don't blame her. It's not a home. It's a place to stay.

"This is nice," she forces, and I laugh, giving her a 'come on' look. She makes an exasperated face and chuckles. "Ok, fine. But it's not that it's not nice. It's just… sort of…"

"Boring?" I supply.

"Undecorated," she says diplomatically.

"Decorating hasn't been high on my priority list."

The three of us stand looking at each other, then avert our gazes to something boring and undecorated around the room. Maybe they're realizing this is the first time they've been to visit me since I moved up here. Maybe they feel bad about that. I think I would, if I were a parent.

"So…" I clear my throat. "Not to be rude, but why are you here?"

"We're taking a road trip up into Colorado, then over to Lake Tahoe. Probably through to the coast, and we'll drive down to San Diego." He adjusts his ball cap. "Trying not to get bored in retirement, honestly." His eyes go to my mom. She gives him a frosty look. "She's getting sick of me."

"I'm getting sick of you rearranging my house," she says.

"Our house," my dad amends.

"Hmph," she growls.

"Can I get you something to drink?" I ask, before this can devolve into what looks like a well-traveled argument for them.

"Little early for drinking," my dad jokes, and my mom

smacks his arm. "Doug, don't make jokes like that around Gabriel."

"It's ok, Mom," I assure her, walking into the kitchen and retrieving three glasses from a cabinet. I fill them with iced tea. "It doesn't bother me."

"Are you, uh…" She accepts the tea from me, holding tightly to it. "Are you, um…" She coughs, uneasy.

"I'm not drinking, if that's what you're trying to ask. I haven't had a drink since the night of the DUI."

She blinks at me, taken aback at my easy use of the word. She never refers to it by what it really was, choosing instead to call it my 'trouble' or 'problem.'

She recovers, and asks, "Do you keep track of the days? Like other…people?"

"Other alcoholics?" I raise my eyebrows. "No, I don't. I don't want to know the exact number. It's irrelevant to me." I look my parents in the eyes, first my mother and then my father. Maybe it's the way Avery encouraged me while she was here, or the fact she faced her own issues with her father, but I feel stronger under my parents' gaze than I have in a very long time. "I don't struggle with wanting a drink, either, in case that's your next question. I go to AA, and some people there say every single day they fight the urge to have a drink. But I don't. Ever, at all. I damn near ruined my life. I injured somebody. Me, a person who swore to protect people." A lot of what happened still feels surreal, even though I lived every nightmarish moment of it.

My mom's pursed lips tremble. My dad nods slowly. He hardly said a word to me after everything happened. In some ways, his disappointment in me runs deeper than my mother's. She wears hers on the outside, like a badge on her shirtsleeve, alongside her grief over Nash. With my dad, it's more something in the air around him, a slow leak.

He sips his tea. "There's a way to get you back out there. Back on a crew." He sets down his glass and leans forward, elbows propped on knees. "They're assembling a hotshot crew made up of ex-cons. You'll be right on the fire line, face to face with fire on the ground." Excitement trickles into his voice. He misses the thrill, the feeling. I understand that. But I don't want it for myself.

"I don't want to be a firefighter, Dad." These are words I should have said a long, long time ago. If I'd been honest with them, and myself, maybe I could've avoided all of it.

The muscles near his jaw flex, and he crosses his arms. "What are you going to do instead? Hide up here in the mountains? Slowly run out of the money Avery set aside for you?" He blows out a heavy breath. "You're good at fighting fires, Gabriel. You have a natural talent for it, and you're wasting it."

The unspoken portion of his sentence twists like a knife in my heart. *You're throwing away what Nash wanted more than anything.*

For so long, I tried to give my parents what they've been missing since Nash died. A son like the one they lost. I can't do it anymore. I shouldn't have done it in the first place.

I push back from the table. "I want to show you something."

CHAPTER 20
GABRIEL

I use my key to let us in the back door at work.

My mom shuffles her feet, hesitating. "Is this ok, Gabriel?"

"I used a key, Mom. I think that means I'm allowed to be here." Instantly I feel bad for my sarcasm. I'm on edge, knowing what I'm about to do. "Follow me," I say, leading the way to Camryn's arch. "This is for a wedding." I pull off the sheet, and step aside. If I tell them this is Camryn's arch, it will invite questions about Avery. Me seeing her here in Sugar Creek isn't a secret, but telling them will only end up with questions that don't have answers.

My mom circles the arch, her hand hovering an inch above the wood. My dad stays in place, studying one portion of it before moving on to another.

"This is stunning," my mom says appreciatively. "Look at all the detail." To her credit, she looks like she means it. It's her stiff posture that communicates she still doesn't understand why I want to be here, in this room that smells of sawdust and glaze. She peers around the wood shop. "I still can't believe you left Phoenix to come all the way up here. You're an assistant to the owner? Why?"

"I'm—"

"Gabriel!" Joel comes from behind us. He's smiling at my parents, his hand already out for introductions. He makes them himself, pumping my parents' hands enthusiastically.

"What are you doing here on your day off?" he asks me.

"Just wanted to show my parents where I work." What I really mean is, I wanted to show them I fucked up, but I'm not a fuck-up. I've been seeing myself that way for too long, and I have to show them it's not ok for them to, either.

It has to start with me. That's what I decided on my way over here, driving alone as my parents followed.

"You must be so proud of Gabriel," Joel says, smiling and nodding.

My mom smiles tightly and lies through her teeth. "We are very proud of him." My dad echoes my mom. Joel must pick up on the insincerity, because he steps over to the arch.

It's the biggest piece in the shop right now, and the most impressive. He raps two knuckles against one pillar, the sound staying close by because the wood is solid. "He has more talent in his pinky finger than I have in my whole body. I couldn't have made this into half of what you see here."

My mom's eyes widen. "You didn't make that?" she asks Joel.

He shakes his hands and rolls back onto the balls of his

feet. "No way. That's far beyond my artistic abilities. This piece is Gabriel's work."

"Gabriel…you made this?" Her astonishment sends pride coursing through me, with a vein of irritation nestled in there, too.

"That's my work, Mom."

My dad clears his throat, shifting from foot to foot. "I didn't realize you could make something like this, Gabriel."

Joel pats my back. "The kid is good at many things. Let me show you these coasters he made." He waves at my parents, urging them to walk with him. I follow behind, listening to Joel tell them about the first time he saw me with my burn tools. "I watched him for a full five minutes. Couldn't say a damn word, I was so fascinated by it." He picks up the set of coasters.

"My grandson added these to our social media, and it's been blowing up with comments. People are asking where they can order these, and I don't have a damn link yet. I don't like missing out on sales." Joel glances at the door that leads to the reception area. "He's supposed to meet me here to add them to my online store, but he's late."

Joel hands the coasters to my mom. She studies them. Her eyebrows lift at the one with Avery's monogram. *Previous monogram.*

I shrug one-shouldered at her look, and a corner of her mouth lifts.

"Anyway," Joel says, "I have work to do in my office while I wait for Mason. It was nice to meet you both. I hope to see you again."

My parents say goodbye, and then it's the three of us once more.

"Why didn't you tell us you were this talented?" My mom sounds disappointed, but I don't think it's directed at me.

"Gabriel," my dad says my name gruffly, and then nothing else.

I ran into fires with him. Obeyed his commands. We risked our lives together, always knowing that even if we followed protocol and did our best, things could go sideways. Where are his words now? Why do they escape him?

I look at the ground, gathering my courage, then meet my mother's gaze. "The better question is, why didn't you notice? I bet you already know the answer."

Tears well up in her eyes, but they don't deter me. She'll be ok if she hears my truth. If Avery can do it, I can too.

"I'm not Nash." My hands tuck into my pockets, and my shoulders wind up, hovering near my ears. "I've tried, but I'll never be the person he was going to be. I can only be me. If you don't want to accept that, I don't know what to tell you."

"Gabriel," my dad starts, the admonishing tone light but still present. "We never—"

"Yes, you did. Nash was the one who was going to follow in your footsteps. He was going to be the son you could brag about. Then he died, and I tried to fill his shoes. It was wrong of me to do it, and it was wrong of you to let me." I gesture around at the room. "This is me. This is what I love to do. I am still recovering from the worst choice of my life, but I'm getting there. I'm done trying to give you the son you lost." I point at myself. "I'm the son you have."

One loud sob escapes my mom. She covers it quickly, and my dad grabs her, pulling her in. He kisses the side of her head, whispering, "It's ok, Corinne," in her ear.

I feel bad. Not because I've hurt her, but because she still can't hear Nash's name without losing it. I turn for the door. My parents can see themselves out.

"Gabriel," my mother says when I'm halfway there. I stop, but I don't turn around. I look down at my shoes, the laces blurring. I wish I didn't care so much. I wish there wasn't a little boy living inside me, wanting only for his parents to love him for who he is.

She touches my shoulder, stepping in front of me. I'm bigger than her, and taller than her, but she folds me into her body like I'm a child again. "I'm sorry," she says. She says it two more times, her voice a whisper. I close my eyes, and then there's a palm on my back. My dad. It's the only form of apology he's capable of.

"We love you, Gabriel. We love the person you are. We don't need you to be"—she gulps—"Nash. Just be yourself from now on."

They hug me again after that. I catch movement from the sliver of Joel's office window that's visible from here.

"We'd better get going," my dad says, voice gruff.

I walk them out to the RV they've rented for their road trip. My heart feels lighter, though I know better than to think a few words can sweep away years of hurt. All journeys begin with a single step, and that was ours.

"I'm driving down to the valley next week to deliver that arch." We stop in front of the vehicle. "It's for Camryn. Avery's sister."

Mom's eyes light up. "Is that right? Do you think you'll get to see Avery?"

"Maybe." A flicker of hope swells in my chest.

"You should try," she says, nodding quickly, "I mean, if you want to. If you think that's what is best for you."

I try not to smile at her attempt to stay out of my business. "We'll see. Enjoy your trip."

She hugs me goodbye and goes around to the passenger side. My dad waits for her to be out of earshot, then says, "If you want to leave your relationship with Avery in the past, that's your business. But if you don't…" He lays a heavy hand on my shoulder. "Don't let anything stop you from going after what you want. You deserve to be happy. Whatever that means for you."

I nod once, swallowing back my emotion. My first non-fire related piece of advice from my dad. Better late than never.

"One more thing," he says, patting my shoulder. "I wasn't sure if I should tell you this, but a bunch of the old crew is getting together to honor Ryan. They're doing Pat's Run. Matching shirts, all that. They asked about you. Told me to invite you."

"I'll consider it." Am I ready for all that? To see the guys again?

He climbs into the large vehicle, and with a last wave from my mom, they lumber down the road.

CHAPTER 21
AVERY

The way it was.
My lips on yours.
Your hand in mine.
I thought we were fine.
Fine isn't what we were.
I broke us.
Choked the life from us.
The wolf arrived.
And I surrendered.
I'll retrace my steps to show you.
If you're not done, neither am I.

I toss aside the chalk pen, peering down at the poem I've just finished copying onto the chalkboard. Spill The Beans entries lie scattered on the table.

Since I came back from Sugar Creek, I've chosen sunny and uplifting entries. Today, I didn't feel like it. The longer

I go without Gabriel, the more I miss him. I've been home a little over three weeks, and this pain in the center of my chest grows bigger every day. It's not like it was when he was in prison, when I desperately wanted him and couldn't have him. This is more like yearning, because he's out in the world, attainable. I fantasize about hopping in my car and pointing it north, about—

"Is Avery Woodruff here?"

My heart turns over at the sound of that familiar voice, saying my old name.

"Uh," Laramie flounders, glancing to where I sit, tucked in a quiet corner of Gem. She looks back at the man in front of her.

"There isn't an Avery Woodruff here," Laramie says, placing so much emphasis on my former last name that Gabriel catches on right away.

His head tips up slowly, lowering at the same pace. "Right. Avery Burke. Is she here?"

Laramie glances my way a second time, meeting my eyes. I nod my approval, but Gabriel doesn't wait. He turns, following Laramie's gaze.

Our eyes meet, and everything in the space between us ceases to exist. The bitter scent of coffee, the low hum of conversation, the scream of grinding beans, it's all drowned out by my racing pulse.

If my hands weren't curled into fists, my fingernails leaving dents in my skin, I might press down on my chest to keep my heart in my body.

He's walking toward me, each step measured, and all I can think is that I don't know how I will survive this. I've been proud of myself these past few weeks, knowing I tangoed with Gabriel and walked away upright. I've been waiting for that growing hole in my chest to peak, thinking if I could just make it to the apex, I'd be ok. It would fill in, I'd heal and scar, like before.

Seeing him now makes me doubt the end exists for us.

He stops beside the chair on the other side of my table. He's wearing jeans and a long sleeve shirt. It's nothing special, except somehow it is, because it's on him.

"Hello." His voice is low, husky, the tenor making me bite my lower lip.

"Hi," I manage after a few heavy seconds.

He exhales a thick breath, eyes darkening. My skin prickles.

If closure is what Sugar Creek was supposed to gift us, it looks like we missed the mark.

Gabriel grips the back of the chair, looking down at the chalkboard. "Your work?" He sounds impressed.

"Yeah. In exchange for free coffee and baked goods."

Gabriel skims the poem. "That's a valuable trade."

"I like to think so." I point at the wall. "It goes up there."

Gabriel pulls out the chair and sits. His long legs spread out under the table, one of them pushing between my legs. I resist the urge to capture him with my calves and squeeze.

"I'm delivering the arch for your sister." He looks around. "I wasn't expecting to arrive at a coffee shop."

"This is Cam's place. And Dani's, too, but Cam operates it. Anyway, they're getting married out back. That's why you're delivering the arch here." I take a breath.

Gabriel smiles knowingly. "Why are you nervous?"

"Who said I'm nervous?"

"Nerves make you ramble."

I frown and flick a crumb off the table. Gabriel is here, on my turf. It was different when I was in Sugar Creek. Having him here, in Gem, unsettles me. It feels like he was missing from this scene all along.

I choose not to respond to Gabriel's question, forging ahead with the reason he's here. "The outside area is gorgeous. You can't see it from the street, but I promise, it's worthy of a small wedding ceremony."

Gabriel adjusts his sleeves, pushing them up on his forearms. I toy with the charm on my necklace.

"So," I start, folding my hands together on the table.

"How have you been?" Gabriel says at the same time.

We laugh awkwardly. "Go ahead," Gabriel says.

"I've been good. Writing a lot. Putting the finishing touches on Cam and Dani's bridal shower. That's one of the things I was supposed to be doing in Sugar Creek." I give him a sideways grin, a slight heat building on my cheeks.

The corners of his lips tug, the tiny grin knowing and mischievous. "But something distracted you."

"Something distracted me."

His fingertips land on the crook of my elbow, sliding down the inside length of my forearm. My toes curl, my stomach tightens. He asks, "Are you almost finished with the book?"

"I'm three quarters of the way through."

He clears his throat. "Are your hero and heroine going to get back together?"

A loaded question, if there ever was one.

"I'm not sure." I avert my eyes, as if looking away from him will decrease the pain seeping into my chest.

My phone, lying on the table between us, lights up with an incoming call.

"Sorry," I apologize, reaching for my phone. "My air-conditioner is misbehaving, and I'm waiting on a call back from the repairman."

Gabriel takes back his hand from my forearm, gesturing at me to answer.

The call is from Bayer Heating and Cooling, telling me a technician will be at my address in approximately twenty minutes.

"I'll be there," I confirm, hanging up.

"I can probably fix whatever it is," Gabriel offers. "If you'd like."

I clear my throat. I've become accustomed to calling out for home repairs, but there was a time when Gabriel fixed whatever was broken in our home.

Except for himself.

Has that changed? He certainly seems capable of fixing everything, including himself.

"Next time," I answer, scooping up my purse and jamming my laptop in its case. "I need to get going." I step away from the table, but Gabriel's arm shoots out, stopping me.

"Can I see you again?"

I look into his eyes and there it is, in vivid detail. Our shared history. Not just our marriage, but our time in Sugar Creek. That too, has been written into our story.

"Yes," I answer. Feelings of overwhelm have me hustling out of Gem, pausing once I reach the exit because I've realized I haven't given him my address.

I guess it's on me. The ball is officially in my court.

Turning back, I peek at Gabriel. I would've bet a

hundred dollars he was watching me leave, but he's not. He's attaching the chalkboard to the wall. He steps back and looks up at the words I've written. I can't begin to imagine what he's thinking. What he's feeling.

———

It's NOT until the repairman leaves that my heightened emotions begin to wane. Sagging against the front door, I drop my chin to my chest and rub at my eyes. Ruby bounds straight for me, pawing at my calves. I push off the door and take care of all her needs.

I don't cry, but I feel like I could. I could throw my head in my hands right now and cry until I run out of tears.

Nothing about my life is how I thought it would go. How I wanted it to be.

Gabriel was my everything, until he wasn't. I was forced to move on, forced to learn who I was as an individual. That feels important, special. Something that can't be brushed aside, forgotten, wiped away like it never existed. There isn't a reset button, only a gathering of experiences.

It's not only my belongings, my home, my new car. *I loved someone besides Gabriel.* When I'm old and looking back on my life, I'll consider Hudson a special part of it. He helped me heal, and he helped me learn about myself.

I take a shower, and after I'm done I open my nightstand drawer. What I want is in the back, hidden from view.

The cool metal slides over my skin, shiny and still a perfect fit. The diamond on my ring finger glints in the dull overhead light. I didn't think there would ever come a time when I wouldn't wear this ring.

I reach back into the drawer, feeling for the slide of my fingers over a smooth surface. There it is.

Two pieces of white printer paper, each bearing newspaper articles. Gabriel cut them out and used packing tape to give them a homemade laminate. I gaze at the images, these significant moments captured in time.

Gabriel, mid-step from a burning home, holding me in his arms.

Gabriel, standing in front of a minister, bending me backward while kissing me.

I did not save the articles about his DUI and sentencing, but I know they referenced the way we met. Cam told me how they chronicled our trajectory, and our spectacular crash and burn.

Gabriel was a memory, vivid and tangible, but a memory nonetheless. Not anymore.

I keep saying we're finished, as if it's synonymous with being done.

Our marriage is finished.

But are we done?

CHAPTER 22
GABRIEL

"Sorry I'm late," Camryn calls out, rushing through
Gem toward my table.

Avery left half an hour ago, and I've been waiting here
since.

I stand up to greet Cam, holding out my arms.

Cam hugs me around the waist. First she's tentative,
then she hugs me hard, like she really means it. "It's good
to see you again," she says, stepping back. "I wouldn't
count Sugar Creek as seeing you, since we didn't speak at
all. You were too busy standing in a downpour with my
sister. Congrats, by the way."

My head tilts, eyebrows cinching.

"All the sex," she explains. "Congrats on all the sex
with Avery."

A breath of laughter streams from my nose. Cam is still
so…*Cam*.

Rubbing the back of my neck, I say, "Thanks?"

Cam holds my gaze for a long moment, and God only

knows what she's thinking. Whatever it is, it seems she decides not to give those thoughts a voice.

"Do you want to show me where the arch belongs?"

Cam snaps out of her thoughts, clapping once. "Yes! Come on."

I follow her through Gem, down a hallway past the restrooms, and step into an outdoor space behind the coffee shop.

Camryn indicates where she wants the arch. I look around, trying to ascertain how I'm going to get the arch to where Cam wants it placed.

Avery was right, the outdoor space is impressive. Vertical cedar boxes house greenery, and string lights swing overhead. The top half of the back of the coffee shop is a windowed wall, and the windows are still open from the morning. The music is low, the grinding of beans periodically punctuating the sound, and it's altogether a great atmosphere.

"Do you have a way to get the arch back here?" Cam's eyebrows draw together.

The arch and its maneuverability isn't at all what I want to talk about, but this is my job, and Joel's business. So, first things first.

"It'll be fine," I assure her. "Let me back the truck in here."

I go out to the delivery truck and drive it around behind the store, backing it up to a spot where the pony gate can swing open and allow me to move the arch inside. Using the hydraulic lift, I get the arch to the ground and on a large hand truck. Slowly, as if I'm wheeling a tower of Fabergé eggs, I make my way to where she stands. Cam watches the process, arms crossed.

"Grab that side," I instruct, and together we lower the hand truck until it's flush with the ground. Cam helps me lift the arch, adjusting it inch by inch until it's in place.

Cam runs the back of her arm over her forehead. "That's a lot heavier than it looks."

"Solid wood," I explain.

She's searching the arch, eyebrows pinched in the same way Avery does when she's concentrating.

"Over here." I point out what I know she's looking for.

She smiles when she sees the small addition. "Dani will love that." Her grin turns proud, and slightly starry-eyed. "Thank you for adding it, Gabriel. I appreciate it."

I nod. "No problem. This is nice, Cam." I gesture around. "I didn't know you had it in you." I wink at her, and she lightly punches my arm.

"I'm just the idea person. A friend of Dani's manages the social media for us, and we probably owe the success of this place to her."

"Was Spill The Beans your idea?"

"Dani's, actually. Who knew it would be so popular?"

I nod, my hands sliding into my pockets. Spill The Beans was the first thing that came up when I searched Cam's name on the internet. I hadn't planned to look up Cam, but when a search for Avery yielded only outdated social media and those articles from Domenica, I felt desperate. I'd only been out of prison a few days, and I finally had a phone again, and I was starving for anything that was remotely related to Avery.

We're quiet, but I think there's a lot we could both say. Finally, Cam asks, "Is there anything else I can do for you?" She thumbs behind herself. "Feel free to grab a coffee and something to eat for the road. On the house."

"Actually." I cross my arms, preparing to be stonewalled. "I'd like Avery's address."

She hesitates. "I don't know if that's a good idea."

"Why?"

Her arms cross. "She's worked hard to get over you. I know you all..." she falters, "*reconnected* in Sugar Creek. But I'm serious when I say I don't think she'll survive you breaking her heart another time. I don't want to see her go through that again. I was scared for her back then."

I give her a meaningful look. "I remember how scared you were for her."

"Gabriel." She shakes her head back and forth, eyes pleading.

I'm not backing down. "You owe me."

She looks away. "No."

"Camryn?"

"No."

"Yes." My tone is low, and firm.

Her arms fly out to her sides. "Why? What is the point? What will it lead to?"

"I don't know. I just...can't leave her alone. I love her."

"Of course you do." She rubs her fingers over her cheeks, eyes rolling upward. "Whether or not you love her isn't the question. I'm not debating that." She shakes her head. "Think of her, instead of yourself."

"I *am* thinking of her."

Camryn squeezes my shoulder. She looks exactly like Avery used to, back when pity was her primary emotion toward me. "Avery still loves you. She always will. And if you love her like we all know you do, you need to be honest with yourself. Do you really believe you're what's best for her?"

Her words carry the sharp swiftness of a machete. She may as well have filleted me right here beside her wedding arch.

Her gaze softens. "I'm sorry, but you have to face the possibility."

My jaw clenches, and my reserve steels. "You think I should walk away with my tail between my legs, head down. And I could. I really, really could. But that would be taking the easy way out. If I do that, I take away Avery's choice. I did that once," I remind her, and she winces. "I won't make that mistake a second time."

We stare at each other, a face-off. I remember the day I met Cam, when she was nineteen and uncertain about life, when Dani was her best friend Danielle and she wanted nothing to do with college.

Camryn holds my gaze, then breaks. "Get out your phone," she says, sighing and looking at the ground.

I hold it between us and wait. She recites the address, and I enter it in.

"Thanks. Enjoy your arch." I hop into the delivery truck and steer it onto the main road. My jeans and long sleeve won't cut it here. I'm already sweating, and I need clothes and such to stay for at least a few days. I hadn't planned on staying, but I knew as soon as I saw Avery that I can't be without her again. I'll fight for her until she tells me to cease.

I stop into a store and buy shorts and T-shirts, then walk next door and purchase toiletries. I have everything I need now, except a place to stay.

I pause in the truck cab, my forward momentum stalled by the fact I have Joel's delivery truck. I'm almost positive he doesn't have another delivery scheduled for ten more days, but I need to be certain. And I need to ask for time off, though that's really out of respect and consideration. Joel won't deny me time off work. In the six or so months I've worked for him, I've yet to take a sick day, a personal day, or be late for work.

I call him, and I'm right. He tells me to enjoy my time in Phoenix, and he says it with enthusiasm. We hang up, and I sink back against the seat. Next up, lodging.

I could check into a hotel, but there's somewhere else I should go.

The truck rumbles to life, and I turn out into the busy street.

———

NOTHING about my childhood home has changed over the past six months, or the time I was in prison, or really in the years leading up to that, either.

I guess that's why I don't love coming here.

But I need a place to stay, and it doesn't cost me anything to be here. So, here I am.

I drop a few groceries in the fridge, then make my way down the hallway to my old room. Nash's photos line the wall, leading the way to his door. It has been years since I've gone in his room. Does my mom still dust it every few weeks, like she used to?

It makes me think of Avery, and what she said about the way we cling to our hurt. Just look at how tightly my family has held on to Nash, as if he can be found between the pages of old books, or the trophies lining his shelf.

I pause, my hand hovering in the air above his door handle, then open it.

Sunshine peeks in around the blackout blinds. It smells stale, and old. For a while, it smelled like Nash's cologne, but that filtered out within a month of his death.

Off to one side are boxes stacked three high. The rest of the room looks like someone could be living in it. Exactly like it was the last time I stuck my head in here. I step inside, making my way slowly around the room. Everything in here belonged to Nash, but this isn't where I feel him. He lives in the center of my chest, where I still love him. He lives in my mind, where his memory is never far.

I step out and close the door behind me. There's a photo of him and I on the wall, and I give it a light fist bump. "I love you, Brother."

I keep going to my room, tossing the bags on my old bed. Aside from the furniture, everything else in the room was converted into a guest room and office. My desk now houses my dad's laptop, my mother's ancient desktop, and an old framed photo of the two of them from their third date. My posters are gone, replaced by a triptych of the Pacific Ocean. The bedspread has a ruffle along the edge.

I remove the items I purchased and lay them out on the dresser, then sink back on the bed and look at the ceiling. The last time I slept in this room, I'd just gotten out of prison. Everything felt foreign, like returning from a long vacation. Minus the vacation part. Driving my truck again felt like an out-of-body experience. Muscle memory took me through the motions as my brain marveled at the remote familiarity. It took me fewer than three weeks to know that this was not the place for me. I needed to get out, and find my own way.

Here I am, six months later, back in this room.

Dreaming about Avery, once again. Trying to be someone worthy of her. Sometimes I wish I could crack open my mind, parse through its contents. Remove what I don't like, add in what I think would make me a better person.

If that were possible, I'd have done it a long time ago.

I used to feel like it was all inevitable, like I was doomed to succumb to the way I felt inside.

I don't feel that way anymore.

Hope, I believe it's called. Trust, even. I trust myself now, in a way I didn't before.

I trust myself not to hurt Avery again.

But it's not about me. Not anymore.

It's about her.

Us.

CHAPTER 23

AVERY

I'm sitting at my desk, staring out the window, my fingers poised on my computer keyboard. The skinny limbs of a mesquite tree sway with the breeze, and large, waxy white flowers spring from the arms of an old Saguaro. Normally I love this view, but today I cannot appreciate it properly.

My coffee has gone cold and my mouth feels as though a desiccant packet is sitting on my tongue. I'm immobilized by my thoughts.

Suddenly, this book feels a thousand times more difficult to write.

Or not, depending on how I look at it.

Within these pages, I have control. I am the puppet master. Pull a string, and an arm lifts.

In real life, I have no control over what anybody does.

Jill emailed me this morning, saying she looked forward to discussing the book in person tomorrow at the bridal shower. Between planning the event, writing the book, and my general angst, I haven't had time to be nervous about meeting her.

I'm shifting my attention back to my manuscript when there's a knock on my front door. For a quick second my brain misfires and thinks somehow it's Jill, showing up to surprise me. That's not possible, considering when she emailed and the time it would take to travel from New York to Arizona.

It's probably Camryn coming to check on me and make sure I haven't forgotten some detail about tomorrow's celebration.

I check the peephole.

Gabriel.

I swallow against the flutter in my chest, then swipe under my eyes and tighten the messy bun tied on the top of my head. I wish I weren't wearing my pink pajamas and fluffy Christmas-themed socks, but then I remember Camryn's words from my first day in Sugar Creek.

Only Gabriel would find you physically attractive in your current state.

I push down my churning stomach and acidic nerves and open the door.

Gabriel straightens, as if he wasn't really expecting me to answer. He fills the space of my walk-up, making it appear smaller.

"Hi." His gaze roams my face. "Can I come in?"

I look down at myself as I back up to allow him in, silently cursing the salsa stain on the thigh of my pajama bottoms.

Gabriel steps inside. He doesn't touch me as he passes, and still there's an electric current between us. It's so strong he might as well have his hands all over me.

He pauses in the entryway, which is also nearly the middle of the living room, and only a few steps away from the kitchen. "This is nice." He looks up at the ceiling. "You have fire sprinklers."

"I remembered what you said, about houses built in this area after 1990 all having sprinklers."

His hands go into his pockets, his shoulders lifting halfway to his ears. "I'm glad you thought of that, when you were looking for a home."

Gabriel's gaze slides over my place, peering around like there's more to see. There's not. Aside from the small living room and kitchen, it's just my bedroom and the bathroom.

He strides over, sitting down on the couch. "Did you sell our things?"

The couch is new. The coffee table is new. Every piece of furniture in this place is new.

"I sold some. Others I gave to Salvation Army." I wonder what this is like for him. In a rented cabin in Sugar Creek, we were in neutral territory. Now he's in my home. It has to be uncomfortable.

I close the door and sit beside him. "Should I ask how you found out where I live?"

"Camryn told me."

My head rears back in shock. "Camryn?" Why would she do that? That seems out of character for her, to not at least ask before handing out my address.

He sits back, one ankle crossed over the opposite knee. Then he leans forward, elbows resting on his knees. His right leg bounces.

I watch, fascinated by his restlessness. "You ok?"

He looks at me. "Yeah. I'm—" His eyes focus on my hand. Specifically, the fourth finger in on my left hand.

My wedding ring. I didn't take it off last night. I showered with it on, slept with it on, applied moisturizer with it on. This wasn't an absentminded mistake. I knew it was there, felt thrilled at its heaviness, the same way I did when it was first placed on my finger.

My thumb pushes the ring around my finger as I scramble for what to say. Gabriel fills in the silence by asking, "How often do you do that?"

"This is the first time I've put it on since I took it off." Sliding the ring onto my finger means conjuring up the day he put it there, and I already spend plenty of time with my memories.

A timer dings. I stand. "Come on."

He follows me into the kitchen. I stuff my hands into oven mitts and pull a coffee cake from the oven.

Gabriel peers over, eyebrows drawn. "So that smell isn't a candle. I forget you're competent in the kitchen now."

I can't help my proud grin. "More than competent. I'm good."

"Do I get to be your taste tester?" His expressive eyebrows lift hopefully. We could be back in our old kitchen with the outdated cabinets and the counter chipped in one corner, dancing to music Gabriel has chosen while dinners burns.

That feels like another life. A parallel universe.

I remove two plates and two forks. Gabriel takes a knife from my knife block and cuts two slices of coffee cake. He uses his fingers to pull the first slice from the pan, placing it on a plate and licking crumbs from his finger before lifting the second and plating it. He hands the second slice to me.

We eat in silence after Gabriel compliments the coffee cake. He takes my empty plate, stacking it on top of his own, and places them in the dishwasher. I don't mention that I wash my dishes by hand. What's the point of using the dishwasher when it's just me? By the time the dishwasher is full, everything in there smells gross. I wash as I go.

Gabriel leans against the counter. I do the same against the opposite counter.

He's watching me, waiting for me to say something, but I don't know what. How do you choose what to say when there's a sea of words to choose from? How do you choose what to say when you're not sure there's a point to any of it?

"Avery?"

It's only my name, but it's really not. It is strain, and torture. Pain, and hope.

Gabriel drags a hand through his hair. "Would you consider trying again with me? If we lived in the same place? I know we talked about it in Sugar Creek, but…" He trails off, but it's not because he doesn't know what to say. It's more like he has too many thoughts, and he needs to decide which one to voice. Like he, too, has a sea of words swirling in his mind.

"Gabriel, I—" I cut off, pressing the heels of my palms to my eyes.

"I know you're scared, and—"

He stops talking when he sees me shaking my head. It's true that I am so scared, terrified out of my mind. The very thing I want the most also carries the ability to decimate me. But, there's more. "It's not only fear. It's *trauma*. And just because I objectively understand trauma is something that can be dealt with, doesn't mean it's not hell getting through it."

Gabriel vaults over the small space, taking me by surprise when he grabs my hands. "I'm sorry, Avery." Intensity fires up his brown eyes. "I understand now how important choices are to you. I want you to choose me." He gestures from his chest to mine. "My choice is already made. I don't think I ever had one. For me, it was over from the start. It's different for you. I made it different. I know that, and I am sorry. I haven't officially asked for your forgiveness, because I wasn't certain I deserved it. But I'm here, right now, asking for your forgiveness."

My heart slams against my breastbone. "You think you deserve it now?"

His head shakes. "I will endeavor to deserve it. I will work to deserve it, always."

I take back my left hand, swiping at a lone tear. Light catches my ring, sending colorful prisms onto the wall.

"You're my wife," he chokes out. Moisture gathers in his eyes.

My eyes tighten, too. "You know I'm not."

I thought we'd traveled difficult terrain in Sugar Creek, but it was just the surface. There is hurt to wade through on both sides of the answer. I lower my hands from my face. "I don't know what to say."

"Say your truth. What else is left? What more is there to lose?" His defeated posture makes me want to cry.

I stare into his eyes as the memories trip past my brain on a slideshow. "We were good, Gabriel. God, we were good." My voice quakes with my conviction. "We were beautiful, until we were tragic. I can't see how the hell we're supposed to come back from that." I palm my chest, my heartbeats pushing against my bones. "I want to, more than anything. But what if there's too much damage? Sometimes, things can't be fixed, and you have to let go."

"Time," he pleads. "Time is how we come back from that. Right now I have nothing but words. Words and promises." I'm already shaking my head in response, but he's nodding, as if he can cancel out my refusal. "Give me time to show you that it will never happen again, because now I understand what drew me to it. I don't need to escape, because all I want is right in front of me. I wouldn't trade this feeling of belonging, of being right in the world, for anything. Ever. You don't have to say you believe me right now. I don't need you to. All you have to do is say you believe me"—he jabs a stiff finger at the ground—"today. And say it again tomorrow, and the day after that, and the day after that. The days will turn into weeks, the weeks into months, and then it will be years. I will spend every moment for the rest of my life proving it to you over and over, day in and day out. You're going to see it in the tiny moments when nobody is looking. You're going to see it when all eyes are on us."

He gulps air, and continues. "Remember in your book, you talked about irrevocable shifts? The accident, the DUI, prison, all of it, those were irrevocable shifts. Trauma that alters brain chemistry. Alcoholism could have killed me, and it nearly ruined my life. It's poison to me, Avery. Poison. I want nothing to do with it, ever. Not just for you. For me, too."

I want to believe him. I want him to be right. I want a crystal ball, so I can peer into the future and know the outcome. "I'm not sure if giving us another chance would be the most indulgent thing I've ever done for myself, or the dumbest. I love you. To this day." I stab the air with a pointed finger as I speak. "To this very moment. I never stopped loving you, even when I moved on from you." My hand drops. "But how foolish would I be if I just accepted your words? I cannot skip off into the sunset with you. The sunset might be a mirage, Gabriel."

He presses a fist to his lips, pushing until his lips lose color. He breathes deeply through his nose and removes his hand, his lips blooming pink as the blood refills. Tears shine in his eyes.

I want to hold him, to soothe him, so desperately. I don't though, because that won't help us. My job now is to tell my truth, even when it hurts us both. "I know it's easy to look at what went wrong in our relationship and see the headlines. But there's more to it than that. I walked on pins and needles for months, never knowing if you'd be drunk or sober when you came home. Do you know what that does to a person's mental state? All the lies I had to tell, to keep your image intact? I lied to people I love. I lied to myself. And I was lonely. So fucking lonely."

"I will be sorry for the rest of my life." Gabriel leans closer, planting a soft kiss against the side of my head. "I believe, with everything in me, that there is goodness ahead of us. That we are meant for a new beginning. What we had before, we can have again. I do not doubt my ability to treat you and our marriage like precious gifts. I only need one chance." He pulls away from my head and stares deeply into my eyes. Into my soul. "I will not let you down."

I blink away the moisture in my eyes, soaking in all of

his earnest words and his conviction like a Gabriel-soluble sponge. "I need to think about all this."

His gaze is long and meaningful. "I'll be at my parent's house."

"You're not going back to Sugar Creek?"

"Not yet." He strides to the front door, still fully visible from the kitchen. He opens the door, then turns back. "You don't trust me with your heart right now, and that's understandable. But I trust me. Nobody will hold me to a standard higher than the one I'll hold for myself."

He steps out the door and closes it behind him.

CHAPTER 24

AVERY

I'VE SPENT ALL MORNING GETTING READY FOR TODAY'S gathering. I'd planned to assemble thank-you gifts last night, but after Gabriel left I sat on the couch and stared at the wall for a solid hour. Then I went to bed and woke up throughout the night, the strength of Gabriel's words reverberating through my mind and pulling me from sleep. Finally I got up, finished putting together the thank-you bags around four a.m., then found a few more hours of fitful sleep.

I look and feel like a zombie, but I've plastered on a cheery disposition and smoothed a truckload of concealer under my eyes.

Cam is supposed to stay away from Gem today. I want her to walk in with Dani so they can experience the surprise together. Considering she's just peeked her head out the back door, I guess that's not happening. She sticks out her tongue when she catches my exasperated look.

"I know, I know," she calls, watching me arrange vases

and candy jars of varying heights. "I just wanted to see if you need help."

"No, you didn't," I respond, and she laughs.

"Ok, fine, I'm making sure you're alright."

I stop what I'm doing. "Why wouldn't I be alright?"

"Well, Gabriel's in town, so—"

"So you tripped and fell and my address came tumbling out of your mouth."

She laughs, then slaps a hand over her lips. "Sorry, I know you're mad, but that was funny." She walks closer, until she's standing next to me. Using my scissors, she cuts open three bags of lemon hard candy and pours them in a jar. "I'm sorry about that, but he said he wanted to talk to you, and he looked really sad."

"Since when do you care if Gabriel looks sad?"

"I don't. I know you have unfinished business though, and it seemed like maybe it would be good for you to talk. Plus, I heard how much tension there was between you two."

"Who told you that?"

"Laramie."

I throw up my hands. "Maybe I should buy a billboard and use it for announcements."

She opens a fourth bag of lemon candy and dumps it into the jar. "Don't waste your money. Write it on the chalkboard instead. Which, by the way, you're fired. That poem is depressing."

"That poem is beautiful." I pour a mountain of Skittles into a tall, thin vase.

"You should ask Gabriel if he wrote it."

I glance sideways at her. The candy clinks against the glass. "You think?"

She shrugs. "You could literally sum up your entire relationship with that one poem."

"He asked me to take him back. And for my forgiveness."

Camryn doesn't seem at all surprised. "What did you say?" She dips her hand in the candy as I pour. More scatter on the table than end up in her hand.

"I love him, Cam. There's no denying that. But it's a lot more complicated than it looks from the outside."

Cam chews the candy. "It looks pretty damn complicated from the outside."

"I don't know how to trust him again."

"I know." She shakes her head. "Actually, I don't. But here's what I think. Everyone, at one point or another, hurts the person they love the most. How can we not? Real love demands we strip ourselves, and bare our souls. It is a vulnerable, messy affair, and nobody escapes unscathed. I think the point, at the end of the day, is to decide whether you can forgive Gabriel's mistakes, and move forward. If the promise of the future is enough to make you forgive the past, then do it."

I stare at my normally irreverent sister.

She gives me a look. "I know, I know. Give me heart arrows and call me Cupid. I've been reading a lot about love and marriage lately." Cam plucks a napkin off a stack and wipes candy coating off her hands. "What does he say about drinking?"

"He swears he's sober. That he doesn't even want a drink. He called it poison."

"Do you believe him?"

"Yes," I say quickly, without having to think about it

first. The word, its meaning and its weight, sinks in. It's the first time I've let myself fully make that decision.

I resume my task of loading up ornamental jars with colorful candy. "It's all a lot to take. To think about. You know, if Gabriel had never done what he did, Hudson wouldn't have entered the picture. I can't decide if that's another mark to add to his tally, or if maybe there's a part of me that doesn't hate that I got the opportunity to know Hudson."

"I get it." Cam gathers the empty candy bags. "You also figured out how to sell a house, buy a house, adopt a dog, write a book, and probably a whole mess of stuff you don't even realize."

"I wish Gabriel hadn't needed to do what he did in order for me to learn all that."

"Yeah, well..." Cam shoves the empty bags at me. "That's not what life handed you, my dear." She checks her watch and backs away. "I need to go get ready. I'll see you in about an hour."

She leaves, and I keep working. I can't shake what Cam said about the poem, and it being from Gabriel, so I go in Gem and find Laramie.

"Hi," she chirps when she sees me. "Need more caffeine?"

"Sure." I lean a palm on the counter as Laramie steps over to the espresso machine. "I have a question about the Spill The Beans entries."

She nods me on as she works, so I ask, "The ones that are typed out. I'm guessing they're emailed?"

"Yep. They come into Gem's general email inbox, and I print them out. Usually I just copy/paste them into one document, and then cut them so they fit in the fish bowl with the handwritten entries."

"Can you show me the emails from last week?"

Laramie hands me a coffee, then her fingers fly over the screen used as a cash register. "Here," she announces, rotating the screen so I can see. "The top four emails are the most recent." She points at the chalkboard behind my head. "Including the one you chose."

I see it right away.

AVeryQuestionablePoet.

My hand goes to my stomach. I drag in a breath. Laramie's eyebrows pull together in concern. "Are you ok? Should I call your sister?"

I shake my head. "I'll be alright. It's just… I know this person. AVeryQuestionablePoet. I know him."

Laramie, who knows nothing of what I've experienced in the past few years, seems to understand the gravity of the situation. She nods solemnly. "Is the poem meant for you?"

"I think so."

Someone walks up to order. Laramie rotates the screen back to her. I float away, out to the space where I'm hosting the bridal shower, and force myself to focus on the finishing touches. I straighten chairs, tweak the photo board, rearrange the flowers on the gift table.

The entire time I think about Gabriel. About his poem.

Guests arrive, and the bridal shower is underway. In the back of my mind, lurks Gabriel.

———

Cam and Dani are hamming it up. Or, Cam is. Dani prefers to let Cam have the spotlight, but she can't escape it entirely today.

They're opening gifts now. They've lived together for a while, so the gifts are more fanciful. Not a hand mixer or knife sharpener in sight.

Jill in-person is just as terrifying as she is in electronic form. She's quick, witty, snappy, and though she is petite, her aura towers ten feet tall.

She has just sat down beside me and announced today we're going to mix business with pleasure. Her eyes are intense as she says, "The last few chapters you sent over were killing me. My stomach is in knots. Is she going to forgive Gabriel?" She holds her hands out to the side, eyebrows lifted.

"I haven't decided yet." The answer is true for both me, and my character.

"Great job, because I'm on tenterhooks." She taps the center of her lower lip, eyes scrunching. "I wonder about the divorce though."

"What about it?"

She shrugs. "There's something missing. I went back and reread the scene and it left me thinking there needed to be something more to it. Why does Gabriel divorce Avery?"

"Because he's sitting in prison feeling ashamed and he thinks he's showing her mercy." It's awkward talking about myself in the third person.

Jill's head moves slowly back and forth. "No. The book needs a better reason. Something more tangible. Gabriel's character needs something that forces him to make a choice like that. Maybe he's in a fight with an inmate, or someone comes to visit him." She makes a clucking sound with her tongue. "Think on it."

"I will." I'm not sure what to say. Not only do I have to make the right choice for me, but for my characters, too. Are they the same thing?

Cam sinks down into a seat beside Jill, her grin stretching the length of her face. "I bet you both feel you already know each other pretty well."

"We were just discussing Avery's book." Jill swings her shoulders to face Cam. "Have you read it yet?"

"She read the first half to me, but I'm not up to date on the rest."

Jill's eyes light up. "Maybe you can chime in on something. I think Gabriel needs a better reason for having divorced Avery. Something is missing from it all." She surveys Cam. "Thoughts?"

An odd emotion flits across my sister's face. Her gaze meets mine for a fraction of a second, then skitters away. "Hmm," she says. "I don't know. Better let Avery handle it. She's the creative sister."

I hear it, and I see it. Camryn's higher pitch, the unease in her posture.

Jill doesn't know Cam well enough to catch any of this. She chatters on, moving from my book to the upcoming wedding. I smile and nod where needed, but I'm not paying attention to what's being said.

For the sake of propriety, I tell myself I'm mistaken, but I know what I saw on Camryn's face.

Guilt.

CHAPTER 25

AVERY

It takes me three hours to get Camryn by herself.

She's picking up pieces of wrapping paper that didn't make the first trash pick-up. The last guest departed ten minutes ago, and Dani left right after to take Jill back to her hotel. We are alone. I can tell by the way Cam looks at me she knows what's coming.

There isn't a whole lot more to be done. The party rental place won't pick up the table and chairs until tomorrow. The leftover food has been wrapped up, and the back of Camryn's car holds their gifts.

I sit down in a shady spot under an awning. Cam tosses the trash she collected in the outdoor bin, then walks over to me. She stands in the full sun, arms crossed. "Are we going to do this now?" She sounds reluctant, but also defiant. Bold, considering I know she's guilty of something.

"Do you have something to tell me?"

Cam pulls out the chair beside me and collapses into it. "Before I say anything, you should know I'm really sorry."

I don't have patience. "Cam, I'm going to need you to spit it out. Now."

"I went to see Gabriel when he was in prison. Near the beginning of his sentence."

"While he and I were still married?"

She nods.

"Why?"

"I was worried about you. Honest to God, you were scaring me. When Mom died you were so capable. You just…just…rose up and took charge. Like you weren't as devastated as Dad—"

"I didn't have a choice, Cam. Dad's way of coping was to pretend we didn't exist."

"This was different," she insists. "The light inside you was snuffed out. You were a robot Sunday through Friday, and then on Saturday you came alive. I was with you one morning, watching you get ready to visit Gabriel, and it was like you were waking up from the stupor you placed yourself in the other six days of the week. I knew as soon as you left your visit, you'd go back into it. That broke my heart. I realized the only thing you had to look forward to was seeing him on Saturdays. All week long, your thoughts focused on that one thing. I couldn't watch you live like that." She takes a deep breath. "So, I went to see him. Dad had questions about his taxes, and I knew you'd be helping him and weren't going to see Gabriel as early as you normally did."

Goose bumps cover my arms. I know what's coming.

"I told him how you were doing, outside of your visits to him."

A lump forms in my throat. "How could you do that to

me? I had it under control. I was going above and beyond to keep his spirits up."

"At what personal cost?" Tears well in her eyes. "I didn't know he was going to divorce you. I swear I didn't suggest it."

"What did you think he would do?" My tone is sharp.

"Not that." Cam runs her hands through her hair, pulling as she goes. "I thought he would talk to you. Comfort you. Try and go deeper, help you figure out how you could find some happiness Sunday through Friday, too."

"Are those the words you used?"

"I don't remember exactly."

"Did you suggest he help me find happiness?"

Her mouth hangs open, her lower lip shakes. I see a sliver of Cam as a child, needing to be soothed. "Maybe?"

"Dammit, Cam," I whisper forcefully, then groan in frustration. "If it weren't for you…" I let the thought die out. It's not fair to say it's Cam's fault, because what Gabriel did was not outside of his wheelhouse. Gabriel will sacrifice for those he loves. His dreams, his hopes, his passions, he'll set them aside for others. I used to see his selflessness as something to aspire to, but now I'm not so sure. Maybe our desires never really go away, but sit inside and fester, waiting for the opportunity to surface. Gabriel might have let me go even if Cam never went to see him. Maybe our marriage was bound to go up in flames.

"I wanted to tell you, Avery. I promise, I almost told you so many times. But you were doing well—"

"You mean, when I lost my temper and then my

career?" I blow out an angry breath. "Is that when I was doing well?"

"After all that. You were putting your life back together. You were starting your book and meeting Hudson, and—" she cuts off, looking down at her hands. "I shouldn't have gone to see Gabriel. I should have done something else, maybe involved Dad and Lara, or—or, something. I don't know what."

I'm mad at her. Furious. But something is there, reminding me she's not entirely wrong. I lost myself after Gabriel went to prison. My world revolved around when I could see him again. I survived the week, just so I could get to Saturday.

"I don't know what to say to you, Cam."

"I don't like what I did, and I hate that I kept it from you. I'm sure you hate me right now, and I understand."

"I don't hate you, but I am so, so mad at you."

"I know. And I'm sorry. From the bottom of my heart, I am sorry for meddling."

Dani walks from Gem's back door. The tension must be visible from a distance, because she halts.

"Does Dani know?" I ask.

Cam turns to look at Dani and nods. "I told her when I got home that day."

I don't blame Dani for not telling me. Of course she wouldn't betray Cam's trust.

Dani walks forward cautiously. "Everything ok here?"

I purse my lips and nod.

Dani holds out a hand and Cam takes it. "Avery knows I went to see Gabriel in prison."

Dani sucks in a quick breath. "Wow. Things got serious after I left."

"You have your aunt to thank for that," I tell Dani. "Her creative musings clued me in."

Dani looks confused, and Cam promises to fill her in on the drive home. "What now?" Dani asks, glancing from me to Cam.

Cam looks to me for a response. I shrug. "I guess we just keep going."

"I meant about Gabriel," Dani says, pointing back at Gem with her thumb. "He's in there."

CHAPTER 26
GABRIEL

Cam and Dani sent Laramie home and snuck out the back. On their way out, Cam reached for a knob on the wall and turned down the lights. She made a face and promised that would be her last time meddling in our relationship. Somehow I doubt that.

Avery walks in, her gaze zeroing in on me. I stand up from where I'd been sitting, waiting for her. I make my way over, as does she, and we meet somewhere in the middle. Reaching out, I brush her cheek with my thumb. She leans into my touch.

"Did you come here for coffee?" she asks.

"No."

She blinks up at me, face still cradled in my palm. "Why are you here?"

"There's no staying away from you. Not for me."

Her lips tug into a shaky, emotional smile.

I hold her gaze, and say, "I have done so many things wrong. I have been stupid, and reckless, and selfish. There will not be a day when I don't regret what happened in our marriage. I've fought my demons and pain and grief, and now I'm fighting for another chance with you." Her lower lip quivers, and my other hand lifts, thumb gliding across the length. "I won't stop fighting, unless you ask me to. And I pray you don't." My throat thickens. "You are the hill I want to die on."

She whimpers. It's only a tiny little moan, but it speaks volumes. She's going to allow this.

Me.

Us.

"Kiss me," she whispers, pushing herself up on tiptoe.

I do better than that. I grip her backside in my palms, and lift her onto me. She wraps her legs around my waist.

We stare at each other in the half-light. I hold her with one arm, and press a hand to the nape of her neck.

She places her palms on either side of my face, the tip of her nose pressing to mine.

"Come here, baby." The nickname returns without fanfare. Almost like it was always present, waiting at the tip of my tongue.

Avery's lips meet mine. We kiss softly. Slowly. Savoring something that is old, and new.

The most precious thing.

My tongue swipes over her lips, and she opens. She tastes sweet, like candy.

"Take me home," she whispers against me.

"To your place?" I clarify. My parents' house is empty, but I would much rather be in Avery's bed.

"Sure," she answers, in a way that makes me think she might not consider it only her place for much longer.

We take Avery's car, leaving Joel's delivery truck where I parked it down the street from Gem. I drive. Avery touches me the entire five minutes we're in the car. Hands in my hair, nails grazing my forearm. I take the turn into her parking spot a little too quickly, and glass in the trunk clinks together.

"Candy jars," Avery explains. She's out of the car and walking to her front door, and I'm jogging to catch up.

"Where's the fire?" I joke, nipping at her neck while she unlocks the front door.

She turns around, winding a hand into my hair. "In here…" She taps two fingers over her heart. "Are you going to save me again?"

I gently push her back against the door. It swings open and we fumble our way in. "How about I sit in the fire alongside you, and we let it smolder for the rest of our days?"

"Fire." She kisses me. "Smolder." Another kiss. "Let it burn."

I laugh against her lips. She's already unbuttoning the front of her dress.

There aren't any more jokes after that.

There is touching, and loving, and kisses that taste like apologies. We hold each other close, and our eye contact says it all for us.

After, when Avery is lying over my chest, I tell her, "I don't love you the way I used to."

She lifts her head, her gaze curious. "Explain."

"It's tangible now." My hand caresses her bare back. "Something I can hold in my palm. Love feels different after you fight for it."

She places a kiss on my chest, right over my heart. "I love you, Gabriel."

God, how I've wanted this. *Her*. I wasn't sure I'd ever

have it again. A profound and overwhelming sense of gratefulness fills me. "You are my beginning, and my end."

She looks up again, her fingertips tracing my jawline. "Your poetry skills are much better than questionable."

I'm about to ask how she figured it out, but she's kissing me again, and now I'm rolling her over again, and the question disappears into a tangle of limbs.

This, right here, is what life's all about. Loving beyond measure.

Growing and listening and adapting.

Together.

CHAPTER 27
AVERY

"ANYBODY HOME?"

"Back here, hon," my dad calls. I'd bet a crisp twenty he's in his office.

I beam at Gabriel and take him by the hand. It's been a solid week since we got back together. He had to return the delivery truck, so we spent a few days in Sugar Creek. I finished my final chapters while I was there, and sent them to Jill. I haven't heard back yet. Hopefully no news is good news.

I pop into the office. Gabriel stands in the hallway, out of view. "Hey, Dad. I have a surprise."

He removes his glasses and sets them on the desk. "Is it about your book? Did you finish?"

"It's not about my book. And yes, I finished." I reach out into the hallway, and pull Gabriel into the room.

"What the hell?" my dad says, astonished. He pushes back his chair and rounds the desk. His arms open, and Gabriel gives him a long hug, and solid pat on the back.

"It's good to see you," Gabriel says when they break apart.

"Gabriel," my dad puts a hand on his shoulder. He shakes his head like he can't believe what's in front of him. He sends me a questioning look. "What's going on?"

I deliver a condensed version of Sugar Creek. My dad's gaze switches from me to Gabriel and back again. He waits until I'm finished to ask, "Are you officially back together? Is that what all this means?"

"We're back together. Officially." We discussed taking it slow, but given all the history and time in Sugar Creek, we decided to do what feels natural, whatever that means. No extensive thought, no should be or shouldn't be, or considering what other people might think.

I'd assumed my dad would trip over himself welcoming Gabriel back into the fold, but he's regarding Gabriel with a wary gaze that confuses me. "I trusted you with her the first time around, and you betrayed that trust. One day, if you're lucky enough to have a daughter, you'll understand what it was like to watch my little girl suffer."

Shock freezes my expression in place. I've never heard my dad talk like this. He loves Gabriel.

Gabriel nods once, maintaining eye contact. "I'm sorry I made you experience that."

My dad inclines his head toward me. "If Avery has decided she trusts you again, I'll go along with that. I'm all for second chances and learning from mistakes." He eyes me meaningfully. "Lara is in the backyard. Let's go tell her. She'll be so happy for you guys."

Gabriel backs out of my dad's office. Instead of following him, I throw my arms around my dad. My dad hugs me back.

"You sure?" he whispers.

"I'm sure."

"I have a shovel," he says, louder.

I chuckle. "And you know places where a body will never be found?"

"Exactly."

"Message received, sir," Gabriel says from the doorway.

CHAPTER 28
GABRIEL

"Loser wears his underwear on the outside of his clothes for a day."

I'm not sure who said it because I'm bent at the waist, stretching my back before Pat's Run, the 4.2 mile race that's minutes away from starting. I look sideways and watch Gutierrez cup his hands around his mouth and crow, "What if we don't wear underwear?"

Plotnik, who always did love to place a bet, frowns at him. "You're a piece of work."

"What?" Gutierrez shrugs. "Bro, it's Phoenix."

Nobody asks Gutierrez what the hell that means. They've been with him so long, they don't need to.

I listen to the familiar shit-talking from my old crew as I stretch my calves, my hamstrings, my arms.

"Don't worry." Casella jostles me with his elbow. "You won't be the one wearing your underwear outside your shorts. We all know it'll be Tomcat over there."

Tomcat, aka Thomas, sits on a pony wall, eating his third race-sponsored donut. The guy absolutely cannot say no to a donut. They're his kryptonite. At this rate, he'll likely be vomiting halfway through the race.

"How about," I say, taking a break from stretching my calves, "we make a different bet? If I win, you all have to wear your underwear outside your clothes?" This way, Tomcat may still be on the losing end, but he won't be the only loser.

The crew's collective gaze is on me. Gutierrez points at my chest. "You have yourself a deal, hero."

The crew knew I was coming today. I was registered to run with them. They had a custom-printed shirt ready for me, to match theirs. The front says Phoenix FD, the back says Running for Ryan. Nobody acted like anything big was happening when I walked up. There were hugs, the muted *thwack* of solid back slaps. Gutierrez boomed, "What's good, buddy?" and hugged me a little harder than the others. He and I went to the academy together.

I hadn't allowed myself to feel how much I missed these guys. These friendships.

The race begins.

They all keep up.

Halfway through, Tomcat peels off and pukes in a potted palm tree.

One by one they slow their pace. Gutierrez is the last, and he's trying to pass me. As the finish line banner comes into view, I turn on the afterburners and sprint. He's not expecting it, and yells something I can't hear.

Avery and my parents are waiting at the finish line. I run straight to Avery, who's bouncing on her toes, her smile wide and proud. My mom and dad clap for me as I plant a kiss on my girl. Endorphins stream through me, concealing the screaming burn of all my muscles.

Mom holds out her arms for a sweaty hug, and my Dad delivers a hard squeeze to my shoulder. "Proud of you, Son."

The rest of the crew trickles over the finish line. Even Tomcat, accompanied by Casella.

"Lookin' green around the gills, Tomcat," my dad bellows.

"Donuts, sir," Tomcat responds, and my dad shakes with laughter.

The guys are all enthusiastically greeting Avery. It's been years since they've seen each other. Plotnik lingers, urging Avery off to the side and speaking quietly to her. She nods, accepting whatever it is he's saying, and smiles graciously.

We have reservations at a nearby breakfast spot. In the car, Avery hands me a package of wipes. "I love you, but you stink."

I hold up the package. "Baby wipes?"

"Read the front," she says, shifting into drive. "Man wipes."

Avery glances in her rearview mirror. My parents are behind us.

"How are you?" she asks, glancing at me quickly.

"I'm good. Really good."

I read the follow-up questions she hasn't yet asked, and answer them. "Everybody was normal. Like nothing happened. I was nervous when I first walked up, but then it was all ok somehow."

"They love you."

I ball up the used wipes and toss them into an empty plastic bag on the floorboard. "What did Plotnik say to you after the race?"

Avery signals her turn. "He apologized."

I don't need to ask the reason for the apology. He was with me that night, before I made the choice to drive. Of my entire crew, he tried the hardest to contact me after. Once, he tried to see me in prison. I refused his visit.

Avery parks. She opens her mouth to speak, but stops, jaw dropping and eyes bulging. Her car is surrounded by men wearing underwear outside their shorts. Gutierrez has his hands out to the side and shuffles like a crab. Avery laughs until tears roll down her face.

I climb out, pointing at Gutierrez's crotch. "You're wearing underwear."

"Can't free ball when you run," he quips.

Avery takes a picture of the mayhem, with me at the center.

The guys go into the restroom and switch their clothes.

We eat an obscene amount of pancakes. My dad insists on picking up the tab. He sits beside me, and tells everyone about my work in Sugar Creek.

He brags.

About me.

Avery's hand finds mine, and she gives it a squeeze.

———

AVERY

I watch Gabriel speak, the way his mouth moves and how he gestures.

He explains to a crew of rapt firefighters how burning wood in a controlled environment can lead to art.

"You always knew how to do this?" Plotnik asks, eyebrows lifted.

"Yeah."

Tomcat sits back, his plate of pancakes mostly untouched. "You've been holding out on us, hero."

Hero. It still fits, despite everything that has happened.

The guys are talking, asking questions, and getting out their phones to look up Intricate Wood Works on social media.

I hope Gabriel sees how loved he is. How much he belongs, simply by being himself.

I watch him hold court, and my mind wanders. In his expressions I see the man he used to be, back when we were new. What he looked like the first time I saw him, wearing all that heavy gear and appearing in my room, lifting me up and carrying me to safety. Our first handshake, our first kiss, the fireworks detonating in my stomach. The thrills, the glory, the agony, the angst. I see it all. I think I'll keep some of it with me. Not to hold over him, but to remind me of what we carry between us, how fragile it all is.

Day by day, I plan to shed some of it. Let go of what hurt and keep what made us good.

All of this, everything, is a choice.

I've chosen to be here, to show up, to forgive, to love.

EPILOGUE
AVERY

"That was the last one." I sit back on my heels and toss the packing tape on the ground.

Gabriel picks up the box and adds it to the stack on the table. Our dining room is unrecognizable. Every inch is piled with boxes.

"Are you sure you closed the store?" I ask, eyebrows raised. I want the holidays to be about us, not Gabriel's business or my next book. Jill supports my holiday break, especially because I'm on deadline for the second of the three-book deal she secured for me eighteen months ago. She wants me to return from my break inspired and ready to write.

So do I. So does my publisher.

"It's closed," Gabriel reaffirms. "Mason changed it all earlier today. Every product says we're not currently accepting orders, and there is a banner as soon as the page loads that announces we're taking a break for the holidays."

"Perfect." I blow a stray hair from my face and hold out a hand. "I have to pee."

Gabriel helps me up. "You went to the bathroom twenty minutes ago."

"Feel free to have a talking-to with your son," I call over my shoulder as I waddle from the room.

Six more weeks to go until delivery, and I'm huge. And I can't find a comfortable position to sleep in. And I'm constantly being kicked from the inside.

I love every second of it.

Last year, Gabriel and I had a house built on the outskirts of Sugar Creek. We hosted a housewarming party and invited all our family and friends. Everyone was confused when the music switched from top hits to Canon in D Major. Gabriel and I walked from the house, him in a navy blue suit and me in a lemon yellow dress. Everyone swore they were shocked, except Camryn, who loudly announced she saw it coming a million miles away. That night, we said 'I do' a second time.

Our home has a large wood shop in the back, where Gabriel works. Joel retired from Intricate Wood Works, and Gabriel took over. Gabriel spends his days working with his hands, and creating. Mason runs his online store and social media. His wedding arches have become something of a wedding status symbol, but he is careful about how many orders he accepts. Gabriel is purposeful with how he spends his time. His priority is me, and this sweet boy I'm carrying.

My phone rings in my purse as I'm turning off the

bathroom light. I lumber over to where I left it on the kitchen counter, nearly missing the call.

When I see it's Jill, I glance at the time. It's late for her to be calling.

"Hey, Jill," I answer.

"Are you sitting down?" Her brisk voice thunders across the connection.

"Um, no. Why?" She sounds excited, so I don't think the news is bad.

"I don't want to be the reason you deliver that baby early. Maybe you should sit down."

"Spit it out, Jill." I'm pretty sure my smile comes through in my tone.

"I received an email from a production company. They want to know if the TV/Film rights are available for your book."

"Wha— What?" I look around for a chair. I think I really do need to sit down.

Gabriel comes in from the backyard, feet stuffed in unlaced boots. He didn't wear a coat, and now he's rubbing the cold from his forearms. He stops when he sees whatever look is on my face.

"What's wrong?" he asks, hurrying to me.

"Jill." I point at the phone. "TV. Film. Book." I hold my hands out to steady myself. "Sweet Jesus. Oh my Lord."

Gabriel grabs the only chair not loaded with packages and guides me to sit. He hits speaker on my phone.

"Jill, hi," Gabriel says. "What's going on?"

She repeats herself.

Gabriel's eyes grow large and he mouths '*Are you flipping kidding me?*'

'*I know!*' I mouth back, arms slicing the air in tiny, chaotic movements.

"What do you think?" Jill asks, voice crisp. "Should I say yes?"

"Yeah. Yes." My hands are at my mouth, fingers tapping my lips. "This is insane."

Jill informs me she'll write the person back right now, and get back to me with their response. She hangs up, and I stare at my phone. The baby kicks, and reflexively I reach down and press into the spot.

Gabriel lays his palm on mine. "On a scale of one to ten, how badly are you freaking out right now?"

"One thousand," I reply.

Gabriel laughs. "Me too."

I look up at him. It seems prudent to inject some cautious optimism into my thoughts. Just to hedge my bets. "This could be nothing, you know. They could decide it doesn't translate from book to screen."

Gabriel lowers himself so he's balanced on the balls of his feet. He brushes hair from my face, his hand staying on the back of my neck. "Or, it could be something."

I smile at him. My husband. "We'll just see what Jill has to say and go from there."

Gabriel offers me a hand and helps me stand. My belly bumps into the stack of packages closest to me, and the top three teeter and tumble down to the ground.

"I'm happy your talents are in such high demand, but I won't be sorry when gift-giving season is over. I'm ready to have my home back."

Gabriel is on the floor, retrieving the package that slid under the table. He hands it up to me. I'm placing it on the top of the stack when I see who it's addressed to. Mr. & Mrs. Hudson Donahue. It's a Phoenix address.

"Did you see this one?" I run a finger along the printed postage.

Gabriel reads where I'm pointing. "I didn't notice it."

"Me neither." I'm the one who stuck the printed label on all these packages. I'd done so many I eventually stopped paying attention to names.

"How does that make you feel?" Gabriel wraps his arms around me and my belly.

I turn around. My stomach bumps against his. "Good. I want him to be happy."

He brushes a kiss on my lips. "I want him to be happy too, as long as it's not with my wife."

I smile against his lips. "I love you."

Gabriel carefully folds me into his arms. "I love you more than you will ever know."

He's wrong. I know how much he loves me.

How much we love each other.

Some people claim love makes a person weak, but I disagree. Real love forces a person to do the hard work. It will ask you to get uncomfortable, to expose the wound, to confront what hurts you most. That requires strength. Fortitude. And above all else, compassion.

I understand now why some marriages simply don't make it. Living and loving through one another's growing pains isn't easy. It can seem insurmountable. It can *be* insurmountable.

But we did it. Through grace, or luck, or stubborn hearts, and maybe a little of all three, we wound up here.

Camryn recently asked me what I would do if I were handed a magic wand. Would I erase the fractured path

Gabriel and I traveled to get to where we are today? The simple answer is, no. We may never have ended up in this place if we didn't go to war with our demons. I've embraced everything it took to get us here. So has Gabriel.

We are different the second time around. We are intentional. Careful. Considerate. Hard-won love is sweeter.

Gabriel leads me to our bed and tucks the extra pillow under my stomach. He climbs in behind me and kisses my shoulder.

Four weeks later, Nash Woodruff arrives quietly into the world. Corinne and Doug wait with my dad and Lara outside the delivery room, and Corinne sobs when we introduce her.

Later, when visiting hours are over and it's dark outside, Gabriel climbs into the bed with me and the baby. The pad of his thumb rubs over the side of Nash's tiny, dark head of hair.

"Thank you for naming him Nash," Gabriel murmurs.

"There was no other name for him," I whisper.

I close my eyes, and allow the happiness to seep into me. Life hasn't been, and won't be, perfect, but I'm going to hold on to the moments that are. I'm going to keep them close to my heart, where I can feel them always.

The End

AFTERWORD

Dear Reader,

I wrote What We Keep over a two-year period. Halfway through the novel, with my heart battered and bruised and exhausted from what I was asking of the characters, I wrote these words on a Post-it note:

THIS BOOK IS A JOURNEY.

The note stuck to the bottom of my screen for the second half of writing the book and through many rounds of edits. I needed something to remind myself what I was attempting, using an unconventional story structure, to accomplish. Avery and Gabriel are sent on a journey of love, loss, and learning. I asked them to examine what happens when, even with the very best intentions, we don't tend our own garden. What wounds shape us, making us who we are? What do we keep close, even to our detriment?

Perhaps you recognized Jane as a character from Our

Finest Hour. I wanted to bring closure to that storyline, so I gave Jane an opportunity to reveal why she left her daughter. If you're among those who noticed this returning character, I hope you feel Jane (redeemed? No, not quite.) *explained* herself in a satisfactory way.

Thank you for joining me on the messy journey to Avery and Gabriel's happily ever after. The road was long and the fight was tough, but I hope that in the end, the trip was worth it.

Xoxo,
Jen

ALSO BY JENNIFER MILLIKIN

Hayden Family Series

The Patriot

The Maverick

The Outlaw

The Calamity

Standalone

Here For The Cake

Better Than Most

The Least Amount Of Awful

Return To You

One Good Thing

Beyond The Pale

Good On Paper

The Day He Went Away

The Time Series

Our Finest Hour

Magic Minutes

The Lifetime of A Second

ACKNOWLEDGMENTS

Readers. The first acknowledgment must go to you for being on this journey with me. I am so very grateful to you for reading my work, for spending your precious time in the worlds I create, for letting my characters have a little of the love in your hearts.

Erica. You read this book when it was in its original form, when it was a barely molded lump of clay. You helped me form it, to make it into the story it is today. Thank you for your honesty, your streaming consciousness margin notes, and your support.

My editor, Nicole Purdy. You always make me look harder at the characters, go deeper into their minds and motivations and thoughts. Without you asking, "How did the character feel when this happened?", What We Keep might not pack the same emotional one-two punch.

Forever grateful to my beta readers, Crystal, Julia, and Kristan. Your honesty makes me better.

My husband, Luke. Twenty years together, and though it hasn't always been perfect, it has always been worth it.

ABOUT THE AUTHOR

Jennifer Millikin is an Amazon Charts bestselling author of contemporary romance and women's fiction. She is the two-time recipient of the Readers Favorite Gold Star Award, and readers have called her work "emotionally riveting" and "unputdownable". She lives in the Arizona desert with her husband, children, and two

dogs. With seventeen novels published so far, she plans to continue her passion for storytelling.

facebook.com/JenniferMillikinwrites
instagram.com/jenmillwrites
bookbub.com/profile/jennifer-millikin